HANGTOWN

A NOVEL OF THE OLD WEST
THIRD IN THE PLATTE RIVER WALTZ SERIES

BY KEN CONSAUL

ACKNOWLEDGEMENTS

Edited by Samantha Ettinger

TABLE OF CONTENTS

CHAPTER ONE 1
CHAPTER TWO 10
CHAPTER THREE..34
CHAPTER FOUR...1
CHAPTER FIVE...1
CHAPTER SIX...23
CHAPTER SEVEN...34
CHAPTER EIGHT 41
CHAPTER NINE..56
CHAPTER TEN..78
CHAPTER ELEVEN...94
CHAPTER TWELVE 106
CHAPTER THIRTEEN 124
CHAPTER FOURTEEN..135
CHAPTER FIFTEEN 163
CHAPTER SIXTEEN..177
CHAPTER SEVENTEEN 188
CHAPTER EIGHTEEN...201
CHAPTER NINETEEN...217
CHAPTER TWENTY..223

SOME HISTORICAL PERSPECTIVE AND
A WORD FROM THE AUTHOR

The two prior installments of the Bonner series chronicled our young couple's adventures on the trek across the frontier of the early west. The Growler Brigade concluded with Josh Bonner reflecting on how his life seemed tied to rivers. One reader lamented I had left the reader and the Bonners knee-deep in a freezing river. Hangtown is where the reader can dry their feet, sit around the campfire and catch up with Josh and Elizabeth and their friends.

When gold was discovered in early 1848 at Sutter's Mill, present-day California was an unsettled country with a few settlements along the coast and at the Spanish missions. The population, not counting the Native Americans, was estimated at about thirteen thousand; slightly more than half were Mexicans who were in charge until the conclusion of the Mexican War in 1846. The balance was mostly Americans, a number of them soldiers and militia veterans from the battles that created the Bear Flag Republic. There was a contingent of French refugees from the troubles in France, some South Pacific islanders, some Chinese, and a scattering of South Americans. Other than the *ranchos* of the land grant Mexicans, most of the commerce was a trade in cattle and hides. San Francisco, then *Yerba Buena*, was such a trading post with perhaps six hundred permanent inhabitants.

Alta California, as the territory was known, was primarily a wilderness of people living along the coast and in Spanish land grant ranches. At the conclusion of the Mexican War, *Alta California* became an American territory nominally governed by a small military garrison. There was no civil or criminal law and the holders of land grants were uncertain their property claims were even valid. One of these was John Sutter who obtained loans and land grants during the Mexican domain. He settled far inland in the foothills of the Sierras near present day Sacramento and called his world New Helvetica, named after his native Switzerland.

Even after gold was discovered, little changed. Once word traveled across the region, the people came to the foothills and, mostly from curiosity, tried their hand at panning for gold. Most found a little. A few found some paying amounts. No one claimed anything. They would just pan until they found no more and moved on to a new sandbar or bend in the rivers. They would leave their pans and plates of gold on the table in their tent and no one disturbed them. It was almost a picnic atmosphere and a diversion from everyday toil. Eventually word spread to the settlements and, as the stories grew, the towns and even the army garrison emptied out and fled to the hills. Ships arriving to trade heard tales of easy riches and the officers and crews joined the exodus to the gold country.

Unfortunately, placer mining has a season in California. In the late spring through early fall the rivers are shallow and miners can stroll along the banks and try their luck where they will. The upstream canyons with the gold bearing rivers were steep and so deep that some stretches never received any direct sunlight. Once the rains came and the rivers became torrents the gold hunters had to retreat to the foothills, eke out a living as best they could and await the next warm season. Meanwhile, troops of people from around the world have heard the news and are swarming to *El Dorado*. Over the next few years the population of California will swell by hundreds of thousands. Almost all will be young men from the United States determined to make their fortune and return home to a life of fame and leisure. The reality will be that nearly one in six will die and be buried in shallow graves if they are even that lucky. Many arrive from around the world to prey on the miners by hook or by crook.

There is no government and the military is plagued by desertion. There are no towns beyond the temporary settlements where miners gather to resupply and huddle during the despairing wet winters. There are no jails, no postal system, and no way to secure a claim to land or to mining rights. This is the land of good fortune the Bonners have chosen and they try to make the best of it. Together with their friends Jubal, an ex-slave and Duncan Shipwash, an eccentric British mining engineer they band together to make a place for themselves and to wrest the gold from the new country. They eventually form a partnership with a company of men who have arrived from Albany, New York. They have chartered a venture to stick together and share the wealth of their labors.

It's time now to make some apologies to the discerning historical reader. I have taken some liberties with historical accuracy and sacrificed them on the altar of the all-demanding story.

First, it would be unlikely the Bonners would meet an organized group of prospectors from the East at the time they did. The discovery of gold in California did not reach the settled United States except in drips and drabs until around September of 1848 when President Polk confirms the richness of the find and sets off a fever in the East. Companies were formed by the hundreds and came to California overland, by boat around Cape Horn, or by boat and a trek across Panama and Nicaragua. In any case, the journey was months long. The Albany enterprise comes into our story around early December of 1848, nearly a logistical impossibility. Their labor was needed to exploit what became known as The Dry Diggings, along the South Fork of the American River. The camp near these deep gravel diggings was simply a convenient camp spot along a trade trail. It eventually earned its moniker of Hangtown and eventually became the current day city of Placerville, California.

The story ventures far afield from Hangtown itself. It meanders from Sutter's fort to the nearby river encampment of the *Embarcadero* to the estuary of the Sacramento River and to the neighboring gold camps of Auburn and Gold Run. Today all of these could be visited in a single day on scenic highways. At the time the journey between these points was arduous and dangerous. The only roads were following someone else's wagon ruts through wetlands, up and down hills, through forests, and across rocky rivers and tributaries. I freely admit I have not only sacrificed history, but the geography itself to the story. I condensed time and distance to move the plot along.

In the story our intrepid company employs a placer mining device known as a long tom. During the early days of the Gold Rush, most mining was done with pan, pick, and shovel. Some miners made crude rockers, a rocking cradle-like device. The long tom did not become prevalent until perhaps 1852. I beg your indulgence in the liberties I've taken. I think you will enjoy the Bonner's continuing saga and you might even learn a bit about gold mining and society in *Alta California*.

For those who would like to know more about the California Gold Rush, I heartily recommend:

They Saw the Elephant by Jo Ann Levy, University of Oklahoma Press.

Days of Gold by Malcolm J Rohrbough, University of California Press

PREFACE

Elizabeth Bonner was in a pique as she stomped across the footbridge spanning the unnamed creek dividing the nameless mining camp that had become their winter home. When she was incensed, she knew she was not good company so a retreat to the winter shelter would ruin an already morose day for Jubal and Duncan Shipwash. Both had remained behind, declining to participate in the miners' court and its foregone outcome. Elizabeth walked the quarter mile to the big loop in the South Fork of the American River below where the partnership washing operation was set up.

She had no desire to see two men hung, but the gall of the men who shooed her away from the court was exasperating. Did they expect her to give the key testimony against the two murderers and then retreat to the kitchen to bake cookies and dust the furniture? She resolved not to bring her brooding temper home and drive her friends out of doors. She would remain here until the deed was done and Josh returned. She needed to cool off and to that end she commenced pacing back and forth along the creek.

When the miners cut the approaches to the bridge and set the split logs firmly in the bank, the stream had been only a couple feet deep and the surface was ten feet below the logs. The depth and volume of the water had been steadily increasing ever since. The water was no more than four feet below her and incrementally rising every day. The cascade was filled with brush, branches, and other debris flowing south to join the American River. If it rose much more, the branches would strike the underside of the bridge. Maybe the bridge would wash away and the camp would be split for months. She imagined being marooned on the south side of the camp while Josh, Jubal, and Duncan Shipwash stared back at her from the north bank, a scant twenty feet away but separated as surely as an exile on a forlorn shore. She was letting the imaginary scene play out, relieving some of her ire at the men in camp when she saw the crowd escorting the two condemned men away from the camp on the other bank of the river. Gaveling men to death was something to be done in the bosom of the community but carrying out the sentence required seclusion and distance from the public square. They could not abide such dirty business where they rested their heads at night and conducted their affairs by day.

The procession ended in a grove of sycamore trees, now mostly bare of foliage save a few withered, yellow leaves dangling from the branches. The ground below little more than a dank carpet of brown and tan. A few men left the crowd and wandered about, seeking suitably sturdy limbs. The congregation halted, patient or perhaps hesitant to take this final measure of the verdict. A tree was selected and the solemn throng shuffled forward. No one hurried lest they perceive themselves a mob instead of a community gathered for an unpleasant but necessary duty. The two convicts were nowhere to be seen, enveloped by those who would now carry out the sentence of the court.

From within the crowd, first one rope, then another flew upward and down again, the nooses dancing above the heads of the gathering. Clumsily a circle opened in the middle as individuals pulled back from the condemned as if a dozen paces would transform them from participant to casual observer. The ends of the rope were heaved into the gathered crowd. Many pressed back against their neighbors but some hands accepted the rope and formed a line. The rope hung slackly back to the limb above, then straight down. For some minutes the crowd was silent. Elizabeth was too far away to hear any words being spoken. The verdicts were read, the men were given a chance to say their final words, perhaps someone said a prayer and then the slack was taken up. Two bodies rose, their hands bound behind them, until their feet sought some non-existent purchase above the heads of the upturned faces. The ascent was accompanied by a collective gasp from the witnesses, like a mutual intake of breath. The sound carried across the river. To Elizabeth it sounded almost like an uttering of astonishment at what was happening.

~~~

Josh Bonner was in the crowd. Somehow a length of rope had found its way into his hands. When it had been cast over his head, he instinctively reached for it. Gazing along its length he traced its course up and over the branch. Other men formed up on both sides of him and turned away from the condemned. Perhaps it was a mercy he would not see the execution he was to now be a participant in. He wrapped a loop around each hand and waited. Through the length of hemp, like a fish nibbling on the bait, he could feel the movement behind him. What man had the will to slip a noose over another's head and adjust the knot against the trembling neck? Josh couldn't imagine. Perhaps one of the judges saw it as a duty. Josh didn't look and didn't want to know. He stood straight and still, awaiting the order to march forward.

His hands began to sweat. He dried them on his pants and took his grip again. The verdict was read to both men at once. One of the men spoke last words, a mixture of remorse and a final cursing of those who condemned and would now take his life. Josh thought he recognized the voice as Jacobsen. He imagined he could feel the doomed man's words through the rope but willed himself not to look. Pastor Fredericks said The Lord's Prayer. Josh found himself mouthing the words. Others did the same but no voice besides the pastor's rose above a murmur.

There was no order to march. A miner stood at the end of the line before Josh with his hand raised. A moment passed and the arm dropped. Josh strode forward, almost walking into the back of the man ahead of him. For a second, the effort was sloppy, then they strode forward in unison. They took up the weight and moved until the miner at the end held his hand up for them to halt. The man in front of Josh stole a glance over his shoulder. They exchanged a brief look of horror before the man turned away. Like a fish with the hook now in its belly, Josh could feel the dying man kick, seeking footing that was now forever departed. Mercifully, someone took the loose end of the rope, wrapped it around a tree trunk and hitched it down. Josh and the other men, their terrible work complete, released the rope as if they held filth. This was a mistake, dropping the hanged man a foot and strangling a moaning gurgle from the victim. Repulsed, Josh wiped his shaking hands on his pants. The wiping did as much good as did Pontius Pilate washing his hands after condemning Christ.

Josh looked up at the rope, watched it jiggle, then settle in to its work. To his surprise, there was a smattering of men clapping their hands. Whether the applause was for the work of the executioners, the satisfaction of justice, or an acknowledgment of an odious task completed, was anyone's guess. Josh was certain of one thing. He needed a drink.

Josh was not alone. Everyone needed a drink and set off at a respectful pace back to the camp for a shot of whiskey and the encouraging conviviality of men who were still among the living. There was little talk as they proceeded. Nearing camp the crowd thinned, bound for the various crude tent saloons. A few wags tossed out witticisms that elicited only silence and some baleful stares. No doubt, with hands and nerves steadied by ardent spirits, the mood would turn more ebullient and the same jokes received with better humor. Liquor would steel men's resolve and loosen their tongues. Josh wanted no part of such society. The memory of the rope dancing in his hands was too vivid and too personal. At a barroom someone might recall his part in the proceedings and speak to him. Better to drink at home than to have to disclose his part. He started for French Bridge across the American and then turned west for the trek to the diggings and home.

Elizabeth was waiting on the creek bank for him when he crossed. After the verdict had been read, the men had sent her packing. Silently she stormed from the outdoor court and away. There was no trace of anger in her bearing now. She must have watched. She put her arm in his and rested her head on his shoulder.

"I started to watch but when they were strung up I had to turn away."

"I couldn't watch either. It was bad enough just being there. I need a drink, maybe two or twenty."

Entering their winter quarters, Jubal and Duncan were sitting on two packing crates and playing checkers on a third. The two players greeted them with concerned stares. From their faces it was apparent they didn't want to discuss the hangings.

"It's over", is all Josh said on the subject. He retrieved the brandy and almost drank from the bottle. He stopped, poured a shot for Elizabeth and himself. He lifted his eyebrows to the checker players, silently asking if he should pour them, as well. They both nodded, Josh got down two more mugs. There were no toasts and no discussion. Josh tossed back his drink and poured another. The balance of the day passed quietly, really no different than any other since their arrival in camp, six weeks ago. Time to reflect on how much had happened   in   the   interim.

CHAPTER ONE

After striking a partnership with Shipwash, Josh and Elizabeth left his camp the next morning. Not wanting to consume the mining engineer's dwindling supplies, they hiked down the Middle Fork and reunited with Jubal who had been keeping watch on their two carts and mules. When they arrived they found him washing dirt from the stream with a dented miners' pan. He grinned when he spotted them approaching.

"Guess Ah'm bound to be a miner, too," he said, producing a worn pouch and plucking a couple of what Shipwash called 'pickers' for them to see. A picker was smaller than a nugget, more substantial than flake, and bigger than gold dust. Picker was an apt moniker. Jubal followed the pickers by dumping out a little more than half an ounce of dust into his palm.

"While I was waitin', a man come by and offered me gold to haul his goods down to some 'bark a dero' or somethin'. I told him I was waitin' for you. He showed me where I could look for gold. Even showed me how to pan. Gave me the pan when he left. We split what we found."

"Found any since he left?" asked Josh.

"Little bit. Some other folk saw I was findin' and they started pannin' on the other bank. Guess they didn't want to share a gold mine with a colored man." Jubal didn't seem angry about being discriminated against. Probably a leper could have mined by himself just as well.

"Thinking' about staking a claim?" asked Josh.

Jubal seemed puzzled by the concept.

"Lordy, no. I ain't never owned no land. Don't know what would happen if I tried."

"A mining claim is different than owning the land. I guess all this land belongs to John Sutter. I was told he owns fifteen thousand acres here. All the land around Sutter's Fort." Elizabeth stated.

"Sutter's Fort," said Jubal. "That's where the man was going to 'depart-adero' from."

"We'll probably visit there to get re-supplied. For now we are headed to Gold Run camp where we are to wait for Duncan."

1

"That reminds me. While you was gone that Coody man come by. He had a new wagon and team and was headed for that fort. Mr. Billings was with him. They was both drunk as lords."

The three of them set off for Gold Run. As they rode, Josh explained how they were all partners in new claims and showed Jubal the nuggets they had prised from the quartz seam in the desolate canyon near the middle fork.

Before long they began to pass the tents of miners along one of the tributaries to the American. There were signs of excavations tested and abandoned. Men were digging and washing sand all along the streams. Most looked up and waved but quickly returned to their labor. As they approached one lonely camp near the trail, the flaps of the tent parted and a dark-haired man seated inside called to them.

"You headed to Gold Run?"

"We're supposed to meet someone there," Elizabeth answered. "Why do you ask?"

"Dang, it's a woman," The man said to someone in the tent. The dark-haired man came out and stood by the tent.

"Well ma'am. There's sickness in Gold Run. My friends just returned from there and they is all laid up."

"What kid of sickness? Fever?" asked Josh.

"Didn't know you was particular in your plagues but the answer is the bloody flux."

Having lost their parents to cholera on the road to California, the Bonners were taking no chances encountering the disease or its symptoms again. They reversed direction without taking another step. Elizabeth was riding their friend Charlie Quill's horse. If he remained in Gold Run she would have to return the horse later.

"You said you were meeting someone. Are they already in camp?" said the dark-haired miner.

"No, he's coming down from the Middle Fork," said Josh.

"If I'm still here I'll try to pass on a message if you tell me where you are going and who to give the message to," the miner offered, repeating, "...if I'm still here."

"Duncan Shipwash is his name, an Englishman. Got a bum leg, might be riding a mule. Tell him we went to Yerba Buena."

"There's no reason to go to Yerba Buena."

"Why not?"

"No one left in the village. Wasn't more than three hundred there before the gold. They all left and came to the hills. Probably not twenty people left. Sacramento's where you want to get fitted out."

"Sacramento?" said Elizabeth. "Where's that?"

"Down river from Sutter's Fort. Things is cheaper there than the fort 'cause of the freight. You got mules so Sacramento's going to be cheaper."

"Thanks, mister. I'm Josh Bonner. Didn't get your name."

"Carolina Carl is what they call me. Say you got any medicine for my partners."

"Sorry, Carl. We don't have anything for what your friends got."

Carolina Carl shrugged and ducked back in the tent.

The Bonner party, what was left of it, headed down the road, for Sutter's Fort and Sacramento.

~ ~ ~

Since morning, gray clouds had been piling up against the mountains. As the day cooled the clouds let loose with a light, steady drizzle. Before they got too wet, the Bonners stopped and retrieved rubber ground sheets from their packs. Rather than cut a hole for their head like the ponchos the Mexicans wore they draped the sheets over their shoulders and depended on hats to keep them dry. The rain accompanied them the rest of the afternoon and into the evening as they made a wet camp along the trail. It hadn't let up when they arose and set out again for Sutter's Fort.

As they approached the fort the throng of miners on the move began to close in around them. It was too miserable a day to exchange pleasantries or even a tip of the hat as strangers came near. Occasionally, they had to move off the trail as a teamster pushed his way into the hills, trying to get somewhere before the ground beneath his wheels turned to mud. By the time they arrived at the settlement, it seemed like the whole world had gone mad and converged at the rude camp by Sutter's New Helvetia.

When they arrived they never even saw the famous fort of John Sutter. There was so much activity and confusion it made no sense to compete with the frantic pace of commerce. The business of finding gold would not be interrupted by nightfall or rain. They made camp on a level spot away from the melee and made ready to sleep under the carts. Rain dripped from the branches and pattered on the oilcloth cart covers. Supper was cold biscuit and ham as tough as the bark of the dripping trees. As the evening wore along, the revelry and noise from around the camp ascended to new levels, fueled by various ardent spirits. When sleep finally came it was fitful.

The Bonners awoke to find the rain abated, leaving a persistent dank chill in the air. The morning was comparatively quiet as people were beginning to stir. The business of mining prevailed over everything. Josh and Elizabeth walked along the muddy path between makeshift businesses. One tent, declaring itself a tavern, had the flaps pulled back. Inside there was a mud floor with a plank across two barrels serving as a bar. A similar arrangement behind the "bar" held a keg, bottles and glasses. A man in a dirty apron was asleep on the planks.

Food was what the Bonners sought. It was too wet to build a fire. Josh and Elizabeth set out to forage while Jubal remained with their gear. Somewhere in this madhouse of commerce someone must be offering meals. Occasionally the aroma of brewing coffee drifted towards them, momentarily overpowering the stench of the overcrowded gathering. One establishment under a tarp was offering biscuits and red-eye gravy with a slice of beef for two dollars. It was a "bring your own plate affair." The alternative was to use the previous diner's plate. The Bonners moved on.

Rounding a corner they saw a line of men queued up in front of a tent. A man was doing a brisk trade selling oranges at one-quarter ounce of gold for a dozen. The store owner had boxes of limes and lemons at equally exorbitant prices. Fruit was certainly a luxury but just the appearance of colorful treats in the drab, muddy surroundings drew miners to his wares. Elizabeth and Josh joined the eager throng. She kept her hat pulled low, hoping not to be recognized as female. The ploy worked until they got to the counter. Two Mexicans were running the store. One doled out the prisings while the second weighed the gold. There was no bargaining, the storeowners pleading ignorance of English. When the one weighing the gold saw a woman before him, he snatched the hat from his head and grinned broadly.

"*Buenas Dias, senorita,*" he said, offering an orange to her.

"*Senora,*" replied Elizabeth, anxious to do business and avoid drawing a crowd. "How much?"

"*Un cuarto de onza doce naranjas.*"

"What did he say?" she said, turning to Josh. He shrugged his ignorance

"One quarter ounce for twelve," said the vendor.

"For sixteen," Elizabeth protested, insisting on a bargain.

"*Nada de inglés,*" replied the vendor, still grinning and offering the single orange.

"Hell, he speaks English," said Josh.

By this time the crowd was catching on there was a woman amongst them. They began to crowd around.

"Just buy the oranges and let's git," Josh urged.

They left the store with the dozen they bought and the one as a gift to the *senora*. It was the best they were going to do in such a frantic sellers' market. They carried their treasure back to camp in a scarf. Soon the air about them was fragrant with the smell of fruit. Oranges were not an unheard of luxury back in Illinois as steamers carried them upriver from the south. Still, oranges were an indulgence. Here in the muddy camp, the first fruit they had enjoyed in months was an impossible luxury. The three of them went through the dozen in no time. Passers by inquired where they obtained them. Happily they gave directions. Their faces and hands were soon sticky with juice. They cleaned up and set off for the landing at the junction of the American and Sacramento Rivers, about five miles away.

Finding the way to the river landing was more an exercise in avoiding being run down by wagons than in following a trail. The traffic, the mud, the noise of commerce and revelry, and the smells were the same as the camp by the fort. The trio who trudged into the melee were tired, wet, and hungry. The animals needed forage and water. Jubal took them to the river while Josh and Elizabeth set off to find food. Inland the ooze gave way to drier footing as the elevation rose. It seemed a little more ordered once the cacophony of sound and smells of trade by the landing was left behind. The young couple stood at what passed for an intersection in the camp. From somewhere the smell of baking and cinnamon enticed them to the south and over the crest of a small rise. There they discovered the source of the aroma, a tent with a sign proclaiming 'apple turnovers, fifty cents'. The flaps of the tent were closed. A small placard read 'sold out for now'. The tent was sealed up but someone was baking inside. Heat rose from a metal stovepipe at the rear of the tent. Josh approached the tent and called to the folks inside.

"When will you have more turnovers?"

"Sold out. Come back in two hours." It was obvious the question was a familiar one. Josh and Elizabeth walked away, disappointed but determined to return. They hadn't gone ten steps when a voice rang out from behind them.

"Josh? Elizabeth?"

Turning they were greeted by the grinning face and red beard of Carl Van Volk, his head poking out the tent like a deer trophy mounted on a wall. Recognizing the couple, he threw open the tent and came forward with his arms open.

"Welcome to Von Volk Family Bakery. Come in." He clasped them both over the shoulders and ushered them into the new enterprise. The now familiar plank on two barrels marked the sales counter. Some pine stumps served for seating. Calico cloth was strung from side to side, dividing the store from the bakery. It was delightfully warm inside. The fragrant smell of baking enveloped them.

"Please, my friends. Sit down and rest. I can offer you some cider while the latest batch cools enough to eat."

"B'God, Carl. You are already in business," said Josh. He was amazed at how quickly things happened in the camps. "I thought you were bound for the gold mines."

"We were. We came here to get outfitted but Providence put us in the bakery business. Now I think there is more gold to be made in this tent then in sifting ore from the streams."

Carl told of their journey from Auburn camp and how they had run into a teamster whose wagon had broken a wheel. The teamster offered them three hundred dollars for their wagon on the spot. Of course, they couldn't sell their wagon and have all their possessions left at the side of the road. The teamster had been carrying supplies to the Auburn camp when his wagon broke. He'd been carrying canvas, picks and shovels, and, most importantly, three barrels of apples and three kegs of apple cider.

In an instant, Carl Von Volk saw his future. He negotiated the purchase of the apples and cider in exchange for one hundred fifty dollars and the exchange of enough furniture to make room for the barrels in their wagon. The teamster helped with the transfer of goods and gave Carl a receipt for the purchase in case the owner somehow didn't receive payment for the goods.

Once in Sacramento they obtained enough canvas, poles, and rigging to make a store and another tent for their animals and possessions. Providence smiled again and led to a man who sold them a folding sheet metal oven. They were able to buy flour, lemon juice, and the other basics to bake in. They elected to sell turnovers because pans were in short supply as mining implements and went for fifteen dollars each. They leased a town lot from a man who purported to be the owner. The rent was one hundred dollars a month and cheap at that exorbitant rate because it was on the backside of a knoll and therefore segregated from the regular business district. This suited the Van Volk family because the raucous nature of the camp was not suited for the girls, Wilhelmina and Mary. The smell of baking and cinnamon was all the advertising they'd needed.

"This is our second day in business, and we have made more in that time than I made in a month cutting leather in the boot factory at home. The girls peel apples and mix. Hannah bakes and I run the storefront. We are so glad we came to California, and we have you to thank for it, my friends. Two weeks ago we were slogging through the Humboldt Sink. It's a miracle. More cider?"

Josh certainly didn't refuse but his interest was drawn to the canvas covering the tent.

"That's quite a spread of canvas, Carl. Mind sharin' with me how you came by it?"

"I'll get you some turnovers and then tell you. It's quite a story on its own."

Van Volk left the Bonners to get them the anticipated pies.

"This seems perfect for the Van Volks," said Elizabeth. "I can't picture the girls hauling gravel to a rocker, can you?"

"A bakery couldn't be better. They stay inside, warm and dry. Not like us miners."

It was Hannah Van Volk who brought them a plate of six turnovers. Each was a square with the corners folded up and pinched off to hold the filling. The corners were a little bit dark but not enough to deter the miners— starved for anything home-baked.

"Carl just told me you were here. I scolded him for not telling me the instant he found you. Let me fill your mugs with more cider."

"Thank you, Hannah," said Elizabeth. "These look delicious."

"Bah, they're burned. I'm still learning this folding oven but the customers don't complain."

"Carl was going to tell us the story about the canvas," Josh said, pointing at the ceiling.

"I'm sure he'd take credit for the find. He went with the owner to look at town lots. He left me and the girls, and all our possessions next to that madhouse at the river. While we were waiting for him to return, a man brought a rowboat to shore. Just as he got near the shore, the boat swamped and dumped his cargo overboard. He was loaded with sails from one of the ships abandoned in the river. I offered him two hundred dollars if he would drag the load to dry land. Now we have shelter for our animals and ourselves. Carl thought I paid too much for it, but when I found out he agreed to rent a lot for a hundred dollars a month, he sang a different tune. It took nearly all our money to start the bakery. With hard work and a little luck we will make it work."

Josh and Elizabeth stayed a bit longer, toured the kitchen and said hello to the Van Volk girls. The girls were peeling and slicing apples while Carl mixed the slices into pie filling. The Van Volks were getting ready for the next opening of the bakery. They invited the Bonners and Jubal to bring their gear to the bakery and stay with them as long as they liked. Josh took two pies back to Jubal and then returned to the Volk's tent with all their belongings. After greetings were exchanged Jubal took the animals to the pastureland behind the tent for forage.

Within the hour there were nine dozen tarts ready for sale. Josh and Elizabeth volunteered to help where they could. Carl opened the tent and Hannah took a tray out into the muddy thoroughfare and announced they were open for business. She could have saved the effort. Miners scrambled to the tent, and the pies were gone within twenty minutes. The Van Volk bakery closed up the tent flaps for the day. Between tarts and cider the bakery was richer by over eighty dollars. They had taken in nearly three times what Carl had earned in a month as a leather cutter in the Ohio boot manufactory.

The happy family was settling in for the evening, but the Bonners were restless. They needed to meet Duncan before he ventured to the blighted camp of Auburn, and they hadn't done a thing to get outfitted. Josh wanted to get going right away.

"Carl says there are ocean going ships all up and down the river. Says he hears there is over a hundred in San Francisco Bay just abandoned by the crew and even the officers headed to the gold. The ships' boats litter the shoreline. I aim to take one tonight and visit one of the abandoned ships." Josh said.

"You're going to steal a rowboat and then go board a ship like some pirate?" asked Elizabeth.

"The rowboat's are abandoned, too. Besides, I'm just going to borrow it. The ships are abandoned so I'm going to salvage one. We can get some sails, some lumber, and who knows what else."

"Plunder it, you mean."

"All right. I'm going to plunder it like a pirate."

"Not without me you aren't." threatened Elizabeth, defiance clear in her words.

Josh tried to sputter a retort. Women shouldn't plunder ships.

"Would you take Jubal along and leave me to hike up the trail and wait for Duncan? How long would it take before I…"

Josh didn't bother to protest. The danger to a woman on the road was far greater than climbing aboard an empty ship.

"I DO know how to row a boat, you know."

He could only nod.

Elizabeth whooped with delight at the coming adventure. She crushed him in her embrace, spun him around twice, and planted eager kisses on his face. It took about five seconds for Josh to forget why he objected in the first place.

"We'll go tonight. Ride the current downstream. We'll need a couple lamps from our gear."

CHAPTER TWO

The nightlife of the camp was already at a fast trot as they made their way to the river's edge. The saloon tents were ablaze with light, and the patrons' outlines wove and staggered in silhouette on the canvas sides. Vendors called out their offerings as Josh and Elizabeth passed. Josh was carrying a leather sack of tools he might need, some provisions, and blankets. Elizabeth walked just ahead of him holding two lanterns and a sack of clothing. The mud thoroughfare was full of men, all seemingly dressed alike in heavy pants, muddy boots, plaid wool shirts, and slouch hats. People seemed to be walking in all directions. No one paid a whit of attention to two more people in heavy cloth coats and shapeless hats trudging through the crowd. Everything was for sale. Hasty deals were struck with a handshake and an exchange of the precious dust. Wagons were being loaded. Teamsters called to their teams and swore at the foot traffic. Mules brayed and deals were done. The stacks of goods seemed to stretch for three hundred yards along the riverbank. Everywhere lanterns bobbed.

Along the gravel beach, yellow moonlight shone on abandoned goods. The couple stepped around several boxes of broken crockery. Burst barrels and kegs lay among their spilled contents. At the water's edge bolts of cloth were strewn, trampled and soggy in the muck. Several hams bobbed in the water. Only a few men wandered or stumbled along, perhaps seeking some form of solitude from the crush of commerce not a hundred feet away.

Several ship's boats had been dragged ashore and overturned. Propped up on either or both ends they served as impromptu shelters for some. Small fires near them illuminated the residents within, huddled together like dogs in a kennel. No one even looked up as they explored the beach. Just two more fortune seekers in battered hats.

There were probably two dozen boats either pulled up on the shingle beach or riding to anchor just offshore. Josh and Elizabeth tried moving some of the grounded boats but couldn't budge them. They did find a pair of oars that hadn't yet been lifted. Holding their lanterns high they waded to the tethered boats. The current was steady but not difficult to contend with. They selected two, both about twelve footers, picked up the mooring lines and set off into the stream. Once away from the camp they fixed a line between them, set the lamps in the bows and drifted in the current. There was hardly any rowing to do. Once in a while an oar was dipped to keep the boats on course.

They drifted along in silence. A quarter moon gave just enough light. The lanterns were dimmed to just a glow. The river broadened. Reeds and rushes leaned slightly downstream obscuring both banks. Frogs serenaded them while bats and night birds swooped by overhead. Occasionally a fish jumped. When either Josh or Elizabeth felt the need to speak they did so in whispers. The night seemed to demand hushed voices. After the hustle and confusion of the camps the hours drifting in the silent stream became dreamlike, placid, and timeless.

Before long the river broadened and the effect of the current slackened. They rowed in earnest, adding the squealing of the oarlocks to the evening's symphony. Soon they soon began to feel the tug of the ocean's tide so many miles away. Josh, being a waterman, could read the ripples and eddies of the current. He navigated them around sandbars and sunken snags. As the water of the river mixed with the tidal delta, it chuckled against the hull. Slack tide was gone and they had to row against the flow. It was after they'd navigated the point of a long wooded island; the masts of the ship came into view.

Two stubby masts protruded above the treetops. The yards were crossed and bare, sails stripped from the rigging. Clouds scudded across the moon and the silhouette faded back into the night. They rowed the boats close to the shore, where the effect of a rising tide was less. When the moon reappeared, Josh scanned the channel, expecting to find a ship at anchor. There was nothing. Then he saw the stern of a ship protruding from the tree line. The ship wasn't at anchor. It was aground.

As they rowed closer a side-wheeler steam packet revealed itself, just barely large enough to rate being called a ship at all. She was aground by the bow and down slightly by the stern. Firmly beached forward, the ship swung with the tides. There was the slightest of lists. Her hull was sprung somewhere. They rowed underneath the counter of her stern cabin. The rudder hung splintered and useless from the pintles. On the transom the victim's name was painted in gilt. *Julianna Dolce* out of Valparaiso. The captain and crew of the *Julianna Dolce* had steamed a long way to kill their ship in California.

She had foundered on her port side. They could hear the paddlewheel on that side slowly being ground away between hull and shore. Forward, the hull groaned and protested the patient but inevitable destruction. The Bonners pulled their craft along the

11

starboard side, around the silent side-wheel and found the gangway. A rope ladder with wooden rungs hung from stanchions. The ship's boats were gone, the davits trailing lines into the water as if fishing for the missing longboats. Josh clamored up the rope ladder. Elizabeth tossed him a line and he made fast to a cleat. Elizabeth scampered up while he was tying off.

"Your brother used to tell me tales of ghost ships," said Elizabeth. "This is better than any of his stories."

Josh turned in surprise. Not at the revelation, but at the fact he hadn't thought of his brother since they crossed the Sierras. Ned was probably a first mate by now. They had parted company when Ned departed down river to New Orleans where he shipped out as engineer on a steamer. Maybe the steamer was carrying passengers to California, and they might meet up in gold country or at *Yerba Buena*. While Josh had written to family telling of their parents' death on the trail, perhaps word had never reached him. It would be terrible if they met and Josh had to break the news. The odds of a random meeting were slim at best. No sense dwelling on the subject. It was time to explore the *Julianna Dolce*. Time to see what salvage and plunder awaited the newly initiated pirates.

The *Julianna* was a trim little brig-rigged ship to augment the steam. She was less than a hundred feet to be sure. In an earlier life, she had probably plied between ports on the Chilean coast. A boat this size would be perfect for shipping between the ocean and Sacramento, probably not drawing ten feet under the keel. Unfortunately, after her grounding, the crew abandoned her to an unkind fate on the shoal. Forward was a deckhouse and a raised bow deck with capstan. There were signs of other visitors. Besides a tangle of loose rigging on the deck, kegs, boxes, and other flotsam littered the deck. Kegs fetched up against the bulwarks as the tide and list dictated. The topsides were capped with a pale painted wooden rail. The most noticeable feature was the black void and exposed timbers where long straight sections of deck boards had been removed and taken away. The mast had been stripped of spars up to the topmost yards. If the Bonners were going to be pirates they would have to be content with the leavings of both the crew and more enterprising buccaneers.

Elizabeth called out to anyone aboard. After the silent passage and quiet night, the sound of her raised voice rang out across the water and into an empty sky. Josh was about to scold her but she was doing the proper thing. Perhaps only the crew had abandoned the *Julianna*

12

Dolce, and the captain and officers had shown fealty to their ship and station. Her hail brought no response other than the bark of a dog somewhere in the distance. They were alone on a derelict boat with only the sounds of frogs and night birds for company. They split up and began to explore.

Josh went forward, examining the crates and barrels on the deck. There was too little light to read what the contents were but Josh didn't want to turn up the lantern. Some of the burst kegs had spilled white powder. He could identify another mess by the smell of molasses. There would be ample light and time when morning came.

He stood by the open wound where the decking had been pilfered. He peered past the boat's ribs at standing water in the bilge. It reflected the moon and clouds above. Perhaps the hull wasn't sprung and the rains had caused the listing of the craft. A rank smell drifted up, robust and piercing but not quite rot. The prospect of going down in the hold of an abandoned ship in the dark gave him the shivers.

Kicking in a door opened up the deckhouse. It was fun to be a pirate but he couldn't escape the feeling he was violating the ship itself. He entered a cookhouse, dominated by a large cast iron stove set in a bed of sand. It was as cold as a tomb. He turned up the lantern enough to see the rest of the layout. It was obvious the provisions had been plundered. The crew, afflicted with gold fever, probably cleaned out the stores and implements. Not a pot, pan, or knife was left behind. The shelves, where stores should be, were picked clean. There was a half full water butt but even the ladle was gone.

Going back on deck he found another door. It swung freely on its hinges. He took this as a good sign the hull wasn't sprung out of true from its spell on the beach. As he entered the crew quarters, he was expecting hammocks. Surprisingly, he found bunks along both the port and starboard bulkheads with a common table and benches in the middle. The foremast protruded through the overhead, table, and deck. There were hooks around the circumference of the mast, empty but probably for coats and foul weather gear. It would be nice to turn up some sea boots. The table ran the length of the forecastle but lay bare. Some of the bunks had firm bolsters. Others were bare boards. No blankets or bedding remained. There was little left of the crew's personal effects, only a few books in Spanish. When the sailors left they took all of their lives they could carry.

Going outside again, Josh examined the structure of the deckhouse. It looked well made with long horizontal planks fixed by wooden pegs to the frame. With his knowledge of boats he knew the wood used would be chosen for its lighter weight, unlike the oak deck. He could take away enough material to build a shelter without sinking his dinghy with hardwood.

On either side of the deckhouse there were doors, closed, locked, and undisturbed. Digging through his tools he picked a hefty iron bar and pried open the lock. The interior presented a small storage locker. Josh stepped in and turned up the lantern's wick. He took one look around, backed out on deck, and turned the lantern down to just a short orange bar of light. He'd stepped into a paint locker. In the instant of illumination he spied waxed boxes of pigments and barrels of solvents to mix paint with. If any of these had been leaking he could have blown himself and the forward half of the ship all over the landscape. Reaching back in he rolled out a small cask. There was no label but it smelled of tar, and the ends of the staves were black and tacky with the stuff. Tar was a valuable find.

The other locker, when he pried open the lock, contained an even greater find. Here was the sail locker. Bright white sails were bagged and stowed in racks. Even better was the discovery of a large bolt of heavy sailcloth. The new white material almost glowed in the moonlight. He pulled out about five feet of the material from its home. More remained on the shelf. The stiff cloth was truly a treasure. With it he could build shelter. With the contents from the other locker he could mix up paint and make the shelter waterproof. They had yet to find gold and jewels but lumber, fabric, and paint were as rich to him as any treasure buried by Captain Kidd. Enough for now anyway.

~ ~ ~

Elizabeth first explored the quarterdeck, accessed by stairways to either side. She was drawn to the large helm wheel. It was connected to a drum that moved the ropes to the tiller. Giving the wheel a tug it moved a few inches either way. The broken rudder, under the stern of the boat, had jammed the wheel. Where the compass should reside was an empty space. Probably the captain or navigator had removed the precious device and put it away for safekeeping.

Descending the steps she entered the companionway to the officers' quarters. Turning up the lantern revealed four doors on the port side. Each of the cabins was empty but she found the missing compass in a box filled with sawdust. Another door revealed the head. Across from the cabins was a common area for the officers. At the very stern of the boat was the captain's quarters. The door was locked.

While on deck she had heard Josh prying open a door. She was off to find him when he stepped through the companionway from the main deck. She held up her lantern and pointed at the locked door.

"The door to the captain's cabin is locked."

"I have just the thing, m'lady," he said, brandishing the pry bar.

"I want to do it." Elizabeth held her hand out. "If we are going for plunder than I want to do my fair share."

Josh acceded, nodded to her and surrendered the metal.

"May I hold the lantern for you?"

Elizabeth curtsied, turned, jammed the bar into a gap by the lockset. She set her grip and wrenched hard against the wood. The wood screamed, splintered, and the door sprung loose. She kicked it so hard it hit the wall behind it and sprung back at her.

"What fun. Let's see what was so valuable it needed to be locked up."

Peering into the cabin they were, at first disappointed. No ancient chests of gold doubloons, silver pieces of eight, or shining jewels spilled over the sides of the chest. The cabin was nearly bare. The floor strewn with books, papers, and an upturned pot of ink— leaking between the boards of the deck. Josh touched it. It was dry. The spilled molasses was fragrant and fairly fresh. This proved visitors were aboard after the crew departed. How did they get past the locked door. Looking up, the skylight was unlatched.

They hung the lanterns from the beams overhead and began to explore. Elizabeth picked up some of the books. They were all in Spanish. There appeared to be several ledgers and the ship's log. If nothing else, the presence of the log indicated the crew had gone for good. They dug through a couple of cabinets but didn't find much. One appeared to be the captain's private food stores. Empty but for a broken jar of preserves. Another was a weapons locker, also empty. On the floor before it Josh picked up a couple small tins of percussion caps and a paper sleeve of wicks that would fit their lantern. In the hanging clothes locker hung an ornate dress uniform and some gleaming buckled shoes, abandoned as impractical. The drawers held some handkerchiefs and silk stockings. There was a bunk with a heavy bolster left behind. Looters hadn't taken it. Underneath the bolster were boards that could be removed. It contained bed linen and most importantly, blankets. The only really good thing they'd found was a small cabin stove, just too big to be readily portable and fastened securely to the deck. It would be added to the Bonner plunder.

Josh and Elizabeth had been up since daybreak and it was now surely past midnight. The thought of an actual bed, inside, under a roof, with a stove to take the chill away put an end to their reconnoiter of the *Julianna Dolce*. Josh retrieved some scraps of broken barrel and crate and started a fire. Elizabeth made the bed. It was narrow but a thousand times better than sleeping under a cart, lying on an oilcloth groundsheet.

Their chores completed they turned down the wicks of the lanterns to extinguish them. The stove was drawing well and a cheery red glow beamed out of the grates in the iron door. They stripped off their sturdy miner's clothing and left it in two piles on the deck.

The quarter moon was lower now, reflecting off the water outside and in through the stern windows. The moving water made yellow light dance over their skin like startled fish flickering off their bodies. The two lovers stood before each other with the red and yellow light competing for attention. Together they made for the fresh bed and entwined, tumbled into it. Their lovemaking was frantic, intense, and somehow more satisfying for its brevity. They lay entwined in afterglow and did not speak. Both watched the yellow, flashing fish dance in yellow squares on the ceiling. The moon had not yet set before both slept. While they rested, the tide ebbed. The *Julianna Dolce* settled once again into its own bed of sand. As if the boat were falling asleep, she listed a bit more. The sleeping lovers took no notice.

~ ~ ~

They slept late, a luxury they had not afforded themselves in, it seemed, a thousand years. By the time they woke, the flickering overhead reflections of the night before had been replaced by yellow slashes of sunlight on the cabin walls. They lazed away the morning, watching the slashes become rectangles on the deck, shorten, shrink to bars, and eventually vanish. They got up before the daily cycle completed. The sunlight was warm through the glass; they bathed in it like a half-remembered memory of childhood. All the scene lacked was a large tabby on the window bench, cleaning its paws. Morning's bright intrusion gave the looted cabin a forlorn, violated look.

There was another intrusion into the, otherwise, blissful domestic scene. Josh detected a trace of the same pungent, dank odor present as he stood over the open deck boards. Elizabeth, like a pampered duchess, remained under the covers. Josh stirred the fire in the small cabin stove back to life and dressed as he made his way on deck. He stepped into a bright, windless day. Overhead, small patches of gray clouds hung as motionless in the sky as the rest of the morning over the earth.

Looking aloft, Josh could see some of the spars in the topmost rigging still remained. Their sheets and halyards intact. Those who pillaged the ship earlier had run out of nerve as they scaled the mast. Josh knew he could use both the spars and the rope. He was willing to test his nerve for what he wanted. A task needed doing and he was the only one there to do it. The decision was settled but could wait until he was fully awake.

He strolled the deck amidst the litter, looking for anything salvageable. The broken barrels might once have contained flour and sugar, but the rain had spoiled them. Whether it was crew or scavengers the work had been done in haste. Both flour and sugar were valuable commodities. He prowled until he made a discovery as worthwhile as a pouch of gold coins. Under a stairway a wooden crate caught his attention. It weighed about twenty-five pounds. He was astounded when he read the stenciled label. The box contained nails. In their haste to leave the *Julianna Dolce*, not everything of value had been taken. Their trip would yield canvas, paint, the small stove, nails, and whatever his courage could harvest from the rigging.

Throughout his tour of the deck the oversweet, piercing smell hung in the still air. He wondered how to get below deck. Between the two masts was an intact hatch cover, battened and secured against the weather. Taking the knife from his belt, he cut away the lashings that secured the cover. He walked down one side, cutting as he went. Halfway down he cut a lashing and the hatch popped up, releasing a foul stench he wouldn't have been surprised if it could be seen. He backed away, involuntarily wrinkling his nose and fighting the urge to vomit. As the hatch had popped up, tightly woven cloth sacks were revealed. He held his breath and finished cutting the remaining lashes. The hatch was too heavy, so he retrieved an oar from one of the launches and levered it sideways. The sacks were rice. When the decking had been taken, rain got into the bilge. The lower tiers of rice had soaked up the water expanding to fill the hold and press the top most sacks tightly against the hatch cover. The expansion may have breached into the forward hold, releasing the stench he'd detected earlier. It was also possible the swelling rice had expanded the hull's planking. The now fermenting cargo and sprung boards could well account for the ship being down by the stern.

"What is that God awful stench?" Elizabeth bellowed, her words distorted from the cloth held against her mouth and over her nose. "What's rotting?"

"Rice! I'm not sure if it's exactly rotting but something nasty is going on below."

What to do about it was something best left for later. For now they maneuvered the cover back in place. From their meager supplies they made coffee on the small stove and warmed up the last of the tarts the Van Volks had given them. Closing the cabin door kept out the worst of the odor but enough lingered in the cabin to serve as reminder. Breakfast was quiet. Each took refreshment in company with their thoughts. Josh was turning over the hurdles of re-floating the *Julianna*, a natural train of thought for a boat mechanic. Elizabeth was turning over other possibilities. She poured over the options before she spoke.

"Why don't we winter here instead of hauling off to some mining camp?"

Somewhere in the back of Josh's mind, unknown to him, a similar thought must have been swimming around. He was only startled that it was Elizabeth who gave voice to the idea. His mouth hung open uselessly, before managing to stammer a reply.

"What about our claim? What about finding gold?"

"We'll have to ask Duncan. I don't think there are any claims. People just seem to be digging where they want and moving on if they don't find anything. I know one thing I haven't seen is a courthouse. Don't you have to go to court and file something?"

"I've seen some diggings where the prospectors marked their spot by leaving a shovel or pick on the spot."

"Leaving a shovel is like leaving a blanket to mark a picnic spot at a Fourth of July celebration. We're talking about gold."

These weren't new concepts for Josh. They'd popped into his head as they were headed back from Duncan's camp.

"I guess we just don't know how it works."

"That's a reason we partnered up with Duncan. We certainly can't camp out all winter and protect our spot. The river's are rising and we could get cut off for months."

"Suppose I can't keep this tub afloat? Then what?"

"I don't think you would let it founder. Besides, the water doesn't seem like it would sink all the way. Surely, you can prevent it from tipping over."

"Mebbe," Josh considered the options. "If that's the plan, then we ought to sink it now where we want it sunk."

"If it doesn't work out, we load up our salvage and head up river. Build a shelter and wait out the winter. Right now we're dry and warm with a roof over our heads."

The idea was gaining on Josh. The disadvantages of being away from the gold and the trading posts were losing ground to wintering on the derelict *Julianna*. If there was sickness in the camps it was better to be away.

"What about our horses and mules?" He was getting tired of being the one contrary to the idea.

"They can stay on the island. We can gather forage if we have to."

"Food, what about food for us?"

Elizabeth smiled. "You like rice?"

~ ~ ~

With the plan settled upon there were things to be done and new problems to work out. Neither of the Bonners were discouraged by the prospects. The last six months had been one challenge, setback, or obstacle after another. Life wouldn't seem normal if they didn't have something broken to fix or challenge to surmount. The list seemed endless. There was nothing to do but bend mind and muscle to the task.

Much of the morning was spent in simple work that left their mind free to prioritize and gauge the next move. They explored and scavenged as they set about a general housecleaning and disposal. Elizabeth worked in the stern cabin. She opened the gallery windows to let fresh air in and the trash out. Josh found a smaller hatch cover aft of the main mast. Removing it he was able to descend below decks down a ladder. The bilge was awash with water and rice, as if a layer of maggots floated in the slop. He stripped off his trousers before climbing down. The ripe and fermenting rice in the hold almost drove him out. With a lantern he ventured to the stern to certain whether the splintered rudder might have opened the hull. The water was deepest and dirtiest here. The best he could determine by feel was the hull hadn't been sprung. The steering quadrant above hung precariously over his head, twisted and useless from the rudder's grinding motion. The air was close, stifling. Before he became too nauseous, he had to climb back to the sun. The swollen cargo was a major problem. How could he possibly empty the entire hold?

He wore the sludge from the bilge like gravy. Stripping off the rest of his clothes he climbed overside, down the rope and wooden boarding ladder, into the launch, and then rolled tentatively into the river. Alongside the *Julianna* the water wasn't much of an improvement over the bilge. He paddled under the stern gallery and arrived just in time to be pelted with a sluice of dirty water that came flying from the gallery windows. He had barely managed to splutter out a wet protest when the bucket followed the cascade of scrub water.

"Dammit! Elizabeth. You almost brained me," he yelled.

Elizabeth's head appeared in the window above. She seemed more curious to find him there than aghast at almost killing him.

"I see you found a bucket."

"Yes. In the privy. There was a mop and the bucket was in a cubby behind it."

"In the head, you mean."

"Yes, I almost hit you in the head," Elizabeth sighed, treating him to a contrite smile. "I'm sorry."

"On a boat, the privy is called the head. You found the bucket in the head."

"Yes. *In the head.* I said I'm sorry."

Josh tread water below, looking up at his wife who was starting to see the humor in dumping the sludge water on her husband.

"You mean, 'I'm sorry, Captain Bonner', Don't you?"

"Yes, of course, Captain Bonner. Hold there just a moment, please." Her head and shoulders disappeared back inside. She was back in short order.

"I see you've neglected to put on your uniform."

The fancy captain's uniform discovered in the locker cascaded down on him. The coat and trousers were followed by the hat and buckled shoes. Josh wrestled himself free from the uniform and looked for his wife but she had disappeared. Moments later she stuck her head back out.

"How deep is the water?"

Josh stuck his arm straight up and let himself sink till his feet touched sand. His hand was still underwater.

"About ten feet," he said after he popped to the surface.

Elizabeth's bare body leaped from the gallery, her figure blocking out the sun for the moment before she splashed next to him. She was only underwater for a second before she surfaced, gooseflesh from stem to stern.

"Lordy, that's cold."

"It's warmer than what we were wading in a few days ago."

"Wading is not the same as diving in," she said through chattering teeth. "Did we bring any soap?"

Josh stroked to the launch.

"There's some in my possibles bag, I think," he said as he climbed up and over the stern of the launch. He foraged a bit before holding up a hunk of brown soap and a nubby square of cloth.

"Me first," he shouted, claiming finders' rights. He dunked both soap and cloth in the river and commenced a vigorous scrubbing. Elizabeth swam over and hung on the transom until Josh plunged in for a rinse. Pulling herself up and over, she started to wash when she saw that Josh was treading water and enjoying the view.

"You wouldn't peer at a lady as she attends to her bath, would you?" She scolded.

"Why yes. Yes I would."

"You cad," she protested, false outrage and modesty overcoming her.

"More like a scamp, I think. We are husband and wife, after all."

For the moment, practical matters took priority over what promised to be an exciting afternoon. They retrieved their clothes and set to scrubbing them as best they could in the bucket. Soon they were both scrubbed clean and scoured pink. Their clothing was spread on the *Julianna's* deck to dry. There was no rush. They wouldn't be needing them anytime soon. Laughing they disappeared through the companionway.

~~~

Josh awoke with Elizabeth's armed draped over his chest and her body spooned close to his. With great care he extricated himself. Wrapped up in a blanket; he climbed out into the last of the afternoon sun, now bereft of warmth. The scattering of clouds was gone and a breeze had come up, causing a chill to run across his skin. The deck retained some residual heat and warmed his bare feet. The clothing was still slightly damp and beginning to flutter in the wind. He gathered it up in case it became gusty. Their clothes smelled much better than when they took them off.

There were so many things to do Josh didn't want to waste even an hour of daylight. Looking up at the rat's nest above, he decided it was time to scale the lines and see what could be done with the remaining yards and rigging. It would be better to wait until the tide floated the *Julianna* off the bar and she righted herself. Aground, the cant of the decks was more pronounced. Peering upward, he guessed the mast was only two or three feet out of plumb. Nothing he couldn't cope with. Still, he faced a choice before his ascent. He didn't want to put on the clean but still damp clothes. Nor did he want to climb to the highest point for miles while naked. He could not see any other people from where he stood but it might be a different story when on display eighty feet in the air. He compromised, returning to the cabin and grabbing a suit of long, red underwear from one of the bags. He told Elizabeth, still abed, what he intended. She nodded sleepily as he went back above deck. He climbed up on the rail and put his bare feet on the tarred ropes woven to form a tapered web for the crew to go aloft.

Looking up as he climbed was disconcerting. The rope web narrowed as it reached the first landing. This gave the appearance of standing on railroad tracks and seeing the illusion of the tracks vanishing into nothing. Combined with the list of the boat, looking up soon made him dizzy. He knew it was no good to look down as he climbed, so he kept his eyes on the job in front of him. Feet on the horizontal, hands on the vertical, he recalled what his brother Ned had taught him. One hand for the boat, one for yourself. This was good practical advice and Josh repeated the mantra as he climbed. As he climbed he realized why sailors went up the ropes barefoot.

Before long he reached the first landing on the mizzen. The tarred shrouds passed through a rectangle in a slotted platform. He was able to squeeze through and stand on the slats. Not pausing for a moment to gawk about he swung on to the next and final set of ratlines.

He was gaining confidence as he climbed, but his self-assurance dwindled with each new handhold. The listing of the ship was far more pronounced than it appeared from the deck. While gravity pressed him against the ropes he clung to, his climb was going to end at the next landing and he would be retrieving yard and line at an angle that wouldn't quite clear the deck if he fell.

Before long he hauled himself through the last lubber's hole and found himself enclosed by a waist-high metal rail designed for lookouts to scan the horizon. The yard he wanted was still at least a dozen feet above his head and would require climbing the topmast itself. He balked at the idea. What would he do after he climbed?

It was time to survey where he was. Away to the north the land was a vista of low brown hills. They were sheathed in a grass that gave the appearance of a velvet blanket draping the landscape. The few trees he could see were in the gullies between hills where they were nourished by runoff on the slopes. In the spring, the new green growth would be magnificent. He could see small knots of cattle and horses grazing unattended. Miles away the red tile roofs and white adobe walls of a substantial homestead were nestled in a copse of trees. No fences broke up the pastureland. He figured he was looking at one of the large *ranchos* of the *Californio* estate holders.

To the west and south he found himself surveying a huge delta of natural channels, river estuaries and marshland. Even this late in the fall the wetlands teemed with all variety of birds. Long-legged herons and egrets lifted off and flew short distances, then resumed their graceful fishing in new waters. Migrating geese stalked the many islands. Ducks of all varieties were in abundance floating in sheltered waters and among the reeds and grasses. Ungainly pelicans swooped here and there low over the water. Above all, hawks soared and circled like kings of the air keeping watch over their subjects.

Josh was enjoying the marvel of his perch and watching the birds when his eyes locked on the masts of another ship lying in the channel between two islands. There was activity on the ship and she wore a full suit of yards and furled sails. The ship was too far away to hail but close enough he could see men working on deck. There was no one in the rigging but sailors were emptying the holds. As Josh watched a cargo net of barrels and bundles was hoisted on a yard and swung overside to a waiting raft. On shore a queue of wagons awaited.

This captain was taking no chances on losing his crew to gold fever. He had anchored in the channel and secured the boats. The crew never left the ship or were given an opportunity unless they chose to swim to shore with just the clothes they wore and whatever they could tow. The teamsters were manning the rafts and loading the wagons. He watched one depart and head up the river where it would pass the *Julianna Dolce*, the teamster perhaps wondering what tale she told. As the wagon drew by his roost he discovered they were not on an island. The channel had eroded near the shoreline and had dug away at the bank, creating a kind of cape he had mistaken for the passage between shore and island.

Josh soon began to wonder what sort of spectacle he presented up here amongst the spars and ropes and blocks clad in his red underwear. Wait till he started scrambling around in the rigging.

He began to lay out a plan for climbing and retrieving the yard. There were two pulleys either side of centerline fastened to it. He followed the ropes upward and saw they joined at another pulley set into the mast itself. Walking aft he saw where the line emerged from the mast and ran down to a cleat bolted to it at about the height of his knees. What a relief. He wouldn't have to climb. He could simply lower the yard to the platform he was on and then...and then what?

He could see no line to retrieve, fasten to the spar, and then lower it to the deck. First things first. He unhitched the halyard from the cleat and felt his feet pressed hard into the wooden platform. Even lowering it to the railing was almost more than he could manage. The yard finally came to rest on the tilted railing. He needed to secure it while he calculated his next step. The end of the halyard had a round knot, a Turk's head tied in the bitter end. Josh berated himself for not bringing a knife along. Enough slack remained he could pull the knot down to his chest. He gnawed at the salt-hardened rope until it loosened. He pulled the halyard through the pulley and took several wraps around the yard and rail to secure it and then analyzed his problem.

With the ship listing he figured he could shove the wooden spar off the low end of the platform so it would clear the rail and land in the water where he could retrieve it with one of the launches. He started to push. It slid rather easily and he was pleased with his strategy. That was until the spar rotated and one of the pulleys caught on the rail. The yard swung outward and plunged down. Josh could only watch it fall and hoped it cleared the rail. It didn't.

It struck the deck on a shallow angle and with a booming clatter. The spar bounced up once, hit the rail, and tumbled into the water. *Well*, he thought. *At least it ended up where I wanted but it's probably busted all to hell.*

Elizabeth was poking at the embers in the small stove when she leaped up at the sound of a crash reverberating

through the whole ship. Earlier, Josh had mentioned trying to retrieve one of the remaining yards from the mizzenmast. He must have fallen and now lay broken and dying on the deck. She rushed to the companionway but halted at the hatchway. She wasn't prepared to see his mangled body leaking life out through the scuppers. She stuck her head through the doorframe and just as quickly withdrew it, perhaps to lessen the impact of death. She saw nothing. Gathering her courage she took a longer look. Nothing looked amiss. For a moment she mistook the clothing Josh had gathered together for his body. She even moaned a bit before realizing her mistake. She stepped out and looked to the quarterdeck with dread. It looked the same as it ever was.

"Ahoy on deck," came a voice. She spun around searching for the source. The call was repeated and she looked aloft. There stood Josh, alive and whole in his red underwear like a cardinal in a tree.

"Josh. That crash," she cried. "I was certain you'd fallen and were dead."

"No such luck," he called down. He pointed to where the spar had been as if its absence was all the explanation needed. Elizabeth stared at him, puzzled.

"I was trying to lower the yard when it slipped. It hit the deck and bounced over into the water. I'll need to retrieve it."

With her terror relieved, she tried to sound angry like she was scolding a child who had narrowly escaped injury.

25

"Then you better come down and do it before you really get hurt," she called to her cardinal.

"Are you wearing anything besides that shirt?"

She plucked at the plaid shirt like she had never seen it before.

"No."

"I'll be right down."

Josh took in the panoramic view once more before beginning his descent. When his eyes found the nearby ship, no one was moving. Sound carries well over water and the crash had caught the attention of the crew, teamsters, and raft men alike. Work had stopped and men stared at the distant spectacle of a man in red long underwear cavorting in the rigging of the derelict. Josh waved his arm sheepishly a couple times in greeting. A few men waved slowly back. He began his descent before the laughter began. The sound slipped over the water to his ears. His face was nearly as red as his long johns.

By the time Josh plopped down from the rail to the deck, Elizabeth had finished dressing. She'd looked pretty enticing from the masthead, clad only in the heavy shirt. Now she looked like any other prospector they'd seen in the camps. He took her hand and she followed him to the outboard railing. There in the water floated the renegade spar, apparently none the worse for its journey.

"You risked your life for that?"

"It was the spar that fell, not me. I wasn't never in no danger."

"What do you plan on doing with it?"

"Plenty of possibilities. Mebbe a ridgepole for the roof of a cabin. Mebbe I could rig up a mast so we could sail one of the boats back to Sutter's with our loot."

"Looks too heavy for the boat. Probably sink it or make it turn turtle."

"Make a damn fine beam for a cabin though, wouldn't it?"

"I thought we were staying here."

"Just till we can get back up the river and work the gold," countered Josh.

Elizabeth thought that a fine idea but she still was peeved about Josh, if only in her mind, getting smashed on the deck.

"Guess you better get to work then before it drifts away."

~~~

In one of the rowboats, Josh secured the spar with the line still attached to it. The end where it had struck the deck was splintered. Elizabeth was right. It was way too bulky and long to use as a mast for a sail on the launch. He towed the spar under the boat davits and made it fast to one of the trailing lines. By the time he climbed aboard the last of an orange sun was disappearing. Josh started for the stern cabin.

"You aren't getting in my bed with those feet

Josh stood first on one leg and then the other to see what had drawn his wife's ire. The soles of his feet were flecked with tar from the ratlines. Elizabeth handed him the bucket and the soap. It took nearly half an hour of scraping and scrubbing until his feet met Elizabeth's approval.

~~~

The next morning marked the day of their departure and return to the landing up the river. Josh explained the *Julianna* wasn't grounded on an island but on the end of a short peninsula. He had told her about the other ship and the queue of wagons waiting for cargo to haul upriver. Without a spar to construct a sailing rig there would be no way to row both boats and their loot against the current. They would hide their plunder in the scrubby woodlands and then buy passage on one of the freight wagons that would eventually come by. Josh first towed the spar from alongside the hull off into a nearby cove. After the effort to retrieve it, the thing had become something of a fixation with him. Returning with the skiff, he hooked on to the lines trailing from the davits. Together with Elizabeth they were able to lift first one boat from alongside and bring it on deck, followed by the other. Josh then took the rope ladder from the boarding port and moved it to the other side. He made a crude sling from one of the salvaged sails and bundled the paint, tar, and crate of nails inside, then lowered it from the port davits until it hung above the marshy ground alongside. He unloaded each item and walked into the undergrowth to find suitable caches for their plunder. He had to wade into smelly water, mud, sand, and dead weeds to do so. He'd have another spell with the bucket and soap before this day was done.

Meanwhile, Elizabeth gathered up and packed into bags what they had brought with them. She placed the discovered bed linen in the compartment under the bedstead. The small cabin stove was too valuable a find to leave in place. Elizabeth took a scuttle and removed all the embers so it could cool. The stove would be unbolted and hidden until they could return. Soon, her chores were done and Josh had yet to return. She had time to explore.

Climbing the stairs to the quarterdeck she stood behind the wheel and imagined herself at sea, guiding the *Julianna Dolce* from one exotic port to another. Looking astern she spied several men on the hills across the river. They were afoot but attempting to corral several of the cows that foraged on the velvety hills. As she hadn't seen anyone but Josh for the past three days, her interest was piqued and she made her way to the stern rail to watch their activity.

She was several steps away when she stopped in her tracks. The stern quarterdeck of the ship was stained in dark brown splotches, puddles, handprints and footprints all muddled together. The stains couldn't be anything but dried blood. The stern quarter could only be the scene of a desperate and fatal struggle. Had the ship been boarded by pirates while steaming upriver. She didn't think so. The bloody sprawl was too concentrated. If pirates had boarded the fighting would be widespread or at the boarding port, not at the point highest above the water.

The herders across the river forgotten, Elizabeth paced back and forth at the perimeter of the fight scene. She tried to isolate some of the footprints and duplicate their movements. The bloody footprints overlapped, intersected, and disappeared in smudges and stains of gore. She tried to find some direction or ebb and flow in the stains but none could be found. On the railings and stern bulkhead there were smears of bloody handprints. She could see where men slid, stumbled, and died as they slashed and stabbed. She could make no story, no sense or reason for what she saw. She sat and stared, trying to see into a bloody past. That's where Josh found her when he returned.

Whatever words he was about to speak were throttled into silence by the shock of what he saw. Like Elizabeth he strode back and forth, seeking some sense to the melee painted in the lifeblood of those who fought here.

"Jesus, what a rumpus this must have been. Can you make any sense of it?"

"I don't think it was pirates. I'm thinking not all of the crew went to the mines for gold."

"How'd you come up with that?"

"All the fighting, or at least the end of it, was here where people were cornered. There must have been some sort of argument and it got out of hand." She concluded with a sweep of her arm to encompass the scene.

"I think you're right. Remember the empty arms locker where I found those primer caps. The crew might have mutinied and the officers armed themselves to knock down the rebellion."

"I don't think *Julianna* would be a wreck if the officers put down a mutiny. Do you?"

"My guess is the crew waited until the officers were all on the quarter deck and then broke into the weapons. They killed the officers and dumped the bodies over the rail."

Elizabeth stepped to the rail and looked into the water where they had been swimming. She imagined them cavorting in the water while murdered men lay in the mud below their feet.

Josh could read her mind and offered a different theory.

"I think the ship was underway when it happened. The bodies were dumped in the river and the crew ran the boat aground. They certainly couldn't take it to any landing. So they looted what they could and skedaddled."

"I guess we'll never know," said Elizabeth. "The only thing we can be certain of is there was murder done right where we're standing."

"I doubt anyone will return, but I'll be damn glad to put some distance behind us. There's just one pistol between the two of us to defend ourselves with."

With that said, the Bonners departed the *Julianna Dolce*, crossed the peninsula with their two sacks of belongings and began to hike upriver, following the trail of wagon ruts headed towards Sutter's.

~~~

Eventually, a wagon was certain to come along and they could offer gold for a ride. The rutted road often strayed inland from the soft ground at the river's edge. Rushes, reeds, and tangled undergrowth kept them on track as they trudged along. At one point they turned to look back. The masts of the *Julianna* were still visible. After a time they looked again and saw only trees. It was good they had to walk. Distancing themselves from the ship would avoid questions. Mostly they passed the time in silence until Elizabeth spoke.

"The crew that mutinied, they were probably a regular crew."

"I suppose so. What of it?"

"I don't think the captain would ship out with a crew of criminals. Some of the crew probably had families and ties to homes in South America."

"From what I've seen, men who make their living on the water are ones that seem to find trouble on land. Some are running from their past and some are just running. Not sayin' they is a bad breed but they ain't the same as regular folks," Josh explained. He knew his brother Ned had gone down river just to get away from the boring life of home in Cairo, Illinois.

"I'm thinking they were expecting to leave the ship and go hunting for gold. Maybe they just went crazy when the captain wouldn't land them ashore."

"Guess everyone here has gold fever, but we've seen claims marked by shovels in the dirt and tents with gold just sittin' out in plain sight. Other than some drunks fighting over who knows what, there hasn't been any violence," Josh said. "There don't seem to be much point in fighting over the gold when you can find it most everywhere."

"How are we any better than pirates ourselves? Its like we are moving into a man's house while everyone is at the funeral."

"It's different with boats. There are salvage laws for derelicts but I admit I don't know how to do it proper. Besides, we didn't touch anything that wasn't abandoned. Its not like we broke any laws."

"That's just it. There isn't any law. There isn't a constable, sheriff, judge, or even a jail. Even if we were certain of what happened back there, who could we report to? The army is supposed to be in charge, from what we've seen, most of the troops just walked off their posts and grabbed a shovel. I think things are going to change come next mining season and it won't be for the better."

Josh was about to agree when they heard the approach of a team and wagon coming from behind. Elizabeth stepped back out of the way as Josh waved his arms, hoping the wagon would stop. Josh was counting on the rarity of encountering travelers as reason for the wagon to pull up.

The teamster was alone on the seat. He cracked his whip over the horses' heads to speed past the two tramps by the roadside. Just as he approached, one of the miners threw their hat on the ground and shook loose her hair. The teamster pulled up on the reins and yanked on the handbrake for all he was worth. The horses, confused by the contrary commands, eventually stopped but they had passed the couple, about a hundred feet. As the wagon passed, the teamster squinted an appraising look at Josh but only for a moment. He gazed at Elizabeth and snatched his hat off his head, holding it respectfully over his chest.

"Glory be! I ain't seen a white woman in over a month. Not meanin' any disrespect ma'am but you are the pretties thing I've seen in…well I don't know how long. What are you two doin' out here all to hell and gone?"

Josh and Elizabeth had worked up their story and Elizabeth told their tale.

"We came up the bay in a skiff. When we got to the river we couldn't row against the current so we left it in a sandbank and started walking. All we have is what we could carry."

I s'pose you be headed up to Sutters and wantin' a ride?"

"We can pay."

"He can pay," said the teamster, nodding towards Josh. "I ain't going to charge a woman."

Elizabeth produced a US gold Eagle and displayed it between thumb and finger. "How about ten dollars United States coin for the both of us?"

Whether the teamster was suspicious or just curious, he wasn't yet satisfied.

"You two from that wreck a ways back? I heard there was someone climbing about in the rigging like a madman."

"We rowed past that wreck just about dawn today," said Josh. "Didn't see anyone aboard. Course we wasn't lookin' for anyone either. We put ashore some ways upstream. Hard to tell how far on the water. Been walkin' ever since."

The driver cogitated on the story, taking his chin in hand to help his thinking.

"How far is it to this Sutter's Fort?" asked Elizabeth.

31

"I'm only going as far as the landing so that's what you get for your ten dollars. It'll take about six hours if the road holds. If'n it don't, then…" The driver shrugged his shoulders. He removed a filthy glove and offered a callused hand to assist Elizabeth so she could perch beside him. Josh climbed up by himself, assisted only by a suspect look from the teamster. Josh offered his hand.

"Josh Bonner. This is my wife Elizabeth. We hail from Cairo, Illinois."

"Lewis Werther. Erie, Pennsylvania." Werther gave Josh's hand a single pump and held out his paw for Elizabeth. "Lately from Monterey."

Both Bonners knew Monterey was the provisional capitol and where the US Army was garrisoned. Werther was telling them he was an army deserter without actually saying so. Josh and Elizabeth feigned ignorance. The teamster could well be telling them to mind their own business.

Undeterred, Elizabeth tried to draw Werther into conversation.

"Have you tried finding gold?"

"I gave panning a whirl. Found a enough to call it a livin', but I'm a born teamster and I'd rather ride this hard seat than muck about in a freezing river."

Werther spat a brown cud towards a puddle to accent his distaste for freezing rivers.

Josh leaned forward to speak.

"We aim to get rich and then buy ourselves a big ranch like the ones we heard about." Josh put on his most innocent face and most naïve tone. The farce must have worked. Werther looked at him with disdainful eye and wrinkled nose. Maybe their ruse worked, maybe not.

An axe, a shovel, and a shotgun rode in the box by the driver's knee. None would be handy against a person sitting next to you. Werther seemed gruff and uncommunicative. Of course, Josh didn't expect him to start bragging about deserting his position in favor of the greater glory of Lewis Werther.

For the Bonners' part, they told him where they were from and that they were married. The rest of their tale was a pack of lies. Embellishing their story would surely trip them up somewhere along the line.

Elizabeth sat between the two sphinxes. Werther was willing to talk to a pretty lady so she kept up a banter about the countryside and questions about the camps. Werther tried to keep up his end but it was a lot to ask from a man who spent his life looking at the ass end of a mule team. Elizabeth did her best to appear as empty-headed as the geese she queried him about. Before long they fell into an agreeable silence, punctuated occasionally by Werther spitting out his tobacco cud and replenishing his chew from a plug in his shirt pocket. He made no offer to share and the Bonners didn't ask.

CHAPTER THREE

The morning after Josh and Elizabeth departed; Jubal saddled Josh's sorrel, Natchez, and fixed up a pack rig for his own horse, Chicory. He was going to retrieve the British mining engineer, Duncan Shipwash. Having never set eyes on the man, Jubal would have to rely on Josh's description of him and the fact he had a bum leg and was on foot, leading a mule.

The Bonners had parted ways with the engineer on the Middle Fork of the American River while Jubal waited at the trailhead to Gold Run. Now he would head back to the American, hoping to intercept the Brit before he set off for that pestilence-ridden settlement. If need be, Jubal would venture up the river but damned if he was going to ride into a town beset with the bloody flux. He decided he would ride as far as the tent of the miner from Carolina and ask if Shipwash had passed that way. If not, Jubal would follow the crude map Josh had given him to their claim. If Shipwash had gone somewhere else, Jubal would track him down. If the Englishman had gone on to Gold Run, he could go hang.

On the trail west the custom had been to leave messages along the trail and mark the spot with a colored rag or something a passerby would take note of. There might be one of these frontier post offices where the road crossed the American. He'd just have to wait and see.

Few people were headed up into the gold fields. Twice he had to leave the trail to make way for teamsters hauling freight to some small settlement. Teamsters made their money by the mile and they gave no warning of their approach. Of course, it was hardly necessary as the racket they made could be heard half a mile away. He would move out of their way. The drivers never halted but both looked him over as they stampeded by. Whether they were surprised at seeing a colored in these parts or were amazed anyone would head up into the hills this late in the season was anyone's guess. Either way it made no difference. The encounter only lasted a few seconds and then the sound of their passage soon became a memory.

Miners returning from the hills, either afoot or on horseback, were more common. It was easy to tell those who carried a poke of riches and those who had not struck. The former walked with the stride of a successful man, measured and sure, eyes alert and looking forward.

The beaten man traipsed, weary, broken, and looking through eyes that envisioned a barren and difficult winter. As Jubal passed them on the road their reaction to encountering a black man didn't differ with their measure of success in the mines. While most took no notice of him at all, some nodded or spoke a greeting. Others, ingrained with some natural hostility, either stared him by or looked expectantly for some signal of deference as if they had met midway on a footbridge. These few, Jubal met with a disinterested gaze but nothing more. His days of tugging a forelock or snatching his hat from his head were over. He knew this could lead to unwanted trouble but a man had to live by some principles. Putting up with a few sullen looks wasn't about to make him turn aside.

Soon he reached where the path to Gold Run crossed the Middle Fork. He found the spot where he had panned while he waited for Josh and Elizabeth to return from their expedition. As he expected, there were several bottles with messages hung on twigs. The recipient's name was visible through the glass but this did Jubal, who could not read, little good. Not knowing Shipwash he could not recognize his handwriting so he would wait for a friendly miner to help him out. No one came by so eventually Jubal headed north towards Gold Run. He would go as far as the tent camp of the Carolina miner who was tending to his ill friend. If there was no word, well then, he would figure out something when he needed to.

When he arrived at the site of Carolina Carl's tent site no one remained. Where the tent once stood was a plain wooden cross and a cairn of smooth river stones. There were words on the cross and a date. Upon the cairn of stones were three flat bottles with messages in them. The roadside grave was a good place to leave a note for a friend. The first two miners who came down the trail ignored Jubal. He received nothing more than sneers when he asked for help reading the messages. It was downright unchristian to be treated so poorly. But he told himself, it could have been worse. Besides they were coming from the pestilence camp.

The third miner was also coming from the camp but he seemed in fine spirits and he hailed before he arrived, wishing to buy a horse. He had his poke of gold out already.

"Sorry, suh. These be fine horses but they belongs to my boss." Jubal was angry with himself for playing the docile Negro servant but he had a mission to accomplish. "He'd skin me if I was to sell off his animals."

35

"Is he nearby? Perhaps we could go to where he is and I could strike a bargain with him."

Jubal saw his chance and wouldn't have to plead for help.

"I don't rightly know where he be, suh. He said he would leave me a note with directions." Jubal gestured at the grave and the bottles. "Trouble is, I cain't read."

The stranger stopped in his tracks. He peered at Jubal and bit his lower lip before saying.

"Then why would he leave you a note?"

Jubal beamed his most solicitous darkie smile. "He figured a fine gentleman like yourself would eventually come by and help out. And now you've arrived."

The stranger laughed. "Your boss sounds like a clever man. Let's look over these messages. Perhaps I can make a deal with your boss if he's nearby." The stranger picked up a bottle and read the name through the glass.

"This is for Henry. Would that be you?"

"No suh, My name is…uh…Joshua. Boss calls me Josh."

The stranger retrieved the bottle stuck on the top of the makeshift grave marker.

"This one says Virgil. Name on the cross is Elias Shaw. He'd be twenty-six if he'd lived."

Picking up a third bottle, "Here we go, Josh and Elizabeth."

"Elizabeth be my missus. She's back at Sutter's."

The stranger pried the note from the bottle with a twig.

"Carolina Carl told me of the pox in Gold Run," the stranger read. "I've gone back up to the old camp. Will wait for you there, as I don't know where you may have gone. Duncan."

"That be him. I'd best head up the river."

"The days kind of run together but I think this is dated yesterday. How far is the old camp?"

Jubal didn't want the man tagging along in an effort to buy a horse. Of course, he had no idea how far the old camp was.

"It's a purty far piece. Most half a day ride if the weather obliges."

The prospect of hiking up into the canyons of the Middle Fork had no appeal to the stranger. They broke company. The stranger continued south, and Jubal began his trek up river. As they took leave, Jubal called after him.

"Suh. You come from Gold Run Camp. Is there pox there still?"

"There is, but it's confined to the lower part of the stream below the camp. I just passed through so you needn't worry about coming down with the bloody flux."

"I was worried some. Thank you."

Jubal rode Natchez up the stream with Chicory placidly following behind.

~~~

Duncan sat shivering in his hastily erected tent. He'd managed to get a feeble flame going in the damp twigs he'd scavenged along the shoreline and was brewing up a cup of tea. At least he could warm his insides. Yesterday, he hadn't gone much more than a mile upstream when a surge of water from some storm in the distant peaks overcame him and soaked his packs. Unable to proceed, he and his mule had become stranded on a rocky shingle, cut off by the rising flow and unable to scale the steep and muddy slope above. The sure-footed mule had been able to scale the hillside far enough to graze on the fringe of vegetation. No such good fortune for Duncan. He could scramble up as far as the mule but the gradient was steep. If he was going to scale it and escape the beach, he'd have to crawl on his belly, abandoning the animal and all his gear. The mule seemed unconcerned and satisfied munching the vegetation. Duncan realized if the water didn't recede or soon someone didn't come along he would be eyeing his trusty animal as dinner. He gnawed on a piece of ham, its flavor improved with the dousing of his tea steeped in the cup—he appraised his situation.

The torrent of water showed no sign of abating, and he had passed no camp coming down from the claims. The other miners had given it up for the season, so he could not expect rescue from that direction. While he had scant food, enough to perhaps wait for the crest to recede, the danger was in lying wet and exposed to the elements with only a tent for a roof and damp blankets on a rocky mattress for a bed. A healthy man could perhaps negotiate his way over the boulders past the bend in the river but his lame leg had so little strength, being swept away was almost a certainty, one he was not yet willing to risk. He was wondering if the mule could swim the chill waters to safety while he clung to its tail. He hoped his situation never became so desperate he would be tempted to try. He could console himself with being able to warm his hands and innards with the tea. Looking at the gray sky he offered up a short prayer that the Almighty did not release another storm before he could formulate his escape. He was shivering himself to sleep when he imagined he heard a human voice. The roar of the stream was such he couldn't make out any words. It was only the novelty of a sound other than the river making him believe salvation was near. He recognized his condition was deteriorating and hearing things made him suspect his decline might be more progressed than he perceived it to be. He abandoned the meager shelter of his tent, stood and looked about, prepared to be cruelly surprised by a trick of his own mind.

Nothing had changed. The river still thundered by, the shingle shore was still damp, the slope just as muddy. Wait! His mule had stopped grazing and was looking at something. Shipwash swung his gaze around and up to the top of the slope near the bluff that cut off his escape. Just as he turned a rock flew past his head and struck the beach with a sharp crack. Out of instinct he ducked, then chanced another look at his attacker.

It was a black man who had tried to brain him. Their eyes met and the man yelled something. Whether it was some sort of threat, Duncan could not discern over the churn of the stream. The man thrust his arms forward at waist level. His palms were open and waving back and forth, waving away his mistake. Duncan realized the Negro had just been trying to get his attention. He risked a smile and waved back. The black man's lips moved but no words carried. The lips parted in a smile and he returned the wave. Then he motioned for Duncan to remain where he was and the figure disappeared behind the crest of the hill. Duncan decided to oblige the request, as he possessed no inclination or means to do otherwise.

~ ~ ~

That was a close one, thought Jubal. *Josh sends me up here to find their new partner and I damn near brain him before even speaking to him.* He'd located his quarry but he needed to figure out how to get him off the beach and back down to Sutter's Landing.

Traveling upstream, Jubal had come to the same barrier barring the Brit's retreat. Jubal explored a way around. He got to a point where he would have to hold on to the rocks in front of him and swing his feet over the hungry river to a safe foothold. Jubal figured he could do it but there was no way for his horses to get by. While he'd been exploring the route, Jubal saw the thin line of gray curling upward. At first he thought it might just be mist before deciding he was looking at smoke from a campfire. He fell back and tried the bluff. Right below where he wanted to ascend was a vertical rise of about ten feet. He retreated back down the river to where both he and the animals could get above the grade of the water. The going wasn't too tough, other than having to cut through a web of brush and low branches barring the path. This done, he reached the bluff and led both horses up the slope. There he spied Shipwash.

Retrieving a rope from Natchez' saddle and another from Chicory's pack, he joined them, tied a loop in one end, passed the rope around a fallen log that looked permanently set. He then tied the bitter end to the horn of Natchez' saddle. Natchez was no cow pony but the passage west had presented similar circumstances. He knew what a rope on the horn meant.

Jubal put the loop around his waist, took the coils of rope in hand and let it take his weight. The slack went out of the winding around the log and tightened the pull on Natchez. Taking his cue, Natchez planted his feet and became an observer to the human's antics. Long before the length of line gave out, Jubal found himself looking over a cut in the bluff. If he was to fall he would be sure to break an ankle or a leg for sure. Gingerly he let himself down over the drop until he dangled and hung like bait on a line. The bank was undercut so his feet could gain no purchase. He felt Shipwash's hands on him, steadying his descent. In another moment he was standing on solid ground. Jubal stepped out of the loop and secured the rope end to a root sticking out of the bluff. Natchez was a steady horse but no sense taking chances.

"I'm hopin' you be Mr. Shipwash. Josh sent me to find you."

"Then you found my note by the roadside grave. I decided to stroll back to my original camp and instead found myself marooned on this beach. How nice of you to become marooned with me."

Shipwash offered his hand in friendship. Hesitantly, Jubal accepted, shook hands, and now their fortunes were entwined. Instantly, Shipwash's spirits picked up.

"Like Robinson Crusoe, I have my Friday."

Josh had forewarned Jubal about the eccentric Englishman, so he wasn't too surprised by the odd remark. If Josh wanted the man retrieved, he would retrieve him. Still, he kind of had the feeling he had when entering a pen of nervous goats as a child. Best he could figure, this was a Tuesday but let the man think as he wanted.

"How'd you come to be stuck here?"

"I walked in along the shoreline. Inconveniently the river rose and curtailed both advance and retreat. Together we can wait for the river to settle or we can plot our escape."

"My thinkin' is we get off this beach. This river be likely to rise as it be to fall."

"The eventuality has been a concern. Given that my bad leg prevents me from escaping on my own, I shall defer to your judgment."

Jubal had heard preachers use more words and say less but not within recent recollection. He scanned the shelf of land they stood on. Where he had come down the bank was eroded by the flow. The upstream slope was steep but manageable for a man in good shape.

"I'll go back and you pack up your gear. I'll haul the gear up the rope, then you."

"And then Cyrus?"

Jubal wrinkled his forehead, again questioning the man's sanity.

"My mule. His name is Cyrus."

"I get you out of here, then we be thinkin' on the mule."

"Cyrus."

"Cyrus, then. We won't leave him behind."

"I couldn't bear that."

Jubal traipsed toward the steep bank, called back to Shipwash.

"Best be gittin' a bridle on Cyrus."

Shipwash was spurred to action and started preparing to leave. It wasn't more than the work of a few minutes to pack the tent and small assortment of gear he had broken from the pack. With bridle in hand, he advanced towards Cyrus. Jubal had been trying to scale the steep upstream slope but was sliding back nearly as much as he advanced. Retrieving an item from his gear, he offered it to Jubal.

"I tried using this to climb with but hadn't succeeded. Perhaps you will have better luck."

Jubal took the rock pick and tested its heft. Satisfied with his grip he stretched and drove the tine into the slope. He managed to pull himself along until the lodgment pulled loose and he slipped down.

"I'm afraid it was designed for chipping, not climbing."

Jubal was about to return the tool before an idea came to him. Swinging the short pick sideways he etched out a foothold, tested it and began on another. It was dicey progress because the footholds were not as much use as handholds. Jubal ended up going more sideways than vertically but before long he was standing on firm footing. From there he crept past branches and through the brush until he was once again above where he had earlier descended. Duncan had, in the meantime, affixed his gear to the rope. Jubal brought it up with ease. Not so the Englishman. For the first part he was simply deadweight. Once he was able to secure purchase the ascent was easy and soon the two stood, slightly winded, on high ground.

When they turned their attention to rescuing Cyrus, he was nowhere to be found on the rock shingle. Looking upstream, Cyrus followed the route Jubal had taken. Trying to make his way to where his master now stood, he had become entangled in the underbrush. With a plaintive look, he brayed his displeasure. It took longer to cut a path through the chaparral than it took to bring the miner and his gear up to safety. Jubal marveled at the adeptness of mules. Somehow the mule had pursued him up the slope with just natural sure-footed instinct. No horse could have managed. Natchez and Chicory must have also recognized the accomplishment, welcoming the newcomer to the fold. Together, three beasts and two men managed to get back to the road crossing the river before dark. They made camp away from the trail, away from the clatter of passing teamster wagons, and under the shelter of towering fir trees.

Dawn found Jubal and Duncan already on the road to Sutter's Landing. Cyrus had inherited much of Chicory's load so Duncan could ride. The mule complained but such is the nature of mules. They rode single file on the verge of the trail. In the branches mockingbirds trilled and hopped from limb to limb. Crows squawked like old men awakened from their sleep. Occasionally the sun rising over the mountaintops managed to peek through the cover of clouds and splashed color and shadows about in fleeting glimpses.

Duncan's left leg and hip began to ache with the inactivity of the saddle. Periodically he would pull his foot from the stirrup and pull his knee upward to flex out the stiffness. It was better than walking. He was kneading the muscles in his thigh when a man stepped across the trail and stuck a cap and ball pistol in his face. The man seized the reins of the horse. Ahead, another man with a long knife accosted Jubal. The procession came to a halt. The man with the pistol spoke.

"Both of you, let's see your hands." Duncan placed the accent as Irish, furthering the outrage of what, at best, was to be a robbery by highwaymen. Duncan complied, holding his hands wide, palms down.

"Now where would you and your nig-nog be headin' this dreary morning?" said the Irishman, displaying a surprisingly white grin.

Duncan knew, once he was revealed as an Englishman, the robbery could well escalate and he might end up covered with leaves in the forest.

"We were headed to Belfast to hang some Irish rebels but you've saved us the bother." The grin vanished.

"So, tis a fine English gentleman I'm going to—"

Duncan's right arm flashed up and over the rogue's head. From somewhere a sabre appeared in Duncan's hand. The arm slashed down. The Irishman raised his gun hand to protect himself and caught the blade on his forearm. The impact drove the arm down and the pistol dropped. If it discharged, the report was not as loud as the man's howl of outrage. The outrage turned to a cry of pain as the man examined the long diagonal slash and the white flash of bone among the dripping wound. He turned his face to his attacker just in time to recognize and duck away from the killing blow to his neck. The Irishman ducked under the horse's neck and fled to the cover of the woods.

His companion retreated back across the trail. Duncan, with only one leg in the stirrup, spurred his mount forward. Duncan leaned down in the saddle and locked his arm straight with the bloody blade extended. By the time the highwayman had taken four steps, the horse, the rider, and the deadly blade were upon him. The tip of the blade pierced the man's clothing and back, glanced off his shoulder blade, and tore free in a spray of blood. The would be assassin, gasped, fell in the road, then jumped up and scampered away into the cover of the trees. He still grasped the knife he had earlier threatened Jubal with.

Jubal had remained frozen during the whole reprisal. He jaw hung open for some time before he found his tongue.

"Lordy, Mr. Shipwash. I never seen the likes o'that. Two armed men done for before I could blink twice."

Duncan had dismounted and retrieved the pistol from the mud. It had discharged on impact but the mud prevented the hammer from striking the cap. He decocked it and brushed the muck from the works.

"Jubal, the man you see before you is a man diminished from the vigor of his youth. I was formerly Lieutenant Duncan Wallace Shipwash, late of the Ninth Light Hussars, a Company regiment stationed in India." Duncan laughed, whether as victorious champion or a release of tension, even he could not tell.

"I never reckoned you even had a weapon. That's a wicked blade."

The Englishman examined the sabre as if it had magically materialized in his hand. Picking up a handful of yellowed leaves, he wiped the gore from the blade.

"Yes, a wonderful weapon I keep in my bedroll mostly as a keepsake. I never thought I would have occasion to use it again." He laid the hilt across his arm and presented it to Jubal. "Would you like to examine it?"

Jubal took the weapon and cut the air above his head a couple of times.

"It is double-edged so it can be used as a slashing weapon but its real use is for thrusting. You witnessed both its applications to good advantage. See how the blade is curved?"

Jubal looked along the flat of the sword.

"In a charge, the hussar holds the blade out before him. A man's ribs protect the vitals from a blow delivered overhand. As an upward thrust the ribs open and invite the steel. The curve allows the rider to pierce the enemy. He then rotates the hilt upward, releasing the victim and not de-horsing the rider." Shipwash pantomimed the sequence. Jubal tried the motion for practice.

"My charge was ineffective as the horse was not at a gallop and I had but one foot in the saddle." Duncan sighed. "Mostly, due to lack of practice, I also missed my target."

Jubal returned the sabre, copying the same formal presentation with which he had received the sword.

"You was in the army?"

"I will elaborate when we're reunited with the Bonners." He put the pistol in a saddlebag. With the sabre still in hand and with some difficulty, he regained the saddle. "Let us journey forth."

Jubal had retrieved the Hawken rifle he had briefly thought about before Duncan took the initiative.

"Shouldn't we track those two down?"

"To what purpose? There is no sheriff or jail to welcome them. If we captured them we would most likely be compelled to finish the bloody work, and I have no taste for slaughter. They are sorely wounded. I suggest we let nature take its course and call the outcome justice even if we never know what justice that is."

It took some cogitation on Jubal's part to understand the Englishman's words. Finally he nodded agreement.

Shipwash pointed the blade down the road.

"Let us proceed."

CHAPTER FOUR

As Jubal and Shipwash were riding towards Sutter's Landing, Josh and Elizabeth were doing the same. Lewis Werther, the teamster, made camp under his wagon. The Bonners set their ground cloths under the low branches of a fir tree and made beds ready. Together they gathered kindling and soon had a fire going with the teamster and the Bonners sitting on opposite sides of the flames. They were digging through their rucksack for the usual meal of coffee, biscuit, and dry ham when Werther spoke.

"Put that away. I got a treat for you. A Mex came by camp this morning selling *tamales*. If you ain't had them before, they is a right fine change of pace."

From a metal lunch bucket he produced a dozen concoctions wrapped in corn husks, like tubes of dough. He handed them to the curious couple.

"Is this like a corn dodger or something?" asked Elizabeth.

What had been a rather tense atmosphere around a campfire of strangers was succumbing to the presence of food shared and enjoyed. Probably the beginnings of civilization began with a meal shared by strangers over a campfire.

"There's corn meal in it but it has a filling. The Mexicans make up a dough, spread it on soaked cornhusks, then they put a filling on it, wrap it up and steam it. These is already cooked, we just need to steam them again till they's hot."

"What's inside?" asked Josh. His face showed he was wary. Still, he had eaten rattlesnake on the trail.

These are peppers and *papas*. Potatoes. There's some cut up jerky in it, but I can't vouch for what it is. Might be goat, which is damn good eatin'. The peppers got some bite to 'em so you might want to start off small."

At the bottom of Werther's lunch bucket there was a perforated platform. He put water in up to the bottom of the grid, put the *tamales* in standing up, popped the lid on and hung the pail over the fire. After a few minutes of steaming the aroma sneaking out of the pail put aside all trepidation.

1

Josh and Elizabeth took cautious bites at first, having never eaten Mexican food before. The spices and the peppers had some heat but no surprises. The first *tamales* disappeared quickly.

"These can get a mite dry. You might put a dab of this on them. I'll warn you first. It's pretty hot stuff." He proffered a small bottle containing a burnt-red colored sauce. The Bonners sniffed at it, hoping their nose didn't get singed for the effort. It was hot but not unbearable and had kind of a soapy, pleasant aftertaste.

Werther slathered on the sauce, trying to show the newcomers how accustomed he was to the local fare. He overdid it and gulped water from a canteen to the delight of his guests. Perhaps he overdid it on purpose as whatever tension of strangers at a common camp dissolved in laughter. Still, when they turned in for the evening, all slept fitfully and with an eye open to danger.

In the morning they resumed the last leg of the journey to Sutter's landing. As they plodded along, Josh inquired if Werther knew of a wagon they could buy.

"You'll need a team, as well, I might know of a rig could be for sale."

"We're headed to meet friends at Sutter's. They might already have acquired a team and wagon."

"Guess we'll find out when we get there," said Werther, flicking the reins to urge his team to a better pace. The horses ignored him as they wore along the muddy rode with the river passing on their left with as much enthusiasm as the mule team.

~~~

In the early afternoon they arrived at Sutter's Landing. The melee of commerce continued unabated even though it was the Sabbath Day. The Bonners' arrival was heralded with as much fanfare as their surreptitious departure. With the possibility of acquiring a replacement wagon, they continued on to Sutter's Fort. From the landing to the fort, the pace of travel slowed with the stream of traffic between the two outposts.

Sutter's fort was the commercial center of Sutter's New Helvetia, a settlement built on debt and slow repayment. Up until the discovery of gold, Sutter's had been a way station on the way to nowhere. Sutter had acquired a massive land grant from the Mexican government which, after the ouster of Mexican rule, was to be called into question. The fort had grown up around a large two-story central building. Connected to the main building and forming the exterior palisade was a series of blacksmithing, weaving, tanning, baking, and other cottage industries serving the needs of New Helvetia. Among the shops was a distillery as John Sutter enjoyed not only his drink but entertaining his friends. Most of the trades had been abandoned as the workers abandon the drudgery of toil for the promise of fortunes at their feet. Sutter had leased space within the walls to traders and merchants, but the tent barrooms and gambling dens springing up made do in tents on the mud streets before the fort. Outside the fort the scene was much like the camp at the *Embarcadero* on the riverfront. A free for all of trade, gambling, drinking, and provisioning operated all day every day.

Werther bypassed the throngs roaming idly around the camp and approached his destination from the perimeter. The merchant who had chartered his wagon spotted their approach, waved a welcome and left his pile of goods for sale in the charge of two men who lounged on the stacks, serving as both clerks and security. From a distance neither man appeared competent or even interested in the tasks assigned.

"I didn't order any miners, Lew. The market's fair flooded with them already." As the merchant approached he discovered one of the shabby miners was a woman. Even with her hair up and hidden under the near-shapeless hat, there was no disguising the fair complexion. Elizabeth was getting used to her disguise being seen through and the reactions she generated. American women were as uncommon as grand pianos in the mining camps.

"Lewis, please tell me a shipload of beauties has landed at Yerba Buena." He stepped forward and offered a hand so she could dismount.

"Stephen Collier, ma'am. Proprietor of Collier and Associates, supplier of essentials to the prospectors." Raising a thumb over his shoulder indicating his loafing employees. "You might want to forego an introduction to the associates part of the enterprise."

"Elizabeth Bonner, Mr. Collier. And this is my husband Joshua." Continuing the fiction she pumped his hand vigorously.

"Yes, of course. Well met, I'm certain, Mr. Bonner." He waited till Josh stepped down before offering a welcoming handshake. The delay was compensated for by Collier's enthusiasm.

3

"If you've come to make your fortune, and who here hasn't, then I can provide you with all of the essentials. Top quality goods at a fair price is what I offer. Lewis should have an assortment of new clothing somewhere on his wagon." Sensing his comment might reflect on the mean state of the couple's attire, he backtracked. "Ah, I only mean you appear to have traveled a long ways. Say, Lew. Where did you discover these fair wanderers?"

Not to be distracted from procuring a wagon, Josh answered, continuing the farce tale they first laid on Werther. "We came upriver by boat as far as we could, sir. Then we began walking and Mr. Werther was kind enough to offer a ride."

"And fortuitous chance has deposited you here before the man who can supply all your needs. Remarkable how these things work out?"

"We have friends waiting for us back at Sutter's Landing. Mr. Werther indicated we might find a wagon for sale if we continued on to the fort. If you have a wagon for sale, then we can do business."

Collier looked up at Werther, cocking his head in inquiry.

"Teague," said Werther.

Collier's shoulders slumped and his head drooped forward at the word.

"Ah yes, the unfortunate Mr. Teague."

"He still up at the fort?" asked Werther.

"Yes, they've set aside part of the main building as an infirmary. I've heard he has managed to get around with a crutch. He's a tough coot. Might even pull through." Collier pointed at the adobe plastered two-story building. "Teague is either abed in that building or within the walls somewhere. Whether he still owns a wagon or not is anyone's guess."

On the way to Sutter's Fort, Werther had told them Teague's story. They never learned his first name. Teague had come west in 1845 with John C. Fremont, the famous explorer and hero of the Bear Flag Rebellion in California. Once the dust had settled after the Mexican War, Fremont received public office and a large tract of land. The men who accompanied him and fought with him got a mere handshake and a thank you, and were sent on their way. They drifted about California or went back to where they came from. Teague made his living as a teamster and had partnered up with Lewis Werther, eking out a living

4

carrying goods from the ports like Monterey to the ranches and sparsely settled outposts in the interior. When gold was discovered, like every other person in the territory, they gave prospecting a whirl but soon found they could make more from transporting miners and goods than from standing knee-deep in freezing water and wandering through the valleys and hills of the numerous watersheds.

One day not long before, Teague was securing a load on his wagon when a drunk, in an alcoholic exuberance, fired off his rifle, startling Teague's mule team. The team lurched forward and the iron-tired wagon wheel rolled over Teague's foot, crushing three toes. Neither Werther nor Collier, having business to attend to, volunteered to help.

Josh and Elizabeth entered the gates of the fort. The interior was nearly as tumultuous as the camp outside. A large crowd mingled in front of the fort's distillery and saloon. Inside the main, two-story building they were directed to a physician's office. Two doctors were treating common complaints and injuries for an ounce of gold per each consultation. When they asked about Teague, one of the doctors, in a voice blasted by brandy and a stumpy black cigar, instructed them to go outside the fort to a room underneath the front bastion serving as a hospital. Failing that, they should try the saloon or to a storeroom converted to the convalescence of patients. They were warned the hospital outside the fort was reserved for those with contagious pestilence, explaining that was why it was outside the fort proper. They tried the converted storeroom first, hesitant to contact whatever assortment of disease resided in the isolated sick room.

At the converted storeroom were several attendants, relatives or friends, of the people crowded into hastily constructed beds. They were hard at work trying to keep the hospital decently clean for those under their care. It was a losing proposition. The atmosphere was foul with the stench of urine, human waste, and decaying or infected bodies. The only saving grace was the quiet inside as compared to the uproar outside. Before they entered they asked about Teague and were directed to a man sitting on a bench outside a few doorways distant from the sick room. There sat a man in buckskin pants underneath a dingy but clean nightshirt hanging halfway to his knees. He wore no hat over his balding pate. A wool scarf was draped over his shoulders like a priest's short stole. One foot was swaddled in a long bandage reaching to the calf, the bottom of which was muddy from the man's hobbling about. His voyages were aided by a crutch fashioned from a peeled branch with a scrap of blanket tied as padding to a fork in the branch. The other foot bore a brushed but muddy boot, partially laced but untied. A nearly empty bottle of brown liquor kept him company on the bench.

"Mr. Teague," said Josh as they approached, Elizabeth slightly behind her man.

"I'm Teague, as if it's any of your business," the man said. He squinted up at them as if looking into a bright sky. He was both far-sighted and drunk. Both conditions may have contributed to his delightful personality.

"Lewis Werther said we should seek you out. We're looking to purchase a wagon."

At the mention of his partner's name, the squinting fell away and his demeanor seemed to improve, if only slightly.

"Lewis sh'da come along with ya. He sent along a jug of whiskey, d'in he? This swill they pass off as rum'll be the death of me." Teague took a large pull from the bottle as if to demonstrate. They noticed there was no cork for the neck. Teague grimaced and gave a single shudder as the liquor galvanized his innards. The Bonners thanked heaven Teague didn't offer to share.

"When we left him he was busy with Mr. Collier. When we see him we'll pass on your request," said Josh.

"And then who be you two again?"

"Josh and Elizabeth Bonner." Elizabeth stepped forward.

"A woman? Glory be. Let's get a look at ya." Teague brought back the squint and seemed to be satisfied. "Pull up and set a spell why don't ye?"

"A spell of my feet would be wonderful but we have friends we need to catch up with," said Elizabeth. "Lewis said you might have a wagon for sale."

"Lewis's right as paint on that score. Trouble is I ain't got no team. Sold two of 'em to pay for my foot and my keep. Lost the other two at cards. Wagon's no use to me now. Its over behind the main building, or it was last I was able to get over there. Go and have a gander and mebbe we can talk."

Josh could tell the wagon was different even before he pulled the oilskin tarp off. Teague's wagon looked like an oversized version of the kind of cart found on a railway platform. It was completely flat behind the driver's box though there were open wooden frames that fit into slots on the bed. Most unusual was both the front and rear wheels, wooden with wide iron tires, set completely under the bed. It was designed for large loads that could overhang the bed, and the wide wheels were designed for the muddy paths in the mountains. Josh could see it was well built and cared for. It would take at least four horses or mules. It was perfect and he resolved to own it.

Teague was still on the bench when they returned. He'd moved the crutch to a position in front of him like he was going to get up and walk. That wasn't going to happen. Teague was having a hard time sitting up. Still, he managed to speak without slurring.

"Looks to me like some folks is about to make me an offer on my wagon."

"We've got two hundred and fifty collars gold," said Josh.

Teague leaned forward and tried to spit his disgust at the offer. He managed only to spit on his own pants.

"The price is four hundred fifty dollars and you have to do something for me. That's my price."

The asking price was not high considering everything associated with gold prospecting was exorbitant. The deal would depend on the condition attached.

"What is it we'd have to do?" asked Elizabeth.

"Missy, don't pretend you can't smell the putrefyin' of my leg. The doctor did what he could but now he wants to take off my leg at the knee. Start cuttin' on me like cuttin' off a hunk a sausage. I ain't got a chance of seein' the spring. I want someone to see to getting my remains back home to my family in Providence. That's Rhode Island."

Teague fairly glared at them, almost like he was challenging them to accept.

"Why us? Why not your partner, Werther? Maybe Collier," she replied.

"Don't rightly know why. You two is young and mebbe because you're a woman. That don't carry much on its own, but I got to trust someone. Werther'll see me into the ground, but he's a wanderer. Both he and Collier are men to look after their own interests first. Same with everyone else here. They is after the gold and devil take the hindmost. But mostly because I don't have a lot of time left. I'm a goner for sure."

Teague spat again, wiped tobacco juice from his chin.

"Don't say that," protested Josh. "Lots of people survive losing toes. Even a limb."

"Hell, you been to that sickroom I been in? The only reason I ain't expirin' on a cot in there is cause I can still move. Soon they'll move me to the room outside the fort and that place is just a place to die out of sight. If I do survive, and that'd be a miracle, then you made yourself a good deal. If not, I figure I got to trust somebody, and I picked you two. That's good enough reason I reckon. 'Sides, I ain't askin' anyone to sit by me. I'll have Lewis pack me up in salt before buryin'. You'll come passin' this way again and that'll have to do. What do you say?"

The deal was struck, the details worked out, and a bill of sale made. They shook hands and the obligation settled on Josh's shoulders in the same measure as doubt lifted from Teague's. As they left, Teague asked them to find Werther and ask him to bring a jug of good whiskey and a bottle of laudanum if he could find it. Werther was still at his wagon, watching Collier's help unload and stack the goods he'd brought. The Bonners relayed the request.

"Teague asked me the same thing last I saw him two weeks ago. Told him I was leaving the camps before it got bad up here. Told him I might not be back, too. That ain't the truth, but I didn't want to admit I ain't the kind can be holdin' to a promise like that. Won't be any boats leavin' California with cargo for a long time and promise like that cloudin' a man's thoughts for months and months ain't something I could live with. Sorry to admit that about myself but its just the way it is."

Werther, knowing the young couple had just now taken up something he could not own up to himself, could not look them in the eye. At that moment the Bonners realized Teague had picked them because they were a couple and would have to look each other in the eye if they let him down. Maybe the old soldier and teamster was a better judge of character than they realized. At least they hoped he was.

Teague was prescient about more than just the Bonners. Most who ended their lives in the new land would be buried in hasty graves, often unmarked. Their families would never hear of their fate. Teague, having seen many pass the mortal coil without eulogy or monument, dreaded the same fate and took his precautions.

The opportunities for death were rife in Alta California. Drownings, cave ins, mining accidents, starvation, exposure, and general mayhem helped to cull the herd. Outbreaks of dysentery, cholera, tuberculosis, typhoid, and exotic pestilence imported by foreign immigrants created an even more lethal rate of mortality. The Bonners, after losing their families to cholera on the trail west were understandably conscious of exposure to sickness. Wisely, and to their benefit, they kept clear of local outbreaks of disease. Death in the camps became routine and the populace became inured to death in its many forms. The business of California was gold and business could not take time out for memorializing the fallen.

CHAPTER FIVE

It was long after nightfall when Josh and Elizabeth reached Sutter's Landing. The raucous circus of trade and revelry continued undiminished. The Bonners pressed on back to the landing rather than spend the night in the open or in cramped quarters at Sutter's. The desire to reunite with their friends livened their pace along the dimly starlit path to the *Embarcadero*.

They were welcomed back to the fold with warm spiced cider and a new addition to the menu. Duncan Shipwash had schooled the bakery in the preparation of the pastie, a staple among the miners of Cornwall. It amounted to a thin round of biscuit dough, topped with meat and vegetables, then folded over, crimped, and baked. Wrapped in cloth it would stay warm until mealtime. The Americans took to calling them hand pies. The Van Volk bakery was fast becoming a staple enterprise at the landing.

Bakeries demand early hours and the Van Volk family was getting ready to turn in when the wandering couple strode through the tent flaps. Even after the short absence, the reunion of the adopted families was as warm as any blood relationship. The baker and his wife insisted the Bonners eat their fill, exchanged goodwill, and then retired.

Jubal and Duncan heard the Bonner's arrival but remained in the rear tent. Soon the Bonner's appeared.

"I've walked halfway across a continent to get to California and now that I'm here, I'm still walking," said Josh. "If only I could sleep in the same place twice."

"That's hardly true," said Elizabeth. "We spent two nights on the *Julianna Dolce.*"

"What is the *Julianna Dolce?*" asked Duncan.

"It's a ship, foundered and abandoned down river," said Josh. "It needs some work but we aim to make it our winter quarters." The story of the blood slashed across the quarterdeck could wait. Elizabeth took up the story and described what they had found, how the boat was listing, and outlined their plans for winter quarters, sketchy as they were.

1

"We'll be further from our claims than ever," Duncan objected. It was obvious he was pretty well sauced. Several times during Elizabeth's narration he produced a bright, metal flask from his coat and splashed liquor into his cider.

"For a claim to be recognized, it not only has to be discovered, the miner has to develop it," he added.

"Who is there to recognize any claim?" asked Josh. "There was probably some kind of government here before the war. Mexican laws would apply. Since the war, there is nothing. There's no government, no magistrates, no courts, or even a jail as far as I know."

"During the summer," Duncan replied. "A claim could be marked by clearing off the top layer of dirt and leaving your shovel. Of course, gold prospecting was more of a novelty. A man could leave his washed gold in his tent and no one would bother it. Those days are but a memory, I fear."

"There's bad men about," said Jubal. "Two men tried to rob us on the road back here. Before I could even think about what was happenin', Mr. Shipwash pulled out his sabre and slashed the one with a gun and then stabbed the other. They was wounded pretty bad but they skedaddled. Show them your sabre, Mr. Shipwash."

"It's time you called me Duncan, and it's time I went to bed. When a man is in his cups his tales of bravery tend to polish his heroics beyond reasonable measure. That's a tale for another time."

To punctuate the end of his speech, Shipwash slapped his knees, stood up and nearly pitched forward before catching his balance. Gathering his dignity, he announced his retirement and left the group.

"You should have seen him. It was over in two seconds. Said he used to be a hoosier or something off in India."

"It appears those times hold some bad memories for him," said Elizabeth. "He didn't strike me as a drinker but we hardly know the man."

"I've seen men who drink to settle their souls. It never seems to serve them well," Josh replied.

~ ~ ~

As was their custom, they arose early and greeted the new day. Even rising at dawn, they could hear the Van Volks busy in the bakery. Jubal roused a hung over Shipwash from his cot. The four unpacked plates and utensils from their gear and set out on a quest for food.

Scattered clouds wandered in the dawn sky but there was a promise of sunshine. A sunny day in these climes was welcome relief from the usual leaden sky and damp weather. Below the hill, wood smoke, fog, or a mix of the two hung low across the river. It rose as high as the peak of the tents. Pillars of smoke rose above the bank and then settled in.

The call of commerce at the shoreline had become an underlying theme to their temporary base. Here, on the backside of the hill, the morning was still and serene. It would not prevail. As the Bonner's had followed their noses to the Van Volk bakery, they followed the delicious aroma of grilling meat. Fresh meat had come to the camp.

"That's got to be beef I'm smelling," said Josh. "I haven't had a fresh steak since we ate bison last summer."

"No doubt we'll be eating beef plundered from one of the big *ranchos*," said Duncan.

"What do you mean, plundered?"

"A year ago, all the land belonged to a few privileged *hidalgos*"

"So they are selling off their livestock to get by?" asked Josh.

"I doubt anyone paid for this beef. A year ago all the land was open range, owned by *hidalgos* like Mariano Vallejo, Antonio Romero, and even John Sutter. Everything was open range tended by *vaqueros*. With the discovery of gold, the great *ranchos* have fallen idle. The wandering herds of cattle, sheep, and goats have become fair game for the enterprising."

"Plundered beef smells just as good as beef from a butcher," said Elizabeth. "Let's hurry before it's all gone.

Just such an enterprise tempted the Bonners. The four found an open fire with cuts of meat turning on a spit. A canopy had been erected above two long plank tables and benches. The wandering foursome were not the first at the table but no line had formed yet. The fare was simple. Spiced strips of beef were fried with strips of peppers and cuts of onion. This was ladled onto a large *tortilla* spread with a foundation of bean paste, rolled up and served with coffee and a scoop of spicy rice. Two Mexican vaqueros turned restaurateurs, aided by four *peons*, who turned the spit, tended the fire, and chopped the meat and vegetables, were running the enterprise. Pots of beans and rice hung above the coals and were constantly being stirred.

The Mexican owners displayed no prejudice in who was seated at the table. This acceptance did not extend to the white miners who objected to seating Jubal at a table with them. They of course had no objection to Elizabeth's presence. The segregation raised Elizabeth's ire. Familiar with her moods, both Josh and Jubal awaited reaction like they waited for a teakettle to sing on the stovetop. Before she boiled over, Jubal took his meal to an area behind the cooking area, already populated with Sandwich Islanders rejected earlier. The white miners had no discontent sitting alongside Mexicans. The Mexicans operated the business. Perhaps they feared an objection might result in a refusal of service. The Bonners set apart from the offended group, ignoring them. Other then commenting on the fresh meat and vegetables, they ate in blissful silence. Shipwash, no doubt with a pounding skull and queasy stomach, welcomed the quiet interlude. For the four of them, their bill came to a tablespoon of gold dust, about fifteen dollars. The price was considered outrageous but their experience buying oranges had reconciled them to the conditions of sellers' markets.

Albeit expensive they did gain something more then the best meal they had had in months. Josh had paid particular attention to the plank tables and benches. With Shipwash's assistance, they were able to discover a place where sawn lumber could be purchased. They retrieved one of the carts and painstakingly made their way through the milling crowd to a lot where six men had dug a sawpit and were industriously cutting planks from a wagonload of green timber. Both Jubal and Josh had spent time at the bottom of a sawpit, pulling a whipsaw and eating a cloudburst of bark and sawdust. They expected to pay premium prices for green and unseasoned planks. They were not disappointed. It hurt to pay for lumber when they planned on living on a wooden ship, but they could not cannibalize one part of the ship to replace the missing deck boards that opened the hold to the weather.

It was decided Jubal and Duncan would take two horses and the mule team, along with the bill of sale, to Sutter's fort and retrieve the wagon. They would also buy any fresh fruit or vegetables they might find. Josh and Elizabeth would tour the *Embarcadero* for other necessities. They split paths at the river road and each pair set off on their chores. Their plan was to reunite and depart for the *Julianna Dolce* the next morning. They would make a gift of one of the carts to the Van Volks for their hospitality.

Josh and Elizabeth spent the rest of the day searching out and buying supplies. Still shocked at the inflated prices: they paid ninety dollars for a dozen planks, twenty-five dollars a pair for gum boots, fifteen dollars for some Mexican *masa* to make *tortillas*, and similarly exorbitant prices for lard, whale oil, dried apples, fresh oranges and lemons, and other staples. The expedition required unloading their carts, wending their way through the crowded thoroughfare and back. The pile of supplies accumulated at the bakery. They tried to gauge the volume and weight with their memory of the wagon Jubal and Duncan had headed upriver to retrieve. By the end of the day the couple finally sprawled on top of their cache and soon fell asleep, slumbering sentries upon their vital needs. Snoozing was how Jubal and Duncan found them when they returned. This time their journey had been uneventful but there was news from the fort.

"We found your man Teague," said Jubal. "Said they was fixin' to take off his foot tomorrow. That'd be today now. Claimed he wanted to get drunker than the doctor who was gonna do the cuttin'. Looked to me like he was workin' on a good start."

"What did the doctor say?" asked Elizabeth.

"Din' see no doctor, least as I could tell. There was drunks a'plenty though."

"You may have met a man named Collier," added Duncan. "I gather he was Teague's employer. He seemed genuinely moved by the man's plight. He took us to the wagon and signed the receipt for delivery on his friend's behalf."

Reflecting on the promise made to Teague, Elizabeth inquired, "besides being drunk, how did Teague appear to you?"

"Teague was close to being in desperate straits," said Duncan. "He was pale and bathed in sweat. His lower leg was inflamed tight as a drumhead. Worse, the smell emanating from it spoke to me of gangrene. In India the close heat and humidity made gangrene an almost certain death. I have no experience of the condition in these temperate climes."

Josh and Elizabeth had decided to keep their obligation to the teamster close. Like the tale they had told Werther, there seemed no real reason for not being forthright. To them it seemed right to keep private matters private. On their trek west, all had been open and above board. There was little reason or opportunity to maintain secrets. Here, with the proximity to gold everywhere, the atmosphere reeked of every man and woman for themselves, fostering a furtive reservation about a person's intent. Even back in Cairo, Illinois, small town ways were public ways. Even more so on the trail. Once arrived in California, the Bonners quickly adapted to local custom.

~ ~ ~

The wagon was larger than Josh remembered buying. The supplies purchased fit comfortably on just the wagon. Still, they distributed some of the load to their remaining makeshift cart and their little caravan was ready to roll. Good-byes and promises of return visits were shared with the Van Volks. The two Van Volk girls, Wilhelmina and Mary, presented their departing guests with two baskets of tarts and pasties. The girls were sniffling and tears ran down their cheeks as they presented the gifts, then in embarrassment stole back behind the shelter of their parents. The whole family was on the verge of bawling and once again Josh was struck by how the girls were miniatures of their parents.

Rather than fight their way through the muddy streets and crowds of the *Embarcadero*, the group headed down the back side of the hill and then veered to the southwest and picked up the Sacramento River. The Van Volks watched their friends descend into the blanket of fog and wood smoke shrouding the lower end of the camp. Once they disappeared into the mist the family went back inside to prepare wares for the bakeries daily custom.

Like their earlier adventure along the trace of the Platte, the Bonners let the river be their guide. Once they left the vicinity of the camp the smell of campfires and kitchens disappeared. The fog hanging over the river wove through their journey, often clamping down over them so they could only see a few yards ahead. At other times the mist hung about their knees but was always present. They could not see the river itself and relied on following the reeds and brush that grew on the banks. Sometimes even these became faint shadows and disappeared. They had to pause and listen for the sound of the river's flow. Most of all, it was misty, chilly, and a miserable walk. It never rained but the damp was pervasive and soon everything and everyone wore a sheen of moisture that dripped from the end of their noses and the brim of their hats. The rutted path remained firm but care had to be taken not to misstep into a rut. The pace was slowed, conversation ceased. They ate the Van Volks' gifts as they walked and the food sufficed for what little pleasure the journey allowed.

~~~

The overcast stayed with them throughout the day. The sun never appeared, only hinting at its presence as a somewhat brighter region of illumination. Josh felt he should be near where the *Julianna Dolce* must lie, but even the treetops were vague shapes and there was little hope of finding either mast or spar in the pervasive gray. Josh rode on ahead, scouting breaks in the brush that looked familiar and might reveal the way on to the island. He blamed himself for not leaving a trail marker and as he plunged into one dead end after another he became more despondent. His mind told him he had missed the island completely. A nagging voice told him to ride back-trail. Finally, he dismounted and pushed his way through the brush and grasses until the muck under his feet threatened to pull his boots off. At last he was able to see the river. The other bank was visible or so he convinced himself. If the Sacramento had not yet opened into the bay he still had a ways to go. Looking downstream he believed he could see the confluence. He struggled back to the trail and waited for the wagon to come abreast. After telling his companions what he found, once again he trotted away, looking for the point where the river fed the estuary and then the island.

About two miles down and on his second foray into the brush his effort was rewarded. He was standing in reeds over his head, looking for a firm step to carry him closer to the water. Certain his ears were playing tricks he convinced himself he heard wavelets hitting something solid, perhaps a rock or a sunken log, but he moved to where the sound seemed to come from. He soon found brush broken and tramped coming away from the water. He followed the trail toward the water. His heart lifted and he nearly cried out when he found one of the boats he had hidden when they departed. He was close. He scanned to the west and there, though it may have been an illusion born of desire, he thought he saw a mast and two crossed spars.

Crashing back through the undergrowth, brambles clinging to him and snagging his ankles, he burst back on to the road. Anxious to bring good news, he did not wait for his companions but loped off down the path until he found another opening. It looked recently traveled. Not fifty feet in, he came to what he was sure could only be the island he sought. He could not be certain, casting about for some familiar sign. Carefully, he urged Natchez into the muck. It held and he was on firm ground. Parting some reeds he scanned ahead and there she was, at least the top part of the masts. It must be the *Julianna Dolce* he told himself. He left his doubt and recriminations dead in those reeds and forged back to the road to await the others.

He heard them arrive only moments before he saw shapes in the mist. A more sodden and downtrodden crew he could not imagine.

"We're here," he said, pointing at the gap in the tamarisk and mulefat. "Not more than a quarter mile away. Tonight we sleep dry and with a hot meal for our bellies."

"Thanks be to the Lord," said Duncan. "I can barely envision another step."

"Well, we ain't on board yet," said Josh.

~~~

A warm bed and hot supper might await but not without more work. To gain the island they had to fashion fascines from brush and branches. Bundles of undergrowth were cut, laid out and bound with lashings. These were laid down, packed, and stacked in the boggy approach. The wagon and cart, now riding on a firm bed crossed the twenty feet or so of black goo without mishap. Then the last quarter mile had to be cut wide enough for the wagon. At least the ground underfoot cooperated. It was sound enough footing but wet enough much of the undergrowth could be uprooted with the turn of a shovel. The rest was just beaten down by their passage. Soon they stood on the gravel shore with the *Julianna's* curved wooden hull and battered side-wheel before them. Josh scampered up the broken frame of the wheel and tossed the rope and wood ladder down. Soon they all stood on the deck of their winter home.

Elizabeth was the first to notice.

"Someone has been here," she said, pointing to the muddy footprints that crisscrossed the deck. They ran back and forth everywhere. The cover to the hold was off as well.

"Looks like they took some bags of rice. We should thank them for saving us some work," said Josh.

More ominous was the trail leading to the officers' quarters. It wouldn't do if they had managed to remove the small stove in the captain's cabin. He rushed through the companionway and, to his relief, the stove was still bolted down. The captain's bunk, which he had come to think of as his own, was smeared with dried brown mud from boots. Returning to the deck, he found his friends at the lockers below the foredeck.

"I think there is some canvas gone and maybe some rope," said Elizabeth. She pointed towards the rigging. "Maybe they helped themselves to some spars. I can't be sure."

"Let's be bringing up that ladder and let's fix that side-wheel so it can't be climbed," said Josh. He couldn't help but think of the pirate sagas he had read of Captain Kidd and Captain Henry Morgan. Thoughts of repelling boarders in those stories came back to him. There might be action afoot and Josh was in his element. It wasn't he looked forward to a clash with grappling hooks, cutlasses, and muskets. He simply enjoyed the prospect of having a task to do that required a plan. Whether his claim of salvage rights was valid or not, he thought of the *Julianna Dolce* as his and he was going to do what was necessary to safeguard his people and property. This was not a boy's fantasy coming to life but a responsibility a man should take by the horns. He set his crew to work.

The sun was setting but they did what they could with the remaining light. Besides pulling some slats from the paddle wheel and pulling up the ladder, they took some additional canvas and lashed a loop across the boarding portals and the anchor catheads so there would be nothing to seize upon and climb up on. It would have to do. Tomorrow they would think of other precautions. Jubal moved the wagon and the cart away from the boat and hobbled the team. He volunteered to sleep ashore and keep watch with the shotgun. They were all exhausted from the trek down and the precautions taken. They ate a quick meal and fell bone-weary into their new bunks.

Unseen, obscured by clouds, the moon reached its zenith and the rain commenced. The downpour drummed on the skylight above the entwined lovers, awakening and inspiring them. In the forecastle, Duncan Shipwash continued his fitful sleep, haunted by his private demons. On the island, Jubal lay comfortably under the wagon. Lying on an oilskin and underneath his familiar buffalo robe, he was comforted by the rain dripping from above. Thieves would not ply their trade on such a night. It was still raining when sleep finally overtook them all.

~ ~ ~

By morning the decks had been washed clean, obliterating the tracks of the interlopers. Somehow it seemed to validate the meager precautions they had taken to repel the unwelcome. The muddy tracks may have washed out through the scuppers but more effective safeguards would be required to secure their stronghold. A simple breakfast was prepared and the day's labor discussed among the new crew of the *Julianna*.

Josh and Jubal scaled the mainmast and walked the rope walkways along the lower topgallant yard. They cast off the gaskets bound about the main course and let loose the buntlines. Below, Duncan and Elizabeth belayed the head sheets. Josh and Jubal descended and in pairs brought the sail down to the deck. It was a wonder the canvas was still aboard. The top course was nearly a hundred feet above the deck yet had not been liberated by the mutinous crew. Perhaps other plunderers balked at inching along the towering spar. In any event, they counted their blessings for its retrieval. The procedure was repeated until they had both the upper and lower topsails on deck.

Back aloft, Josh rigged a hawser through the block at the end of the yard and, using the braces, swung the main yard outboard so they could lift their supplies aboard for stowage. The job had to be completed at low tide so the wagons could be under the lift. As the brig was beached, the listing of the deck and the angle of lift made the task more formidable. Fearing the weight of the wagon might be too much, they brought the cart aboard and secured the wagon with a length of chain between the front and rear wheels. The mules and horses were set on a picket line in the shadow of the ship. Setting off with shovels and hatchets, the four set off to disguise the access point across the isthmus. Satisfied with their work, they returned to the *Julianna* to find her afloat on the flood tide. The canting of the deck and the settling by the stern seemed no worse than Josh recalled at their departure, a good sign.

With the ship afloat, boarding required either a swim or retrieval of the longboats. Soon done, all were aboard, the boats hauled up the davits and stowed inboard lest their presence be seen by others passing by.

The plan they had made at breakfast, on Josh's suggestion, consisted of using the retrieved sails in an effort to staunch the sprung hull by fothering the sails to the hull. Fothering meant the two retrieved sails would be tarred at the perimeters and drawn tightly to the hull, hopefully reducing the leakage through the sprung boards to mere seepage. It would be a temporary measure at best. Even with the gentle cycle of the tides, the grounding would eventually chafe away the canvas. The measure would do until they could empty the hold and gain access for repairs.

The maneuver required someone to swim under the hull and bring the securing lines from the port side to the starboard so the canvas could be secured. The concept belonged to Josh and he was the natural choice to execute the plan. The canvas was tarred from the stores locker. Josh stripped and entered the water. He waded in, dragging the clew lines with him, each weighted with a stone. Once he found himself adrift he seized up the stones and disappeared under the surface and under the shadow of the hull.

The shoal below the brig was gravel so no mud impaired visibility but the turgid flow in the estuary reduced the range of vision to just beyond an arm's reach. The work would be by touch. He would have to work quickly. Slack tide had passed and the ebb had commenced. He could feel the sprung boards as he felt his way towards the keel and the brighter light on the starboard side. Towards amidships the keel hung above his head, perhaps two feet off the gravel bottom. With the stones as ballast he slipped under and soon was able to stand. He came up for a breath and was greeted by three relieved faces peering over the rail. He waved, took a breath and descended to free the first line from the stone. Once done, he surfaced and seized the line to a rope dangled in front of him.

"Don't pull yet. Not till I've brought up the other line and made the sail lie fair."

He dove before anyone could reply. Soon he resurfaced, line in hand and the hauling could begin.

"I'll lay the sail out flat and you pull when I tell you. When I pull again, just hold your position till I pull the other side in position." This time he waited for an acknowledgement. Three faces, anxious for his safety, nodded back. Shipwash saluted his acknowledgement. As Josh ducked back underwater he was considering the salute a strange gesture.

It took barely fifteen minutes to have the sail fothered securely across the keel and up the inboard side of the brig. Josh ducked under and swam under to position the other sail forward. It was probably his imagination but the keel seemed closer to the gravel shoal on the ebbing tide. This sail would go towards the bow and the clearance was decreasing. At the forward end he could hear the hull as it gently ground on the bottom. No boat in the water is ever perfectly still but his proximity to the hull and the bottom accentuated the illusion of descent. As he pulled himself under the hull his chest scraped against the wooden keel he sensed the motion and faint vibration. The imagery of a great pair of shears closing on his body appeared in his mind's eye. The thought of the severed upper half of his body popping to the surface sent him scurrying under and popping to the surface. His fantasy must have shown on his face as those on board asked what happened. He shook off their inquiries and fixed the ropes so they could be hauled. Diving down he carried their concern as he swam to the stern and crossed under without incident. With the sail laid flat he gave the signal to pull. The edges sealed until there was only a triangular gap on each side of the hull where the water could readily flow. A caulking of rope scraps and tar could wait for another tide to remedy the openings.

The next task before the crew was to deal with the rice in the hull. A miasma of fermenting rice greeted them as they removed the cover of the hold. It wasn't enough to make anyone retch but it was pervasive and unpleasant and would probably get worse. They trundled sacks that were completely dry to the galley at the end of the deckhouse and stacked them against the bulkhead for storage. Those still wet were set by the rail for disposal. By the time they had moved enough sacks to a waist-high depth in the galley they realized they had hardly made a dent in the cargo. There were plenty of sacks left that could be salvaged but many more that had gone bad. They couldn't just dump them overside. There wasn't enough current to carry the waste away and soon their home would be like a sausage in a casserole of rice.

Nor could they truck them to land away from the brig. The refuse would draw vermin, birds, and attention to their location. They were already killing rats with the flat of a shovel and filling up a sack of bodies. The best they could manage would be to load up the two skiffs and empty the bad rice into the channel. It was an immense job for a crew of four. At some point, they would be in the hold with shovels filling buckets with the reeking mess in the bilge. There was no choice. Either the spoilage had to go or they would have to accommodate themselves to the sharp stench and the company of rats.

"I know Americans aren't accustomed to rice with their meals but it was a staple of our diet in India. Besides being almost imperishable, there are more ways to incorporate rice into your meals than I could possibly list," said Duncan.

"Smells to me like a bunch of this rice has done perished already," said Jubal, wrinkling his nose in case no one got his point.

"Well, when kept dry I meant," Duncan countered. "Rice, like beans, kept dry will keep for years. Your potato, on the other hand, will sprout, blacken and rot within a few weeks."

"That may be so but I suspect they tried to sell this rice in Yerba Buena and had no takers," said Josh. "Americans likes their spuds is all I'm saying."

"Indeed they do, the English, as well. I suggest we put it to the test. I've got some dried peas and peppers soaking and I have some onions and spices, too. I'll put together a dish to accompany our meat tonight. I judge you will like it more than potatoes fried in bacon grease."

Duncan rejected all other inquiries while they continued to work in the hold. Sack after sack was moved to the deckhouse and beyond. The spoilage was unceremoniously piled by the rail for later disposal. By the end of the day, a hole in the middle of the cargo had been established so a man could stand and work on the layers. It eased the work but was disheartening as they worked into the hold and saw they had hardly made a dent. As they descended into the sacks, the smell became stronger. A canvas was rigged over the hold to circulate air through it. This arrangement either worked or the crew had become accustomed to the fetid odor. By the end of a long workday, they had dug into the middle of the pile, deep enough they could no longer sling sacks on to the deck. A pallet was discovered while working and this was piled with sacks and then hoisted from a yard braced over the opening. Even so, by the end of the day, everyone's back, shoulders, arms, and legs were singing in protest. The only appendage that seemed to show any benefit was Shipwash's bad leg. The exercise of atrophied muscles had loosened the joint somewhat but at a price of a throbbing that would probably keep him up most of the night. The anticipation of preparing his secret rice dish offset the discomfort. A few tots of brandy didn't hurt the cook's mood even a touch.

In the galley, he set to work with a knife, slicing and dicing while the water boiled for the rice. He cut up some kegged pork, sliced up green onions, added his soaked peas and chopped up the peppers after removing the seeds. The spices he added, regretfully, were not of the curried Indian variety but a pouch of local Mexican spices. In his travels, he had acquired a taste for spices with some heat. His guests were probably not of a like palate so he utilized less chili and more cumin, thinking they might find the nutty and pungent taste appealing.

The aroma of his cooking soon cut through the miasma of spoiled rice and his freshly scrubbed guests were drawn to the table like the children of Hamlin to the song of the piper. A keg of pale ale, procured at the *Embarcadero* was tapped. The brew had cooled in the water all day and was acceptable but suffered from an indeterminate period of storage. All in all, the meal was a hit and there would be no more talk of the superiority of the humble potato. Talk turned to the sale of the rice and their prospects in the commerce at the landing.

Elizabeth suggested setting up a cook pot and letting the smell of hot food draw people to them. After all, the strategy had been a boon for the Van Volk bakery.

"I don't want to start a restaurant, though. I didn't walk across half a continent to slave over a hot stove and become a scullery maid."

"No, of course not," said Duncan. "I will prepare and tend to the pot. We only want the cooking to serve as our advertisement. Our customers' noses will counter their prejudice for potatoes. Perhaps I can procure some spices from the locals. Dried peas, peppers, and onions are available at other markets."

"Should we even be selling?" said Josh. "Suppose the owners come along and recognize the bags as their own? How do we explain that?"

"I say the ship and cargo belong to us as right of salvage," said Elizabeth. "As to the owners, we both saw the scene on the quarterdeck. The owners and officers are at the bottom of the river, I fear."

"What about those has kilt 'em?" asked Jubal.

"If any of them are about and recognize the rice sacks, what story could they tell? Are they going to lay claim as their right by murder and pillage? I welcome countering the tale of some murdering rogue from who knows where over that of a young wife and a gentlemen like Duncan."

It was agreed they would dip their toes in the sea of commerce. Elizabeth and Duncan would take a wagonload of rice sacks to Sutter's Landing and join the parade of merchants on the beach. Duncan would cook and Elizabeth would do the dickering.

~~~

After a breakfast of Duncan's tea and reheated rice, the monotonous chore of moving and sorting sacks continued. The sodden sacks were beginning to accumulate. Soon they would load them into the boats and dump them downstream. Josh and Jubal were working in the hold, and Duncan and Elizabeth were lifting and bracing around a load when Elizabeth spotted a sight that nearly caused her to let go the line. Duncan, noticing her distraction, followed the nod of her head. They set the load down where it hung.

"Come up on deck, you two," she said. "You have to see this."

Once on deck they all stood at the rail and marveled at the approaching spectacle.

Approaching them from downstream was what appeared to be a military company, or so they first thought. As the formation drew near, the lack of military precision was evident. A collection of men dressed in black trousers and suspenders, topped by green shirts and matching kepi hats was advancing up the riverbank in columns of four abreast. While the columns were sloppy the files were non-existent. No effort was being made to march in step as soldiers would and no mounted officer led them. Three wagons of supplies followed the procession. Two men carried small green pennants hanging listlessly on staffs. American flags were flying from each of the wagons. A ragged and tuneless chorus of Yankee Doodle could be heard. A few men had rifles slung on their shoulders. Others had holstered pistols.

"Do you suppose the government has sent soldiers to maintain order?" suggested Duncan. "Perhaps this is the first contingent."

"I'm thinkin' those ain't soldiers," said Josh before glancing at Elizabeth and correcting himself. "I'm thinking those aren't soldiers. I never heard of any American soldiers in green uniforms and soldiers is usually...are usually all bearing the same arms. And where's the officers and sergeants."

Just then one of the men spotted the group on deck. He waved and the rest of the group waved and cheered.

"Nope," said Elizabeth. "Definitely not soldiers."

Josh tossed the rope ladder overside and climbed down.

"Wait here. I'm going to find out who they are."

"You'll wait for me and I'm going to get your revolver and holster. You aren't going anywhere without me."

While the other two remained aboard, the Bonners loped along, hopping over fascines in the boggy approach and slipping through the disguised entrance. They began trotting to meet the group as they trudged upstream. Once the approaching company spotted them on the trail, whatever frail discipline they had failed. The columns disintegrated and the men surged forward. One man separated himself from the group, holding the mob, for the moment, at bay. Perhaps in an effort to remind his men of their military organization, he saluted them and executed a sharp about face. Then, unseen by his charges, he grinned and approached.

"Jack Luder," he said by way of introduction. "The gaggle of honking geese you see behind me are the Greater Albany Argonauts. As you might have surmised already, our purpose is gold, whether fleece, dust of nugget, we've come to claim our share." He extended his hand. Josh accepted, then Elizabeth with Luder throwing in a curt bow at no extra charge.

"Are you boys a militia?" asked Josh. "Did the government send you?"

"Some of us have military experience but no, we are not a militia and no, we were not sent by the government. We're a private concern, organized for the purpose of enriching ourselves with gold."

"But the uniforms, the flags and such?" said Elizabeth.

Luder laughed. "Before we left Albany we trained like a military unit. The idea was to instill discipline even though we don't have a commander as such. On the long voyage we exercised as a group, ate as a group, and drilled as best we could on the ship. We were pleased with the results, then we came ashore in the bay."

"What happened then?" asked Elizabeth.

"What happened was we couldn't decide whether we had landed in Bedlam or Gomorrah. Within an hour, men had gotten roaring drunk, gambled, and a few just deserted. Some even took up with ladies of dubious reputation." Here Luder blushed but did not elucidate. "The trade in goods was frantic. The prices of supplies and animals were far beyond anything we ever expected. Only gold was acceptable specie. Even silver coins were refused. It took us four days to supply and round up the crew you see before you. Thankfully, some order has been restored now that we are headed to the gold fields."

Josh was about to ask exactly where they thought they might go when Duncan Shipwash traipsed up from behind. Introductions were made.

"Mr. Luder, Jack if I might be so bold," said the engineer. "I see you have two of the new long toms on your wagons. Those are a good choice and just the thing for placer mining. Just the right approach for an organized crew."

"I'm glad you approve, sir but is our method any of your business?"

"Sir, I meant no offense or intrusion. I simply mean to point out that washing gold from the streams will be a difficult and dangerous pursuit while the rivers are in flood. It may be months before profitable placer mining can be attempted."

Luder seemed taken aback by the new knowledge. He and his company had not anticipated a long delay before their quest could begin. Luder was turning over their near future in his mind. The possibilities were painted on his face and they did not look positive.

"Mr. Luder, I did not mean to discourage you. I simply wanted to suggest another means whereby you could better employ the sizable labor force at your command."

Luder balked. "There is no one in command. We all share equally but I have been elected as one of the managers."

Before continuing, Shipwash looked in turn at the Bonners, as if he was asking permission. Not knowing what was on his mind, they made no objection.

"Placer mining is simply locating and retrieving the surface gold carried downstream through erosion. The weight, as you know, causes the suspended particles to settle when the velocity of the water can no longer support the weight. I'm afraid you and your companions have arrived during the erosion period. The rivers are in full flood, too fast and deep for successful results."

Luder was a man used to finding solutions. It was plain he was confronting a problem completely unanticipated and one for which he could furrow out no solution.

Shipwash appeared not to notice the man's confusion. He continued.

"A pan or a cradle can be worked by one man. The Long toms require three or four men working in concert. Your enterprise is too large for one method and too small for the latter. The company will quickly disband if not directed properly."

17

"I'm thinking you wouldn't have brought this up without a solution, granting I acknowledge there is a problem to be solved," said Luder.

"Indeed. Perhaps I might have a moment to confer with my partners. Thank you."

Duncan took each of the Bonners and led them out of earshot.

"There was a matter I meant to discuss with all of you but had not the chance. The arrival of these cove fellows could be auspicious. I'd like to suggest we invite them aboard to discuss a proposition."

"Auspicious?" said Josh.

"Fortunate," answered Elizabeth. "There's over twenty of them and all armed. Can we trust them?"

"In my recent experience, robbers tend to skulk about. I don't believe a band of brigands would march down the road singing "Yankee Doodle." You two fair ran to meet them, if I recall." replied Duncan. Curious as to Duncan's undisclosed proposition, they nodded ascent. Duncan turned to Luder and his Argonauts.

"We would like you to come aboard the *Julianna Dolce* for an evening of discussion about how you all might successfully take home your fortunes from these hills."

There was no discussion amongst the Albany Argonauts. At the mention of finding a fortune a cheer went up and the matter was settled. They led the troop to the brig.

~~~

Shipwash had prepared another, larger pot of his rice creation and served it out. Duncan, the Bonners, and the elected officers of the Argonauts—Luder, Weber, and Fellowes—were seated around the wardroom table. A bottle of brandy set before them. Glasses glittered in the yellow light of an overhead lantern. Duncan let his story unfold.

"As I said earlier, any attempts at washing gold while the rivers are flowing is dangerous, cold, difficult, and most likely will be discouraging. They will soon tire and wander away seeking fortune on their own. Almost certainly most will fail miserably."

He looked around the table for a contrary opinion. Finding none, he continued.

"Geologically speaking, this area is new, in constant turmoil. Rivers and streams are created, diverted, and run dry. The beds, gold bearing beds I might add, remain. No doubt a person with a watchful eye could locate these ancient streams. The trick is knowing which ones are rich with the color and where, ages ago, did the gold become deposited."

Leland Weber, a former secretary to an Albany legislator, spoke. "Why are you telling us instead of working these dry rivers yourself Mr. Shipwash?"

"Because your presence has brought what cannot be purchased locally at any price. Labor and particularly labor comprised of men determined to work the metal from the earth."

"And what do you bring to the table besides this delicious rice concoction?" asked Fellowes, a taciturn miller.

"My partners and I, you met the colored fellow Jubal earlier, bring knowledge and expertise. We already know of such a site. I know how to work all types of mining: placer, deep gravel, and quartz vein. Gentlemen, I suggest a partnership. If you decide against such a venture, I shall instruct your men in the proper use of the pan, the cradle, and the long tom. You go on your way and carry our best wishes for success with you."

The three guests looked at each other, obviously anxious to speak privately.

"I suggest we each and all retire to discuss the proposition and then convene over coffee in the morning."

The guests rose, but before they could thank their hosts, Shipwash produced a piece of parchment paper he unfolded on to the table. From his pocket came a pouch that he spilled out on to the parchment. Pure gold dust and a palm full of decent-sized nuggets glittered in the yellow lamplight.

"Gentlemen, I offer proof of my expertise. Feel free to examine the goods."

If the three men hadn't had the fever before, they were instantly now infected. They leaned over the table. Each picked up a nugget and tested its heft. They fought to resist the fever. Josh and Elizabeth scooted back from the table, wary of what the sight of gold might portend.

"Damn, Shipwash!" said Luder. "You sure know how to make a sale."

"Not so fast, Luder," said Weber. "We need to discuss this amongst ourselves and with the men."

"If any of your partners need to see for themselves what is to be had, I shall leave this sample here on the table for their perusal," offered Shipwash.

"Aren't you afraid it might be stolen?" asked Fellowes.

"Should I be? Would any of your men throw away a fortune for these trinkets? If, in the morning, I find there is gold missing, I know we don't have a deal and you gentlemen have a far greater problem.

"What's that?" asked Fellowes.

"Need I answer? It would mean you have a thief within your company."

~ ~ ~

"What were you thinking?" exclaimed Elizabeth. "First you take twenty strangers into our midst and then leave your gold out on the table for the taking."

"It was my poke I put out as a carrot so it will be my loss if it wanders away. I apologize for the hasty invitation. The sudden appearance of the Argonauts caught me by surprise as well, but I saw an opportunity I did not want to let slip from our grasp."

"This deep gravel prospecting, you mean?" said Josh.

"Indeed. I mentioned earlier there was something I wanted to discuss with you but the appearance of this crew of hungry gold seekers could bode well for a new venture," revealed Shipwash. By way of apology he added, "I admit I perhaps acted hastily but I couldn't let the chance just march away."

"What's done is done and it will play as it will," said Elizabeth. "What is this deep gravel technique?"

"We've seen some success at placer mining but we may find our claim worked by others by the time the rivers subside. We might even find that productive hole completely gone, washed away. In any event, our collection will suffice to sustain us through the winter and spring. We need to find another source of gold and deep gravel is the means. Deep gravel is digging in streams where there is no present source of water to wash gold in. Either the ore must be transported to the water for washing or the water diverted to the ore. Such an undertaking requires organized labor, something that is virtually non-existent in the districts."

"So you took it upon yourself to suggest a partnership with Luder and his crew. What about our partnership?"

Duncan, perhaps indignant that Josh would think of abandonment, nevertheless contained his pique.

"Our partnership and sharing arrangements remain intact. I am suggesting our partnership partner with their company. If you approve and they accede to the concept, then the details can be arranged."

"I'm going to get Jubal. Should of done it before. You'll need to explain this to him."

Some of the Albany bunch were fixing up berths in the deck house. Others, having recently been confined to a ship, were bivouacking on shore. Josh found Jubal on the foredeck by one of the anchor cat's heads.

"What are you doing up here?" he asked. No answer was needed. Jubal had, over the course of their travels, taken up moon gazing.

"Mostly staying out of the way of those new men on board. They is friendly enough but I don't think any will put up to sharing a bunkroom with a colored. I was about to go ashore and see to the animals. I'll bunk down there where I got my things set up already."

"Duncan has made these Albany boys a proposition between them and us. We'd like you to come and hear what he has to say."

Jubal declined. "I don't know minin' or partnerships' from magic. Whatever you think is right is right with me."

"Jubal, we're talking about your future. You really should have a say."

"I'll know my future when it shows up. The way everyone here runnin' 'round crazy with the gold and the tradin' and with movin' about one day to the next, it don't look like the best place to be countin' on plans."

Jubal was never one to offer an opinion and it was a long speech for him. In case he might have offended his friend, he bade good night and went to bunk with their gear and stock.

Josh had been all caught up in Shipwash's big plans. Hearing Jubal's fatalistic view set Josh adrift and squarely between the two extreme positions. Not one to be content letting life just happen to him, he decided he would rather undertake something and fail than to just exist. He returned to the table and added Jubal's consent to the enterprise being hatched under the light of a lantern.

Duncan continued.

"If we are able to partner up with our labor force, it will be only for the dry digging site I know of. Our existing partnership remains and this is particularly important for the quartz veins we discovered in that dry gully. There lies the richest prospects but the most expensive to extract. I don't believe anyone will even explore the gully before we can return."

"We already took out all we could find," said Elizabeth.

"You only extracted with a spoon what was immediately visible. That small gully is rich with quartz seams of gold. To mine those it requires mining in the most traditional sense. The veins must be followed by tunneling into the earth and removing the seam. Quartz mining requires a considerable investment in equipment and most of all labor. We need a means to acquire the equipment, and this partnership with Luder's group will provide the needed capital."

Josh saw Shipwash's plans cavorting off into a distant and uncertain future. The contrast between Jubal's fatalist prospects was even more profound. Still, he would stick with the engineer. Besides, Elizabeth seemed to be in full concert with Shipwash and trying to turn her head was nigh on impossible once she had decided on a course.

Before turning in they discussed the terms of the proposal they would make to the Albany men, settling on a one-third share as their goal, with Shipwash taking half of the third. The division seemed fair as the other partners had no idea where the deep gravel was or what to do when they arrived. They retired to their bunks, leaving the poke of gold lying unattended on the table.

CHAPTER SIX

The gold remained undisturbed as the parties reconvened in the morning. The Albany company suggested the Shipwash partnership should retain twenty percent of the proceeds after expenses. Shipwash countered with a third share of the gross. The negotiations went back and forth through several pots of coffee. They settled on a thirty percent share after direct mining expenses such as shovels, picks, barrows, and shoring were deducted. Labor and the cost of feeding and housing was to be borne by the Albany fellows. When the placer season resumed, Duncan would show the men how to build a cofferdam in the streambed so ore could be worked without standing in the flow and how to divert water for washing. This was predicated on being able to establish and record a claim when it became possible.

As a last condition to the agreement, the Albany company was to be provided with as much rice as they could carry in exchange for helping the scant crew to offload and dispose of the spoilage. In exchange they would provide two days of labor and no more. A simple agreement was drawn with Shipwash as arbiter of all technical details and with the elected officers of the Albany group to resolve issues of personnel. Shipwash signed for the partnership and Luder, Fellowes, and Weber as agents for the company.

Right after breakfast the men set to work. Swollen and burst bags of fermenting rice were loaded in bails, hoisted aloft, and deposited in the launches. A crew would row the almost swamped craft into the channel and shovel, then dump the mess. They rotated so everyone got a sample of the fetid atmosphere in the hold. As the rice was removed, air was better able to circulate, and work in the bowels of the ship became at least tolerable. At the end of the agreed labor, the company departed, taking six hundred pounds of good rice with them and leaving the hold less than three feet deep in a sludge of swollen rice. At least now the task before the original crew was not so daunting. With the hold mostly emptied the *Julianna Dolce's* trim improved. She was still down by the stern but much of the list when she was afloat on the tide was gone. Josh felt with a few more days' earnest labor he would be able to clear the bilge pumps of the mess clogging the intake. The effort they had put into fothering the canvas seemed to be holding. With the cargo gone some of the sprung boards could be seen. Rice clogged the seams and would require cleaning and caulking to make the *Julianna* to right.

At the rail, the four partners watched the Greater Albany Argonauts march away, still managing only a phantom of military precision. They had departed with just a few hours of light left, now even more anxious to make their fortunes. Their flags flew and they sang "Oh Susanna," a song that was just becoming popular when the Bonners left Missouri. The procession entered into the trees and the sound of their chorus was instantly swallowed up. A few more minutes and the four found themselves alone in the world again.

"By spring those boys is goin' be damned tired of rice," said Josh.

"I'm damned tired of it now and I hardly et any," said Jubal. "I been up to my hips in it for near a week now. I sleep with sacks of it against the walls and the galley is piled near to the ceiling."

"So now you've taken to sleeping aboard?" said Elizabeth.

"I aim to, startin' tonight. Those boys left the bunkroom a lot cleaner than they found it."

"I think such courtesy is a good portent for the future of our prospect. Even though the company would prefer digging for gold, they didn't shirk at relieving us of the cargo."

"When do you have to leave?" asked Josh.

"I gave them directions to their new camp and they plan on a day provisioning at Sutter's. I can travel faster and arranged to meet them along the South Fork of the American in three day's time.

"Elizabeth and Jubal should accompany you as far as the landing. Perhaps they can sell some of the rice. We need fresh meat and vegetables too. Mebbe we could trade for some fruit. I'll stay aboard and work on repairs."

"Duncan, show me some ways to fix rice. I need to learn some if I'm going to peddle rice to miners and besides, I'm so hungry I could even eat it," said Elizabeth. Her stab at humor wasn't all that funny but they all responded, needing a bit of relief from a difficult and tiring day.

~ ~ ~

Josh watched his three friends roll away, his wife and Jubal on the wagon, and Shipwash on his mule alongside. He finished securing the rudimentary anti-boarding shield over the gangway and looked at the sky. The sky above was bright blue with scattered clouds. Away to the northwest a bank of mottled gray promised rain. His first order of business should be to replace the missing deck planks taken by earlier scavengers. He'd have to work quickly scarfing in the replacements, then cover them with canvas. He could snip rope ends to mix with tar later. Water kept out of the hull was water he wouldn't have to pump or bail.

As he worked the sound of his tools seemed to be the only sound in all Creation. No mockingbirds sang, no gulls squawked, and no crows cawed. Josh saw this as sign the storm coming would be a knocker. He was making good progress and worked amidst a pile of cutoffs, planer shavings, and sawdust when he noticed the debris began to move along the deck. A wind was announcing the approaching storm. Looking to the sky he decided he could finish the board he was working on and then he would retreat to the warmth of the cabin. Within the hour he was watching the rain cascade down as gusts of wind blew the drops against the stern windows. The chop in the estuary was rocking the now unburdened vessel. He couldn't help but think of his friends on the road and how they would pass a miserable night.

~~~

Arriving at the *Embarcadero* the trio was not as beaten by the storm as Josh imagined. Sheltering in the trees had provided a windbreak and a partial canopy above. At the muddy thoroughfare that was becoming the main street of the camp they split ways with Duncan as he left to rendezvous with Luder and the rest. He might even catch them on the trail, as they certainly would not be able to resist the temptation to grab a pan and wash sand along the way. The storm had passed but the sky still spit an occasional sheet of rain. The path up the hill was a quagmire of mud and discarded rubbish. As they passed one of the saloon tents, one with a sign proclaiming it the *Sacramento Belvedere* from a crudely painted canvas banner, they came upon a body lying in the mud, next to the plank entrance. The man was clearly dead and the body had been arranged with hands over the chest. Pebbles had been placed over the man's eyes. If originally there were coins instead of pebbles they had passed over the bar to pay for drinks. What was remarkable was the bar was open for business and many men were inside, probably as much for companionship as relief from huddling in a damp tent or brush *remuda* during the storm. Men came and went but no one paid particular attention to the cadaver nearly under their feet. From the size of the gathering inside, a corpse on the doorstep didn't seem to be hurting business any.

Elizabeth, always attentive to possible epidemics, halted the wagon and examined the body for clues as to the poor man's demise. There was no blood except for a dried rind on the open lips. Curiously the skin was puffy and presented a pale, yellow-orange, not quite as deep as the flesh of a pumpkin. This man had died from some pestilence she had no experience with.

"Scurvy, ma'am," said a man leaving the bar. "He ain't the first you'll see others laid out just like him. We're organizing a burial party inside."

"I've heard the term but nothing else," said Elizabeth. "Is it contagious?"

"No ma'am. Not far as I know. I only thought sailors got the malady. It's from not eating proper. Vegetables and fruits. Citrus juice is supposed to put the victim back on the mend."

"Weren't there a couple of Mexicans selling oranges?"

The man laughed. "They sold out at a dollar apiece, some say as high as three dollars. Delegations were organized to go to the big ranches and see if they can bargain for lemons and limes and such. The Mexican boys was drafted to act as interpreters."

Elizabeth's mind wandered to the small cask of lemon juice they had acquired. Little good it did her as the cask was stowed in the galley aboard ship.

"How many dead?" asked Jubal.

The man gave Jubal the sharp eye, reluctant to answer a query from a Negro.

"How many?" asked Elizabeth.

"Half dozen I know of, but them is just the ones out on the street. No tellin' how many died alone in tents or huts." Tiring of the conversation the man touched his hat, bid good luck and entered the saloon. By now the tent was bulging from the crowd inside. Jubal slapped the reins and they moved on to the bakery.

Already there was a line outside the tent waiting for the next batch of goods to be offered for sale. The men were quiet, many with blankets over their heads against any future rain. Two women headed the line, apparently ushered to the front by the miners. Rough as the camp was, women were still held in high accord. Jubal drove the wagon around back to the canvas sided structure used as the stable. Hannah

Van Volk heard their arrival, peeked through the curtain and disappeared. Moments later she returned with two cups half full of apple cider. She pressed a cup into waiting hands.

"You've heard of the scurvy outbreak?" she asked.

"We saw a couple victims laid out on the way here."

"I'm told only fresh fruits and vegetables will allay the progress. We have the dried apples, some dried peaches, and the cider. Drink up now and no arguin."

"Does the cider combat the disease?" asked Elizabeth.

"No telling for certain but its about all we have. We had a cask of lemon juice but its gone, so we have what we have."

"None of you have taken ill?"

"God preserve us, no."

"I was told parties had left for the big *haciendas* to try and procure fruit. May fortune smile on them."

"And if the landowners will sell to them," said Hannah. "They have their own to think of."

"I doubt it will make much matter whether they want to sell or no," said Elizabeth.

"How's that?"

"Mexico lost the war, and many don't believe the *Californios* have any claim to the land and particularly the gold on it."

The conversation drifted on and into family, bakery news, Elizabeth's story of the *Julianna,* and meeting the Albany group. Jubal had listened intently when they talked about the scurvy and the news of how the Van Volks were getting on. He had been brushing and drying the animals. The work was nearly automatic so he could pay attention to what was being said. He waited until there was a lull in the conversation before interrupting.

"Thank you for the cider, ma'am. Something that tastes that good sure must be good for you, too."

"Until we get some citrus, I hope it will suffice."

"Miz Elizabeth, what shall I do with this rice?"

27

Distracted by the conversation, Elizabeth seemed to have forgotten why they had returned. She made a gift of a hundred pounds of rice to the Van Volks along with Duncan's recipe. Perhaps, she suggested, they might add a rice dish to the baked goods menu.

If Elizabeth was going to entice miners to buy their sacks of rice she was going to need ingredients. Supplied with silver and gold she left the bakery to ply the market stalls at the landing. Once she had hastened away from the cinnamon and sugar smells of the tarts being prepared she was overwhelmed with the atmosphere of filth permeating the camp. Chamber pots and garbage were dumped in the street to join the droppings of livestock, discarded bottles, and other trash. If smell were to be the measure, then the hill behind the camp could be judged the more genteel neighborhood. She wrinkled her nose and longed for the smell of fermenting rice on the ship. Pressing on, she was able to buy a whiskey bottle of the pungent Mexican spice cumin, a string of garlic, more dried peas, and a small sack of dried peppers. Even these basics were in short supply and reflected prices paid by men desperate to allay the new scurvy threat. At four dollars each she procured two old chickens for the pot. Trudging home she had to wait as a wagon passed in front of her. Its cargo was a double layer of the dead being collected for burial. The feet of the corpses danced in unison over the bumps and dips of the thoroughfare. The wagon stopped for another passenger. At least this one had been shrouded tightly in a bound quilt. The man had friends enough to prepare the body for burial. The mass burial effort indicated there was some minimal organization in the camp. If so, it was only because of the season proscribing any concerted effort at mining. Come spring most of the inhabitants would scramble into the canyons and arroyos to seek their fortunes. She reflected, if the effort to dig privies had been made earlier, the effort needed to dig graves might be diminished in direct proportion. Thankful for the gum boots she wore, she trudged through the mire and ordure back to the bakery and wished herself back aboard the ship, snug in her cabin with the stern windows and the skylight above.

~~~

Josh, instantly awake and moving at the first alarm, grabbed his Walker Colt and the Hawken rifle. The yipping howl of coyotes and the nervous cries of Natchez drove him to the deck. From the rail he could see the sorrel stallion fighting against the hobbles. The pack of coyotes was not on him yet but their baying cry was all about, celebrating the find. Before long they would come for him, nipping at his fetlocks and trying to bring the big horse down so they could tear at his soft underbelly.

Josh tossed the rope ladder overside and started to scramble to the ground. As he went over the rail he spied the shovels they'd been using to clear the hold. He grabbed one of the spades and tossed it over. He had but seven shots, and there was no telling how many of the scavengers there were. With his pistol holstered and the rifle slung over his shoulder he hit the ground running.

The first coyote, a well-fed tawny thing, emerged from the brush into the clearing where the animals were picketed. The animal did not attack. It simply pranced through with its distinctive light-footed gait. The appearance served its purpose. Natchez fought the hobbles, hoping to free his hind legs for defense against the marauders. He was whinnying piteously as Josh hurried forward. The first varmint had disappeared in the undergrowth but another emerged on the near side of the frightened mount. This one moved in a more threatening manner, slung low, more deliberate in its steps. Intent on its approach, not till the last moment did the coyote hear Josh running. It swung around to face the threat. Pulling its lips back to expose a set of sharp fangs. A growl told the intruder to leave the pack to its dinner. The growl was suddenly cut off as Josh swung the edge of the shovel up from under using the momentum of his charge to enhance the power of his swing. The spade caught the coyote right under the jaw, lifting its head back in a spray of blood. The growl turned into a gurgle as the wounded animal staggered forward, seeking the safety of the brush. Whether or not it made it, Josh didn't know as he had already gone by. One, he thought. How many more?

Seizing Natchez' bridle he was nearly lifted off his feet as the horse reacted. Josh had no thought of cutting the hobbles. Natchez would bolt with him underneath and being low would expose himself to an attack from the coyotes. Besides, his knife was lying on a towel where he had left it to dry after washing up after dinner. With his master present, Natchez settled some but not enough to content Josh. He was close up to the animal and could not see a charge from the far side of the beast. He would have to depend on Natchez' reactions to signal the quarter of approaching threat. Even unable to strike out with its hooves, the horse's natural reaction would be to swing its hindquarters towards an attack. Three fat coyotes emerged from cover. Josh drew his pistol but Natchez was swinging him around so he couldn't aim. He needed to step away to shoot. He nearly fell when he tangled his legs in the shovel he'd dropped to grab Natchez' bridle.

The three coyotes fanned out around Natchez' rear. They feinted and shifted, seeking an opportunity to press their attack. As the horse rotated to counter the threat the hunters rotated in unison. The circular movement brought one of them into Josh's line of sight. He'd already unslung the rifle and brought it to bear. The range was minimal but the lack of light prevented an accurate sight picture. The crack of powder and an orange flash from the muzzle illuminated the clearing for the briefest of moments. A howl from his target rewarded the shot. The creature had taken a tumble but brought its feet under it and hobbled back into the brush. Whether the wound was mortal or not, Josh could not tell. It was enough the animal had retreated. Useless except as a club, he lay the rifle on the ground. Quickly, his night vision returned and he scanned about for the two others but the shot had scared them into a hasty retreat.

Having no doubt they would resume the attack, Josh decided it would be best to flush them so he crashed into the underbrush, praying the coyotes were not so bold as to attack a man. Standing still would embolden the pack. With the Colt in hand, he turned right and blundered toward what he discerned as motion. He nearly stepped on the coyote he had wounded. It lay on its side, breathing shallowly with its tongue in the mud. No sense wasting a shot.

There was yipping in what seemed to be a half-circle spread out before him. He stood between the hunters and their quarry. From the sounds he guessed there must be half a dozen yipping and snarling canines anxious for their dinner. A snarl close by on his left was followed by the appearance of a bold, aggressive tooth-filled muzzle. It lunged forward a step, challenging for the ground. The Colt roared and the coyote's boldness was rewarded with death.

Josh had only his pistol. There would not have been room amongst the undergrowth to effectively swing the shovel. Still, with one more kill he felt he had the pack on edge, it was time to press the attack. He pressed deeper into the brush, swung to the left and charged as best he could through the clinging branches. He pushed until they yielded or broke but still he moved forward. He heard the yipping retreat before him but he could hear them close up behind him as if they meant to lure him in. An impulse took him and he howled wildly like a wolf. The release of tension was glorious. Tension and fear leapt away on his feral call. He turned, crouched, waited. A coyote padded on his right, seeking a better angle. He fired and the animal yowled. Josh didn't think it was a howl of pain but more the voice of surprise. He pushed towards the now vacated turf and in a dozen hard-fought steps he emerged back in the clearing, his face and arms scratched and bleeding.

His appearance must have startled Natchez as the animal's bladder let go loudly enough for Josh to hear over his own quickened breath. Three shots left. He knew there were more in the pack than he had shots, and he would save two as a last, desperate measure. He seized up the shovel and cocked it back over his shoulder. He stood poised, turning in anticipation to face a new attack. None came. Natchez, with the instinct of animals, had settled down and now nickered and blew. Minutes passed with his nerves on the sharp edge of waiting. The coyotes it seemed had given up.

Suddenly, a tumult arose in the brush. A yelping and snarling of frustrated animals and the squeals of an animal being torn alive. The coyotes had turned on their wounded comrade and conceded the ground to man and horse. Josh fired once more to where he thought the sound emanated. There was no change in the wild sounds of frenzied animals at the feed. Josh undid the hobbles, re-slung the Hawken and led Natchez back to the side of the ship. He would spend the rest of the night on deck, sleeping on but one ear.

~~~

Duncan discovered no Albany stragglers who had fallen out from the march. There were men trying to pan the swollen waters but none wore the distinctive Albany green and black. He found the company intact on the near bank of the South Fork of the American. They could go no further, the river being too fierce. They must have just arrived. Men lay under wagons or under canvas awnings slung low between tree trunks. Duncan had cautioned them they would have to move once he arrived. The site he meant to prospect was some quarter a mile away amongst the trees. Hidden away from the amateur prospector the ancient stream was disguised from the novice eye by a blanket of overgrowth.

He joined Luder and some of the others and shared out a pot of coffee, already sweetened to the point of being unctuous. He bade Luder to accompany him to the site of their new venture. They left with the crew beginning to pack and move. When the two returned, they would find out where and how far. The two riders disappeared into the woods.

Soon Duncan found the one remaining bank of the ancient stream. At a low point, the two horsemen mounted to the top and meandered along the overgrown watercourse. The other bank, over the ages, had eroded and only a few found hillocks, no taller than a man, remained. Duncan rode along with purpose, the ground gaining its familiarity. Duncan was close. He surveyed the ground below intently. Luder rode along behind, his gaze below equally intent but blind to what lay before him. Duncan stopped, motioned Luder up beside him.

"There. Do you see the long arc below, the curve of the primal stream?"

"I reckon."

"No reckoning about it, there lies our dry diggings. Try to erase the trees and plants from the scene and look at the watercourse from just the bed and what remains of the embankment."

"I think I can see it," offered Luder with little conviction.

"Never you mind. I will try to explain. Once the American River or at least a branch of it, ran down below the bank we stand upon. Some prehistoric upheaval diverted the path of the water to another, probably its present course. You have rivers at home, do they not meander so?"

Not waiting for a reply, Shipwash continued. "As the water enters a curve the water on the inside of the arc slows and the water on the outside of the arc speeds up to keep apace. If the arc is a sharp one, the water on the outside will begin to swirl in an effort to rejoin the slower inside flow. This will create an eddy and an erosive rotation. Picture a wheel rolling over a pavement. The roiling action cuts away great chunks of the outside bank, carrying the sediment and the gold down stream. As the gold bearing sediment flows it will settle along the inside, slower flow, dropping the heavier minerals to the bed. Action of the water will make the gold settle to the bed and collect in crevices, later to be covered with more settlements from the stream as the seasonal flow diminishes. At this place, the long arc is present and the gradient is reduced, making this an ideal spot to prospect."

Luder laughed. "As you spoke, the picture came to me like opening a door to a lighted room."

What Duncan didn't explain, because he didn't know, was just how much of an excavation project would be involved. There was no telling how much spoil would have to be removed to reach the bed of the ancient watercourse. He had collected samples, marked them and washed them, mapping the locations on a hand-drawn map of the area. Picking the most likely spot to find color he had excavated to nearly three feet before he found even black sand. The washed pans produced gold in dust form but only a few grains, perhaps a dime per pan. There were no nuggets at the shallow depths. The weightier metal would have worked its way to the bed.

Pulling his map from his saddlebags, he consulted his markers and dismounted. With shovel and sacks he clamored down the slope.

"Let us take some samples back to camp. There won't be much but just the sight of color can bring glittering riches to the tired mind. In other words, we shall infect the men with gold fever."

CHAPTER SEVEN

Elizabeth and Jubal had risen before the sun with the bakers. She prepared a kettle of rice, spices, dried peas, and some shredded goat meat they had acquired the evening before. The broth from the braising of the goat was used as stock in the mix. She guessed at the proportion and variety of added spices, most being as unfamiliar to her as anything more than the base preparation of the rice. She was rewarded with an enticing aroma wafting out as the lid of the kettle trembled away and steam puffed out. She was tempted to peek inside but Duncan had cautioned her to wait, lest the rice become sticky. After the prescribed interval, she removed the kettle from the heat, letting it set a bit before opening. She was concerned the Mexican spices might be too bold for the American tongue. Tasting the results, she feared she might have erred on the side of caution, her recipe was somewhat above bland. Jubal agreed and they cut up an onion and added some salt until in agreement they had approached success.

It was almost time for the bakery to greet the hungry miners and tradesmen with apple turnovers and peach tarts washed down with strong black coffee. Even before sunrise, a line had begun to form.

Slinging the kettle from an iron rod, Elizabeth and Jubal were going to carry the pot outside and offer samples in the hopes of selling rice out of the back of the tent. As they passed through the bakery's meager dining area they were halted by Hannah Van Volk's startled voice.

"You're not going to go out front with that, are you?"

"Yes, we were going to offer samples as an enticement to buy our rice."

"Don't be daft. Set that kettle up on the counter and station yourself behind it with a ladle. Those who bring bowls or cups can be enticed at a dollar a ladle full."

"Oh, I don't know. This isn't exactly American food. I may have no takers."

Her remark elicited a laugh, not just from Hannah but from her two daughters who stood beside her, ready for the morning custom.

"These men will eat anything prepared by a woman. The smell might not compete with our cinnamon but it will sell. Coffee and pastries ain't exactly stick to your ribs food. Besides, if it wasn't for what food these men can buy, they would soon be eating rats cooked over the heat of a lantern."

When the rough dining room opened the miners flooded in. Within twenty minutes the bakery's first run of the day was exhausted. Many of the miners perched on the stump stools to converse with others. Some took their purchases with them. Elizabeth had only made three dollars from her rice concoction. She was disappointed in sales, not realizing the lack of sales was not because of her wares but because the customers had brought no plates or bowls. Once the remaining guests had their fill of coffee, it freed up their cups and a short queue developed at her station. Even those with cups had neglected to bring utensils so she was viewing a room full of men eating either with their fingers or with knives. Soon many removed the blades from their mouths long enough to compliment her on the new offering. Better yet, some came back for seconds. Hannah and the two girls left her alone in the dining room. The next round of baking needed preparation. Elizabeth, despite the display of hardware, felt no alarm. The men were curious and she suspected those who came for seconds had disposed of their initial timidity and bought a second helping just for the opportunity to speak with her. It wasn't long before she was scraping the sides of the kettle, leaving two customers disappointed. She lingered with them, exchanging banalities about the weather and comparisons with their womenfolk left behind. Once the last one passed through the flaps of the tent she realized she had not once suggested the customer purchase dry rice. Caught up in the final success and kind attentions, the idea had fled from her mind. Oh well, there was always lunch to be served. She closed up the tent flaps, put out the sign and lugged the empty kettle back to prepare for the next onslaught.

"If you have another kettle, I'd make up a double batch. Word'll spread in the camp and you'll sell out quick," said Hannah.

"Really, do you think so?"

"Why Elizabeth, would you doubt me. I've been in the bakery business almost two weeks now and I know my customers," laughed Hannah, amused by her own overnight success. "Brew up some more of your burgoo and we'll all have some lunch when it's ready."

~~~

Josh had not spent a restful night, what little of it remained. Lying on deck every sound he heard from shore became swarms of four-legged predators or two-legged boarders with knives in their teeth. He would freeze at each click, snap, or rustling of the brush. He scolded himself for such foolishness and would just starting to relax when yet another sound caused his eyes to snap open and his hand clutch for his pistol. As soon as the sky above began to wake he gave up sleeping as a useless enterprise. In the quiet hours before the sky lightened behind the distant mountain he thought the sound of the coyotes yipping at one another had moved away across the river.

Sitting on the main hatch, huddled in a blanket and watching his too hot to hold mug of coffee cool on the deck between his feet, he began to come up with a plan to rid himself of the coyote threat. Thirty minutes after finishing his breakfast he was climbing the ratlines to the maintop, the Hawken rifle slung over his shoulder. If the pack hunted at night they must sleep during the day. He didn't think they had made dens nearby so they might wander about in daylighbt. He had a good vantagepoint and an accurate rifle. He might be able to pick them off one by one or make the area so hazardous they would move on.

It was a chilly morning, but the sky was clearing except far in the northwest, which held the promise of another storm riding in. He wore his coat and kept the blanket about his shoulders, constantly scanning the land for telltale movement. Down the estuary, no ships were anchored or off-loading. No wagons came or went. Across the river, a small herd of cows grazed contentedly. Offhand, he wondered who was milking them. Perhaps he might wash up a pail and row across. It was cruel to leave a cow un-milked he told himself. It might prove a worthwhile expedition.

Considering the alternative was to work single-handed in the hold, shoveling, hauling, and dumping the spoiled cargo. Milking cows would be almost like a vacation. Just about everything left in the hold was loose, spoiled stinking rice. Until it was dumped he had no chance of operating the pumps. Every bit of what remained would have to be shoveled into a sling, hoisted onto one of the dinghies, rowed away, and dumped. It was miserable labor and made worse by working alone, at least for the time being.

Huddled on the mizzen top his gazed wandered over the land below. Across the river he spied a coyote patrolling the shoreline above the cut headland. The presence of the animal on the opposite bank made him think the pack had moved on after counting its losses from the night before. His eyes found the herd of cows. They were moving away, calves protected within the herd. It looked as if they were surrendering the field to their unwelcome visitors. He watched them until they were out of sight, taking his dreams of fresh milk with them.

The lone coyote was still investigating the shoreline. He would trot along to another vantage point and then peer down to the muddy flats, hoping for a washed up fish or a drowned rabbit perhaps. He'd stop on occasion, pausing to taste the air for the scent of a threat. There was little breeze to waft anything his way.

Josh's elevation gave a good measure against detection from across the river. He was half-hidden by the mast. He moved further behind and brought the Hawken to rest on the mizzen cap and against the mizzen topmast. No target was visible when he sighted along the barrel. Had he been detected? He estimated the distance to where he had last seen his quarry at a bit over two hundred yards, a difficult but not impossible shot. Slowly he slid the buckhorn sight forward, click by click until his best guess was two hundred and fifty yards. He brought the hammer back to half cock and tried to slow his breathing, to relax his upper body and to wait.

While scanning the far headland for movement he speculated about the coyote. Was this individual one of those who he had done battle with the night before? Was this one a single hunter or had the survivors swum the river, perhaps to target the cow herd? Perhaps there was a separate troop with the two tribes observing the river as a natural barrier between territories. Either way, if he could manage to convert this one to carrion it would draw others, and he could eliminate them one at a time. Even if he never got another shot, if any animals remained on this side they might cross over for an easy meal, he would be rid of them, at least for the time being.

Back from the edge of the bluff, Josh detected the movement of grass and the back of an animal as it moved to his left. The coyote paused, moved slowly towards the bank. Josh brought the hammer back to full cock and waited for his quarry to appear. What wind there had been dropped away. It carried no foreign scent to the canine's nose. The beast turned, presenting its flank. Josh drew the hammer back full. His finger found the set trigger, pulled it and the Hawken was on the knife-edge of discharging. The animal walked along, paused. Josh held his fire, uncocked the rifle and contented himself with observation.

37

Last night, with the pack a threat to Natchez, he had felt no compunction about wading into the slaughter. Even less, though in retrospect it was probably foolish, did he regret charging into the undergrowth. His blood was up and fear had not overtaken him. The animals had come to do him harm. He had no regrets.

This lone coyote, and perhaps it was one of the marauders, was no immediate threat to him and even less so being across the river. It was living as nature intended. Josh had killed men in anger and killed game for food. He bore no remorse for either. Killing even this mean creature because of what it was seemed senseless. He brought the Hawken down, knowing maudlin sentiment might cause him to rue the decision. He stood, waved his arms and howled against the morning. Seconds later the bushy tail was disappearing upstream.

~~~

The excitement generated by Duncan's demonstration of gold washing was somewhat tempered with his description of the scope and nature of the work involved to relieve the dry streambed of its treasure. The company had, to a man, been thrilled as he taught one of the men the technique of washing gold in a pan. In order to avoid any disappointment he had, on the sly, introduced a bit of gold from his poke to select samples, not trusting a dime's worth in the rim of a pan to bring jubilation to his audience. He wasn't trying to deceive the men. He simply wanted to enhance the experience. His foil had the desired effect. The men crowded about and cheered as the precious metal gleamed in the rime of black sand in the washing pan.

While the flush of untold riches was upon the prospectors he patiently explained the workings of erosion and how and where the river would secret its wealth. He had their full attention as they envisioned returning to Albany with each man rich as Midas. The trouble began when he entertained questions. It was soon brought to his attention the site he proposed was over a quarter mile from the water needed for the final separation.

He explained the alternative the ore would either require transport to the water or the water would have to be directed to the excavation site. Duncan proposed that both alternatives be commenced simultaneously. After barrows and tipcarts had been constructed, the fine oar could be brought down to the river and the rocks and spoilage could be transported upstream to begin construction of a dam and diversion to bring water to their excavation. At the river site, a sluice gate could be built to provide water to power the gold machines they had purchased in Yerba Buena. This could begin producing color within ten days or two weeks time. For the long term, they could dam off and divert water from the South Fork into a pool and carry it down to the distant site in flumes constructed from lumber sawn from the trees that grew around them.

On the trek from the Sacramento estuary to where they now stood, the march had crossed, with some difficulty, the Middle Fork of the American and probably a dozen small tributaries and forks of various other watercourses. The men wanted to know why they couldn't just take pick and pan and begin producing gold that very day. After all, they had heard tales of hundred dollar pans and of men picking fortunes from sandbars right at the thresholds of their tents. Many complained they had not come to California to labor in a sawpit or to haul and dump dirt for a dam. Men would be getting rich while they built calluses and sore backs.

"What you didn't see as we marched was men standing shoulder to shoulder panning the rivers. There is a season to this placer mining. Think of the rivers like a farm. There is a season for sowing and a season for reaping. In the winter the rains carry gold from far in the mountains to the rivers. The rivers are in flood now and the gold is coming to us from above. As the rains cease and the snow melts, the rivers will slow and the gold will drop to the beds, adding to and replenishing the wealth in the bars and banks yet unformed. The time of reaping will come. To venture into the canyons and pan in the rivers might result in some accidental finds, but it would be akin to discovering a tomato in the garden in December."

"I'd rather take my chances panning than having nothing but sawdust in my beard as reward for a day's work," came a voice from the rear.

"Did I mention the quest for the single tomato will probably result in drowning or starvation," explained Duncan. "Not two weeks ago I became stranded on a bank as the river rose around me. I would have certainly been swept away except for friends who discovered and rescued me. Believe me friends. Our best prospects for immediate rewards will be right here. We only need excavate the dry gravel down to sand and bedrock to begin seeing results."

"And how far down do we have to dig to reach the gold?" said a young man with just the first dusting of a beard upon his face. The others voiced their assent to his question.

"It could be four feet or four yards down, perhaps more. That's why you must prospect before you mine. But, from the samples I brought down..." His words were overcome by objections and complaints. Perhaps, Duncan reflected, it might not have been a good plan to "salt" the sample pans. Not that the men could be blamed. Gold fever had infected them from two thousand miles away and their expectations had been building since the first blush of the malady struck. The realization gold mining was hard labor was a lesson only experience could teach.

Luder stepped in. Discipline needed to be restored and his military background could be employed to restore it. Duncan retired to his tent. He ate his dinner pondering the various sample jars, wondering which might point the way to the most likely beginning dig.

CHAPTER EIGHT

Hearing Jubal's hail from ashore, Josh extricated himself from the hold. He poured a bucket of water, only slightly warmed by the thin winter sun, over his head and toweled away the muck on his legs before sticking them into the trousers he'd shed before his descent. Rushing to the rail he greeted his bride and friend with a wave and a fair imitation of coyote's yipping chant.

Once aboard, Elizabeth and Josh embraced and kissed as if they hadn't seen each other for three days. Jubal, feeling uncomfortable, wandered over to the hold and peered in.

"You're going to need more than a bucket of water to make you appealing," said Elizabeth.

"Thought you said you appreciated a working man."

"I think I said I liked a man who worked. You are ripe."

"Been trying to clear the hold and I discovered something. Come see."

He led the way to the far rail where several wooden crates were stacked. Excelsior was visible along all four edges. Josh pulled up the lid and picked up a heavy white mug.

"Under all that rice is a layer of crockery. Mebbe a hundred crates like these. Plates, bowls, and mugs. There's some broken stuff and it needs a washing but I think we could sell it."

Elizabeth examined another crate of plates.

"I'm not certain. I recall a big stack of chinaware sitting on the beach at the *embarcadero*. We could try I suppose. We can give some to the Van Volks."

"It's got to be worth somethin'," said Josh.

"We'll sell it as is. I don't aim to take up washing dishes."

"They need to come out of the hold. They are full of rice and this wood wool is leaking out. Either will foul the pumps."

"Well, we sold all the rice. It was a slow start and we had to undercut the price of potatoes but all told, we took in over four hundred dollars. Now I have something to show you. Jubal!" she called. "Show Josh what we bought."

Jubal unslung the bag he'd carried over his shoulder, removed a bundle and unwrapped it on the deck. Inside were two unusual looking pistols.

"Cost forty dollars apiece with the bullet mold and horn. The man didn't have any powder but we managed to buy a pound from another," said Jubal.

Josh whistled at the price. His father had paid thirty-five dollars for a Walker Colt revolver. Revolvers weren't unheard of but the Walker was a larger caliber than the earlier patent Colt Patterson. Some considered the Walker a jinx gun as the namesake Texas Ranger captain had been killed soon after taking delivery of a pair. The pistol was Josh's prize possession.

Josh had seen pistols like these before but they were still not in common use. They too were called revolvers but they differed from the Colt models with a rotating cylinder. These had revolving barrels and were sometimes called turnover pistols with two shots or a pepperbox with four to five barrels.

Both were beautifully crafted Belgian Mariette Brevettes. Each rotating barrel had a nipple for a percussion cap. Some other types had rotating barrels but the user had to remove the fired cap and replace it after each shot. These simply required rotating the barrel until it locked in place. Pistols like these had not been possible until about twenty years ago when the fulminate of mercury percussion cap replaced the flintlock and pan pistols of old. The pepperboxes were usually short barreled pistols, purposely so because the weight of four or more barrels made an unbalanced weapon.

Colt's revolving cylinder model was a vast improvement and almost perfectly balanced. Josh's had two spare cylinders. He could fire six shots and then slip in and cap a fresh cylinder with six more charges. He was not foolish enough to carry a loose cylinder with the nipples primed. With these two additions, the three had the firepower of a platoon of soldiers.

"I have plenty of powder, lead, and caps. I wonder if my caps will fit."

It was found they did and the three of them spent the next hour shooting the turnover guns. As expected, short barreled pistols were only accurate to about twenty paces and once half a dozen rounds had been fired, the barrels became almost too hot to rotate. A single glove sufficed. The pistols had a ring trigger guard so a glove on the shooting hand made it awkward to fire. The shooting was fun and they discovered a use for the crockery.

~ ~ ~

Duncan was enjoying his breakfast coffee and some cornbread with currant jelly when Luder joined him as he walked the bank of the American. He was devising a sluice gate in his mind and seeking a likely spot for its placement.

"Did you find a likely spot to tap?"

The Albany officer had inquired at an importune time. Duncan had a mouthful of dodger. He pointed to his mouth and chewed hurriedly. He swallowed and replied.

"I've found several likely ones but I have to consider the terrain we have to transport the ore over, as well."

"Well, transporting it won't get any easier." Luder hesitated, rubbing the back of his head like a boy caught at mischief. Finally, he relented.

"Two men packed up and left in the middle of the night. Guess they couldn't wait to get rich. Word is they headed up this river here. Going to prospect the banks."

"Then they may rejoin us soon," said Shipwash. "This South Fork is one of the faster running streams and much of it upstream lies in narrow cuts that can only be approached from above on steep banks. They either will get discouraged and return to us or their bodies will float by. Please convey these two alternatives to the remaining men."

This was not a good sign, thought Duncan. The men needed to be kept busy. He'd make his decision where to place his gate and then they would relocate camp to the deep gravel site. Luder was already walking back to camp after bringing the sour news.

"Jack," called Duncan. The man turned to him.

"The desertions now leave us with an even twenty in the company. Is that so?"

"Twenty it is with one man in that number ill today."

"The Albany partners' share of the enterprise is based solely upon its contribution of labor. Is that not so?"

"It is," Luder replied.

"And now that number is diminished by two men. There may well be more deserters. In light of that possibility I believe we may have to discuss the arrangements further."

"Perhaps. I'll discuss it with Fellowes and Weber." Luder waited for an acknowledgement but Shipwash was already deep in contemplation of the task before them.

As an officer in an East India Company regiment Duncan had held military authority over a squad of men. Since leaving Company service he had managed only his own affairs. He longed now for martial prerogative and a strident sergeant major to see his orders followed upon. This collection of Albany Argonauts might have uniforms and flags but they had no discipline. These were citizens, self-organized to chase a vision. Their idea of military discipline did not even allow their leaders to be called or to act as officers. They had lost men already at the bottom of their ship's gangway and now two more striking off on their own. No doubt, faced with hard labor and no immediate reward, others would follow suit. His own ardor to develop these dry diggings may have led himself and his partners into a poor association.

First things first, situated below an embankment of the river the grade and nature of the ground could be used to tap the river. A small confinement could be constructed from the initial excavations and a shallow downhill grade would provide sufficient flow to operate the gold washing machines. The grade from the diggings was not so far or so steep that the return trundling of empty cards would be onerous.

He set to work organizing work parties. Carts would need to be built, planks sawn or cut for a short sluice run. Clearing of the ground and initial excavations could begin and someone needed to return to Sutter's Fort or the *Embarcadero* to seek a slab or iron sheeting and a frame to construct a sluice gate. Perhaps some mortar and lime could be obtained, as well. He added wheels for the carts and barrows to his list.

Shipwash was able to absorb himself in the organization and planning of these practical manners. Concerns about his labor force were set aside. He was dependent upon Luder, Fellowes, and Weber to keep their men in line. Clearly the Albany boys would never accept direct supervision from a stranger, a foreign stranger at that. His role must remain technical.

Duncan was pleased, or at least partially relieved, when he returned to the diggings and the newly relocated bivouac. Someone with military acumen had set up a company street of tents on high ground above the diggings and in the shelter of trees. The tents were evenly spaced and straight with a common dining and common area at the end. The ground had been cleared and leveled. Rocks had been placed to mark the confines of the central street and, down on the backside of the bluff four men could be seen digging a privy. Duncan could hear the ring of axes in the distance. Most pleasing to his eyes was the complete lack of men loitering. Every man was working in concert with his fellows. Duncan joined Luder and Weber who were working through a list of tasks and the stowing of goods in their proper places.

"Where is Mr. Fellowes?" asked Duncan.

"Elias is off with a woodcutting party," replied Luder. "They are felling trees and digging a sawyer's pit for planking. You said the mining will require planks and we will need planking for the floors of our tents. Most of these men are townsfolk. We can't expect them to winter in the mud. We've set up a tent for you, too."

"That is much appreciated. Thank you. I get so caught up in the practical aspects of recovering and processing the minerals, I often forget to attend to my own comforts."

"Your mule's comfort has been attended to, as well," said Leland Weber.

"Ah, Cyrus. I'm surprised he hasn't quite abandoned me, the amount of neglect I heap upon him."

"Cyrus seems a tractable enough creature, as far as mules go," said Luder.

"Just so, I notice the long tom gold machines have been unloaded and set up. Perhaps I might intervene. The smaller box goes below the long one, not above it."

"We had some discussion about that. Decided we'd wait for you to set us correct."

"Perhaps tomorrow we could arrange a demonstration. If we could transport one of the machines down to the water's edge at a convenient location as well as a barrow or two of excavation, it might serve as encouragement to the men."

Even as he spoke the words, Duncan knew he was running a risk. If the excavations produced nothing, the men would be discouraged. Honestly he did not expect any color in the first layer of the overburden. He would have to ensure the first prospect went deep enough to approach the richer deposits. He suggested that the excavation at the most likely prospect site be commenced, explaining why. Luder and Weber agreed and Weber set off to make it so. Certainly not as satisfying as having a sergeant major snap his heels and about face, but this was a different place and time.

~ ~ ~

One or two more days and the hold should be clear. Slinging the crates of crockery up on deck was a right bit easier than shoveling soaking, swollen, and stinking rice on a shovel. Josh was already envisioning dismantling and clearing the chain pumps. The fothering operation had markedly reduced the leaking into the hull but the depth in the bilge was becoming a concern, far more than seeing to repairs of the steam engine. The water in the bilge was now the ballast of the ship. Relieved of her cargo the *Julianna Dolce* now floated free within the confines of the small inlet. A small warping anchor was run ashore and dug in to prevent a tide from pulling the wounded craft into the channel. Not being able to manage the bower anchors, spring lines were run from amidships and staked ashore, keeping the boat roughly centered in the inlet.

With the end of the onerous clearing of the hold in sight, the three crew members began to settle into their winter home. Personal and household items were brought aboard and stowed. Empty shelves began to fill and regular meals could be served at table. Clothes were repaired, washed, and laundry soon adorned the rigging. Rain, fog, and wind no longer had to be endured. Being able to just step inside to a warm and familiar cabin brought as much vitality to the crew as any bodily nourishment that left the galley.

On fair days they took a crate of plates ashore and practiced with the pepperbox pistols. Ungainly and poorly balanced, accuracy at anything over ten paces became more a matter of luck than practice and skill. Compared to the Walker Colt, the shooter might as well be flinging stones. During one of their shoots it was found one of the casks of powder obtained at the landing had been adulterated and was of a coarse grain to begin with. It might better be suited to Fourth of

July fireworks but as a propellant it was worthless. It was decided to load up more rice and a dozen boxes of crockery and head back to the landing and perhaps to Sutter's Fort to sell and then buy supplies. They would make a gift of plates to the Van Volk bakery in appreciation for their hospitality and provide them a share of the proceeds of rice sales as part of their informal business relationship.

Jubal was elected to make the journey on his own. Upon his arrival he was to extend an invitation to the family to come visit the ship. It was doubtful they would come, as a visit would mean closing a flourishing business. Still, the courtesy should be extended. With a clear night and a canopy of bright stars showing a prospect of sunny weather, the next morning was set for Jubal's departure.

The methodical loading and packing the wagon had become routine. The road back to what passed as civilization would soon become familiar. While the route might become familiar, the dangers of the road could never be. Jubal departed with a pepperbox in a makeshift holster by his knee and the shotgun in a rack across the footboard. He also carried extra provisions some medical supplies to treat an injury. Beyond those precautions he would be on his own.

Extraordinary, at least in Jubal's mind, was he was being entrusted with not only the task of bargaining the goods but carried eight ounces of gold dust in a brown glass bottle. Never in his life had he ever had so much as a few dollars in his possession. As a slave in Missouri he had sometimes been rewarded with a few coins from his owners or from other farmers to which his labor had been hired out. Working for Josh's father had mostly been for room and board and five dollars a month that was mostly spent on used clothing or an occasional celebratory bottle. Of the half pound of dust he carried, two ounces of it was his. Just over forty dollars; eight months labor in Illinois. In California, the money would buy him a shirt and pants and a bottle. Still, he was almost overwhelmed with gratitude for the trust and responsibility given to him. He would not disappoint. He popped the reins, called out to the mules and pointed their noses to the river landing.

~~~

The morning's first wagon brought Duncan, the long tom, and four men with picks and shovels from the camp down to the riverbank. Another wagon followed close behind with the first load of excavated gravel. It would take several more wagonloads just to get below the level of gravel. It was hard digging and a burden to place on the

47

wagons. Duncan could as well have the men dump the spoil at camp but he knew he would need it at the embankment to make a raised bed ditch from the river to the long tom. The gravel would be dumped along the embankment and the four-man crew could begin digging from the top of the bank down to the level of the river, tossing the dirt and rock down to build up the ground behind them. They began the excavation on the bank side of the embankment, anticipating the arrival of a sluice gate from Sutter's. If one could not be had, they could build one with a wooden frame, bolstered by rock and slats that could be removed or added depending on the flow of water. Once the gate was in place, they could dig out to the river and begin. Approximately eight-foot of cut was needed to reach the water level. The material taken out would raise the dirt behind them to about six feet and then run in a ditch gradually down to where the tom would be set up at waist level where men would work it from the ore delivered. It was ambitious but necessary. It was Duncan's hope the project would be complete by the time the men at the dig site had reached gold bearing ore.

"Perhaps now would be an opportune time to wash our samples. Please gather round."

With his four man digging crew and a pair from the last wagon delivery, Shipwash produced the jars of sample ore from the dry bed. He handed out buckets and asked the men to fill them from the river and deposit the water into the half cask he had brought. The men would have to scale the embankment and then descend the slope to the river. The work involved just to retrieve a few buckets of water should impress upon them the necessity of building the gate and sluice.

Sitting on a stool before the cask he produced one of the sample jars and dumped half its contents into a broad flat tin pan. A crescent shaped ridge had been tapped into the bottom just before the sides sloped out.

"See here, this little ridge will trap the color behind it," he explained as he began tossing out the larger pieces of gravel. "As you are panning, keep your eyes open for any large bits of gold, called pickers. Panning works best for dust and flake. We wouldn't want to lose anything larger."

Holding the pan at a slight angle, with the hammered ridge at the lower extremity, he commenced a fluid motion that quickly produced an elliptical current in the pan. As he washed he let the lighter material slosh out on the ground.

"Won't that let the gold slop out?" asked one of the men, poking about in the discards with his fingers. Duncan explained the weight properties of gold and how it would always seek the lowest levels. From there he expanded the pan's actions into the natural workings of a watercourse and how and where the gold was deposited. All the time he kept up the pan's action, occasionally replenishing the water in the pan. He pointed out the white bit of quartz and explained how quartz was a good indicator of the presence of gold, though it was much lighter and would remain with the discards.

Eventually all that remained in the pan was a thin crescent shaped bank of black sand lying on both sides of the ridge in the pan's bottom.

"When you are excavating, black sand is an indicator that you are near where gold might lie. Gold is two to four times the weight per volume of the various minerals in the black sand. While the black stuff serves to tell us we are close to our quarry, it then becomes a problem as it is the last bit of material separating us from the color." Here he passed the pan around the circle for the men to examine. Duncan had spied some bits of flake as he panned. His hope was one of the men would also spot it. None did and the pan was returned to him.

"What I call black sand is a combination of minerals, mostly iron or iron oxide like hematite, sphalerite, or chromite. There may also be lead present. Because they are oxides they are, in nature, black in color." He could see he was losing his audience and concluded, "Other than their color, they are of no interest to us."

He added more water and returned to his panning but in a shorter abbreviated stroke.

"Our object here is to get the black stuff to jump the ridge, leaving gold behind." He paused to take a brush and move the" jumped" sand out of the pan. From start to finish he had expended about ten minutes of uncomfortable work. The sample he worked was not one of those he had embellished from his poke. It was one he was curious about himself and he could finish his demonstration with the 'salted' sample ore. When done with this first pan, he passed it around so all could see the two or three flakes and a tiny, tiny bit of gold dust that remained. Even the five or ten cents worth in the pan had the desired effect on the collective. It took no more than the slightest sample to bring on a bout of the fever. How well he knew the feeling.

"Let us each take a turn with the remaining samples. You first Mr.?"

"Dryden, John Dryden," the man said, taking the pan while shaking Duncan's hand with the other. "I used to be a clerk in a bank, but now I'm going to make enough to start my own bank."

Duncan took Dryden's fever as evidence of the success of his demonstration. He dumped the remainder of the first sample into the pan and set to work educating his class. At first Dryden spilled as much water on himself as where he wanted it to go. Duncan sent the rest of the men for more water and coached his first student until he was at least competent. By the time the water bearers returned the pan was down to the black sand line and was once again passed. This time one of the men spotted a glimmer and tried to pick it out without success.

"The finds are too small to pick out. Let us continue to wash."

This pan and the next two samples produced some color, but each man was thrilled with his first find. By the time the last two men washed out the sample Duncan had added to, the men were fairly dancing with delight. There would be joy in the camp as the word spread. The whole of all the samples hadn't yielded more than three dollars worth and most of that from the adulterated pans. Still, the purpose had been served. By this evening the Argonauts would be outdoing each other with tales of how they would spend their fortunes.

Luder arrived, wondering why the wagon and crew had not returned.

The men showed him the fine gold they had accumulated from the samples. As their leader he tried to restrain his enthusiasm but his gaze darted frequently to Shipwash as if he was some miracle worker. It was time Duncan brought them back from their flight of fancy.

"Gentlemen. We have barely washed four quarts of ore in the last ninety minutes. As you can see, the pan is an inefficient method for production. While its merit lies in testing samples, we may have lost a fourth of the gold we salvaged during the wash. Let us now examine and demonstrate the gold washing machine you brought with you."

There was risk in working the long tom. If no color was found, the elation could as easily swing to discouragement, then discontent, and possibly more desertions. On the other hand, if gold was left in the riffles at the end of the demonstration, the work of constructing the gate, sluice, and the extensive excavation could proceed with the promise of gold as return for the labor. Duncan was playing a hunch.

The last wagonload of spoil, still standing where it arrived, appeared to have enough fine material to produce something. How much remained to be seen. The ore on the wagon showed some promise, bearing enough fine material to merit testing. If he had doubts, he would have used the machine back at camp with no ore just to show how it worked. As they say, the proof of the pudding.

"Gentlemen, we will need a continuous flow of water for this to operate. Let us commence."

If the ore proved out even a little it should impress upon the men the necessity of developing the gate and establishing a reliable flow of water for operation. It wouldn't take more than a few trips up and down the embankment to impress upon them the worth of their project.

Duncan spent an inordinate amount of time adjusting the machine for the right pitch to establish a proper flow. Periodically he would step back to appraise his work. Satisfied, he then set the machine to level side to side. Not until ready did he call for the wagon to be moved and the first shovels full of prospect be loaded.

"We will soon fall into a routine but before any water is introduced, all of the large rocks and debris should be removed and set aside for our future use. If you come across any white or stained bring it to me, please. Quartz is as much a precursor to gold as the black sand." Duncan was ready to commence the demonstration.

"As I'm sure you are aware, the purpose of this mechanism is to increase the amount of material to be washed. Please, let us begin. One man will shovel ore into the upper end and a man on each side will remove the worthless rocks to a barrow for disposal." He moved men to their station as he spoke.

"As the ore washes down trough the wider end, it spreads out and, at the end, tapers slightly upward. This directs the finer material over this perforated plate. Here, two men will work the gravel over the plate and the fine sand containing the treasure will fall to the riffle below. Do I have a volunteer?"

He did. "Begin working the material over the plate, ever mindful to rescue anything that glitters. As the spoil accumulates, shovel it away. Now let us examine the lower mechanism." Duncan was warming to his work and the men caught his enthusiasm.

"See how the material continues to flow down to these battens. These battens serve the same function as the ridge in the washing pan. Gold will be trapped behind these "riffle bars", retrieved and once again pan washed to remove the last detritus."

The long tom was more efficient than the one man 'cradles' that worked a shovel of ore at a time. A single miner would rock the cradle back and forth while picking out rubble. At the end of each rocking motion, a slight jerk was added to aid separation. The cradle was far more productive than the pan and the long tom left the cradle behind for both efficiency and production.

"Even as much an improvement over other placer methods as the tom is," he continued, "it still will not catch everything. The cloth trapped what was called "flour gold" that would otherwise end up in the spoils pile."

"Keep a careful eye. Always be on the watch for the holy nugget too large to pass through to the lower machine."

"See how the particulate that passes below is left largely unimpeded save for the action of the water flowing ever downward. This accumulation of unwanted material burping out the end must be shoveled aside. Add more ore to the top of the long trough and keep repeating, shovel after shovel after shovel." Duncan was so excited he clapped his hands and threw in a couple of dance steps.

At the end of the day, or more optimistically several times during the day, the riffles were cleaned and set aside for final washing. The gold remaining in the final wash was then put in a fry pan, dried over a fire and stored away before the fry pan was used to prepare the evening meal. Tons were processed to produce ounces, day after day after day. The expectations of finding riches by picking up nuggets during a leisurely stroll along an idyllic bubbling brook were soon dashed as the reality of placer mining set in.

Shipwash's demonstration was perhaps an extreme example but illustrated the vital role supplied by water. Water brought the gold into the streams and no ore could be processed without a reliable supply. This became apparent as the first half dozen buckets of water were dumped, the rubble removed and the smaller material moved forward inches at a time as more buckets were laboriously filled and carried back to be dumped and the process repeated. The men bringing ore and picking through the tailings relieved the water bearers every half hour and the ore moved on. The men complained but good naturedly, still riding the euphoria of the first gold produced by their own hands. Luder, not holding himself above the rest, joined the rotation. Duncan, with his bad leg, contributed by sorting as the material passed by him in the trough.

Dryden, like a child bringing an apple to the teacher, presented Duncan with the first piece of quartz. The engineer called a halt to the workings in order to teach a lesson.

"John Dryden has brought me the first piece of quartz," he said, holding it aloft for all to see. "In itself completely unremarkable. No doubt you have encountered quartz near your homes."

No one replied. They were grateful to have a respite from the tedium, even if it was for just a piece of white stone. Undeterred, Duncan continued. "The geology of this land is new, meaning it was largely influenced by volcanic activity. As the activity beneath the surface rumbled, gold and other minerals were liquefied and began moving to the surface. They accumulated in fractures in the rock, most notably quartz." Duncan passed the rock around so they could see the empty crevices.

"As the molten gold cooled it is retained in the fissures. Time and weather conspire over countless years releasing the gold. Erosion carries the color to the stream so that companies of men from Albany, New York can retrieve it and become wealthy men. Even when walking keep your eyes tuned for quartz. You might just turn over a piece with the vein still intact. Then it can be pried out with a knifepoint or even a spoon. Hopefully, in our excavations, we will uncover a vein of gold and we simply follow the reef of quartz to find the gold. Quartz, men. Quartz!"

The men went back to work. The effort required to wash just the few shovels of ore in the tom impressed the men with how vital a supply of running water was. Four men, two on each slope of the bank filled, passed, and emptied buckets just to move the fines a hand's breadth along. If the wash produced nothing, the demonstration could well be a disaster. The joy of washing gold in the pans would be forgotten. Frustration could build and more men might desert to try their luck directly in the swollen streams. So much depended on what was left in the riffle box.

By the time all of the ore was on the perforated metal and men poked about looking for color another wagon of spoil arrived with a curious driver. Duncan saw the material was much like what they were processing. The driver dismounted the box and came to observe.

"Eureka!" shouted one of the men. He looked about at the others. "I've always wanted to say that." He pointed to the material left on the sheet metal. The light shown on a bright piece of gold flake.

"I thought about picking it up but was afraid it might break."

"If it breaks, its iron pyrite just catching the light right," answered Shipwash. He squeezed in among the curious and lifted the flake and a bit of sand on a knifepoint. This was surely an omen, a good omen. Peeking under the tom he saw there was only water passing through. He dipped a bucket in the half cask that was catching the runoff from the lower section and took it to the upper end of the top section.

"Let's wash a few more shovels worth before we see what we've trapped. Look lively, men!"

Once the upper tom was cleared of any small material and the lower section was again running clear, the lower machine was pulled clear and every remaining bit behind the riffles was washed into a pan, Duncan showed Luder how to do the final cleanup. Luder crouched over the cask of water and sluiced it again and again. Duncan, with his practiced eye saw the appearance of color and almost clapped his hands with delight. It would be better if Luder or one of the other men crowded about were the first to see the flakes and dust lying in the final bit of black sand.

A moment's more labor and the men were nudging each other and getting excited. Shipwash could see they hadn't accumulated much more than a dollar's worth behind the last ridge in the pan but he knew it didn't take much to bring back the fever. He pointed to the two wagons of ore.

"There are two wagons with gold bearing ore on them and they are just from the first level of excavation. I don't know how deep we need go but the quantity and quality will improve as we near the bed of the dry stream."

The men were eyeing the ore on the wagons like looking at a Christmas goose. They saw riches but weren't looking at the labor required to separate the gold. They had already forgotten the bucket after bucket of water carried from the stream to the machine. The three hours spent sampling had yielded no more than four dollars for five men, six if Luder's late arrival could count. Most of the find had been from Duncan's poke. With the fever upon them, the labor seemed trivial.

"We can't wash all this with buckets. Dump these wagons and build up the bank so we can tap the river. Captain Luder, perhaps you might see to bringing us more material." While more material would be necessary Duncan was more interested in spreading the fever to the rest of the camp. No doubt Luder would infect the rest of the men.

Duncan's plan was to construct a work area below the water level of the passing river. He would then excavate partially through the embankment and install a sluice gate. Hopefully, the men sent back to Sutter's could obtain a frame and have an iron gate fabricated. Once that was in place, they could begin to cut away on the other side of the gate, setting pilings and rock to prevent the water from cutting away at the bank once it was breached. Rocks could be piled in front of the sluice gate. Water could still come through. All in all, this was a productive day all around.

CHAPTER NINE

Elizabeth was straddling a bench in the stern cabin of the *Julianna Dolce*. Pressed between her knees was a coffee grinder she was turning unconsciously as her mind wandered. She and Josh had been alone on the boat for the past two days and, unless lovemaking was considered work, little had been accomplished. Having her knees pressed against the grinder reminded her of pressing her knees into Josh's sides as they embraced in the berth not eight feet and an hour's span of time ago.

The grinding of the beans filled the cabin with their aroma and the promise of brewed coffee replacing it shortly. Fondly she recalled the sweetened, canned milk they had once added to their brew. The last of it had gone by the wayside on the other side of the Sierras. She should have asked Jubal to look for some as he bought stores at the landing. The canned milk made her think of fresh milk and churned cream and butter she'd enjoyed back on her parents' farm in Illinois. The fond recollection did not go so far as to include the skimming of the cream or the churning that produced the remembered sweet butter.

Grinding coffee, lovemaking, thick and sweet canned milk, Illinois, cream, butter. How the mind wandered as she gazed out the stern galley windows without really seeing. Then it came to her. How many times had she looked out across the river to see cows pasturing on the far side? Perhaps there was a farm where she could buy milk, cream, and butter. Someone must surely be tending to the milking. If not, it would be a kindness to the animals to relieve the burden in their udders. She knew how to milk a cow. She'd done it nearly all her life. She had buckets and she could row one of the skiffs across the estuary and look. She would do that very thing and she would do it today. She pressed her knees tight against the grinder and set to her task with purpose.

~~~

Josh gazed down into the hold, now nearly clear of the pudding of spoiled rice. He hadn't done anything with it for the past two days except fiddle with the pumps, trying to see what it would take to get them operating again. He wasn't looking forward to the drudgery of shoveling the muck out and disposing of it but he didn't want Jubal to return and find the work untouched. No bathing in hot water in the tub he'd fashioned from a hog's head and heated on the galley stove. No sponging of Elizabeth's delicious skin or lying about with her under the sheets of the bed and listening to the water lap against the hull, watching the reflected light dance off the cabin overhead. Josh was steeling himself to an unpleasant day of toil when Elizabeth bounded over to him with excitement painting her face. He'd grown cautious when she was in one of these moods. Perhaps she had come up with a new way to spend the day in carnal abandon but more often her enthusiasm for impulsive adventures made him cringe. Once worked up, she would not be denied.

"Didn't you say you saw a farm from up in the rigging? Away, over the river there." She pointed the way in case he had forgotten where the other side of the river was.

"Yes, but it was miles away; probably a good five hours walk. Maybe further."

"And cows. You saw cows, too?" The plan was unfolding in her head.

"Not every day. Just sometimes, they seem to just graze as they please."

"Do you ever see anyone tending to them or herding them?"

"Nope. Never saw a soul over the river. 'Spect there is some at the farm or *rancho* as they are called here."

"Scamper up in the rigging and see if there are any cows to be seen."

Josh trying to make sense of her rapid-fire questions, looked at her, puzzled.

"I'm going to row across and milk them, silly," she exclaimed. "We'll have milk and cream for our coffee. It will be grand."

"It's too dangerous," said Josh but he knew he'd already lost.

"Pshaw on dangerous. I can row a boat; I was raised on a farm. I can squeeze a cow's teat with the best of them. Besides, you said you've never seen a person there."

"There's coyotes."

"A pox on coyotes. We haven't heard them yipping for days."

Josh put both palms over his face, thinking. No argument was going to take root.

"Take a pepperbox with you. Powder and ball, too. I'll watch from the masthead," he added.

"Nonsense. Why would you spend a day perched in the rigging to watch someone milk a cow?"

Josh held his hands palm up in front of his chest, defeated. He had to concede her points were sound. The coyotes were gone and there had been no people. There should be no danger except getting stepped on by a bossy.

Elizabeth donned the worn but comfortable boots she had trekked halfway across a continent in and wore a gingham dress. The day seemed to call for a dress. She was tired of dressing in miner's clothes and, if she managed to get to the *hacienda*, being dressed like a woman would be the polite way to call on someone's home. She gathered an enamelware, two-gallon milk can and washed two buckets, one for the milk and one to sit on. These she stacked for ease of carrying. A cloth shoulder pouch contained her lunch and armament.

Setting off across the estuary in one of the skiffs was easy going until she reached mid-channel where the influence of the in-flowing river caused the boat to slip sideways. She adjusted her course until out of the current and then hugged the shoreline until she was abreast of the *Julianna Dolce*. It was the first she had viewed the entire ship since they had discovered her. She rode high in the water with just a bit of a list, one she had grown accustomed to as a sea-wife. At first glance, the boat seemed trim and ready to put to sea. A second look revealed the stripped spars, rigging, and the demolished rudder. The crushed side-wheel was on the port side, against the shoreline. Elizabeth pulled the skiff up on the narrow shore and tied off the painter to the exposed root of a cottonwood. She used the root to pull herself up to the bank. She turned to wave at Josh. She didn't see him until she looked aloft and found him at the mainmast platform. She waved, turned, and set off on her walk.

It was winter, nearly Christmas, and the pastures before her were broken and bleached by the remorseless summer sun. The grasses laid down or were trampled. There were trees, now nearly bare of foliage and brittle bushes all along her path. With the off and on again sequence of storms, new growth was poking its way out of the earth. Fresh buds could be seen on the tamarisk and manzanita. She climbed the little knoll where she often had watched small herds of cattle through the stern windows. The crest of the mound had been nibbled to stubs, the hill giving the impression of a monk's tonsure.

The sky was a pale blue, the color washed out with the first really bright afternoon they had enjoyed in many a day. Above, a lofty layer of cirrus strolled across the sky from the northwest. From her modest elevation she looked north but saw no sign of the *rancho* she hoped to visit. Turning south, only the masts and spars of her ship remained. Josh was still in the rigging and they exchanged waves before she again set out.

~ ~ ~

"We appreciate the thought, Jubal. Really we do," said Hannah. "But we can't use them."

Jubal looked at her as if he had never heard such a strange declaration. The Van Volks ran a bakery and served food and drink. A gift of crockery plates, mugs, and bowls surely would fit the bill.

"Don't look so confused," she laughed. "The problem with owning dishes is they will have to be washed."

That made sense but didn't answer anything. Hannah explained.

"We have to take the wagon down to the river to get water for our own use and for baking and cooking. We go way upstream of the camp and then have to fill the barrels and haul them back up the hill. We do it nearly every other day and it's a four hour chore."

"But..." Jubal protested. "The river isn't but a quarter mile right down the backside of this hill."

"So it is," said Willie Van Volk. "The problem is the camp is upstream from that place and every manner of garbage is just dumped in the water. There is no town government and every person down below sees this place as just a temporary stop before they can begin mining in spring. There's no garbage collection or a place to put it. Worse, no one is digging privies. The few that have been dug are at the public houses and gambling houses who don't want to lose their customers. Everyone else just goes into a field, or worse, they go out in the river to do their business."

"So you go up above the camp for water," said Jubal.

"Just so. If we started serving our fare on dishes we would have to wash them and that would take twice the water we use now and twice the time. We just can't do it. Our customers bring their own utensils and plates, even if it's just a piece of bark and a tin cup."

"You'll take some rice, though?" asked Jubal.

"Gladly and we won't accept any as a gift," said Willy.

"No. We'll pay you for it," said Hannah. "We've started serving it up in a spiced dish like you showed us. We buy what's available and the customers are grateful for a hot meal that's different from their regular fare."

"Of course, it takes a lot of water," said Willie, and they all had a good laugh.

It wasn't a great jest but it would have to do. Jubal had an idea and decided it was worth giving voice to.

"How about I do your water run and when you sell the hot rice meal we charge an extra quarter and serve it on the dishes? The miner gets to keep the dish and that might make him keep coming back. I get to keep the quarters."

They all agreed it would be a grand plan and the time saved would allow another round of baking and part of that session would go home with Jubal for his friends on the ship.

~~~

Elizabeth had crested two more long, gently rising knolls as she walked. She noticed as she left the river the land flattened out until it was as unbroken as the land along the Platte River she had walked the year before. Turning full circle Elizabeth could only see the tops of the masts of the ship. Josh was no longer visible. To the north she could see the distant *hacienda* Josh had described. Through the morning haze it almost looked like a mirage. There was a cluster of white plastered buildings with many archways and red clay roofs. There were outbuildings, barns, and livestock in pens. The main house and a large walled patio stood amidst a stand of spreading shade trees and rows of shorter fruit trees. She thought she could see two people who appeared to be sweeping the courtyard in front of the big house. Lying in the flat plain the farm looked like a vision floating in a sea of tan. It would be a jaunt of several hours on foot to arrive. The ground could be covered on horseback in not much more than an hour.

To the west, looking down the gully between hills was a copse of scrub oaks surviving on runoff from the hills on either side. She detected movement in the trees and her first reaction was to reach for the pepperbox. Before her hand found the pistol butt, the movement became cattle, not more than half a mile distant. She decided to walk the crest of the hill, taking advantage of the slight air from the south.

The cattle sensed her arrival and all turned toward her approach. Several calves milled about near their mothers. One was suckling the teat.

The animals were familiar with man. Even when there had been men to attend to them, they lived on a free range, bordered by the river on the south and by who knew what else might restrict their roaming. These were leaner and more fit than the pastured cows she was familiar with back on the farm. They had a bit of wild in their eyes, perhaps better to call it an independent look. Still cows were cows and soon Elizabeth had settled in among them and had commenced milking one bossy with a swollen and painful looking udder. Perhaps she had lost a calf to predators. Elizabeth was falling into the routine of pulling and squeezing as the fresh milk hissed into her bucket. The up-ended bucket she sat upon was hardly as comfortable as a milking stool but the reward was worth the discomfort. Her rear thanked her as she stood to empty the bucket into her milk can. She was rubbing the sore out of her behind and ready to get back to work when the crack of gunfire rent the pastoral scene. Direction was hard to figure in the dell so she began climbing the long slope to the top of the hill. Halfway up there was another shot, a pause, then a third, heavier report. She didn't have to reach the top of knoll to know where the shots came from. Just then two more rang out. Cows, pails, and milk forgotten, Elizabeth tore off at a run for home.

~~~

Josh was cutting and nailing down the last of the planks missing from the *Julianna's* deck and didn't hear the men's approach until it was nearly too late. The men obviously knew there was someone aboard but they were still being stealthy instead of announcing their presence. That made them a threat. They were at the boat, still out of sight when one of them, trying to scale the forechains, slipped and splashed back into the water.

Cursing his own incautious mind, Josh dropped his wood tools and sprang for the cabin where he had left his killing tools, revolver, Hawken and pepperbox, primed and ready. A pouch of powder and ball and he turned for the companionway that gave out onto the main deck. He stopped. If the invaders had come aboard and didn't see anyone, the open doorway would be where they would expect him. He dragged over a bench, stepped on it and lifted up one side of the skylight. He heaved himself up and looked about the quarterdeck. Seeing no movement he put the bag and his arsenal through the opening and on the deck below the coaming. One more look. Clear. He bounded up and over the coaming. He leaped too high on his exit and knocked the wooden frame of the skylight loose. It fell and chafed along his back and legs as he pulled himself clear.

Just as he did, he glimpsed smoke, heard the report and buzz of a ball as it carried over him and buried with a thump in the taffrail. Josh pushed the pistols into the pouch, looped it over his neck, and grabbed the Hawken rifle while the man who shot at him was reloading. He scrambled behind the binnacle at the wheel and risked a look between the spokes. At the bow, there was no movement. The shooter had fired, and gone to ground to reload. No. There was movement. A foot moved next to the capstan. Above the wooden drum a hand appeared, tamping down a charge into a muzzle. The muzzle came up over the top of the drum with a head behind it. Josh took aim with the Hawken but was too late. There was another flash and another bullet went by on the right. The head and muzzle disappeared.

The shooter was probably using an old, worn musket and it pulled to the left. Josh wasn't about to do nothing and let the man true his aim. Josh moved the Hawken's point of aim down to the deck by the capstan. The shooter was apparently sitting down to keep under cover and then rising to his knees to shoot. The range was less than forty yards, acceptable for a musket but child's play for the Hawken. Resting the barrel on one of the spokes of the wheel, he set the trigger. Josh waited, focused on where he remembered the foot appearing. There it was, lower than he recalled. He dropped the buckhorn sight a hair, touched the second trigger and the fifty-three caliber rifle kicked back into his shoulder.

Josh couldn't see through the cloud of smoke but it cleared quickly and he was able to see a white gouge in the deck and a spray of blood behind it. If he had any doubts of his accuracy they vanished on the rising screech of pain coming from the foredeck. The screech reached a level of howling and remained there. A man rose, lurched across the deck using the musket as a crutch. He fell on to the rail, lying flat upon it. He slung the musket over the side and followed it. The last thing to be seen was a foot flopping loosely just below the ankle.

Josh moved to the other side of the binnacle but didn't stand. It was likely the shooter was alone but he might just have been keeping

Josh pinned while another man moved closer. Josh scampered back to behind the skylight coaming and risked a look along the deck. No one. An attacker could be concealed behind the mast but with the man covering him gone, it wasn't likely a further attack was coming. Josh stood with the Walker Colt at the ready and the pepperbox in his left hand. Cautiously, Josh moved forward and then to the rail.

Crashing through the underbrush were three men. Two were carrying the third, who had his arms around their shoulders and hopped on one foot. The other hung useless and jiggling from the broken bone. Two of the men had their hair plaited and clubbed at the neck. They wore filthy pants cut high at the ankle. One, carrying the sole rifle was wearing a boat cloak. They were surely seafarers and Josh would wager they were members of the murderous mutineers, returned to their ship seeking shelter.

The men were too far away to make an accurate pistol shot. Still, he should send them along with some encouragement. He rotated the barrel of the pepperbox two clicks. He had loaded two of the barrels with shotgun pellets. The first shot crashed out and fell short. Another rotation and another charge was sent along, adjust for distance. He had over compensated some. The shot flew over their heads and he saw mud fly as the shot struck. Josh got some satisfaction as he saw the man on the right reach up and grab his cheek as if a bee had stung it. One of the pellets had struck, perhaps furrowing his cheek.

"Boarders repelled!" he shouted after them and danced a little victory jig there on the quarterdeck. Once the euphoria of combat subsided he peered into the distance looking for the vanquished boarders. He could see them moving diagonally from the road north towards the concealment of the forest. The distance was far enough he couldn't be certain but it appeared the wounded man had quit hobbling and was being carried by the other two. How serious had the wound he inflicted been, he wondered?

Walking forward to the capstan Josh examined the gouge in the deck where his round first struck then bounded up to find its mark. Immediately behind the mark was a spray of blood making him think the ball had passed through the foot but he could find no sign of the ball or an impact point. Blood was puddled behind the capstan where the man reflexively withdrew his foot. There was more than he expected and almost gouts of it from the capstan to the rail where the escape was made. The boarder had slit the canvas lashed over the side and squeezed through. The canvas was bloody from the return trip.

Josh didn't suppose the sight of blood would shock Elizabeth but it wouldn't do to let it mar his deck. With a full bucket and a swab he started scrubbing away and rinsing the mess through the scuppers. He'd done with the worst of it and was on hands and knees brushing the remainder when he heard a voice calling his name. He stood and looked across the river where Elizabeth, exhausted and frightened, called his name over and over. When she saw him she threw her arms apart as if to embrace him and then collapsed. Unable to see her beloved until he stood, the relief stole the strength in her legs.

"I'm fine," he called. "Not a scratch. Just had to turn away a pack of rascals wanted to come aboard."

She waved an acknowledgement and lay back in the grass. For some minutes Josh pondered rowing the other skiff over to see her but by the time he'd decided to go she had gathered herself up and started walking the top of the bluff looking for where she'd left the boat.

"By the cottonwoods," Josh yelled, pointing the way. She was still rattled not to remember the trees she had tied off to. Soon she was rowing across, every once in a while turning her head to make sure he was really there and whole. She was unsteady climbing the starboard ladder, taking Josh's proffered arm in assist. Once on solid footing she acted in a very un-Elizabeth fashion, blubbering and carrying on about her relief at finding him unhurt. Her run across the range had allowed her mind to play out dreadful carnage. They kissed, embraced, and then sat shoulder to shoulder against the rail as Josh told her of repelling the attack. He offered to show her where he had hidden by the binnacle and where the assassin's rounds had struck. She had no interest, instead telling him of her jaunt, the hacienda, the dell and finding the cows and starting to milk until the sound of shots sent her flying afoot back home.

~~~

The next night found Josh up in the rigging. It was after the moon had set and a thin haze had accumulated which would burn off in the morning. The evening was as dark as the recent days had been bright and pleasant. Josh's thoughts were as dark as the shade all around.

He was peering towards the distant woods. There, hidden except for a glimmer, burned a campfire. Its smoke lifted up through the bare branches and light reflected off its wisps. His gaze and his thoughts were on the men who warmed at that fireside. His thoughts and vision focused with a young man's fanciful notion he might kill them from afar. In reality he knew there must be a time of reckoning.

The night after the attack he and Elizabeth had made love but it was cautious and unfulfilling. His mind wandered to the threat that still lurked nearby. Each sound, even those familiar ones, would set his mind to racing until, like a child afraid of the dark, he envisioned villains standing on shore gazing up at the stern cabin and plotting pillage and slaughter. Finally the evening's darkest hours found him patrolling the deck, watchful and attentive to sounds he often knew to be imagined. It was ever so unlikely they would mount another siege so soon. They would be licking their wounds and plotting. He had no doubt they would eventually leave their campfire and try again. Their home would not be held hostage to the threat. Must he continue to not burn a light in the cabin, to seal up the skylight, to stop moving about freely on deck or to worry about Elizabeth's presence on deck inspiring the enemy? He could not live with an enemy plotting against him. He would carry his own brand of justice to them. They were mutineers and murderers and deserved no quarter.

Smoke from their fire could still be seen the next morning but a morning spent in the rigging revealed no movement. Knowing they remained nearby meant they had business still. He imagined them cold, hungry, and short of supplies. He imagined them on foot and discovering the animals picketed nearby. Would they expect him to come to them? Could he risk it at night, blundering about to gain their camp? No, he needed to lure them away from their base. How cold he do this with the least risk? He made plans and rejected them for the next half-hour until he detected movement on the road downstream. Two men in a wagon. Not teamsters he thought. The wagon was small and not fully loaded. He guessed it was two Argonauts, recently arrived and making their way to the mining district. Should he warn them of the danger lurking ahead? His mind made up, Josh scurried to the deck. He would have to hurry.

Josh watched the wagon pass from behind the screen of brush. Two men in new wool shirts and hats were driving on, making idle conversation and enjoying the day. Josh did not announce himself. He stroked Natchez' neck, hoping the horse would not nicker and give his presence away.

He gave the wagon time enough to pass a mile or a little less ahead of him and then stepped across the isthmus to follow along behind. He didn't want the travelers to know he was behind them but he also wanted to make certain anyone marking the wagon's progress towards the woods would not see him following. He rode low in the saddle where he could, trying to keep within the tree line near the bank of the river. Often he had to veer back on to the beaten path, always afraid he would lose the vital element of surprise, perhaps providing opportunity to have the tables turned back against him. Even if detected, he could not, in good conscience, turn back. Following behind discretely was no better than leaving the two men as bait. He could not abandon them to face a threat he knew was there.

Once in the forest the road meandered as the trees dictated. There were many turns and switchbacks. A person could see further down the road through the trunks of the trees but seldom directly. Josh detected movement up ahead about the same moment he heard raised voices. Ahead of him was a short straight reach and then a dogleg to the left he could see partway around. Nothing untoward was visible. Through the trees he could see the haunches of a mule, part of a wagon wheel. This was significant simply because the wagon was stopped.

Josh checked the loads in the Colt revolver and holstered it. The pepperbox was stuffed barrel first into a blanket roll behind the saddle. He removed the Hawken from its scabbard and set it across his legs, his right hand on the wrist and a finger along the trigger guard. He advanced down the road. As long as the shouting continued no one would hear his approach. He knew he was visible through the trees but the action ahead would serve as distraction. If he thought he was discovered there would be nothing for it but to gallop ahead.

The yelling continued as Josh came around the dogleg. He recognized the words were Spanish, explaining why he could make no sense of them. At a distance of about forty yards was the wagon he'd been following. One of the miners was standing next to it and getting undressed as he was being threatened with a short-handled axe by the one of the sailors he'd fired at before. Standing on top of the wagon, perched on top of the load was the man in the boat cloak. He was covering the other miner with a musket. The miner on the seat cowered before him, shoulders hunched. Boat Cloak had his back to him.

The man with the axe saw him first and stopped his harangue of the half-naked miner. He looked towards Josh and Boat Cloak turned about. He started to bring the musket to bear. It was far too late.

As soon as Josh had a clear view of the goings on he pulled Natchez' head around to the right. He didn't want to fire over the horse's head. The Hawken was at his shoulder, the set trigger pulled. He pulled the buckhorn sight to the center of the chest and fired.

His aim wasn't low this time. The impact staggered Boat Cloak. He took a step backward and tripped over the back of the wagon seat. He toppled over the seated miner and slithered off the front of the wagon. This panicked the mules and set them off down the road, the miner holding on so as not to be thrown. In the confusion, the half-naked miner grabbed at his pants, pulled them up and took off after the wagon, leaving the man with the axe and Josh on the stage.

The Axe Man swiveled towards Josh, spread his feet and assumed a fighting position, the short axe held up and cocked. The sailor was a terror to look at. His face bore the scars of many encounters and he sported a tattoo on the side of his head, no picture just words in Spanish. His ragged shirt was open revealing another tattoo encircling his neck and down his chest in a geometric pattern. The axe was a wicked looking thing, a handle about two feet long and a blade formed a semicircle. A curved spike protruded from the side opposite the blade. It was obviously designed as a weapon, useless for chopping wood.

Whether the fact he did not flee was either a testament to his bravery or to his desperation. Josh was still mounted and sideways to Axe Man. He drew the Colt and leveled it. Forty yards was a long pistol shot. Josh fired and saw the bullet strike just above the collarbone. Axe man screamed, not in pain but in rage and launched himself towards Josh. Perhaps he wasn't familiar with a revolver and thought both Josh's pistol and rifle were empty.

Josh had never faced a charge like this. His legs gripped the horse for all he was worth. His stomach seemed to climb in his throat, cutting off his breath. Unnerved, still he made himself wait. He raised the pistol and took aim at the snarling face. Axe man did not dodge or swerve. He just kept coming. Josh fired and everything that drove the man towards him in a mad rage instantly quit working. He simply dropped in mid-step. His torso and face hit the ground at the same time and he skidded in the pathway long enough for his slack legs to lift and bend slightly before falling still. There wasn't a convulsion, a tremor, or a moan. It was simply over.

Further up the road Boat Cloak lay where he fell. He was on his side and his legs looked like he was taking a long step. In a way he had, stepping out of this life into whatever waited on the other side. Further up the road, the miner had gathered up the reins and brought the runaway mules under control. They weren't yet calm and he was having some difficulty getting them to back up so he could turn the wagon. Josh waited.

The wagon came slowly, maybe cautiously down the road. The miner stopped as his companion emerged from the woods and mounted up. The pair paused again as they came to Axe Man. They looked down on the corpse, exchanged some words Josh couldn't hear and came forward.

"Mister, I guess we owe you just about everything," said one.

"I was praying for Providence to stand before evil and Providence sent you," said the other.

Closer now, Josh could see the two were related. How could he tell the two he'd used them as bait?

"Evil men they were. I've been following them for some time," said Josh. "I spotted their fire in the woods last night but didn't think I could approach in the dark." He hoped the explanation would suffice.

"My name is Silas Pratt and this is my brother Ebenezer but we all call him Erby."

"I don't know where they came up with Erby but it's better than Ebenezer," said his brother. "Sounds kind of Old Testament."

Josh noted he still had the revolver in his hand. He holstered it and there were handshakes all around.

"Those men were going to rob us of everything, even goin' to take our clothes," said Silas, the half-dressed brother now gathering up his clothes from the road.

"No, they were going to kill you and toss your naked carcasses in the river. They made you strip so they wouldn't get the clothes all bloody."

Silas' face went pale as his exposed torso, imagining how close he had been to a violent end.

"Lord protect us from the evil of men," intoned Erby.

"What can we do to repay you? We owe you our lives," said Silas. Erby nodded his assent.

"You got gold coin?"

"We got some, not much," said Erby, reaching into his coat.

"Then buy your self some weapons when you get to the *Embarcadero*."

"What's an *Embarcadero*?" Erby asked.

"Oh, we got weapons. Two new percussion cap pistols in our sea chests."

"I'd start carryin' them if I was you. This is hard country and getting harder every day."

"But there is gold to be found, isn't there?" Silas inquired.

"Yeah, there's gold but its hard work to get to it. You got picks and shovels?"

"Sure, we don't mind hard work," said Erby. This time it was Silas who nodded along.

"Then you can repay me by burying these two and there's a third one needs to go in the ground."

The brothers looked around, concerned the third villain might be watching them from the woods.

"I wounded him yesterday and they have a camp in the woods. It wouldn't be right just to let him die waiting for his friends to come back. You put those two on your wagon and we'll go back up the road apiece and find their camp."

"Suppose we find him still alive. You aim to just kill him in his bed?" asked Silas.

"I'm hoping I don't have to ask myself that question."

~ ~ ~

Mercifully, Josh didn't have to answer. The brothers and their grim cargo backtracked and cut off the road to follow the tree line. Josh took some rough bearings from the masts of the *Julianna* and cautiously entered the trees with the Pratt brothers, now armed and on his flanks. There was no sneaking about. The floor was littered with leaves and needles concealing tripping roots and twigs that broke underfoot. They may have as well crashed into the woods on horseback.

Soon they smelled the campfire and moved about to approach on two sides.

Josh called out a warning for anyone in the camp to disarm. Whoever was there probably spoke no English but calling out a caution seemed the right thing. As it turned out the warning was unnecessary. The man he had wounded yesterday had died, bled out from his wound. His companions had roughly stitched him up in his blanket prior to doing whatever it was they intended to do with him.

There wasn't much to the camp. Aside from a few cups and pans, there was a small sack with some jerky, some rock hard biscuit and a jar of beef paste for broth. There was another of the wicked looking axes. Erby hefted it and an involuntary shiver went through him as he envisioned the pick end sticking out of his skull.

They put out and scattered what was left of the fire. The body in the blanket was buried where it lay along with the sack of provisions. They didn't look for any letters to find out who he was. None of them were about to right to his kin with the news. The man vanished from the world under a couple feet of dirt and a few stones gathered to keep the animals away for a while.

The other two were buried at the edge of the woods. The wagon couldn't be driven to the campsite and there was no desire to drag the corpses any further than off the wagon. Both men went into a single hole and were covered up. No one said words over them and no one took time to gather even a rock to mark their final resting place. Hardly an hour had gone by since the two had been plotting murder against the now sextons.

"Never thought the first digging I did in California would be a grave," muttered Erby.

Josh told the brothers an abbreviated tale of how he came to live on the ship, easily visible now, how the men they buried were likely mutineers from the ship who had murdered the officers to go find gold. He told them how he had driven them off when they tried to come aboard and how he came to the Pratt's rescue. He left off any references to bait. If they figured it that way, then that's what they figured.

"My wife is with me on the ship. I wouldn't have wanted her to have to see your bodies come drifting past some fine morning."

"And we're mighty glad to be able to spare her such a sight," said Silas.

"That's all thanks to you, Josh", said Erby. "If ever we can do anything for you, consider it already done."

They shook hands, promised to meet again and parted paths. The Pratts left, smarter, armed, and much more cautious about their new home. Josh went home relieved and ready to catch up on the sleep he'd missed.

~~~

The sluice gate was operational. If they could obtain some mortar Duncan would deem it a success. The gate worked but it was hardly the engineering marvel he'd envisioned. In his mind's eye each component snugged up perfectly with its neighbor and together they functioned in flawless cohesion. The reality of what could be built in the wilds with limited materials and tools was cantankerous, rough, and would require constant tending. There was no iron gate to be crafted by a skilled smith. There was not even iron plate to be had at any price. Tree trunks, cut with a slot in each and joined with a similar cross piece were dug into the embankment and braced with stone. A series of rough planks were stacked in the frame. Their removal or replacement would regulate the flow.

On the streamside of the gate, contiguous tree trunks, driven by sledgehammer served as pilings. Excavation from the gate to the stream commenced with a stone bottom laid from the level of the gate's lower frame until water began to seep in. Duncan had rightly calculated, a clear and open channel to the river could not withstand the force of an unabated flow. The stacked rocks would serve as a gabion to tame the course of the water.

All the miners gathered to witness the final connection of channel to river. The last foot of separation hardly needed digging. The South Fork of the American carried it away in a rush of muddy suds and immediately began devouring the bank downstream of the newly formed diversion channel. The whole company scrambled to the diggings and loaded wagons with rocks and boulders as large as the men could load and the mules could move. These were levered up and rolled down into the current, disappearing as quickly as they could be loosed. Eventually, the river had its fill and the embankment was saved by a haphazard levee of rock. It was dangerous work but beyond the expected pinched fingers and toes there were no broken bones or serious calamities. The next day, a Thursday, was declared a day of rest in addition to the usual Sunday sabbatical. Few laid abed but all complained of their various aches and pains as they sewed, patched, and mended their bodies and possessions while embellishing stories of how they earned their injuries.

Duncan, by virtue of his position, did not drive piles or roll boulders. The extra day of leisure was a day for him to further test the ore being pulled from the ancient streambed. From the first shovel of dirt at the prospect hole, the excavation had progressed to a depth of about twelve feet by twenty feet, rising gradually along a ramp for wagon access. The overburden had been hauled and set adjacent to the embankment to a level that was about two feet below the low end of the sluice. Once the gate was opened water could run down and into the mouth of the long tom. The tom was set on a slope so gravity could move the ore along the machine.

With water such a precious commodity, flow at the low end of the contraption was directed into a pond formed by more of the spoil from the diggings. There it would sit until a second ramp and tom could be built and the water in the pond tapped again. This system of terracing and recycling of the water was based on the rice plantations Shipwash had seen in India. In this instance, the terrace plan was limited because at the end of the second pond there was a short but precipitous drop off and the river turned away from the narrow defile. The water from the second machine would once again flow into the arroyo below where once there may have been a waterfall.

The existing built up series of dirt benches, slopes, ponds, and cofferdams were only possible using the excavation from the original dig. Duncan now stood in the bottom filling sample jars and trying to make sense of the history of the now dry stream from the striations in the sides of the pit. For the last six feet or so they had been digging mostly gravel and the promising black sand. Above the gravel mark the sides required more excavation to taper them away from the sides. Otherwise the nearly worthless sand above would fill the void as fast as the shovels threw dirt onto the wagons.

The first day's demonstration of the long tom, paltry though the results were, had exhilarated the prospectors with the prospects of more to come. Despite the labor involved the men seemed to want to wash every wagonload that came from the pit. As the digging progressed, the quality improved and those first piles of gold bearing ore were forgotten, dumped unceremoniously into the earthworks. Already the latest samples were producing two or three dollars a pan. Duncan had been meticulously labeling each sample and marking its location on the plat map in his journal. He expected the samples to improve but markedly so where the ancient watercourse slowed in its meander and dropped its riches. What he was seeing as the work approached the bedrock was an almost uniform layer of color from one bank to another. Perhaps the ancient stream widened at this point and the slower current dropped its wealth in a literal, if not abundant carpet of gold. The image of a carpet of gold brought a smile to Duncan's face. If only it were that easy. There was much labor ahead of them but the steady improvement in quality should be motivation enough. For some, the last few feet of discovery had come too late. There had been two more desertions, among them was John Dryden, the man who had brought him the first piece of quartz. He and a companion had disappeared that very night. They should have stayed. They were pulling quartz out of the ground with nearly every shovel, some few with gold in crevices that could be dug out with the sharpened tine of a fork. Yes. All the signs were present.

The company was fully aware of the improving quality and when Shipwash descended into the pit to dig, poke, and wonder, the men gathered above and watched him explore. Tired, sore, and pained as they were, the prospect of a new test brought them to the edge of the dig. Elias Fellowes was one of them. As an "officer", he took it upon himself to intrude upon Duncan's reverie.

"Is this the day we become rich men, Mr. Shipwash?"

The image of a carpet of gold popped into Shipwash's head. The words nearly slipped unbidden from his tongue.

Cautiously optimistic he replied, "I believe these samples will prove better even than the last. I don't think it too bold to suggest we may all find our selves wealthier men come this next Christmas Day."

His words were greeted by cheers, hats tossed in the air, and impromptu short dances, from the men above. He would map the samples in his journal and then the men could accompany him to the gold machine, as they had begun to call the long tom. Duncan's calibrations were hinting the dry stream was meandering in a long slow bend to the right. He would let the jars prove out before making any recommendation to follow.

He approached the terraced earthworks with the tandem gold machines and couldn't help but take satisfaction in a job well done. Wagons could be driven to the upper hopper of each machine and fed directly from the wagon bed. The water diverted from the river could be metered down a short course directly where needed. The runoff water was collected in the pond and a second gate would meter the water into the second machine. The immediate shortcomings of the sluice gate, the constant war against erosion, were on the other side of the embankment so as not to distract from the efficient scene before him. Duncan could foresee future problems as well. Disposal of the gravel, rocks, and sand would, before too long, create a mountain of debris that would require hauling away before it overwhelmed the site. This future complaint was predicated on the success of the diggings. The mountain would grow only if the ore paid out so the problem would be one bred of success.

Shipwash placed each sample jar on the corresponding pile of ore. He selected one of the five and began to wash with the pan over a half barrel of water. The men hovered over him as he worked. Soon he had to ask them to back up as they were blocking the light. They obliged and were soon rewarded with Duncan's results. He passed the pans, each sample in turn, around the gathered miners. None of the five was extraordinary but each had color. The value was probably less than a dollar per pan but he was washing quarts of ore and there before them were five wagonloads to be tumbled and sifted. The samples had produced no nuggets and no single sample stood apart. He'd learned nothing about the deposition in the old stream. Every layer of depth produced better results consistently across the dig. Certainly two more feet of excavation would reveal all. Of course, a promise of riches in the next shovel or barrow was what kept prospectors filling them.

"Men, pick a pile. They all sample the same. Gold is spread all across the bottom of the dig."

The men debated the choice of piles to work first. One man swore he saw the glitter of a large nugget as he was moving a barrow of ore. They wisely settled on the pile closest to the maw of the long tom.

"Clean up after each pile. Maybe we can learn something more from a large sample."

The crew acknowledged his wishes but almost perfunctorily. They were anxious to run the machines, now certain the ore would produce.

"Take care now," cautioned Duncan. "Don't rush the process. You will send the color gushing out the end."

The thought of losing the gold they had dug from the earth sobered the men. Shipwash climbed the embankment and, for a few minutes, watched men proceed workmanlike and deliberate. He continued on, over the crest to examine the confluence of the gate's channel and the rushing river.

This was the weak point of their operation. He was no trained hydrologist with a career building aqueducts and spillways. The concept he had used was sound but it perhaps exposed too much of the construction to the pillage of the current. The more rubble they dumped to prevent erosion, the less water will be diverted into the channel to the gate. Conversely, without the rubble, the river would soon carry the works away entirely. If only there were Portland cement available to fuse the construction into a single unit.

Duncan stood on the crest of the levee and watched the washing progress. The men worked with the diligence of zealots. The fever was upon them and who could blame men for wanting to better their station in life. Other than Fellowes, the miller, these were not the landlords and merchants of Albany. These were the farm hands, the clerks, tradesmen, and laborers of the community. Other than the families tearfully left behind, they had no store or bank or investment tethering them to the mundane and familiar. Married or not, these men had willingly left friends and family behind to chase a dream of fame and fortune. Every one of them longed to come home laden with gold and tales of high adventure. The gold in California was no fantasy of buried treasure and pirates. A dream lived out in California was one that had a reasonable chance of success.

Each man probably envisioned filling his pockets with nuggets and catching the next boat home. That was fantasy and it was shattered within moments of disembarking in San Francisco. The work before them was difficult, tedious and with more physical toil than any had experienced before. Other than those who had deserted the partnership to strike out on their own, these men faced the reality of prospecting with enthusiasm, good cheer, and camaraderie. The dream was beginning to bear fruit and Duncan was pleased to be instrumental in their pursuit.

Whether the partnership would be able to retain their discovery was another matter. Duncan's gold mining experience in India was within the strictures of either British military rule or under the auspices of East India Company rule. It could be argued Company rule was even more disciplined than regular army.

Subsequently, his experience in South America was under government rule. The government may have been corrupt and capricious but there was still control. The government wanted their share. Greed dictated conduct and violators were certain of retribution for disrupting the dictates of the mines.

Already the lawless and desperate had arrived and spring would bring fortune hunters by the thousands. Many of these without scruples. The crew of the *Julianna* mutinied and murdered their officers. The camps were filling with gamblers and liquor sellers. Others, arriving with piety and manners, were soon corrupted. The two highwaymen he had bested on the road had perhaps once been honest men forced into thievery by the exorbitant prices of survival and the lack of ready access to the gold bearing streams. What would it be like when the castoffs of the world's societies arrived? Who would honor a claim or hesitate to rob and kill for what others had achieved through hard labor? The days of good fellowship and trust were gone. Avarice and villainy would soon dominate.

The company must lay out a claim, perhaps in the name of each member and the agreement amended to share equally the costs and rewards amongst the members. Even with documents drawn and maps and boundaries set, where could they be recorded and how could the claims be enforced. The little settlement by the South Fork was growing. Most of those encamped were awaiting the end of the wet season and preparing for ventures up the river. The first merchants had arrived soon after the whiskey sellers and the gamblers. The miners would be their fair game. The partnership was prospecting potentially rich ground that could be mined year round. It was only a matter of time before the word spread and the camp descended upon their private trove. The enterprise must hold, and the only way to assure cohesion was to produce color and put it in the pockets of the men working the dry diggings. Claiming the stream was one thing. Keeping the claim was yet another.

As Shipwash watched, the men quit feeding the machine and looked up to him. Their gaze alone told him he was needed. Undoubtedly the lower washer had filled with heavy materials and was threatening to overtop the battens in its bottom. It was a simple matter of scooping out the ore and putting it in a bucket for pan washing. One man was using a pan to wash the findings but he was making a hash of the job, slopping out as much ore as water.

He directed the men to fill a bucket with the ore and relieved the man of the wash pan. He demonstrated the easy circular motion necessary and then let the man wash from the bucket. The result was much as he expected, about three dollars of flour gold in the pan but there were also several pickers. The tiny nuggets told him he was on the right track. As they got closer to the dry stream's bed, the heavier gold was announcing itself. He walked back to the camp, leaving the men elated and attacking the piles with renewed vigor.

CHAPTER TEN

Jubal returned with supplies and a pouch of raw gold and gold coin from the sale of the rice and crockery. His success was tempered by the resistance the miners demonstrated dealing with a colored. More than a few simply refused commerce with him. The Van Volks interceded on his behalf. The sacks of rice were moved from the tent behind the bakery to the front counter and the two daughters sold the sacks, getting a better price without haggling with the customers. The miners paid a premium just for the privilege of buying from the girls. Jubal stayed in the background, coming forward only to load the purchases. The crockery sold well but the supply was not exhausted by the time he left for home. Jubal departed with a supply of baked goods, promising to make another delivery soon.

"I was skittery as a chicken with the fox snoopin' 'round the hen house," he said. "I never even seen this much money in my life, much less puttin' it in my pocket. I come out the backside of the camp so no one would see me leavin'. Rememberin' those two highwaymen what tried to rob Mr. Shipwash and me, had me seeing robbers behind every tree. Nearly spent the mules hurryin' back. Stopped to rest them and felt like a mouse bein' watched by owls. Lord above, its good to be back."

"We missed having you here more than you know. We need you here. Josh is about ready to get the pumps working."

"With the hold near empty, I've been able to make up oakum from shredded rope and tar. Took some doin' but I've got most of the sprung boards on the port side fixed up."

"I'm glad to be back just to be able to stay in one place. Guess I just like the routine of knowin' what work I'll be doin when I wake up each mornin'."

Jubal went below to clean up and rest. They would all catch up during dinner. After hearing Jubal's worries about traveling the roads they decided to hold off on telling him of the returning mutineers and the incident with the Pratt brothers. Let him get back into the routine.

"I don't think we realized how difficult being a Negro is for Jubal here in the camps," said Elizabeth. "When he and I were buying supplies I think the sellers thought he was a servant to carry the goods.

There were some hard looks but I put those to men who were jealous it wasn't them along with me."

"Come to think I've only seen three or four coloreds here since we arrived. Damned if I didn't take them for servants myself."

"California is pretty much its own country with no government. What happens if people start showing up with slaves?" asked Elizabeth. "This isn't Illinois where anyone much cared about freeman papers."

"Back home I wouldn't say blacks was treated real well but a black man could own land and make a livin'. Wasn't like they could stay in a hotel or go in a taproom. They had their own places and everybody just minded their own way."

"I don't think people here would give a lick about freedman papers even if Jubal had them," she said.

"Hell, look how the Americans lord it over the Mexicans, even the land owners. The miners just move on and start panning. Sutter's white, but Swiss and miners have moved right into his home. What's it going to be like come spring when more people come and the diggings get crowded?"

"Imagine what it would be like if he were to defend himself from bandits, white bandits particularly. If he shot a white man, even one that was out to rob him, it would be an even money bet he'd end up on trial for his life, if he even got a trial. Hell, even being in possession of a few hundred dollars would probably put him in irons until questions were answered," said Josh.

"California as it stands appears to be a rough place for justice to thrive. Rough enough for a white man to hold on. We were so blind. He was getting hard looks even when we were trading for goods at the landing. They didn't want any truck with him even when they thought he was my servant."

"It was never like that at home. A colored could earn his keep, could spend money and get by without living like a leper. I mean, there was some problems and some people a black didn't want to cross but, for the most part, everyone knew the rules and there was no trouble."

"When we joined up with those Missouri folk coming out here, they wouldn't have taken us in 'cept they thought he was my slave. I never said otherwise."

"You never told me that before."

"Most of the Missouri folk just took him bein' a slave for granted. The scout brought it up a couple times but once Delacroix saw how Jubal took to tracking and breaking trail, he kind of took him on as a student. By then we was all part of the expedition and it never really came up."

"It didn't come up because you were with him all the time and he took orders from you. We can't be with him all the time, but I don't think we should be sending him off to any camp by himself. There's too much can go wrong too quick."

Josh thought back to when they struck the deal with the Albany Argonauts. Purposely they had not admitted that Jubal was in their thirty percent. They didn't need to know but, if it were known, the deal might not have been made at all. Bank clerks and tradesmen might dig gold for themselves but would surely balk if they knew the result of their labor would be going in the pocket of a Negro. The charade would work for now but there would come a time. Neither of the Bonners wanted to consider that part of the future.

Josh was going to wait another day to tell Jubal about the return of the mutineers, the encounter with the Pratt brothers, and the three men buried at the edge of the woods. The dinner went well, and they enjoyed the meat pasties the Van Volks had provided along with some ale procured at the *Embarcadero*. The ale was warm and too bitter but it went down well and Jubal seemed much less jittery than when he first arrived. Josh, after exchanging a glance with Elizabeth, relented and told Jubal about the skirmish and the final outcome. When he first began the tale Jubal became tense but by the end he was almost exhilarated, much like when he told of Shipwash's actions with the other highwaymen. If the interval between leaving the Van Volks and arriving back at the *Julianna* troubled him, he was either over it or didn't let on.

~ ~ ~

With all the work and all the travel, Christmas had snuck up on the crew. The morning before Christmas was much like any other workday. What could be reached of the damaged hull without removing the fothering sail or careening the ship had been done. Josh and Jubal busied themselves taking apart the bilge pump and restoring it to order. There was little to repair but it was clogged solid with spoiled, smelly rice. Parts were removed, hauled on deck and cleaned. The restored parts were laid on the hatch cover in the order they were removed. Soon they would be working and then Josh could pump out the engine room and examine the boiler and engine.

There were no cut boughs of fragrant pine, no wreath on the door, and no tree, but Elizabeth was determined to make something special of the holiday. Taking a skiff back across the river, she set out to recover the milk can and buckets she'd abandoned when gunfire disrupted her milking. Before long she stood on the low hill looking down into the copse of trees where she'd discovered the cattle. The cows had grazed away the forage and had long departed. She found her pails and can but a cow had stepped in one of the pails and punched out the bottom. She hadn't really expected the cows to be awaiting a reunion but she was determined to have milk as a Christmas Day treat. She was prepared to walk to the distant *hacienda*, bent on purchasing milk, cream, butter, or even eggs. She spoke only a few words of Mexican but she hoped not only to persuade the owner to open his larder for gold coin but to establish future commerce. To this purpose she bore a silk bag of rice sealed with wax. She back tracked to the hill where the vista of the pleasant looking home and set off towards it full of anticipation and excited about her adventure all on her own. She was not so naïve as to set off afoot like a child skylarking to market. The silk bag of rice was in her shoulder bag along with two of the pepperbox pistols. About an hour into her walk, large intermittent drops began to fall, spotting the ground and some even raising tiny clouds of dust as they struck. The sky, blue with scattered white clouds when she departed, had consolidated as they struck the mountains and grown pewter bellies, portending an impending storm, now dropping fat dollops in the dust and clacking on the dry grass.

Weather at this time of the year came from the northwest and her gaze naturally turned there. While there was only the meekest of breezes where she stood, the high clouds in the distance were being shorn of their billows and whisking into a mash of gray streamers at the high altitudes. A tempest, born in the frigid Arctic was soon to sweep ashore. The horizon from northwest to west was a mass of dark gray, purple even in its uppermost reaches as the sun touched the loftiest levels. Where she stood, the sun, diminished now so there were only fleeting shadows, as if surrendering its domain to the menace of the storm. In places dark curtains of falling rain blurred the view and served as overture to the concert coming. She could see no lightning yet but her ears were playing tricks, making her think of thunder.

Her gaze turned to the *hacienda* as she gauged the distance. Where she stood was about halfway between ranch and ship. She could march on and seek shelter but it would seem presumptuous on a first visit and, not knowing the duration of the storm, she turned around in resignation. There would be no milk, cream, or butter for their Christmas dinner.

Not until Josh and Jubal climbed from the pump to the deck were they even aware it was raining. When they descended three decks into the ship the sun was shining and scattered clouds lay shadows on the landscape. When they emerged with parts and tools the deck was solidly wet and a thin sheet of water was running to the scuppers. Fat drops rattled on the hard surfaces and pinged on the canvas. Below they were completely unaware of the change.

Standing at the rail, they looked first at the tempest's approach in the west and then scanned across the river, hoping to see Elizabeth returning. The rain increased, streaming down their faces as they waited and watched. Not until a gust of wind shivered the canvas did they seek shelter. They built up a fire in the stern cabin and set to watch across the river through the gallery windows. By the time she appeared the rain was becoming a barrage and a occasional gusts sent the rain sheeting, blurring their vision and setting a scud of gray foam tearing across the water's surface. They watched her board the skiff, shed her parcels and begin bailing out the bilge of the skiff before setting to the oars and rowing across. It seemed she slipped to leeward as much as she gained in progress across. Eventually they lost sight of her among the reeds. Josh was putting on weather gear and preparing to go to her aid when she appeared below the gallery windows, head down and towing the skiff by it hawser. Josh flung open a window and called to her. She looked up, as soaked as if she had swum across and grinned at him. She was on an adventure and having a fine time of it. Her hair hung in wet tangles all about her face but Josh thought she had never looked so beautiful. He wasn't aware of how long he admired her until Jubal, who had sprung to her aid, took over the securing of the skiff and assisted her in boarding. The three met in the companionway. Josh felt a twinge of guilt for only being damp.

"I heard some miner talking about a gully washer. I guess this is what he meant," she said.

"If this keeps up, every gully will be sending the wash water our way."

"I heard gullywhumper," said Jubal. "Reckon it's the same thing?"

"If we had a gully nearby we might could tell the difference, but we ain't," said Josh. "It's all river bottomland but we all seen what happens on the Missisip' when it starts pourin' upstream."

"Seems I recall fishing the two of you out of flash flood not long back," said Jubal

As if for exclamation, light flashed in the open hatch behind them, followed by a crack of thunder.

"Looks like the storm will pile up on the mountains and spend Christmas with us," said Josh.

"We best get the animals and wagons to high ground before the river rises. It's surely going to rise."

Elizabeth retired to the cabin and the cheery stove to revive and change while the rest of the crew donned oiled canvas slickers. The two skiffs were retrieved. Josh went aloft and rigged the jeers to the end of the mizzen yard for support and the two rowboats were hauled aboard, turned hull up and lashed to a grating.

The sailors then became teamsters and ran with harness to the picket line. The rain was steady and the wind constant. When the occasional gust came, the rain pelted them in sheets. The horses and mules paid no more attention to the storm than to turn their backs to it. Josh and Jubal put the mules in harness and tied the horse's tethers to the wagon. In tandem they set off to the isthmus where they discovered they were now on an island. The river had grown some, making their peninsula an island by a scant six feet. The fascines were dumped in the gap and the narrow gap was crossed in short order.

"We'll have to skirt the edge of the woods there," said Josh, pointing inland. "Don't want to follow the river road to high ground in case the river jumps the bank. Hopefully, we can find a way around the trees to a bluff or something."

Jubal nodded his assent and they set off up the road to the tree line. It was barely above the marshy estuary but enough to make solid footing. Before too long the edge of the forest turned and they followed it away from the estuary. The grade was perceptible more from a feeling they were ascending a slope than any visual indicators. The forest thinned as it left the low ground and they soon entered into the trees. Rain still made its way through the tops and there was a constant drip. A picket line was set between trees and the teams hobbled. They then turned on horseback for the ship. Josh wanted to be with Elizabeth and Jubal would accompany him to the isthmus where he would take Natchez back to high ground. After the storm passed he would return.

They rode back with their heads down, hats and hoods pulled low. There were still gusts of wind that threw the rain at them but it seemed fitful. The weather was moving inland and the wind would follow the front. The rain had not let up. The storm would pile up against the mountaintops and play itself out there. They hoped it would play out during the night.

Reaching the path from shore to ship, Josh dismounted, said goodbye to horse and companion and pushed through the brush screen. He found the tide was rising and the calf deep six foot gap was now wider and necessarily deeper. He removed his boots and stepped into water up to mid-thigh. Where the fascines had aided their departure they now impeded his passage across. It was as if someone had dumped bales of hay in his path, making him progress over and around them. Once across it was still soggy going. Water oozed up and filled every footprint left behind. Once aboard the *Julianna* it was Josh's turn to retire and strip by the cheery stove. There was a pot of strong coffee. He splashed a shot of brandy into a cup and filled it from the pot. Elizabeth had warmed a meat pastie for him. Josh devoured one while he savored the coffee, letting it warm him from the inside out.

Elizabeth had laid out dry clothes for him and brushed his boots. As soon as she turned down the cabin lamps Josh knew he would not be needing a change. No sooner than he set his arm around Elizabeth she fairly collapsed against him. They kissed and, without interrupting the kiss, they shuffled over to the bed and fell on the laid out clothing. They rolled about and over one another, stoking their desire. Elizabeth disengaged, stood for as long as it took to peel out of her clothes and sprang upon her lover. Their union was hasty, intense, and over sooner than they wanted.

After, they lay in the rearranged bed, spooning under the covers. The afterwards was almost as pleasant as the lovemaking. The gusts had ceased and the rain fell steadily outside, pattering above their heads, pinging pleasantly on the skylight and tapping on the windows of the gallery. They dozed off and on through the night, twice more they welcomed in Christmas day.

~~~

Christmas morning found the Bonners in much the same state as Christmas Eve had left them. The rain still fell, the little stove warmed a fresh pot of coffee, Van Volk tarts had been eaten and the lovers brushed crumbs from the linen of their repose. Jubal was expected back for Christmas dinner if the weather and tide permitted. The couple lay contented and languid.

This was their first winter in California. A couple of days of rain did not alarm them. In fact they were determined to waste away as much of the day as they could manage. The gusty weather had moved on. The river was up enough to float the ship on the first flood of the tide but the dry, comfortable cabin offered solace and inspiration for a day of extended delight. The storm had, as predicted, stalled out against the peaks and was crying its eyes out upon the land below. What they did not know was how winter worked along the western coast of the continent.

Storms built in the northern Pacific Ocean while wind and current pushed the systems into the Bering Sea. From the Bering the storms gathered momentum and swept down the North American coast before turning ashore. Once they vacated the Bering Sea another storm, conceived and fed in the Pacific rushed in to take its place. As long as the sea and sky remained constant, the process would be repeated like a parade of barrels being rolled down a ramp, as the storms would descend to the southeast before making landfall. Seldom was a single storm cause for alarm but the constant parade of them soon saturated the ground beyond its capacity to absorb. At the lower elevations, the hillsides sent rivulets, then freshets, then cascades of water into the rivers. In the upper elevations, snow fell to depths beyond anyone's experience or even imagination. The banks of snow grew, waiting patiently for spring.

Aboard the *Julianna Dolce* the sun never had the time to cast so much as a shadow before another even greater storm blew in. And blow it did. No intermittent gusts but howls of wind slapping sheets of rain against the hull and turning the estuary to a confusion as the wind waves blew against the now rising current, spewing from the rivers into the San Francisco Bay. The wind blew the *Julianna* up against the bank and, still afloat, she bumped and ground against the muddy shore. Nothing violent but each time a gust passed and released her she would float away only to be gently but relentlessly pressed to the land. Every bump against the bank sent a shiver through the hull, transmitted to the crew. Every shiver a reminder of the hull working against the land, opening seams just caulked, chafing away the canvas stretched over the weakened hull. Their home was in no immediate danger of foundering but each nudge sending a tremor up Josh's legs was a reminder of labor left undone and the constant need to finish overhauling the pumps and correct the trim of the *Julianna,* now down by the stern over two strakes. First hourly and soon after each significant grounding, Josh made the rounds of the deck, peering over the bulwarks at the vulnerable side and several times venturing into the hull with a lantern to inspect the repairs. He'd first descended with his imagination drawing images of water sheeting in through sprung boards and jets spraying across a rising bilge where the caulk had worked. What he found reassured faith in his repairs. There were no open seams and, if water was intruding, it was no more than an ooze when the impact came. He returned to the cabin where the couple lay abed, consciously ignoring the gusts and the impending nudge. After each particularly strong shiver Josh would arise and make his rounds again. The Christmas dinner and celebration now forgotten.

The missing member of the crew was having perhaps a better time of it. True, he was colder and perhaps wetter but not by much. Back beyond the tree line the wind was a factor only as it loosed drips for the tops of the trees. Jubal had erected an awning over the picket line and blanketed each animal. All were being fed and both the animals and their steward were on stable ground. Jubal lay on folded sailcloth in the wagon bed, warm in his blankets and buffalo robe and protected from all but the patter of the dripping rain by an oilcloth cover.

There was no thought of venturing to the ship in this weather and with the responsibilities he bore. A standing roast of beef with Christmas pudding couldn't have enticed him to try. He suspected the isthmus turned island was by now probably sunk. Jubal lay in relative ease, existing on the edge of dozing off until responsibility awoke him and he would lift the edge of his cover to check the well-being of his charges. All was well with them, and he was considering removing his boots when he dozed off again.

~ ~ ~

As with the first storm, the gusts at its front soon abated. The storm stalled against the mountains, joining the earlier front. The storms merged into one turgid mass hanging against the peaks. Here the weather turned dark and threatening. Rain poured down, eroding the slopes and streaming mud and gold bearing ore, along with leaves, branches, and everything loose that could be moved by hydraulics into the already engorged streams. Hundreds, if not thousands of rivulets became freshets, gushers, and mudflows. The rivers became cataracts and soon tumbling floods rushing to the sea. Trees and boulders joined the flow and the rumbling deluge rivaled the approach of a fast freight train. For some, camped on lower ground to be near their claims, the approaching torrent was the last thing they heard as they futilely climbed to escape the charging wall of water.

Fortunately, these fatalities were few in number. Most miners, recognizing the rising water, had abandoned the season for the camps where provisions and supplies could be had as well as the welcome companionship of men. Those with goods on the beach at Sutter's Landing had moved to higher ground and joined the line of men who watched the beach disappear and the seemingly never ending gush of mad water galloped past. With the storm above and the cataract below, the men sought out the company of men as if collectivism itself was insurance against nature's wrath. The restaurateurs, bakers, and in particularly the saloon keepers were blessed and would mark this Christmas Day in memory.

~ ~ ~

At the mouth of the river, aboard the *Julianna*, Josh and Elizabeth had grown accustomed to the occasional bump of ship against shore. Josh dutifully made his rounds but no longer paid heed to the bumps and shivers. It was with little surprise when they ceased entirely neither even noticed. The *Julianna Dolce,* secure in its narrow inlet as a boat tethered in a slipway, was now fully afloat, the inlet sunk by tide and rising water. The central current of the stream had broadened with the mad rush of water to the sea and it now tugged at the ship, drawing it stern foremost into the flow.

Once again the scant crew felt a shiver through the hull and deck, suddenly aware of the absence of movement for some time. What they felt was the *Julianna* coming to the end of its tether on shore. When the Bonner company first set up residence they ran a line to a point of solid ground ashore. Unable to run out the heavy anchors, they had driven a spar into the earth and tied off the line as a caution against their home drifting away. What they felt was the boat snubbing the end of the mooring line as the *Julianna* was drawn stern first into the current. There was no second tremor as the spar pulled free from the mud and dragged through the underbrush and followed the ship downstream.

87

There was another bump as the keel kissed the end of the inlet and plowed stern first into the melee of current and tide. Ships are built to go forward and the current pushed against the bow, sending it towards the shore. For a few tense minutes the *Julianna* swam sideways to the current. Never with enough force to cause the ship to broach to, but an unnatural circumstance for any boat. The bow bumped against the shore, dragged, and the stern moved ahead of the bow. The bowsprit snagged in the cottonwood and willow trees along the bank, holding the boat fast to the shore long enough for the starboard side to run aground, tearing away the paddlewheel. The branches tore free and the ride continued downstream until eventually the end of the sprit was wrenched away and the bow turned from shore, eventually captured by the current and turning from side to side until the bow caught and she swung bow first into the flow.

This was no tempest at sea. The waves were no more than a short, wind-torn chop created by the runoff and a conflicting tide. The ship did not much heel and there was no danger of being swamped. Still, there was no rudder, no canvas aloft that could be swung to control direction and even if the engine was operable the paddle wheels had been reduced to wreckage. The Bonners could do little more than watch the shore pass by. Thinking of their safety, they turned one of the skiffs upright and rigged it ready to launch if needed. Then, unwilling to go below decks, the couple stood at the useless wheel as they drifted with the elements.

Even with the boat swimming in the right direction, the progress was not steady. The canvas stretched across the hull to prevent leaking was now an anchor, almost an underwater sail. As it filled the boat would be slowed and swung from port to starboard in an alarming screwing yaw. The bow would swing towards one shore or another only to be corrected by the current and swung back, only to repeat the maneuver again and again, sometimes bumping over shoals or into the banks. The *Julianna Dolce* was being nibbled apart. There was little to be done beyond attempting to abate the back and forth yaw caused by the fothering sails. With axe in hand, Josh hacked away the belaying lines and the ship steadied her course but there was still no helm. As the ship bumped the sacks of rice now stored in the forecastle shifted, causing a slight list to port. The ship was top heavy with almost no ballast. There was no danger of capsizing but the few degrees of list to the left and the two or three boards of stern trim made for an awkward time on deck.

Eventually the rivers lost their impetus at the confluence with Suisan Bay and the crazy voyage ended in a hapless leeward drift. Neither the rain nor the wind was severe, the worst of the storm front having moved east. The *Julianna* could once again only be described as a derelict. There was no quarter of her bulwarks, rails, or rigging that was not torn or punctured. With the bowsprit wrenched loose there was no tension on the stays and the masts sagged sadly, swaying miserably as the boat yawed. The only constant was relentless drift toward the south shore, barely distinguishable from the water in the fading light

About ten o'clock that evening the *Julianna* struck ground over a submerged bar and, with a final groan, came to rest against a bluff at the bay's southern shore. Aground, the ship heeled against the bluff as if at her final rest. The ship's bell clanged twice, closing out the life of the seagoing packet.

~ ~ ~

By morning the storm had moved on. High clouds scudded across the bright sun casting fleeting shadows on the landscape below. The *Julianna Dolce* lay firmly aground where water met shoreline. The Bonners left the dry cabin and came on deck. The port side list meant Josh had to push open and lash the companionway door. Alarmingly, it now scraped on the deck as the hull had been pummeled out of true by the voyage downstream. The masts, with the forestays and bowsprit gone, tilted miserably towards the land. The rigging sagged mournfully and the few spars remaining swung about haphazardly.

The hull leaned against the dirt bluff, its top only a long step down from the gangway. They literally could step ashore. The loose components of the bilge pump, laid out for cleaning, were gathered in the port scuppers. The housing for the port paddlewheel was barely there, staves missing and the frame hanging precariously crushed between hull and bluff. The starboard wheel was broken and the entire housing and part of the railing had been jolted upward. No doubt the axle was bent. The bow had suffered the most as it was dragged down the shore and over the submerged bars. The last six or so feet of the bowsprit was gone. What remained was wrenched free and skewed drunkenly to port. Both catheads where the anchors were stowed were gone, holes punched through the bulwarks and the anchors lost. Josh descended into the hold, once again filling with water. There was no single breach in the hull but the rough voyage and grounding had sprung the boards. Strings of caulking hung in loops everywhere and water seeped in, trickling down the planking. The *Julianna Dolce* would never swim again. They must salvage what they could.

Josh pulled loose two of the planks he had so recently, lovingly fit to the damaged deck and ran them ashore as gangplanks. The ship was held fast and the receding tide said the next tide would not lift her. There was no rush in abandoning their home. They piled their personal possessions, foodstuff, and what they deemed necessities on the shore and covered the stack with a square of canvas pegged down all around. Only then did they step on land and try to figure where they were.

The bay was much wider and they appeared to have made landfall, rough as it was, at the mouth of a wide channel below two large islands. Directly across from them the bay appeared to be more than a couple miles across. As they walked inland they soon came to the dirt track used by teamsters coming inland from San Francisco. They began walking back towards where they came. Within a short distance they saw the bluff descend down parallel to the river. Water racing down from the mountains had raised the level of the estuary enough so that even a low tide great stretches of the teamster path were impassable. Reflexively, the Bonners looked to the northwest horizon, knowing any following storm would maroon them until the water receded. For today at least, the sky was clear and the sun shone down, turning the flooded land silver. They were cut off.

~ ~ ~

Jubal rolled out of his bunk on the wagon bed, stiff, cold, but dry. He stretched and stamped to bring feeling back to his limbs before seeing to the livestock. They stood much as he had left them. Sheltered under the trees and protected by the awning he'd set up over them, they shuffled about as much as the picket line allowed. The ground they stood on was muddy. What had been a thick layer of dead leaves and pine needles had been stomped into the earth. They were hungry and there was no forage. When they turned from the marshy land into the meadow below the forest there was a wealth of new sprouts coming up in last season's brown remains.

Placing a saddle blanket and a bridle on his Appaloosa stallion, Chicory, then removing the hobbles from the stock, he led the picket line into the meadow and let them graze. When they were done, he'd build a fire from the sticks and kindling he'd kept dry and make himself some breakfast. While the animals grazed Jubal surveyed the sky, enjoying what thin warmth the winter sun provided. It was still a little cool but he stripped off his shirt and let the sun warm him as he walked out the kinks of his two-day confinement. He strolled west to look for a place to water the animals. He hadn't gone far when he found the water had risen, reducing half the meadow to a bog. His gaze wandered over the marsh towards the river, enjoying the birds feasting in the estuary. It took him several minutes of reflection before he noticed the masts of the ship were gone. Where there had been two tall spars sticking up above the line of willows and cottonwoods on the bank, there was nothing.

He knew the *Julianna* could not have sunk or capsized within the confines of the shallow inlet. The rising water must have cast it loose and it drifted into deeper water where anything could have happened. His breakfast could wait but the livestock could not. He led them to a small, firmly grounded slough where they could drink. They insisted on grazing some more as they traversed the meadow back to the forest. He was growing impatient and hurried them along. Once back at the wagons he secured the line and hobbled them again. He put a saddle on Chicory and set out for what had been the site of his shipboard home.

It was not easy going. The narrow band of firm ground between forest and marsh was now sunk and the water extended some ways into the woods. He turned into the trees and continued. It was slow going getting through the underbrush and the occasional deadfall blocking his path but he was able to keep the verge of the tree line in sight and moved forward as best as he could.

He left the trees at a point high enough that a section of the worn earthen track remained and he set off to the west. Before him ribbons of water had inundated the low spots in the road like the tines of a fork and as brilliant as a silver plate in the sunlight.

Coming abreast of the place where they had turned toward the ship there was nothing but reeds and brush sticking up from a sheet of quiet water. The fascines they had ridden across were afloat, making him think the bay was at or near high tide. He headed west along the broken road. Sooner or later he would find the ship and his friends.

Chicory strode through the low places without hesitation. Only a couple of times did the water reach his belly. Jubal pulled up the stirrups and brought his feet up on the horse's back. They trudged on for about three miles as the land rose and fell. At some points he had to swim the horse but he pressed on. Around noon, he paused on a bit of high ground where there were some new sprouts for Chicory to graze on and they both could dry out now that the sun was beaming from straight above them. They pressed on, twice having to swim narrow stretches of water.

On the next bit of high ground Jubal came upon a muleskinner with his team marooned on the bluff.

"I been watching you coming for a while now," the bearded traveler said. "I been stuck up here since last night, and it looks like I'll be making this bluff home for a while more."

The man sported the short beard with no mustache Jubal associated with Mormons. Coming west the train had met several of the Saints. The encounters had been mostly cordial, but the dragoons they met were openly hostile. Given his experience, the few encounters with teamsters had not been pleasant. Jubal was cautious. The man didn't appear to be carrying a weapon, but he would be foolish to travel the road without one.

"Jubal's my name. I'm looking for a ship with my boss living on it."

"I been tryin' to keep my own self from gettin' drowned so I wasn't payin' much attention to anyone voyagin' in a ship," the man said, adding, "Seen one wrecked back a few miles. I didn't stop to inquire."

"Did you see anyone aboard?"

The teamster was lost in his own thoughts, responding. "Mayhap I should have knocked. Would have been drier than this pile o'mud."

Jubal repeated himself. The muleskinner shook his head.

"I was havin' a hard enough time keepin movin' on the road. Didn't give it a thought 'cept to find it curious to see a ship a'tall. Now I'll thank you to move on."

In California Jubal had encountered more prejudice than even in Missouri. Still, this affront took him off stride.

"Nah, it ain't cause you're a nigra," said the stranger. "There's just not enough forage on this mud heap for the both of us. I was here first so I'm claimin' it and you got to go."

Despite a man making claim to something that wasn't his to claim, such practice seemed to be normal for this strange new country. Jubal didn't object. There were more mud heaps to be had. He touched the brim of his hat and set off down the short slope. He didn't look back as he rode. Coming west they had crossed half a continent of land with no law but the wagon train took civilization along with them. There was a group. They elected a leader and everyone pulled together toward a common goal. Once they crossed the Sierras and came to where there was gold fever in the air, all of that seemed to fall apart. Their trail companions, the hotelkeeper Gresham and his wife, the Quills, the Van Volks, the teamster Lundy, had blown apart like leaves in the wind. California was every man for himself and devil take the rest.

Jubal carried on along the wet road for some hours before he spotted the masts of a ship in the distance. It had to be the *Julianna* but she didn't look right. Even at this distance he could see the spars were not aligned. They both sagged drunkenly as if unsupported. Jubal pressed on but twilight found him looking for high ground where he could make camp. He made a cold camp that evening, worried about his friends and vowing to move out by first light.

CHAPTER ELEVEN

Shipwash stood above their excavation. The long ramp down ended twelve feet from the top. Where they were finding paying dirt was now a pond, brown and no doubt with a new layer of runoff from the Christmas torrent of water and rain. Christmas was eight days ago and Duncan guessed it would be yet another week before they could begin working the pit again. A crew was excavating the top end of the ramp to make it longer so they could work new dirt when the pit was dry enough to begin clearing the new silt deposited on top of their find. He was estimating the time lost when Josh joined him.

"Are you getting settled in?" Duncan asked.

"Those Albany boys have been a great help," Josh replied. "We've got a plank floor laid and log walls up about three foot. 'Bout ready to set poles and stretch canvas for the rest of it. Glad to be able to pay the men for their labor until we can get back to mining."

After the desolation wrought by the storms, there was nothing left to do but pick up the pieces. The Argonaut camp was wisely constructed on the bluff above the dry stream but the rains had eroded away part of the bluff and those on the cut side had to pick up their shelters and move. The timing of the storm could not have been worse. They had begun to reach paying ore and the enterprise was starting to make money. Nearly a thousand dollars worth of fine gold, flake, and a few nuggets had proved the worth of their site. The men were excited, eager to work with the promise of gold being realized.

The storms doused their spirits as effectively as the downpour doused their campfires. The smell of both still lingered. Each man barely had thirty dollars in their poke after expenses. They could have earned nearly as much at home without blistering their hands and wrenching their muscles in exchange for a poor diet dearly paid for. Now they could not even earn enough to cover their keep.

The Bonners and Jubal's arrival had been a welcome diversion and he was offering hard coin for labor to set up their home. They had arrived a few days after Christmas with a wagon and cart loaded down with planks, canvas, and supplies. They had even brought three cases of plates, bowls, and cups to hand out. Seeing the devastation of the camp and the pit turned pond they organized a party to go back to the derelict ship and plunder her for lumber and whatever could be salvaged. Of particular interest was the bilge pump, mostly apart on the deck. If they could rescue the pump from the damaged hull and locate all the parts lying on deck perhaps they could pump out the pit and use the pump to wash ore. Jubal acted as guide and was charged with the oversight of Josh's mechanical tools. Two wagons and twelve men left on the salvage mission. The wagons, loaded with canvas, planking, and bags of rice had already returned and left again. They were still working on the pump and would dismantle the entire forward cabin before they left for good.

The camp was still a rough existence but they were a step up from living in mud and eating from tin plates. Being able to get dry again brought up the spirits of the men. Two deserters, caught out in brush hovels draped with cloth, had crawled back to camp. A vote was taken and they were admitted back into the partnership. Forfeiture of anything already earned, a week's share when they resumed mining and latrine duty for a month was the levied penalty for their desertion. They willingly agreed as they wolfed down a hot meal of rice and stringy meat a passing hunter sold them as deer. Perhaps western venison was different than in New York.

While the camp was getting back and getting better, the flume built at the bank of the American River was in dire need of repair. Josh and Duncan hiked down the slope to the river. A wagon returning from dumping its load of over burden passed them on the way. The wash site where the long toms lived was intact except for some breaches in the cofferdam that contained the pond above the lower tom. The elevated plain for the wash operation was built on rocks and gravel washed from the operation. There was little erosion as Josh and Duncan climbed the embankment toward the sluice gate. The going was muddy and Josh helped Duncan cope with the terrain and his game leg.

"See. The gate has not been damaged and the pilings before it remain," said Duncan. They stood above a cut in the bank where the rushing water had removed most of the earth behind the pilings.

"How much is gone?" asked Josh.

"The last six or eight feet of the pilings both up and downstream. See where the water churns white over the shallows there?"

Josh nodded.

"That's where we dumped rock to protect the bank. With the rains, the river rose, even topping the sluice gate. It got behind the pilings and started away on the dirt bank behind. It cuts still at the low end. I'm afraid it might take the bank away completely."

"So we fill it in again," said Josh. "One thing we sure aren't short on is gravel and dirt."

"The wagon that passed us dumping loads of spoil to make a ramp so a wagon can get to the top and fill in the void from above. The river has slowed and dropped quite a bit over the last few days. If we get another storm, I don't know what will happen."

Automatically, the two men looked to the northern sky. It was gray but not the dark pewter of another storm gathering strength for an assault on the mountains. Each day had drizzle but wet hair and rivulets of cold water running down the neck was so common a misery as to be ignored. A storm could come, would come. Of that there was no doubt. One of the first things miners learned when they arrived in California. Everything was a race. A race against the elements, the land, the mountains, and against the other miners. Some races you win. Other you couldn't help but lose. The race became simpler when you could see the difference. The men would repair the sluice gate. Whether the repair would happen before a coming storm destroyed it was an even money bet.

~ ~ ~

The Bonners and the Albany Argonauts were not the only gold seekers making winter camp along the South Fork. Individuals and small groups fled the mountains at the beginning of the winter rains and moved closer to the dirt track that was the supply road from Sacramento. Others came from Monterey and the settlement of San Jose, migrating to the southern bank of the American. Here they camped, waiting for the river to recede and again expose the gold bearing placer sites. For practical purposes the two groups may as well have been in separate countries. In the summer the river was low enough to allow a miner or even a wagon to ford the stream. With the river at flood stage, the two groups could not even shout to one another over the roar of the narrow cataract separating them. Teamsters brought supplies from both directions but their progress was thwarted at the waters' edge. Upstream of the two camps the river flowed through steep canyons. Miners could follow the crest of the arroyos but descent to the river was steep, the slopes were unstable, and the footing unreliable. Some had perished attempting the descent or had drowned in camps on the gravel shoreline, overwhelmed by flash floods. A simple misstep on a wobbly rock would tumble a man into the racing current with only a flash of color above the white water to mark his passage.

The bodies of these unfortunates, at least those not snagged in timber deadfalls or lodged between boulders, bobbed past the mining camps. Occasionally someone would spy a corpse being tossed along but there was no effort to retrieve the remains and bury it. No one would risk their own life to retrieve a dead man. It was doubtful, even if a person floated by alive, anyone would raise a hand to rescue them. The effort was more likely to doom the Samaritan for trying to save the drowning. In the winter the rivers spelled death and the miners were not willing to tempt fate beyond tying their washing to a rope and casting it into the water for a quick, soap-free soak. For most, the American river was a hazard and an obstacle to be avoided until summer.

About a mile upstream from where the Albany group had successfully tempted fate and tapped the river for their gold wash, there was another group of men who saw opportunity roaring past their camp. Half a dozen Frenchmen had abandoned gold hunting for the winter and camped on the north bank about a mile above where Duncan Shipwash and his companions exploited the dry diggings.

Sick of war and political strife the French were uninterested spectators during the Mexican-American War. Gold soon captured their interest. There was little to do to pass the time and eventually someone brought up the idea of building a toll bridge across the river. It seemed like a natural and potentially profitable enterprise. There were tall trees to be felled and the men were sailors, familiar with the complicated rigging needed to move the trees and, like stepping a mast in a ship, to sling the trees across the span. After several failures, they managed to lay split logs across and secure each end of their bridge. They charged ten cents for pedestrians, fifteen cents for a horse and rider, and wagons crossed at a negotiated price depending upon what could be exploited from the teamster or owner of the freight.

At first, the Frenchmen were feted as heroes and great citizens. Their bridge opened commerce and united the previously separated camps. A settlement, as if by magic, appeared. Stores provided staples, supplies, and rare delicacies at exorbitant prices. Saloons and gambling establishments offered cheap drinks and expensive games of chance. For about a month the settlement grew and life went on as best as could be expected. Eventually, idle talk in the barrooms turned the mood against the French bridge operators. Miners made friends over their beer and whiskey and some of those friends might live on the other side of the river. Men needed to cross the bridge to trade or drink or gamble. No one was making any money in the winter hiatus except the Frenchmen. The camp was almost exclusively American. The Mexican and *Californio* contingent had abandoned the hills for the comforts of home in the established settlements and *ranchos*. The only ones lining their pockets were the foreigners. What right did they have to exploit Americans who had taken California and its gold as the proper and deserved spoils of war?

The French bridge builders were soon badgered, bullied, and deposed. The seafarers who abandoned their native France to avoid trouble found trouble following them wherever they went. By a whiskey-sweetened voice affirmation the camp appropriated the bridge, the tolls were revoked, and a grateful public banished the Frenchmen to parts unknown. The first unified action of the new mining settlement was a lawless seizure of another's property and enterprise. If anyone objected to the confiscation, they kept their opinion to themselves.

~~~

With the road of commerce open over the "community-owned" bridge and the camps united it was no surprise that other small isolated camps migrated to the new settlement. Hotels, traders, and public houses set up next to one another and before anyone knew it there were three or four streets competing for the honor of "Main Street". A teamster would set up his stall next to a dentist or next to a hunter selling fresh meat. A saloon and gambling establishment would appear on either side of a freighter's tent. A canvas sided hotel would be under construction, already advertising a dining room and a furnished parlor.

Other than puncheon floors and a few hitching posts in front of businesses the streets were mud, awaiting conversion to dust during high summer. The more ambitious entrepreneurs dug privies behind their businesses. The less civic-minded tossed their chamber pots into the thoroughfare. There was no government and no codes to enforce and no fines to be collected by a non-existent court.

No one seemed to care. During the opening heady days of The Gold Rush, mining camps were notoriously transitory. Hangtown was no exception. One or two dozen set up to work the river and creeks, occasionally washing a particularly rich pan but more often gaining a hard-earned five to twelve dollars for their day's effort. Eventually tents sprang up and a bloom of human society sprouted until a rider came to the camp bearing stories, often just rumors, of a tremendous find only two canyons and a long day's march away. Several times Hangtown almost disappeared. Campsites were abandoned leaving nothing but piles of washed dirt and the cast off garbage and waste of human habitation. Even an outbreak of pestilence could not empty a camp so quickly as the promise of vast riches just a few miles away. The miners were transients. Camps would spring up, disappear, and re-emerge as rumors of nearby color failed to prove out. Only when the elements chased the miners from the canyons did Hangtown take on an air of permanence. What saved Hangtown was the availability of supplies, entertainment, and proximity to the most promising prospecting sites.

Trouble was inevitable at the camp springing up across the river from the Bonner and partnership holdings. It was winter and little gold was being produced. Supplies were expensive. There was little to do and even less work or wages. The saloons, games of chance, and the patronage of the few whores who set up cribs behind the gambling houses relieved the drunk and desperate of what little specie remained in their pockets. Fights were common and disputes over cards, dice, or women ran their course. So far, there had been no serious incidents.

The miners soon organized their own justice system. One of the first miners' court was born in Hangtown and its tenets survived, migrated, and were applied in boomtowns across the country for decades. Most incidents, like fights, were dealt with by a majority vote of those interested enough to gather for the proceedings. Hangtown had no jail and no interest in creating one. Criminal cases were resolved by flogging, banishment, or hanging. Not knowing where on the scale of justice punishment for a particular crime might fall kept most citizens in line. In winter camp, Hangtown's court was novel entertainment with the possibility of a free drink or two thrown in. Cases were adjudicated nearly as quickly as a charade of a court could be convened. A judge, jury, prosecutor, and defense counsel were selected and the trial began. A simple assault case with a black eye or broken nose would garner a fine on the guilty party, usually enough to cover a round of drinks for the assembly. More serious cases took upwards of an hour and the cheating gambler run out of camp, a serious assault would earn a public flogging and banishment.

Civil cases were usually cases of unpaid debt or mining claim infringement. These were usually resolved by the jury, but often a majority rule of the attendees would vacate the jury's ruling and a precedent would be set for future cases. Decisions were rendered, toasts were drunk to celebrate the resolution and the miners' court was born.

The unification of the two camps spurred growth. Growth did not come in the form of civic committees and street commissions. Growth meant more miners and more miners meant more merchants, gamblers, and bars. Theft and violence were passengers in the wagons that came to the new camp. The miners' court would soon have more serious matters to deal with.

The tension in camp was like a palpable stink. There was no doubt some serious transgression would soon occur. The consensus said the first incident would come on a weekend night in or near a bar. Alcohol or gambling would be involved. Men listened to the predictions and nodded their heads in agreement. If there were a camp newspaper the story could well have already been written, lacking only the insertion of the named parties.

When the first murder came, the same soothsayers said they knew all along the reason would be a dispute over a mining claim. Once the camp visit was concluded the miners dispersed into the landscape, vanishing into the gulches and canyons where a meager income could be eked out along the swollen streams. They lived in isolation either by choice or because of financial hardship. This population was scant and miners seldom encroached on another's prospects. There were no claims and no procedures or laws to establish or record one. The miners generally accepted the discoverer of a gold paying site had the rights to the site as long as he worked the site. Industry and perseverance were recognized as the specie that paid for a claim.

One prospector, came to camp for supplies, hurried back to his tent in a secluded arroyo, and poked his shovel into a weed grown old, streambed, dislocated, and dried in some primeval upheaval. The miner recognized the same features as where the dry diggings were producing. His find may well have been accidental but a find it was and it soon proved potentially rich. The prospector's problem, like the Albany partners' was a source of water to wash the ore. Between the bar and the stream were two neglected claims marked by a cairn of rocks at the corners. The two claims hadn't been worked since the summer and the prospector dug a channel across the both to bring water to his dig. The pit began to pay at only a depth of three feet. The miner was bringing up shovels of the paying ore known as blue lead. Within a few days, the prospector had accumulated a nice poke and planned a trip to the camp on the American for a little entertainment and more and better supplies.

Witness to other migrations of miners created by tales of rich finds the prospector vowed to keep his bonanza a secret. He boasted to no one, drank sparingly, and bought his supplies from several merchants. Still, his spending did not go unnoticed.

He had panned during the summer with the two men who had placed the stone cairns where the prospector's channel now irrigated his diggings. The summer season had earned them little so when their neighbor showed up with gold where none had been before it stirred their interest. They followed him back into the canyon. An argument ensued, gunfire erupted, and the first prospector was killed by the two other miners. They dragged the body into the woods and left the remains for the beasts. Their perfidy did not go undetected.

A miner further up the canyon heard the exchange of gunfire. Ever mindful of Indian attacks he grabbed his weapon and came to the aid of his neighbor. Arriving as the body was being disposed of he sought cover behind a timber deadfall and took note of the scene, recognizing the two miners from the summer before. Two days later he was able to slip past the new residents and take his tale of murder and robbery to camp. The site of the crime became initially known as Murderers' Bar but the name became commonplace in the territory. It was eventually changed to Beale's Bar, after the man who discovered its riches.

~~~

"Let's see what this hotel looks like," said Elizabeth. With the camp united they were visiting the settlement on the south side and buying some trifles and generally enjoying the society of others. Much of what they saw was just another version of the *Embarcadero* and Sutter's Fort.

The hotel in question was undoubtedly one of the largest structures around. Other than being big, it was quite unremarkable. A short wall of roughly laid logs with intermittent supports for the canvas walls and roof, capped with pine boughs. Entering, the Bonners strode over a split log floor and a clerk's desk made of a plank on supports and draped with a blanket to complete the illusion of a registration counter. The desk was in an alcove not more than six by eight feet. The balance of the public area was a bar constructed the same as the registration desk but featuring half a dozen wooden chairs and a stained and worn davenport, possibly the only one in camp. The public room was separated from the guest quarters by partitions. The walls only appeared to be substantial. They were simple frames with calico cloth stretched tightly across the frames, providing the illusion of a plastered and papered wall. A boarder drinking in the parlor confirmed the guest rooms were constructed in the same manner with blankets hanging down as doors. This provided the illusion of a solid wall and a modicum of visual privacy. The cloth wall provided no barrier to smell or sound. Beds consisted of a rope and wood cot covered by a thin mattress stuffed with old cloth. For two dollars a night the hotel's chief attraction was a dry roof over the guest's head and what heat could be circulated from the mud and rock fireplace in the lobby. Rough as it was, the hotel offered the miner sleeping on the ground in a lean-to or brush hovel, a welcome improvement in living conditions. A sign announced no unaccompanied women would be accommodated. The proscription was no impediment to the livelier guests. The opportunity to engage in all sorts of debauchery were mere footsteps away.

The Bonners made their way up and down the muck of the thoroughfares, buying basic supply items at scandalous prices. They soon learned other items were available to those who inquired and demonstrated the ability to pay. They were offered fresh meat but even a cursory inspection raised doubts not only of freshness but of source as well. They were able to purchase a ceramic jug of lemon juice, a few jars of jams, and an assortment of cauliflower, beets, onions, parsnips, and rutabaga. They bought some for themselves but most for the company, and Elizabeth insisted on receipts for the common purchases. Staples had been purchased with the collective gold washed from the dig site but these extras were expensed as an investment. It was felt the men would benefit from a more varied and healthier diet giving them the strength to work more efficiently. They were leaving the market with a hundred pounds of victuals and supplies and departing over two hundred dollars poorer. In Illinois a man might work four months for two hundred dollars and consider himself fortunate. In the camps a man needed to earn fifteen to twenty dollars a day just to afford the basic supplies of survival. Few if any made that kind of money prospecting over the winter and fewer could offer that kind of money for wages. No wonder the finer items of trade were bought and sold on the quiet.

They were almost to what had become known as French Bridge when the uproar behind them broke out. Something was happening and anything that broke the routine of camp life was worth turning around for. It seemed like every tent and shelter had emptied into the street. Josh and Elizabeth got up on their cart to see.

Several days before, a miner had come to camp bearing witness against two men who had killed a man for his claim and hid the body. Taking a man's claim alone was sufficient to outrage the populace. A dozen men quickly volunteered to apprehend the villains and bring them back to the settlement for trial. They had returned with their captives and, for all appearances, the apprehension had taken longer than the trial promised to take.

The Bonners met up with two of the Albany men and elected to stay as spectators. A gill of decent whiskey each would make the spectacle more interesting. The impromptu court would never accept the presence of a woman, even one dressed like a miner, so Elizabeth took the cart and retreated to their camp below the Albany one. The word of the trial had spread and some of the mining company passed her as she walked. Normally, they would offer greetings of the day and a simple exchange of good wishes. On this day, the men merely nodded a greeting and, to a man, tugged their hat down over their eyes. The men were off to watch blood sport and Elizabeth knew it. They were like Roman citizens off to watch the Christians be slaughtered in the arena, non-participants but damned if they were going to miss a moment of the spectacle.

As Elizabeth passed the street of tents where the company lived it was almost empty. A few men sat on stumps or casks mending clothes or repairing personal items and the feet of sleeping men, some still wearing boots with holed soles, could be seen under the open tent flaps. A few of these ventured a "good day to you" or "hope the morning finds you well". The words were offered not only in greeting but in hopes she would recognize the speaker as one who did not run to the trial and foreordained execution. She acknowledged each with a smile and a few words in return. Walking home she went by the current dig, still mostly filled with water. Josh was working on putting the ship's pump back together from salvaged parts. Soon she crossed the footbridge across the creek to their separate shelters.

When Elizabeth, Josh, and Jubal came into camp after the wreck of the *Julianna* the Albany bunch pitched right in and helped them cut and split trees for their shelters and to raise and paint the canvas sides and roof. What they did not do and quietly refused too do was build the shelters next to their own. They would not live in proximity to a colored. No one said anything but the footbridge across the creek was hastily laid and the camp was segregated as efficiently as any town in the East divided by railway or canal or thoroughfare. If it had been Jubal alone, he would simply have been told where he could live. If the miners had only known Jubal, as partners with the Bonners and Shipwash, owned a larger stake in the gold venture than any of the partnership men, no doubt there would be trouble.

For her part, Elizabeth had no objection to the segregation from the miners. She valued her privacy that provided relief from their revelry, noise, latrine, and garbage piles. Most were young men who had left wives or girlfriends back in New York. They were awkward around her, either fumbling to utter a simple greeting without a stutter or gushing forth strings of practiced banalities. She had no patience for awkward boys.

Truth be told, she would prefer to be on the other side of the river, watching or at least listening to the goings on of the trial. Men were such fools when it came to women. Since leaving her Illinois home she had crossed half a continent, buried her family, and lived through more trials and terrors than nearly all the happy-go-lucky adventurers in California. Did they think she would press the back of her hand to her forehead and swoon as the details of the crime were brought forth in testimony? Did they think she would break down in tears and plead for clemency for two murdering thieves? She didn't want it generally known but none among those across the river had ever pushed a knife into a man and given the blade a mortal twist. Damn their eyes. She turned to the river, determined to watch the proceedings from a distance. She didn't count herself among the Roman plebeians on the far bank, hungry for diversion and calling their bloodlust justice. She was angry simply for being excluded.

~ ~ ~

Josh had deliberately abandoned the society of his drinking companions. They were amiable enough when the trial had begun and they all were just interested spectators sharing out a flask of whiskey as they lingered near the activities. Once Josh found himself with a rope in his hand marching a man into an eternity, he sought a drink but had no desire for company.

It wasn't as if the two men didn't deserve their fate. Nor was it the hasty formation of the miners' court or the swift and foreordained theater of the trial. Josh had no objection to the immediate execution either. What disturbed Josh was his own, almost mindless, participation in carrying out the sentence. He felt stained somehow, either by accident or instinct and it didn't sit well. Afterwards he drank but only to dull the recollection of how the rope felt in his hands as the man kicked away his life. He felt no guilt but perhaps a regret that he acted upon impulse, not on considered study. The matter deserved reflection and so he avoided his earlier companions and made his way home alone.

Josh was crossing the footbridge across the creek, still consolidating his thoughts but mindful of his steps. When he reached the far shore and looked up, Elizabeth was waiting for him.

"I went down to the river and watched. No one can say justice isn't swift in the camps."

"Christ. They didn't leave them strung up there, did they," said Josh, realizing the hanging site was visible from their segregated camp.

"No. Some men with a wagon took them away. Looked like a man with a Bible may have recruited a party for the job. I almost called across the river to thank them but it seemed out of place to do so."

"Suppose it would," agreed Josh. He would tell her of his part in the affair later, after he'd shed the effects of the drink and reconciled his participation in his mind.

CHAPTER TWELVE

Enough parts of the chain pumps from the *Julianna Dolce* had been salvaged for Josh to get three of the four cylinders working. Since putting it in operation to drain the paying pit, he had disabled one of the cylinders. The imbalance created by an odd number made the actual operation more difficult. Worse, as one side of the pump was easier to operate than the other, men griped about which side of the pump they were assigned. Resentment built with each stroke of the handle.

Only four or five feet remained in the bottom of the dig. The extension of the ramp had cut into new ground and uncovered gold in a ledge of the new excavation. Enthusiasm for pumping had declined in proportion to the gold discovered on the ledge. As long as the ledge existed along the bank of the dead stream, men would rather dig ore than pump water out over the proven pay dirt.

Everything associated with gold mining and keeping the camp running smoothly was repetitive drudgery. Kitchen duty was abhorrent. Latrine duty was worse but not a daily task. Felling timber and sawing planks was considered the worst and the man in the bottom of the pit stood in mud and endured a rain of sawdust. Working with pick and shovel was exhausting and the task with the most nagging injuries. When the men were extracting color most didn't mind the clawing of rocks and dirt from the earth but the gold was always under worthless dirt that required excavation. The only task most men didn't mind was the final wash in the long toms. Even then the men's hands were immersed in frigid water and their fingers abraded by the operation. Sifting out the fine gold and occasional nugget or picker still meant there was a lot of spoil to be disposed of. The men were rotated between chores and the officers did their best to even out the tasks, often sending men to different jobs two or three times in a day. When the pit was full, the pump ran for ten hours a day. Men rotated every hour. Now that they were ahead of the work and finding gold on the ledge, the pumping was reduced to five hours. Shipwash and the Albany captains were trying to reach the paying ore at the bottom of the original dig. At the same time the ledge and its nooks and crannies of surface gold played out and the digging down to what was called the blue lead of gold bearing minerals could be uncovered. There was little rancor in the camp but it was attributable only to a continuing stream of gold. This early in the project, no one was getting rich, no hundred dollar pans had been counted, but for men used to wages of a dollar a day, the five or six dollars coming out of the ground and into their pockets made the toil tolerable. The deep gravel diggings were the envy of the whole encampment. Miners came to watch, to learn and then partner up and disappear into the country seeking similar ground.

Josh had the pump apart and was working on one of the leather gaskets that lifted the water up the pipe and out the discharge. The steel discs on both sides of the leather seal had come loose and the pump was losing efficiency. He was just finishing up the assembly when Duncan approached.

"It's been so long since I've seen the bottom of the pit, I can't decide how much more there is to pump. Five feet you think?

"Mebbe," said Josh. "Makes no difference anyway. We pump till its dry and that's the long and short of it."

"How are the men holding up?"

"How is the ledge holding up?" Josh answered with a laugh. "As long as we bring up color, the men will be fine. They complain all day at the pump and all day I remind them it's a damn site easier to pump than to bail."

"Every day we pick at the ledge I expect it to play out. The ledge isn't what I wanted to talk to you about."

Josh connected the pump rod to the pump handle and he was done.

"Let's walk," said Duncan. "Take a stroll down to the toms."

On their way they had to step aside as a wagon returning from the wash site. The driver helloed about a good cleanup. They waved, picking up the pace a bit. Gold fever, after all, was gold fever.

"Those two men were hanged over a claim dispute," said Duncan, opening a touchy subject. "There will be more bloodshed as more miners arrive and clamor up the canyons. We will need something better than just leaving a shovel at your site to mark it."

"It's understood you have to work a claim besides marking it."

"Exactly. We are the only enterprise here. Twenty-six of us at last count but we're working less than two hundred feet of the ancient stream. We can't keep on working the ground. Someone's bound to drop a shovel right next to us if we don't come up with some rules. And then there's the water."

"There's three men dead over a claim to water."

"Precisely. We can legitimately contend we are working our site on the river but we've got nearly half a mile to traverse getting ore from the pit to the river. Suppose someone decides to put in a mining claim right down the middle of this road we're on? How about where we sleep and eat. How about where we cut our timber? We can't buy the land or get an easement. There's no one with a solid claim to the land that's not being mined."

"What about Sutter? From what I know we're standing on land granted to him by the Mexicans. Hell, almost all the gold being found is on Sutter's land."

"Do you see even one person respecting his land?" said Duncan. "The Mexican government is gone and his claim is gone with it. Sutter doesn't even have a government to complain to or file a grievance with."

"By thunder, you're right. I never even gave it a thought even as the trial was going on. Sure glad you thought of it."

"Wasn't me. Was Leland Weber. He worked in the New York government. He asked me and I said I didn't know. Everywhere I've prospected, from Indian to Peru, the government was there and set the rules and stuck their hand in your pocket as you mined."

"So what do we do here with no government?"

"I say we meet with our partners and propose some rules. We'll keep our interests in mind. Then we go to the miners' court, such as it is, and set rules for everyone. Probably best to send Weber as our man. We're the biggest single interest and I think the other miners, once they see what lies ahead, will agree to a mining district and rules."

"Sounds like you and the Albany captains do more than figure out the cost of flour and bacon. Just let me know what you come up with before we head across and call a meeting."

"Then I'd like to open a recorder's office and keep order until something better shows up."

"Let's just make sure we keep finding gold. We go across and call a meeting, better to go flush with dust. Meetings called by beggars aren't well attended, I reckon."

~ ~ ~

"Did you talk to Duncan?"

"About the claims and the rules and such?"

Elizabeth nodded. "He's right. Without some rules, there will be hangings every week."

"Seems to me his point was without some rules, our dig isn't safe. Neither is where we live."

"Nobody's is, it looks like," said Elizabeth. "We're all on Sutter's grant and he's got no one to complain."

"That's kind of Duncan's point. If there are rules then the hope is men will abide by them even with no one to enforce them. Just having a claim and having it writ down will be enough for most folks."

"Written down, not writ," corrected Elizabeth.

"You're right. I'm sure I've got that writ down someplace."

"If you can write, it would be a surprise to me. What about Jubal's claim? Would it stand?"

"Sad to say, but from what I've seen I'd bet on no. The Americans won't allow a Mexican to have a claim. They ran off the Frenchies who built the bridge, and no Chinese or Sandwich Islander has rights to a claim a white man wants."

"How about Jubal as part of a company, our partnership with Shipwash?"

~~~

Jubal's part was one of the things Duncan was trying to sort out as he met in the meal tent with Luder, Weber, and Fellowes. As far as they knew they were partners with Shipwash and the Bonners. The Albany company just assumed Jubal was hired help and there was no reason for them to think otherwise.

The question became how much dirt could a company claim. Can a partnership of five men claim as much as a company of twenty men, or is it based on how many are in the company? Suppose its based on the number of members and a claim is established, then another partner comes in? Can they claim more dirt? If the company owns a paying claim then that means pushing someone else out or buying the claim for the added interest.

"I say a claim is based on the number of original members. Each man claims a reach of stream or diggings and then gets a percentage of the total. The claim gets no bigger but a man can sell his share or a part of it to someone else," said Weber.

"If a man wants to sell, the partners he's with should get first shot," said Luder.

"That's if you are thinking a share is tied to a specific length of the overall. If we want to keep our dig connected, there will be parts won't prove out but we still need to keep them. A man can sell all of his claim or he can sell lineal feet of his claim but its feet in the overall claim of the company, not any specific feet claimed as an individual," argued Duncan.

"Then how big is a claim?" asked Fellowes.

"If the claims are recorded as individual claims, then they have to be worked to sustain the rights," replied Duncan.

Weber chimed in. "That's the first thing we've agreed on."

"Then the size has to be something a single man can work or at least work on." Fellowes added.

"I suggest two hundred feet in length and fifty feet back from center of the river. River meaning stream, creek, tributary, dry or wet, too. Further I think the discoverer should get an extra hundred feet," said Shipwash.

"Good idea. That will prompt men to do more prospecting with the promise of more rights. Agreed?"

They all nodded and a note was made.

"Surface only, too," suggested Luders. "That means no one's claim can cut off access to another claim. I'm thinking of the route from our river claims to our deep gravel dig."

"What about water rights? "asked Weber. "The court just hung two men over rights to wash water."

Everything they discussed brought up new issues. They had yet to decide how much of a claim a business concern could hold. Companies needed to raise capital so they needed to be able to sell to speculators to raise it. Suppose someone sank a shaft following a promising vein. They shouldn't have to stop because they were underneath a surface claim belonging to another. Will the other miners go along and how much power would the miners' court have. This was all new to Duncan and he was supposed to be the expert in the field. Everywhere he had prospected and mined, the rules of the country prevailed even before the first exploratory pick chipped away at a rock. What that meant was the government claimed prior rights and stuck their hand in the miner's pocket before anyone else could keep so much as an ounce for themselves. These Americans would instantly hang anyone who so much as suggested the government got even a flake from their labor.

This was going to take days just to come up with a plan to present to the others in the camp along the American. Even if they agreed, how far would the authority reach? There were three forks just of this river with tributaries for each. Would those in Auburn on the North Fork agree to rules set up by those on the South Fork. Most troubling of all, who would enforce the claims once a man had paid to record his claim and believe it safeguarded from encroachment? It would be a long night. Duncan poured himself a cup of coffee, thought about a splash of brandy in the cup and decided against it. Adding liquor to a plan usually resulted in poor decision-making.

~~~

The rains returned, not as the sustained deluge leading up to the Christmas catastrophe, but as a constant drizzle over three days. No one saw a shadow for the whole three days. Daylight was almost worse than the night because a person could see how miserable it was. Constant damp and water just seemed to accumulate on every surface and down every neck. It was a wonder the ground could still soak up the water. The only saving grace was the miners hung their spare clothes out to get a natural and labor free soaking. Eventually the sun would return and dry out a change of clothing. Long underwear became the uniform of the day. Few ventured out. Getting dry by the meager and improvised hearths was not a simple task.

At the Albany prospecting site the pump sat idle and the last five or six feet of runoff in the pit became seven feet. Water trickled in from the high ground above. Any attempt to pump would barely hold the level they had. In these conditions morale was a fragile and precious entity. Asking men to stand in the rain and pump would serve the enterprise no more benefit than whipping them for refusing. The setback made it a good wager the ledge would play out before the pit could be pumped clear.

Working the ledge for ore and washing it were tasks preferable to moping about in tents playing cards, smoking, and trying vainly to keep warm. They were there to make money and the ledge was still producing. The miners dug back in the crannies of the ledge, rolled rocks away, and laboriously pulled material from the elevated bedrock. The excavation was more rock than ore. Smaller rocks were carried one at a time to a wagon for disposal. Those that couldn't be carried were levered and pried off the ledge into the stream or rolled away downhill. The ore was rich but there wasn't much of it. It was extracted by spade, trowel, and spoon; dumped in buckets and put on a separate wagon to be taken to the wash site. Occasionally a small picker or even a nugget would raise a cheer along the line. Spirits were good as long as gold was being pulled.

The ledge and dig site in the deep gravel diggings was not lost on the other miners in camp. They knew the New York boys were finding color while the rest of the winter refugees went through their reserves and lived on the edge of going bust. They began accumulating near the diggings and observing the goings on. In order to protect their rights the Albany men each set up a cairn of rocks every two hundred feet along the dry bed according to Shipwash's directions. Each miner was required to spend two hours each week clearing ground and thereby marking the claim as active. A pick or a shovel was left at each site as further proof of an active claim. For this purpose even Jubal was welcomed as an equal participant. Duncan, Josh, and Elizabeth each marked off a claim along the wash site. When someone questioned whether a woman could stake a claim separate from her husband, Elizabeth slammed the objection into the mud.

It quickly became obvious to the spectators no individual could work the dry diggings. A man could dig for a year and not remove enough overburden and rocks to get down to paying sand and bedrock. They would have to form companies of their own. Individual placer miners would partner up with two or three acquaintances and the partnerships would merge with another partnership until a loose affiliation of eight or ten men could band together. The Albany company had marked out over four thousand feet of dry gravel and the embankment above it. More importantly, they could enforce their claim against any competitors.

The newly formed small companies moved up the South Fork or cut across the back edge of the Albany claims and moved, with their pooled resources, down the dry bed of the river beyond where the Albany boys took precedence and then further up the narrow creek below their site. Many crossed the footbridge to the side of this stream where the Bonners resided. No mules or horses. The men would cross bearing awkward and overfilled packs across then scurry away under the watchful eye of Josh, Elizabeth, Jubal, and Shipwash. They did not

112

begrudge the intruders. They had no interest in prospecting in the wild and they wished the men scuttling in front of their shelters good luck as they passed.

Duncan particularly wished these newly formed ventures the best of luck. They were out to make their fortune and, with little competition, gave no thought to claims and rules and filings. Those were issues for men not swinging a pick or straining their backs wielding a shovel. That would change as more people arrived. They would accept the rules and provisions he and the Albany captains were drafting with little argument. The companies would hold sway over the individuals and democracy would prevail. Mining rules would be set in place and recorded to best advantage of those who drafted them.

~ ~ ~

Duncan, Josh, and the miller, Elias Fellowes, were on the far side of the American River walking through the settlement. Their purpose was to find a site to set up the mining claims office. Purposely they had avoided the main thoroughfare with its commotion of drinking and gambling halls and the bustle of merchants competing for attention. The enterprise they were proposing was not one that needed to seek custom. Once the rules had been adopted no miner or company could consider their claim secure without it being recorded. The trio had turned down a quieter byway and walked near the end, almost to where the tents and shelters of the resident miners began. They wanted to be away from the noise and clutter and mostly the filth that was fast becoming the base material of the main streets. Once set up the miners would find their way to their little corner of camp.

Josh and Fellowes were discussing the various merits and faults of undeveloped spots while Duncan was considering requiring a sample of ore be submitted for assessment with each recorded claim. This would require seeking out and buying the chemicals and equipment to validate ore. Conducting an assay was problematic but there were bigger considerations. Those who speculated on claims would submit only the richest samples or even "salt" the claim with dust in order to increase the auriferous content and thereby inflate the value of what might be worthless dirt. Samples tested in good faith would undoubtedly be purer than what was actually mined, casting doubt on his own integrity. He compromised and decided that all claim recordings would cost two ounces of at least ninety percent fine dust, flake, or nugget. If a miner wished to trade specie for dust to submit, the price was to be in natural form, about forty dollars worth. Satisfied with his decision, Duncan was turning his attention to his companions' discussion when a man in a rumpled, dirty suit with cuffs stuffed into tall boots approached them. His shirt was in no better shape and hadn't been washed in a while. The collar was clean and unadorned by a cravat. The man wore a stovepipe hat, or what was left of one. He had a large face, cunning eyes shrouded under bushy eyebrows. The man wore a full beard, trimmed but with the center stained brown by a cud of tobacco that was being worked with enthusiasm. The two men behind stovepipe, for all appearances, were teamsters and were brought along as intimidation. They looked bored with the day but their nonchalance had the look of a pose. Josh was instantly alert and focused on the two ruffians. If there was trouble coming it would be from that quarter.

"You gentlemen appear to be seeking a lot for perhaps a business site. Am I correct? May I inquire the nature of your enterprise?"

Stovepipe was addressing Duncan. The two ruffians stood back but concentrated their boredom on Josh and Fellowes. The teams were set.

"You are correct in your first surmise, sir," said Duncan. "As to the second, you may not inquire."

Unruffled, Stovepipe continued as if Duncan had not replied at all.

"Whatever your business, you will have to do business with Simon Bullard. I am that very personage and honored to be the sole agent for his eminence Captain Johann Auguster Sutter, owner of the land upon which we all stand. Every lot here on Sutter Boulevard must be purchased. The price starts at one thousand dollars and the lot price increases the closer to the main business district." Bullard offered his hand.

"Who will I have the privilege of negotiating with, sir?"

Duncan began to extend his hand before Josh placed his hand on Duncan's wrist and stepped forward.

"You can negotiate with me. My name is Josh Bonner and I am honored to be the exclusive agent for Samuel Colt in Alta California. Now move along."

"Samuel Colt? I don't understand what you..."

"What I'm saying is John Sutter holds a Mexican land grant. You sure as shit aren't his agent and if you and your friends don't get out of my sight I'm going to make everything under that ruinous hat of yours look worse than it already does."

The larger of the two louts with Bullard took three quick steps forward. He stopped after three paces as he found the tip of Shipwash's cutlass pushing into his shirt just below his breastbone. Duncan had the sword concealed in a bedroll he wore over his shoulder. Three steps and the weapon had been waiting for the big man. His companion had stopped feigning boredom and was doing his part backing up his boss and partner with a stead, hard stare but there was nothing behind it.

"Bullard," said Josh. "When I say out of my sight I don't mean just today. If you got a business here I'd suggest you and your two friends put it on wagons and find a new patch of dirt to be Sutter's agent on."

The two teamsters had started to back away. Bullard wasn't done.

"You haven't heard the end of this. We're not finished here."

A crowd had begun to gather. Nothing like a fight to draw people together.

"You aren't paying your hard men enough, Bullard. They're gone and you'd best be after'em."

Bullard saw he was alone, turned and fled up the street. He pulled his hat down on his head like he wanted to hide under it. The crowd cheered as he slunk away. Enthused by the crowd's support, Josh's words chased him down the muddy byway.

"When I say, get packin', I mean you best get packed." Another cheer and the bolder of the men stepped up to slap Josh on the back. The moment passed and the trio went back to picking out a lot.

~~~

A site had been picked and they were walking back to camp when word burned through of a murder a ways up one of the tributary streams of the South Fork. The circumstances weren't known beyond what the rumors speculated but the common thread was of a miner stabbing his wife to death in a drunken rage.

A crowd was gathering in the muddy street of the camp and a miners' court was being convened. Those who served before in the trial of the two hanged men made themselves conspicuously absent. New officers of the court were to be nominated and a jury selected. Once the job was completed, the court would deputize a delegation to apprehend the villain reportedly holed up in a lean-to shelter below a bluff. Shipwash insisted they attend.

"We need to get someone from the partnership as one of the officers of the court."

"Not me. I've had my fill of trials and hangings. These courts are just a sham; nothing more than an organized lynch mob."

"I agree," said Fellowes. "The outcome of the last one was just killing time until they could hang those two."

"All the more reason someone with a conscience and a sense of the law should be a part."

"I'm guessing you have someone in mind, maybe you?" said Josh.

"Yes, at least come along and nominate me as anything but defense counsel."

"Why are you so all-fired eager to be elected?" asked Josh. "You didn't want any part of the last one."

"I only want to get my name recognized. If we're going to present a set of mining rules and claims recording, then we need more credibility than that swindler telling us he was Sutter's agent. I want no part of convicting a man to be hanged but we'll need support for our ideas. I'll do my best to make sure he has a fair hearing but I'll have no part in the hanging."

"Hell, you've already convicted him," said Fellowes.

"Oh, I have no doubt of the outcome. With women being so scarce in these parts, women are seen as needing protection. Come. There's not a minute to be lost."

As it turned out they could have waited. After the recent trial and execution, men were not so eager to play a role in what they all knew would be yet another hanging. When the names of the earlier judge, bailiff, clerk, and attorneys for the case were called no one responded. All those men had made themselves scarce, drunk, or both.

Josh nominated Duncan Shipwash and Elias Fellowes seconded the nomination. There were objections.

"You aren't even an American," came an objection from the throng. The point had weight and a murmur of agreement ran through the assembly. Duncan mounted the back of a wagon to be seen and better heard.

"It is true I am a newcomer to California but are not we all. Who here can claim citizenship in what amounts to a brand new Republic? What law exists here is based on the laws of the United States and the laws of the courts in America are based on the time-honored tradition of trial by jury and right to representation as set down in English common law."

The crowd mulled it over. Duncan pressed his point.

"I was an officer in a cavalry regiment in India. As an officer I served on several court martials. What is more, unlike a lawyer, I was required to act as both prosecuting officer and as defense counsel. I took what was assigned to me and did my best within the law."

While the crowd was not nodding yes, the timbre was shifting and the men were listening.

"I admit none of the cases were capital crimes," he continued. "Most were for fighting, drunk on duty, theft, and other small offenses but the process was the same in every instance. Justice was served."

Shipwash had no more to add. He remained on the wagon, visible to the milling crowd.

"Hell, let him be judge. No one else wants to," came another voice from the crowd.

"Shipwash for judge," shouted Fellowes.

"The remark was unexpected, coming as it did from Josh's side. He turned to Fellowes who just shrugged his shoulders. The crowd finished the job and Duncan Shipwash added criminal court judge to his history. He began a short speech promising to uphold the rule of law and do his best. He was largely ignored as the rest of the court officers were quickly pulled from the crowd and appointed. The appointed submitted reluctantly, most of all the man appointed to defend the accused. The crowd was hungry and ready to begin. It was agreed the bailiff, the judge, and the defense lawyer should accompany the delegation to apprehend the fugitive.

Josh sidled up to Duncan.

"I'm going with you. No telling where Old Stovepipe and his two toughs are but I won't have them sneaking up on you in a crowd. Let's go back to camp and get saddled up."

~ ~ ~

Something between a mist and a drizzle settled on the shoulders and drizzled from the brims of the hats of the dozen men in the posse. They rode under trees that dripped on the men and their mounts. The weather and the gloomy mission killed conversation. No one wanted to be there but all knew it had to be done. Individually each man wondered if the day would bring violence and someone, perhaps themselves, would return to the settlement slung across their saddle.

They were headed south and east across easy rolling hill country to a creek about a mile and a half away. On the tributary several miners had set up their winter quarters. One of the campers was Benjamin Ford and his wife, Mary. Like all the miners, Sunday was a day of respite from the quest for gold. Men relaxed, went for supplies and a bit of recreation. Ford had gone to camp and come back drunk. The next morning Ford had arrived at another miner's site in tears, overcome with regret. He admitted to arguing with his wife. The argument escalated and, in a rage, Ford had fatally stabbed Mary. Eventually Ford settled down and in the spirit of contrition, the miner accompanied Ford back to his camp and found the wife deceased, laid out on their bed with her hands crossed on her chest over a Bible. Once presented with the evidence of his crime, Ford had broken down again and the miner rushed to tell the sad tale. The miner was in the fore of the posse, guiding the group to the scene.

The delegation picked their way up the narrow stream until they were forced to dismount and proceed on foot. Two men gratefully remained behind to tend the mounts. The others pressed on, silent and grim but determined. They had no expectations and each played out various scenes in their mind. Before long they came upon Ford's humble shelter.

The side of a short bluff had been excavated and a berm built along the top of the bluff. Two walls had been built of logs and part of a third wall completed the sides of the shelter. A roof of split logs supported the canvas and brush. The canvas hung down the incomplete side of the structure. Water dripped from the low side of the roof, ran into a crude wooden gutter and filled a barrel at the corner. Two other barrels stood nearby. There was a bench and a table outside along with various mining and household implements scattered about in the cleared yard or hung from the log wall. The canvas curtain was tied to the side, admitting some light to the otherwise dim interior. Smoke rose from one corner of the canvas roof. Someone was home. As shelters went in the gold fields, it was quite unremarkable other than being crafted better than most. The only oddity was four lengths of rope strung from the home to a crosspiece nailed to a tree.

"Mary took in washing," said their guide, solving the mystery of the clothesline. "She charged three dollars a dozen, shirts, socks, or linens. The price was dear but no one complained"

No one commented. The guide continued, more in reminisce than as explanation.

"She'd come by and pick up our bundles. Three days later she'd bring them back clean. I think we paid as much for having a woman to talk with as much as for the service."

"Let's get this done," said one of the men. The speaker was trying to light a pipe in the drizzle. He gave up in frustration and put the pipe away in his coat. "Call him out."

Nervously, the guide urged his horse forward just enough to separate himself from the group.

"Benjamin Ford. Are you there? It's Aaron Summers."

No response. No movement could be seen inside the shelter. The posse began wondering if the smoke was a ruse and Ford, anticipating his fate, was sitting up above them or in the woods, deciding which intruder to drill first. They began to spread out, eyes danced from trees to hillside to the shelter, seeking motion betraying the killer's lair. A dozen guns stood at the ready. Numbers wouldn't prevent an ambush.

"Benjamin. Are you t'home?" called the guide again.

"Hello the house," came another voice.

No answer.

"What shall we do?" said someone to no one in particular. No one wanted to be in charge.

"Maybe we could burn him out," suggested another.

"We don't even know if he's in there," said the man with the pipe. Eyes roamed the hillside and woods again.

"There's no horse or mule. He might've run," said Josh.

"Didn't have one," said the neighbor. "Had to sell it to get supplies."

"By chance he didn't have to sell a gun, did he?" asked another.

The guide shrugged. There was still no answer.

"Thinkin' he lit out on foot, says I" offered another man.

"And left us a fire to warm our hands? Maybe he left a pot of coffee on the stove for us, too."

"You're a contrary sumabitch, Hastings," said the pipe smoker.

Without direction, the men began to argue among themselves. Shipwash saw it was time to step forward.

"We've no choice but to look inside the house," he said, paying the shelter a compliment it didn't warrant. Duncan dismounted, handed the reins of his mount to the guide, and raised his empty hands wide.

"Benjamin Ford. We've heard your wife might be injured. We need to see if she's all right." Duncan took a few cautious steps forward. "I need to come in."

A voice, cracked with fatigue and emotion cried out. "Mary ain't injured. She's dead. I buried her this morning."

"Please. Show us where," pleaded Duncan

"Any of you a preacher?" came the voice. It seemed to be coming from the shelter but sound can be tricky in the hills, especially in the rain. "She would have wanted words spoke over her."

"No. No preacher amongst us. We need to talk to you. Are you armed?"

"Not no more. Powder got wet. If it was dry I'd a kilt myself already."

"I can't be certain of that. I'll have to ask you to show yourself," said Duncan.

"Who are you?"

"Duncan is my name. I'm no one in particular. You need to come out," he said, taking a few more tentative steps, scanning for available cover if needed. "I don't have a gun."

Bitter laughter answered Shipwash's declaration.

"Suppose your friends are unarmed, too."

"In light of what's transpired, they would be foolish not to be."

Time passed with no sound from the hut. It seemed even the rain paused as if in awaiting a reply. Finally, Ford spoke.

"I was there when those other two was hanged."

"Then you know you have to come back with us and stand trial."

Summers came up and joined Shipwash. His pistol was holstered but handy.

"Benjamin. It's Aaron. Please show us where you buried Mary. She shouldn't be left out here in the wild."

A wailing came from inside, then Ford collected his senses and stepped through the canvas and into view. Guns were raised but no one fired.

"Go ahead boys, I kilt my wife and I ain't denyin' it. I deserve it"

"He's not armed," said Summers. "Put up your weapons."

"I buried her in a spot she would like. I'll not have her dug up and buried next to drunks and gamblers."

There was general agreement on that point.

"Leave her be and I'll go with you. No trouble."

Someone pointed out Ford had no mount.

"I can borrow a mule," offered Summers.

"Thank you Aaron. You've always been a square pard."

Ford's hands were tied before him and they walked back to where the horses were kept. A mule was borrowed and they began the trip back to camp. After a bit, Ford began to open up.

"Boys, I done a low thing and I know what's comin'. I deserve no better."

"You never said what happened," said Summers.

"I come home drunk," Ford began. "I been just scrapin' by finding the color. I was down and just went to town for a little change of scenery. Mary never went on a spree. If she went anywhere it was when we needed supplies. I drank up and gambled away a whole week's panning. Hell, it din't amount to twenty dollars. When I come home broke and drunk Mary had just finished bundling up her work. She was tired and mad I'd spent it all. When she started talkin' about how she made more washin' other men's dirties than I made washing gold it turned ugly. I slapped her and she lit into me. Bein' drunk, and I know that's no excuse, I lit back and I picked up a knife off the table and stuck her."

Recalling the scene sent Ford back into despair.

"I knowed it was wrong when I first put the knife in my hand. I knew what was going to happen and I just did it. Oh boys, the look on her face when I stuck her was the awfulest thing I ever did seen. She just looked at me like she couldn't believe what happened. She tried to sit down but she never made it. She fell and looked at me one more time. I swear she never felt any pain but the hurt in her eyes was more than I could take. I run outside and left my poor, dear Mary to die on a dirt floor all alone."

Once Ford began his tale he could no more stop his wailing and recriminations than he could have stopped his knife arm. The riders were determined to be shut of the whole affair by the time they gained camp.

"I'm done with this," said Josh to Shipwash. "Ford done it and he deserves hangin' but I'll be damned if I'll be a part. I'm headed back to Elizabeth."

"Josh, I'm sorry you felt you needed to come along. I'm ashamed of myself for getting involved for the reason I did. I've put myself where I am and I'll see it through. I'll manage to get through these next few hours. I feel like I'm trying to legitimize a mob. This is going to have but one outcome and I'm a fool to think a sham trial is going to put things right."

"It's got to be done. It ain't how a trial should be done but the facts aren't going to change. He killed his wife and there's no goin' back on the fact. What's got to be done ought to be done as best as can be. I know no one here will be a better judge than you."

"It's kind of you to say it but it isn't going to help me feel any better about it. I'm going to get drunk after. I hope I have the good sense to buy a bottle and go home."

"You will. I can't picture you hanging in an alehouse with the crowd. I'll talk to you later."

~ ~ ~

The last kind thing Benjamin Ford did was to confess publicly what he'd done. The trial was over before the gallery could get decently drunk. Shipwash as judge, after the verdict was read, asked Ford if he had anything to say to the court. He did but it was not about his regrets or about his short future. It came out Ford had been pulling one of the ropes at the last hanging and he asked he be allowed to stand on the back of a wagon so when he dropped it would break his neck. He asked that he not be allowed to strangle. Perhaps the miners' court had unpleasant memories of the last execution. Perhaps they were just grateful for his confession but his request was quickly acceded to. He was given a last meal and swallowed enough whiskey to just allow him to stand.

Lots were drawn for hangman and wagon driver. The noose was placed over Ford's neck but it was felt the drop was not sufficient. There was a short delay in the proceedings until a stout crate could be placed in the wagon bed. The rope was adjusted. Ford declined any last words. He was by then too drunk to talk. The hangman drove the wagon away, not stopping to see what he had wrought. It was over for Ford in moments.

The crowd, as in the past instance, adjourned to a public house. The judge and jury were served drinks. When Duncan asked to buy a bottle he was given one for his service. He slunk away to his bed. The hangman did not join the crowd. The wagon, with Ford's body in it, was found tied to a rail the next morning. His civic duty done, the hangman returned to the anonymous life of a prospector.

CHAPTER THIRTEEN

By the end of February, the winter storms had abated to the point where the labor could keep ahead of the runoff in the pit. A ditch and berm had been constructed so the water cascading down the slope above the pit sluiced and carried away some of the future dig. The pumps were kept working so it was even money whether they were keeping ahead of the flow.

The ledge had played out, picked clean and just a granite bench remained. Before it gave up its last flake it had run for nearly a hundred feet and the harvest provided the company with supplies and a small, satisfying poke of gold for each man. The top of the ramp now commenced where the ledge ended and the deep end was back into paying ore. Duncan estimated they were pulling two ounces of clean gold per ton washed. The tailings at the wash site were growing steadily. Another pond had been built and a third tom added. The men realized the more they could wash the more they harvested.

The real moneymaker for the operation was not the mining but the felling and sawing of the wood lot behind their camp. The allure of digging ore with shovel and pick had vanished. Digging a hole was no more glamorous than swinging an axe, eating sawdust, or stacking lumber. The men rotated through the various crews. Both industries were equally exhausting but where one featured boredom the other near constant peril.

The community was growing up around them and the more prosperous businesses, sutlers, saloons, and fancy houses were now featuring wooden floors and walls. There were even a few buildings with wooden roof framing and bark shingling. The structures were a great improvement over the canvas tents and shanties of only a month before but the suggestion of permanence was still an elusive standard.

One of those businesses striving to project a substantial image was the new mine registry of Duncan Shipwash's. After all, who would go to a man in a tent to secure the rights to their claim? Duncan's service as judge at the Ford trial had served him well. He was recognized and when he convened several meetings to elaborate on his mining rights proposals they were well attended and discussed. At the last meeting the South Fork of the American River Mining District was proposed, seconded, and created by an overwhelming voice vote.

Surface claims were standardized at one hundred feet in length and sixty feet back from the center of the stream, active or dry. The original discovery of paying dirt brought in swarms of new prospectors simply on the rumor of a find. To reward the initial miner and to prevent him from being crowded off his own find, the man or organization was awarded an additional contiguous claim. All were to be clearly marked at the corners. A man could hold as many claims as he wished with the provision they be worked in some manner at least every ten days or they became forfeit to the first who could record the vacated claim. The movement of a minimum of one ton of earth or ore was sufficient and allowed a single prospector to protect his claim through the work provision.

A claim owner was allowed to form a company by selling "feet" in his claim. This did not mean a new partner had exclusive rights to any particular reach he had purchased but as a percentage of the entire length of a combined claim. A foot of a hundred foot claim would translate to a one percent stake, a foot of a combined claim would represent one half percent and so on. This allowed miners to merge their claims into one with a single work requirement for the combined reach. Shares within the claim could be apportioned by the rules of the partnership or new enterprise. Labor and material resources could then be pooled to reduce costs and make excavation more efficient.

The downside to this arrangement was the advent of speculation. A miner might offer a sutler, grocer, butcher, or tradesman feet in his claim based on its potential earnings. The worth of any foot in a claim was negotiated based on either the actual or the projected return. This in turn led to miners salting their claim to prove its viability. The prospective investor would be shown to the claim and a sample of the ore washed as a demonstration of its worth. A savvy investor would arm himself with some rudimentary knowledge of prospective sites within a claim and insist the sampling be done at a location of his specification. Buying into or selling a portion of a claim was an ongoing contest of wiles and deception. Disputes were bound to arise and soon the miners saw the need for a permanent or at least respectable board to settle grievances.

Duncan, as the sole recorder of claims, steadfastly refused to participate in any arbitration. He limited his role to recording the initial claim for the standard one-ounce of gold or twenty dollars in coin. He would retain a copy of any future partnerships or shares but his position required strict neutrality. Serving on a committee to settle disputes would easily embroil him and his office in an argument between feuding partners and no doubt one party would accuse the recorder of collusion in a swindle.

Duncan also refused to evaluate or assay any ore brought to him. First, he did not have the equipment or chemicals necessary to refine the gold from a sample of auriferous earth. Second, no miner would bring him anything less than the most profitable sample or even one that had been adulterated in order to increase the value of the claim on speculation. The closest he would come to refinement was to melt the gold brought to him as his fee in his crucible and retain the single ounce in payment. No amount of gold offered could elicit an opinion as to the worth of a claim.

A second, unanticipated benefit to this self-enforced neutrality was he insisted he not serve as judge, prosecutor, advocate, or jury in any criminal matter. Since Benjamin Ford had been hanged and buried in an impromptu grave far from his murdered wife, there had been three more murders. Each resulting in the swift justice of the miners' court and the execution of the guilty party before the sun went down on the day of the trial's conclusion. Two of the murders had been related to claims and mining. The third was between two gamblers over who would be permitted to fleece a mark who came to town with a sack of gold dust and an appetite for entertainment. The survivor was hanged but, if it was any consolation to the condemned, the jury found the victim would have been flogged and banished had he not bled out in the privy behind a tent tavern.

The Mining District, as the only organized body within its vaguely defined fiefdom, soon became the arbiter and enforcer of all matters. Common law and the United States Constitution were relied upon as the basis for all decisions. New laws were made as circumstance dictated. Minor offenses like vagrancy, vandalism, discharge of firearms in camp, or general hooliganism saddled the offenders with fines and public service. A refuse site was declared. A cemetery was established. A public square was dedicated and judgments were handed down providing funds and labor for their operation. The camp was slowly becoming a town. There was still no jail and no one wore a badge. Those convicted of vagrancy still slept where they might but would work off their fines with labor. What had been chaos now settled into a form of haphazard order.

Costs for everything remained high and freight costs kept pace. The cost of a barrel of corn meal would quadruple once it hit the beach in San Francisco and could easily quadruple again depending on the distance and ease of freighting. The Albany company of twenty-seven were now making a profit but more and more of their labor was consumed in keeping the men fed, clothed, and supplied. Luxuries or even the need for the odd necessity entered a sellers' market. Ordering something to be delivered could take weeks even if it were available elsewhere. The Albany men paid. They could not afford to stop digging or cutting timber to venture away.

Shortages became a way of life but soon one shortage threatened the operation of the long toms. At the terminus of the upper assembly was a metal plate punched with holes to allow the fine gold and sand to fall free into the lower riffle box. Tons and tons of material, as evidenced by the spoil piles near the wash site, tumbled down the chute of the toms. The wooden parts could be replaced in short order but the metal plates were wearing out at the punched holes. Large holes meant more grit went through and the final sifting gradually became more arduous and more importantly, slower. New plates were needed but finding them and shipping them were unknown factors. Then Josh came up with a solution.

His former home, the *Julianna Dolce,* had been copper sheathed. Even if the wreck had been savaged there should still be some of the plate left on the hull. He volunteered to depart that very morning to retrieve what he could and to buy other needed supplies. He made a list, accepted special requests from some of the men and carried letters home in the hope a reliable courier could be located. Once packed and ready Josh and Jubal wheeled the wagon down to Duncan's office to inform Elizabeth of his departure.

It was soon revealed the most reliable and settling feature of the recording office was not the new wooden edifice with its two precious windows but the presence of a woman to greet the arrivals as they entered. Just the presence of a woman, especially one so alluring as Elizabeth, some how gave men confidence in the institution. Perhaps it was the general scarcity of women in gold country but more likely the feminine reminder of mothers, wives, and girlfriends so distant in fact but so close in memory, instilled trust in the rugged miners. Soon, miners would not grace the threshold of the recording office without being dressed as cleanly and as orderly as the prevailing living conditions allowed. The recording of a new claim, ordinarily a happy event, became a celebratory social occasion as it allowed men to converse with a beautiful woman.

Josh had no pretenses of social grace as he stepped on to the wooden floor of the office. The feeling he got stepping inside a completed building reminded him of the time they first entered a wooden store at Fort Laramie after weeks of living out of doors or in a cramped wagon. Shipwash's office smelled a damn site better than the trader's store at Laramie. The specie at the fort was buffalo hides and they moldered all about the fort store. He took off his dilapidated slouch hat in deference and gawked out the glass window as if he had never seen one.

"I'm off," he announced. "Going back to the *Julianna.*"

"Whatever for?" asked his wife. Elizabeth was wearing a long pale green dress with a frilly bodice and an emerald green sash. Once the miners began dressing for their visit she couldn't well greet them in muddy boots and coarse workman's pants. She changed in an enclosed office each day and made a show of opening the office with a leisurely appearance on the front porch of the establishment. Duncan, had spruced up, as well. He wore his boots but had purchased several white shirts, a vest, and a cravat. He even sported a watch, with chain and fob, accepted as payment for a recording. The boots and pants spoke prospector, the other accroutements bespoke a gentlemen of commerce.

"I would wager he is on a mission to replace the worn iron plates in the wash machines," suggested Duncan from behind his desk. The desk suitably businesslike was as dearly bought as the window glass.

"Not iron but copper. The *Julianna* is sheathed in copper. It won't be as durable as the iron but I can take as much as I can carry."

"Would it be possible for you to inquire into a few articles for me?" asked Duncan.

"A row or two of books would look right at home in here," said Josh.

"I was thinking of some more utilitarian articles. A small quantity of quicksilver. Some nitric or other strong acid, and perhaps a magnet if one can be located."

Josh wrote down the items on a list he carried in his pocket, then gave Shipwash a puzzled look.

"Those are used in the analysis and refinement of gold ore," said Duncan in reply to the puzzlement.

"I thought you refused to assay any ore?"

"The refusal does not mean I should accept payment for my services in less than acceptable purity. Much of the dust circulating in commerce here is at best sixty percent precious."

"Gotcha." I'm pretty sure I can find a magnet but as for the other?"

"The Sonoran Mexicans working the southern mines utilize quicksilver. Perhaps if you might locate one of these miners?"

Josh put away his notes and made to depart, Elizabeth a few strides behind. Duncan's words chased him out the door.

"No books but perhaps if you can locate some newspapers?"

The couple stood under the shelter of the porch as the drizzle continued. Elizabeth had some questions before they kissed and said their by-your-leaves.

"How long will you be gone? Duncan and Jubal are becoming trying housemates. Neither speaks much beyond their day's labor and the course of the weather."

"I'm sure you will survive the absence of my witty conversation."

"Your conversation is a work in progress but there are other diversions I will miss while you are gone."

She stood close and reached inside his coat, boldly caressing him in public.

Josh, accustomed to her advances, did not but for a moment react in surprise.

"Perhaps you could come back to the cabin. I don't need to leave right this minute," offered Josh.

"That would mean changing from this dress, undressing and loving you, getting dressed again and then changing back when I come back here," said Elizabeth. "While tempting, I'll decline. Let the promise of what awaits your return hurry you back to me. But do take some of my dresses for a pattern.

"Three days at most and I'll be thinking of you the whole time."

They kissed enough for two days apart.

"Button your coat, please," she said. "You're missing me already."

~~~

With nothing but a footbridge across the creek separating their camp from the Albany operation everything they needed for their journey was carried across to the wagon. By the time they snapped the reins and urged the mules forward, both men and the team were soaked. The drizzle continued its dismal serenade as it fell on their hats protecting upturned collars. They put a piece of oilskin across their laps and rolled towards Sutter's Fort with only the creaking of the wagon and tack to compete with the dripping sky.

It was Josh's intention to drive straight through to the *Julianna* before buying any supplies. They would stay with the Van Volks at the *Embarcadero*, salvage what they could, and then stop again for supplies before stopping again at Sutter's Fort to fill out what could not be had elsewhere.

As it happened the road and the fords were in such poor condition they found themselves camping along the way between Sutter's and the landing, much as they had done when first leaving their exploratory mining expedition on the Middle Fork of the American. They made cold camp, Josh in the wagon bed and Jubal in his accustomed ground sheet and buffalo robe under. In the middle of the night the drizzle abated but the travelers, exhausted by the road, slept soundly under the last remnants dropping from the trees overhead.

The morning found them approaching the Van Volk bakery and eatery. In just the couple of months since their last visit the place had nearly doubled in size, featured rough-hewn tables and benches. The construction was still a canvas tent but the family had constructed a frame house with a wood shingled roof behind the business. It was partially painted and two workmen waited for the sun to dry the wood. The house was still crudely built. For windows, empty bottles had been mortared in place to admit light. Plate glass might be an unobtainable luxury but empty bottles were no rarity at the landing.

Just like the last time Josh had come to the bakery the smell of cinnamon was a beacon. Like the first time, a small sign hung over the entrance advising customers when the business would open. This time it was Josh who poked his head between the flaps of the tent and called for Willie or Hannah Van Volk. It was Hannah that peeked out of the kitchen. Her face, red from the heat, beamed a broad grin at him.

"Josh. We are most pleased you come back to us. Wilhelm. Come. Come now."

She raced to Josh and threw her arms around him like a rich uncle come to call. Willie came springing to join the embrace and almost bowled them all over. They dragged him along and saw Jubal following.

"Jubal. You come along," said Willie. "Have you had breakfast? Do you like duck?"

"Where is your pretty wife?" asked Hannah. "You didn't make her hold the horses, you beast?"

"No, she is back at the gold mine, pushing a wheel barrow, she's getting mighty strong, too."

Startled but for a second, Hannah caught the joke and laughed heartily.

"Now you are teasing me, telling me stories." She led them a real table and chairs. The two girls, miniatures of their parents, were seated along with a thin man wrapped near twice around in a long, clean apron. Upon spying the visitors, the girls leaped up, their studies forgotten. They climbed up on their chairs and threw out their arms for a hug. Whatever gloom may have trailed along with Josh and Jubal was instantly swept away with the welcoming of this happy family.

"Enough, girls," said Hannah, clapping her hands for attention. "We are about to open and you must put your studies away. Sit yourselves down. Willie is bringing you a special treat."

As they were sitting the thin man cleared his throat.

"Ah, I am being rude," said Hannah. "This is Harvey Tillman. He works here and teaches the girls. There is no school here, you realize."

"I was a teacher in Memphis, Tennessee. The Pendrake School. Perhaps you are acquainted with it?"

Josh was about to mention he had been to Memphis a time or two but was interrupted by Willie's return.

"Harvey. Bring our guests a plate of biscuits with the duck and gravy. Yes, and coffee, too."

"I'm a pretty fair mark with a fowling piece, too," said Tillman, stepping away to fill the plates.

"We keep Harvey busy. He works in the kitchen and dining room as well as hunting birds for us. The rest of the time he teaches the girls to read, spell, and cipher. There is no school here, you know."

"As I have just told them, father," said Hannah. "Show them our surprise."

Willie had come back to the table with a tray covered with a towel. He whipped away the towel and two glass tumblers of milk were unveiled. There was also a little pitcher with a spout.

"We have three dairy cows. How long since you have had fresh milk? Cream for your coffee, too," proudly declared Willie.

"It's been at least a year but it seems longer," said Josh. "By God, its good. How do you keep it cold? This sure is a treat isn't it, Jubal?"

"Truly is. Best thing I've had since those oranges and that seems forever ago."

"I pay a man to bring me ice from up the mountains. I've got big cans we keep in a metal box sunk in the earth." Willie couldn't help bragging a bit. "We charge two dollars a glass. It's gone in an hour. Of course, we wouldn't think of charging our friends."

"Looks like you are doing right well and you all seem so happy," said Josh as Tillman returned with steaming plates of biscuits with duck and gravy.

Willie laughed and slapped the table.

"We've truly been blessed. And to think it all started with a broken wagon and three barrels of dried apples. Now tell me about yourselves."

Josh told them about the Auburn partnership, the deep gravel claim, the long toms, and the washing gate. He told about the new mining district and how Elizabeth was working in the new claims office with Duncan. Hannah joined them for a moment and heckled Willie back to work in the kitchen. She lingered.

"I am glad to hear you are doing well with the gold. We hear stories about that camp you live in and worry for you. Folks have started to call it Hangtown."

Josh was a bit startled about the revelation but didn't want to enter into conversation about murders and hangings and miners' courts with a woman. Most of all he didn't want to reveal his part in the hangings or the apprehension of Benjamin Ford. It was time to lie a little.

"Oh, we have a camp across the river and far from the main camp. Except for a little footbridge we would be completely isolated from the goings on there. That's why we've come here for supplies and to ask a favor."

"You've done so much for us, it wouldn't be Christian to refuse you anything," said Hannah.

"Elizabeth has taken to dressing like a lady again and she needs clothes, shoes, and lady small clothes," said Josh, blushing at the last indelicacy.

Hannah was not fazed at all.

"Oh I know just the thing. There are two French couples who have cloth and do tailoring. Say no more. I know what to ask for and will go there myself after the crowd leaves. You would just make a mess of it, so I insist. Do you two need anything?

Josh laughed. "I suppose I could use new pants and shirts. We'll leave some extras here so the tailor will know the sizes for both of us. If I tried to order for myself I'd surely make a hash of that, too."

Producing a poke of gold, Josh asked if four ounces would suffice. Assured it would be, Josh told how he was headed to the shipwreck to secure copper plates and whatever salvage he could find and he would need the new clothes quickly.

"Oh, I should tell you," said Hannah. "Not long after you left men came to camp with two wagon loads of rice. There is but one place the sacks could have come from. I fear the boat may be pillaged."

"I haven't given much thought to it but it makes sense. The wreck is right up against a bluff and not a hundred steps from the trail. We'll just have to take our chances on what's left."

With that Hannah went back to work and the two girls came to visit while they ate. Of course they asked after Elizabeth but mostly wanted to show how well they had done their lessons. Each had a small chalkboard and they skillfully wrote out sentences and ciphered arithmetic problems, explaining how they worked the answers. Tillman appeared as capable a teacher as he was a harvester of birds.

~ ~ ~

They were both shocked when they arrived at the wreck of the *Julianna Dolce*. It had been picked clean, hardly more than the ribs remaining. The shoreline was littered with items taken and then abandoned. The corpse of their former home reminded Josh of the bones of draft animals left to bleach along the trail from Missouri. Many of the sheets of copper sheathing had been pried away but the job abandoned. A layer of pitch and tar had been applied to the hull and the copper sheet pressed home and nailed. By the time a plate could be pried away it was bent and creased so as to be useless for anything but smelting and where in Alta California was there a smelter. Josh, familiar with boats had brought the tools to remove the copper nails intact and then carefully shave the copper sheet away. What tar remained could be melted off in a campfire if necessary. It was tedious work, particularly salvaging the nails, but careful attention and diligence soon produced twenty sheets of about two feet by three. The gloves he wore were fair ruined and his clothing was stained.

He'd find some coal oil to remove it but was grateful they were all getting new clothes. These were more patches than original.

Their original goal completed they surveyed the rest of the hulk, as hulk it had become. Stranded not a hundred feet from the road, scavengers had picked the *Julianna* clean. The remaining masts and spars were gone, the deckhouse and even the deck had been salvaged. The bare ribs of the vessel had replaced the strakes above the copper. Only the difficulty of removing the copper plate had prevented complete dismantling. No capstan, no rail caps, no glass, no galley or stove.

On shore, at the ashes of a knacker's campfire, they found the remains of the binnacle. The compass was smashed and the brass stripped away. Digging in the carcass, Josh managed to retrieve four rare earth magnets, used to adjust deviations in the compass. One of Duncan's request fulfilled. Leaving with much less than they expected, Jubal drove the wagon and Josh picked tar from his clothes with the point of a knife.

CHAPTER FOURTEEN

Duncan had been called to the deep gravel excavation. The digging had come to bedrock at about eight feet of depth and the old stream diverted around a granite outcrop that split the stream for a hundred feet. The problem was which side of the old watercourse to excavate. Duncan had been called away to conduct some experimental overtures and guidance. Striking bedrock at such a shallow level and with the resultant invert smoothed over by time and current, nothing had been recovered. With a smooth surface whatever color had not accumulated. Swept over the falls the trail to the next honey hole had to be determined by more than just straight digging.

New claimants came in with fair regularity to record and pay for their staked claims. Miners came in with a sample to be washed, the one ounce fee extracted and the balance returned to the miner. It was no guarantee of absolute purity but having miners bring gold to the office was a lot better than digging it from the earth. Additionally each miner would submit a description of his claim with an elaboration of the boundary markers and whatever crude map they could produce.

Duncan, no great cartographer himself, was creating a rough map of the surrounding area and claims and hung it from the wall. There were as yet no surveyors to make accurate maps and the claims were spread out enough Duncan's chart was sufficient to keep the claims separate. Soon, with the arrival of spring and the exodus into the canyons and arroyos, competition and overlap would require a more accurate method. Elizabeth, in order to pass the time between customers, was making a fair copy of the rough map and labeling the claims by number cross-referenced with a file. It was tedious but necessary work. With Duncan gone, she was alone and kept her pepperbox hidden but handy. She was resting her eyes while lettering when the door opened and a miner leaned in, knocking on the jamb as if asking permission.

As was her custom while in the office to dress as a woman. Today she had on a patched calico dress. The hem had been replaced with some sailcloth that didn't match. Dresses were hard to keep clean when living in a village of mud. The elbows had been replaced and the seat was thin but she refused to draw attention to her behind with a patch. She wore a long cloth coat, distinguished from the miners own coat only by the brooch she had pinned to the lapel. She welcomed the arrival and waved him in.

The miner, knowing a woman was in the office, was freshly barbered, his face still red and scraped from the shave. His clothes were as clean as expected and sported more sewn on repairs than did Elizabeth's. He stared down at his muddy boots, hesitant to track the muck on to the wood floor.

"Good idea," said Elizabeth. "There's chairs on the porch and you can take off your boots and deposit them in that box by the door."

The miner blushed.

"My socks is an embarrassment, Ma'am. My toes is pokin' right through."

"And so would mine be if my mother hadn't showed me how to darn them."

"My ma never showed me how to fix my socks."

"I don't suppose she did. Never you mind I might be offended by the site of a man's toes."

"Thank you, ma'am," he said as he stepped outside to shed his boots.

"I'm supposing you came to put your claim in the books and not to just dawdle the day away."

"Yes'm," he said, forgetting his manners and so snatching his slouch hat from his head.

"And where is your claim?" said Elizabeth. "Come show me on this map and don't be shy about your lack of silk stockings and buckled shoes."

"It's up the creek a piece beyond where your camp is, up past even the lumber stand," he said, putting his finger on the chart.

"You know where I live?"

"Oh, no offense ma'am. There is so few women in camp everyone knows where each of them live. Nothing improper or familiar meant. Its more like back home everyone knew where to go for tobacco or soap or to get your horse shod and where everyone lived even if you didn't know them, you knew of them."

Elizabeth mulled it over and decided there was no harm despite the forward sense of it.

"You've marked your claim, made a map and a description and will agree to work the claim to keep it valid."

"Pardon me, ma'am, but is the proprietor in?"

"He's been called away but is expected to return." She didn't like the turn this was taking and edged a step to where she kept the pistol.

"I've got all the particulars required to record. No offense but I'm thinking the District register himself should do all the paperwork."

"We work together. Why would you need to deal directly with Mr. Shipwash?"

"I'm just thinkin' this is all to make my claim legal and all. I'm not certain a woman's signature on the papers is legal."

The miner saw he was walking an awkward path and corrected himself.

"I mean women can't vote or hold office so I'd just feel better having the official Register of Claim put his signature to everything. That way I'd know my claim was properly done and enforceable."

Elizabeth found herself at odd ends with the remark. The claims being recorded only had validity within the newly formed mining district. The district only had the authority it granted to itself. Once things settled out in Alta California it could be ruled that all of the land belonged to John Sutter through his Mexican grant. She couldn't fault the miners for wanting an elected official of the local authority as signatory on the recording documents. Duncan explained the limitations of the recording to each registrant.

"You are aware all the claims could be denied at some future time. We could all be kicked off of Captain Sutter's land."

The miner laughed. "Pardon, ma'am but I think that horse has already left the barn. Sutter's Mex claim ain't going to hold and we miners don't want to end up in the same boat. No doubt some government is going to form up and stick their hand in our pockets. We all expect that. I just want to have my claim approved by the highest authority we got today and that's the District Registrar."

"Sounds like you've thought this through."

"Well, mostly we talked it through, all the miners. With most mining on hold there ain't much to do except talk. We know there's going to come a day of reckoning and if we end up in a real court of law, the papers I'm waving around ought to the best I can get. This recording is just for today and it let's me partner up with other prospectors or sell part of what I got. It'll do for today."

Elizabeth saw all the man's points were valid. Even as she was a partner with Shipwash she was not on a district official. Even as a partner in the biggest working claim in the area, she would never be elected.

"Well then, let's just get the paperwork started. I didn't catch your name, sir."

"Wade Homely, ma'am." Homely paused for a moment, waiting to see if Elizabeth reacted to his name. She did not. "I come down from The Dalles in Oregon Territory this past summer but I'm originally from Kentucky. I come west to start a distillery and make whiskey. Now I'm diggin' holes and makin' liquor on the side. Curious times is what I say."

"You couldn't be more right. Strange times indeed, exciting though, don't you think?"

"Exciting ain't the word for it. I like my excitement with a bit less danger if you know what I mean. I just want to get this claim thing done and go back to my friends at camp up the far creek."

"Right," said Elizabeth. "You give me your description and map and we'll weigh out the fee. You check back late this afternoon and I'll send someone to fetch Mr. Shipwash for the signatures."

Together they worked on the preliminaries. When Homely left, she examined his map and was surprised at how concise it was. Homely's description said it bordered a claim filed a week before. She completed what she could and waited for Duncan to return.

Around three o'clock, Homely returned. He'd already removed his boots on the porch.

"I'm sorry, Mr. Homely. Mr. Shipwash still hasn't returned."

"I know I'm early but I wanted to let you know there's been another killin' and the camp is all riled up. It looks to work up to a hanging and I'm thinkin' you might be better off at your camp. I'll escort you back if you wish."

Upon reflection Elizabeth now noted there hadn't been much traffic to be seen through the windows. She didn't think she was in any danger but the camp would be caught up in the moment. Level headed and practical citizens would not be thinking of recording claims this day.

"Does the miner's court wish Mr. Shipwash to serve?"

"Uh, no ma'am. Trials all over. Just waiting for the wounded man to die to pass sentence."

"My Lord. What happened?"

"A miner was payin' for a drink with a pinch and caught the barkeep with tallow on his fingers so more dust would stick. The miner called him out and the barman pulled out an axe handle and beat the man down. Busted his skull and he's fixin' to die."

"And the trial is over already?"

"Hellfire…'scuse me ma'am. He dropped him in a saloon full of witnesses. They convened a trial right then and there and it was over in fifteen minutes. They caught him with sticky fingers and the axe handle in hand. Wasn't nothin' he could say to defend himself. He's tied to a chair and the victim is laid on the bar. No doubt he's a goner but they are waitin' for him to die before passing sentence. Others is drinkin' up enough courage and calling for stringin' him up right now."

"Thank you for coming to warn me. I'll take you up on your offer of an escort. We'll take all the paperwork with us and Duncan can finish it up when we arrive there. If you would just wait outside, I'll put on my boots and coat."

~ ~ ~

Duncan stood on the smooth, scoured bedrock of the exposed channel. On the left of the granite outcrop in the center lay an angled decline that disappeared into the unexcavated gravel. On the right, the smooth invert ended and narrowed above what had once been a waterfall.

When this stream flowed any crevices in the bedrock had eroded away and there was nothing to hold any gold in the flow. He was inclined to begin work underneath the overfall. It would be like a natural wash at the bottom, churning and whisking away the lighter material and allowing the color to settle. On the other hand, the left side was on the inside of a meandering. The water would slow and drop gold, as the velocity could no longer sustain the weight of the sediment.

If it dropped on a smooth surface it might well carry to the end of the bedrock but there was no telling how far downstream this might be.

A crew had already excavated both sides of the obstruction down about three feet and there was no sign of either the black sand or the blue clay. What they had removed was worthless overburden to be loaded and taken away. He made his decision and decided to work the fall. It was too narrow for more than two men to work. The crew could spell each other.

With the recent successes of cleaning up the inverts of the dry streams the men had assumed the attitude they were following a rainbow trail of gold to the leprechaun's pot at the end. The yield in the pans had been increasing but they had yet to pull out more than a couple hundred dollar pans. They had been accustomed to hard work and ample reward for their daily labor. Looking at the smooth scoured bedrock, it revealed a stream flowing with enough velocity and volume to keep any gold in suspension. There might well be a valuable pocket under the falls. There could also have been a change in topography since this stream descended at a steep angle. Seismic activity might have increased the flow in this reach or reduced a former torrent to a trickle. After all, the whole deep gravel project had been dry for centuries uncounted. Duncan looked about at the terrain for signs of stratification. There was nothing definitive.

Placer mining, even successful placer mining, could be deceptive for the prospector. While gold could be found within pockets in the bed or even along the banks, the gold did not originate in the stream. It was easy to imagine the proverbial leprechaun shoveling riches into the current at its source, letting the color flow downstream for the picking. The gold came from the erosion of earth and minerals from the hillsides above the banks. Exposed veins eroded and were sloughed off into the water from the sides. Heavier nuggets and growlers would almost immediately sink to the bottom and the dust and fine color would be carried down as long as the flow could keep it in suspension.

The reason there was so little mining during the winter along the forks of the American River was because the richer holdings upstream were nearly impossible to access in the rainy season. The rivers and streams flowed through defiles in the canyons that were so steep a man or a mule could not stand erect or even kneel without toppling over. Only in the dry months could a miner access the best sites by walking up the stream and over and around obstacles, itself a dangerous and difficult proposition.

It was these steep canyons and their winter erosion that fed the waters with gold. Where they were mining now was the remnant of a stream fed by the steep canyon walls. Upheavals and shifts in the earth had changed the course of the river. The topography had changed but the deposits remained. Another concern of Duncan's was the lack of any nuggets or heavier pieces. They had found but a few pickers, none as much as an ounce. This lack indicated they were not near the source of a vein or deposit that could be exploited. At some point in their excavation he expected to uncover a quartz vein like he'd harvested with the Bonners on the Middle Fork. Because the arroyo they'd found was also a dry one, he hoped the site would remain unexplored.

As he was considering the current strategy for the company claims Elizabeth arrived with a companion, Wade Homely. They had recording papers and maps for Duncan.

"There's stretches up the creek where my claim is, looks like this," he said, gazing down into the scoured bottom. "Ain't dry like this though. Peculiar thing is they are flowing the opposite direction from this here."

"And where is your claim again?" said Duncan, turning in his hands the crude map he had just signed but scarcely looked at.

The creek about half a mile south of here, runs into the river. My claim is up way back of the woodlot."

"The one that runs parallel to this dry one?"

"The very same. Folks been callin' it Hangtown Creek cause they do the hangings right across where the creek runs into the river," said Homely. "Pardon ma'am. Ladies don't need to hear such talk."

"I'm not repulsed or offended. I consider all that to be camp business and not mine. Please, Mr. Homely, tell the registrar of the latest trial."

"The Committee isn't going to ask me to participate again, I hope?"

"Nope. Trial's done," said Homely and he relayed the circumstances of the incident and trial.

"What will the sentence be if the victim recovers?" asked Duncan.

While Duncan was relieved his services on the miners' court were not required, it bothered him he now resided on the banks of Hangtown Creek. How would he address his infrequent letters home? The residents of Tyburn village near London must have faced the same dilemma. Setting frontier justice aside, Duncan was interested in something else Homely had said.

The peculiarity of another nearby scoured bedrock streambed flowing opposite from this one was intriguing. Over the ages there must have been an upheaval that changed the topography and grade. If he could find the point where the two geological plates diverged, it was quite possible to discover a quartz vein exposed like the one they discovered on the Middle Fork.

"Of the claims near you, has anyone been finding anything bigger than a picker?"

"Not that I've heard of," answered Homely. "Trouble is there's few places where you can dig a pan with the water up like it is. My partners and me, we been working the cut bank looking for pockets. It's blasted hard working on the side of a hill but we're finding enough to keep us goin' till summer comes. Some of what we found is what I'm payin' to record the claim."

Homely nodded toward Elizabeth who was carrying the papers for signature.

"Yes, of course, sorry to make you wait," said Shipwash, signing the papers using his field notebook as desk. "If you don't mind, I might pay you a visit in the next few days."

"You will be most welcome, sir," said Homely, putting his copies in an oilskin wrapper.

"I'll bring meat for supper. I know most are on short commons."

They shook hands and Homely departed.

"Elizabeth, I'm going to ask you to mind the office for a few days. I need to explore a bit."

"Might as well just close the office for a spell. It's your signature the miners are wanting, not mine."

"Very well, then." He replied. His mind was already planning his prospecting adventure.

~ ~ ~

In the meanwhile, Josh and Jubal had stayed an evening with the Van Volks and were now at Sutter's Fort. The clothes they had ordered were not ready but the tailor promised to freight them to their camp for an additional charge of five dollars. They had no choice and left the *Embarcadero* as shabbily dressed as when they arrived. During their two brief stays at the landing they had become aware of a change in the general outlook of the camp. When they first had arrived, the spirit of the camp had been one of eagerness and optimism. Residents and new arrivals were keyed up, ready for adventure and riches.

Two months of living in the rain and mud had taken the starch out of most miners. The enforced winter interlude of gold digging and stories of new finds and overnight riches had become a respite of survival. The only solace being in simple comforts of friends and an occasional pursuit of relief in a bottle of whiskey. For those that could afford it, some solace could be found in the decline of prices for luxury items, if fresh vegetables and fruits could be deemed luxurious. New arrivals came almost daily and set up the rudest of shelters. The basics like salted and pickled meats, flour, pans, picks, shovels, and other camp equipment still brought high prices. Whiskey prices stayed constant with a reliable demand. The stakes at the gambling tables had dropped and men were seeking labor to sustain themselves through the dismal hiatus. As a result, many of the shopkeepers had left the tent behind and constructed more permanent structures and homes for themselves.

Both the landing and the fort were still bustling with new arrivals and commerce carried on but the earlier eager sense of adventure and riches had been tempered by the enforced passage of the rainy season. It was even more palpable at Sutter's as its location was the last gateway and supply hub for miners headed to the diggings. Diggings they could now only view from afar. Argonauts felt imprisoned with the promise of wealth denied. Eagerness had become frustration and anxiety.

"I see your wagon is holding up well," said a voice to their side. Stephen Collier tipped his hat to them. The hat was new and water beaded on the wide brim. "Perhaps I could interest you in some new head gear. Your present ones seem to be in disrepair."

"Hello, Mr. Collier," said Josh. "Fact is, you do find us in the market for a number of items. Hats, at a fair price, might be counted among them."

"And where is your charming wife? Don't tell me you have traded her for your colored companion."

Josh let the remark pass. "And how are the fellows of Collier and Associates?"

"Lew Werther has gone to the coast. Flour is in short supply but we are hopeful to obtain some in San Francisco. By a miracle John Teague survives, though he is whittled down some. They took off his leg at the knee. He tends to my storefront. Perhaps you might come along to see him and to choose from amongst my humble wares."

Josh nodded. Collier stepped up on a spoke and swung into the wagon. He guided them through the traffic to a side street where Teague sat in a chair tipped against a canvas-covered stack of crated goods. He too sported a new hat and a plaid wool shirt. The stained buckskin pants remained, one leg now abbreviated at the knee. Behind him, in a tent, were planks loaded with boxes of produce. Cauliflower, broccoli, citrus, and onions were on display. Their colors shown like treasure amongst the drab muddy surroundings. Collier, noticing their attention drawn to the produce clapped them on the shoulders.

"Before you, gentlemen, is the finest selection of fruits and vegetables to be had in all of Alta California."

"I thought you specialized in equipping miners with the basics."

"I did and I will. Can't sell mining equipment when no one is able to mine. Those wares are under the tarps. For now we cater to those who demand more than flapjacks and pickled pork."

Collier let himself down from the wagon bed. Teague stood and snatched the hat off his baldhead. The snatch almost toppled him over. A half empty bottle of brown liquor sitting on a cask by the chair might have contributed to the wobble. Teague bumped against the cask and only a quick hand saved the bottle from going over.

"I recognize you. You bought my old wagon but you don't know how to use it. An empty wagon don't make no money." He laughed at his own wit.

"I might be convinced to fill the wagon with some of Mr. Collier's goods if we can come to an agreement. I'll wager you have boots, belts, shirts, pants, and the like under canvas somewhere."

With a customer asking for goods, Collier sidled up, assuring Josh he could fill his needs.

"I'm looking to equip two dozen men," said Josh. "providing we can strike a bargain."

"Just tell me what you require and I'm certain I can accommodate. Have you a list?"

Josh handed over what he was seeking. After a quick examination, one item caught his eye.

"I see quicksilver written here," said Collier. "Is there perhaps a medical need?"

"How's that?" asked Josh.

Collier was looking for a delicate way to inquire when Teague chimed in, "Docs use quicksilver to treat the French pox. Where you been dippin' your wick, sonny?"

Josh knew quicksilver was sometimes mixed into an ointment for lesions and such but he had no idea it was used for venereal diseases. He couldn't imagine the very proper Duncan Shipwash affected with whore's pox. He'd assumed Duncan wished to compound an ointment for his injured leg. Most of all he didn't want to discuss anything of such a delicate nature with the sutler and the one-legged muleskinner.

"I'm going to browse about the fort. Jubal will examine your goods and pick out what we might purchase."

Josh was a bit upset with Duncan for telling him to get some quicksilver without explaining why he needed it, especially to treat a sex sickness. Still, if he needed it, he wouldn't deny him because of some indelicacy. He set off to see the doctors at the sick room where he'd first encountered Teague. On the way he stopped to talk to a man selling cards of buttons, sewing notions, and soap. The man carried his wares in a wooden box and on his person. He could have spared a bar of soap for his own use. As he paid the man with a piece of Spanish silver coin, a voice called out his name. Turning about he faced Tom Billings. The last time he'd seen Billings he'd been drunk and sitting alongside Earl Coody, the muleskinner who crossed the Sierras with the Bonner group. Billings had been the first white man he met in Alta California. He'd accompanied *Senor Vallejo's vaqueros* as a translator. Billings was a guest of the rich *patron* who had sent men to rescue people crossing the high passes before winter closed them off. Billings'

145

attire had suffered some since they'd last met. Other than the mud on his boots he still dressed respectably, though his clothes now bore some patches at elbow and knee.

"Pleased to see you again. Very pleased indeed. Have you made your fortune yet, and how is the charming Mrs. Bonner?"

Josh hadn't taken to Billings even from the first. He struck him as a presumptuous ass and particularly he didn't like the man's flirtatious manner with Elizabeth. The last thing he wanted to discuss were his prospects and his wife.

"I recall you were the guest of a Mexican rancher. Are you still staying at his farm?"

"*Rancho Suisin* is the name. Farm is too bucolic a term for the property if you take my meaning. I am staying with the *Vallejo* family, though their property and holdings are sadly being diminished by the day, it seems."

"Last I saw you, you was with Earl Coody. Went partners with him in a cartage business, was it?"

"So to speak. I sometimes buy a few things and sell a few things. Coody transports them to and from the market. Mostly I use the proceeds to help out my hosts during these confusing times."

"Confusing is a kind way of saying lawless," said Josh.

"That, too. Just look about and see what has happened to Sutter's holdings, overrun by poachers, thieves, and drunks. None of them even so much as giving him a how you do. But enough of the unpleasant. Tell me how you fare and what you are up to."

"Elizabeth and I are partners in a gold mine but nowadays who isn't. We've hooked up with a company of men from New York and we have a mining engineer who has us working some deep gravel diggings near the South Fork. I'm up here for supplies, mostly clothes. Seems mining is tough on clothes. Got a few other items on my list. You wouldn't know where I could get some quicksilver?"

From the look on Billings face it appeared Josh was the only person in Alta California who didn't know mercury was used for whore sickness.

"Our mining engineer wants some," Josh added quickly.

"Indeed, and I might just know where some might be purchased. Unfortunately not here. I visited John Fremont this past summer and he has some veteran Mexican miners working his land. They use quicksilver to bind up with gold from their quartz operations."

"That so. How do they use it?"

"Truthfully, I couldn't tell you. Colonel Fremont showed me a ball of quicksilver and gold about the size of an apple and with the consistency of a ripe tomato. He cautioned me about how handling it could make a person ill and said something about an affinity for gold. I was most taken with the curiosity of it all and wasn't paying much attention to his explanation. Still, I might obtain some for you if you can bear the cost."

"What might that be?"

"I never inquired, though I seem to recall it is extracted from cinnabar which is mined in Spain."

Billing seemed quite pleased being able to recall the nugget of information.

"I'm headed off to see one of the physicians. They say quicksilver is used in medicines so I might be able to buy some from a doctor."

"Then let us be off. If we can establish a value then perhaps I might procure some and then visit you at your mine. Other than trying to assist my host with the day to day travails, there is little entertainment to be had in winter."

At the extremes of the camp a pestilence tent had been set up to mitigate the spread of the various communicable afflictions. Rather than expose themselves Josh and Tom visited the hospital inside the fort. When first Josh had come to Sutter's fort he was looking for Earl Teague to buy a wagon. Teague had been convalescing at the small hospital set up in one of the alcoves along the fort's outer wall. With the influx of new Argonauts the ground floor of the main building in the fort had become the hospital. Sutter had graciously turned over the ground floor of the main building to care for the injured. Sutter now had an office on the second floor. From his original grant of over one hundred and fifty thousand acres, the residence and office at the fort and a plot of farmland was all that Sutter could lay claim to. He'd turned over the management of his affairs to his son and was building a new home at the farm plot.

Josh and Tom watched a doctor patch up a man who had pinched his fingers while loading a wagon. The doctor splinted them, gave the man twenty drops of laudanum and assured him they looked worse than they actually were. Tom commented how he hoped so as they couldn't look much worse and still be attached.

The gray-haired doctor looked over the top of his spectacles at what he took for new patients though nothing apparently was wrong with them.

"Well, what ails you two?" he said testily. "You don't look hurt, drunk, or demented."

"Nothing is wrong," said Josh. "I just came to inquire about buying some quicksilver."

"Pissin' fire, are ye? Drop yer trousers and we'll have a look. One ounce payment before you lose your pants."

"I'm a married man. I have no need for medical assistance."

The doctor sniffed at him as if marriage was some magical inoculation against venereal disease. He turned on his stool and motioned Josh to come near.

"No, sir. You misunderstand. I've been told quicksilver is used in gold mining and I've been tasked to acquire some.

"I've been told that myself," said the doctor, "but I've always taken it for alchemy foorah. What are you supposed to do with it?"

"I've held a ball of quicksilver and gold in my own hand," said Billings. "Supposedly it sticks to gold and nothing else."

"And then what?" The doctor was showing a bit of interest.

"I've no idea," said Billings.

"You've got gold?"

"Do you have quicksilver?"

The doctor went to a wooden chest sitting on a nearby table. He returned with a stoppered, thick blue glass vessel. It looked to contain about half a pint. With a warning to be careful of the weight, he handed it to Josh.

"Why, this must weigh five pounds," said Josh, astonished.

The doctor produced a stone mortar and took the vial back from Josh, pouring about half a tablespoon into the mortar. The glistening liquid formed a cohesive bubble in the bottom.

"If you want to test this with your gold, I'll sell you one pound for..." He hesitated. "Twenty dollars."

"Consider it done," said Josh, producing a small leather poke. The three gathered around as Josh shook out a small spoon's worth into the mortar. The doctor had ready a pestle but before he could begin to use it, the gold began to disappear into the quicksilver. A moment's attention with the stone pestle and the quicksilver looked no different but there was a good pinch of black sand accumulated around it. The doctor tipped the silvery liquid out into a shot glass. It looked no different than when first poured out but the gold had vanished.

"Damn, that's as close to magic as I've ever seen. I'm no chemist beyond mixing up poultices and ointments. Any idea how to get the gold back?"

Josh and Billings shook their heads. So did the doctor.

"Will you sell me two pounds?" asked Josh.

The doctor may not have been a chemist but he did recognize an opportunity.

"Forty dollars and your disappeared gold will be in the two pounds. The look he gave Josh said there would be no bargaining. "I'll toss in a vial for it," the doctor conceded.

Josh agreed.

"Come watch me weigh this out. Two pounds ain't gooin' to look like much so I want you to attend to the scales."

The doctor set a small scoop on the scales, added weight to balance at zero, then added a combination of weights equaling two pounds.

"Satisfied?"

Josh nodded.

The doctor poured the contents of the shot glass into the scoop, then carefully tipped out more mercury from the blue vial. When it balanced out, there was what looked like about two ounces in the scoop. Buyer and seller nodded assent to the measure. Using a funnel, the doc poured the shimmering liquid into another blue glass vial with a rubber coated glass stopper. It was astonishing how the metal moved. It didn't pour like water or cream or even oil. It seemed to just move in one piece all at once. One moment it was in the scoop and the next it was down the funnel and gone. The scale was adjusted and Josh paid out forty dollars in gold dust. The doctor cautioned them about handling it and they departed. The doctor's next patient, a man with his arm in a cast and a sling, was waiting.

"I'd never seen the like before. It's like that stuff just ate the gold up," said Josh.

"I wish I had paid attention when I was at Fremont's. It appears my native ignorance is well served by my lack of curiosity."

"I'm sure Duncan, my partner, will know what to do with this stuff."

By the time they returned to Collier's store, an assortment of goods had been brought out. Collier refused to dicker with Jubal so they waited for him to return. Before they began, Jubal had something of more import to tell. He pulled Josh off to the side where they could talk in private.

"I was with Collier going through the stacks looking for boots when I heard a voice I knew comin' from the bar tent on the next lot. Couldn't place it at first but then it come to me. It was Reverend Clark."

"Are you sure?"

"No. I can't be certain but his is a voice you don't forget."

"I'll grant you that. His is a voice designed to be heard. Did you go and look."

"Couldn't. Collier wasn't about to leave me alone back with his goods."

"I can't say I'd believe a preacher was in a saloon but after he took off with Captain Metzger's horse, I've got to say I've doubts about him bein' a preacher"

"Bein' a preacher don't mean a man ain't greedy. The idea of gold changes a man. Changed us."

"I s'pose so but it didn't turn us into thieves."

"That's so but we been lucky. You're a boat mechanic and I'm a farm hand. Now we mine owners and got more money than ever we imagined. Temptation is harder for those who want."

"How 'bout those dead Indians we found on the trail. Didn't it cross your mind it might have been Clark?"

"Did for a minute but I think it was Paiutes. Clark's greedy and a thief and he's got a temper but I just don't see that kind of bad in him."

"I suppose," said Josh. "Maybe he's still riding Metzger's Trinket."

"And maybe I just heard wrong. Plenty of men talk loud when they's drunk."

"All right. We'll settle up for our goods and then go look into this."

"Settling up might take a bit. The man says he wants fifteen dollars a shirt and twelve for boots."

Jubal was right. Eventually they paid twice as much for half the goods they expected. There was nothing to be done but to go directly to San Francisco with their wagons and even then there was no assurance of supply or better prices. It was becoming a challenge to produce enough gold just to keep the enterprise functioning, much less turn a profit.

~ ~ ~

By the time Josh and Jubal left Collier's store it was nearly dark when they found themselves across the thoroughfare from the tent saloon. The inside of the bar was lit and shadows painted the tent walls. Even though Clark was a big man there was no hope of him posing in silhouette even if he was inside. The odds were against it. The stolen dappled gray was not to be seen and two hours of drinking time had elapsed since they'd talked by the rear of the tent. The sound from the saloon was boisterous but no single voiced carried above the others. Josh moved closer and tried to peer inside as more or less sober men entered and more or less drunken men stumbled out.

Even if Clark was still inside, Josh wondered what was holding him from going in to look. Josh wasn't physically afraid of Clark. Eluding a big drunk was hardly a challenge. His hesitation was based solely upon having his doubts about the preacher confirmed. If Clark was a man of the cloth fallen from grace that was one thing. If the man were a complete fraud it was something else. It would mean his marriage was likely a fraud, too. Deciding that a confirmation of fraud was no worse than not knowing, he stepped through the tent flaps after pulling down his hat and snugging up his coat collar.

If he was concerned about being recognized any anxiety disappeared instantly. With the exception of the bartender in white shirt and apron, every man was dressed in the uniform of the mines. The only difference in attire was the degree of shabbiness and the number of patches decorating the clothing. There were differences in the degree of sobriety but no one paid any more attention than they did the fashion and style of the man drinking next to him.

While Josh had looked into many a rough whiskey seller's tent before, this was his first visit. This unnamed establishment was somewhat improved from those he had seen. Enough booze had been sold the usual plank set on barrels had been replaced by a bar constructed of empty liquor cases. The bar was wider and a log lay in front of the bar as an impromptu foot rail. There was a back bar built of cases and displaying the limited selection of bottles and glassware of choice.

There was an open area between the bar and the tent opening. On either side were rough trestle tables with short sections of tree trunk for stools. Many men just chose to sit on the table edge. One man was laid out on a tabletop. His friends stood guard over him and talked over his prostrate form. If there was gambling it wasn't apparent. Perhaps there was something going on behind the back bar and not seen from the public room. The main room was illuminated by a wire encased lantern hanging from the ridgepole. Two more lanterns sat on the top of the back bar. Mirrors had been set behind them. The mirrors were the only touch of class in the establishment over and above the bartender's white shirt, shabby as it was with filthy cuffs. There was no food and no women. The place was singularly devoted to the drinker.

On closer examination a fiddle player may have provided entertainment. He was asleep with his head on one of the tables, fiddle beside him in a case. The smells of camp and its inhabitants was concentrated in the confinement inside the walls of the tent. No breeze blew through to disperse the miasma of unwashed bodies, smoke, and alcohol. Josh pulled his hat low and tugged his collar high as he wove through swaying men at the bar.

"Shots are fifty cents. Whiskey, brandy, or rum. No beer," said the bartender in a bored voice. "What'll it be?"

"I'm looking for an acquaintance, a friend of mine. I was told he was here earlier."

"So were a lot of people. If you aren't buying then stand aside." The barman made a pretense of wiping the top of the bar.

"Whiskey then," said Josh.

A glass was produced and a faintly tinged brown liquid was poured. The whiskey was either raw or diluted. Josh risked a sip and the liquor went hot down his throat and spread in his stomach with a pleasant warmth. It wasn't diluted. He produced his poke of dust for the bar man to take a pinch. When he looked carefully at the man's fingertips, it did not go unnoticed. The barman turned his fingers up for examination.

"We run a square shop. A fair pinch for a fair pour, says I,"

He took a pinch from the poke between thumb and finger, showing it to Josh before rubbing his fingers clear over a small wooden box on the back bar. He closed the lid before asking if Josh wanted another. Josh had only taken the one sip and put his palm over the glass to decline. The barkeep nodded and went to another customer waving around an empty shot.

Josh counted fourteen customers and none of them were bulky enough to be Clark. Several sported beards that would vie with the preachers. Clark's distinctive room-dominating voice did not stand out above the general din of competing drunk talk. Josh nursed his drink as he watched the goings on. When he finished the bartender descended. Josh pointed to the glass. The glass was filled. Josh produced his poke again.

"The man I'm looking for is a big man. Fat but it's a hard fat. Big beard and a voice that gets your attention like a train whistle."

"Big man, big voice, big beard. This feller got a name?"

"Goes by Dayton Clark," Josh answered.

"Goes by, does he?" scoffed the bartender. "There's a big man with a foghorn for a voice been in here a few times. Keeps the beard close so it probably ain't your friend. Want to pay for that drink now?"

The bartender stuck his fingers in the bag, looked Josh in the eye.

"You want to hear about this friend of yours that might or might not have a beard?"

153

Josh nodded and the man dug deeper in the sack, produced a large pinch and displayed it to Josh before transferring it to the wooden box. Josh downed half of the shot and fought against sputtering.

"This man comes in here couple times a week. He's comes in with two, sometimes three friends. With those boys he goes by Dan Higgins. Think that could be your man?"

"Maybe. Big, broad face, kind of fleshy. Maybe forty years or a little more?

"Could be. It's the size and voice sets this feller apart. A glass just disappears in his hands and he gets louder as he drinks. Ain't pleasant but no one has yet objected."

"Sounds like a lot of men I've seen," said Josh. "How's this man dressed?"

"You might be on to something. This Dan Higgins dresses like everyone else but he sports a black claw hammer coat and a vest. Keeps both clean and brushed. Just havin' clean clothes sets the man apart."

"I don't recall much about how the man I'm looking for is dressed," said Josh. He hoped his face didn't give anything away but, taken with the rest of the description, the coat and vest sure sounded like Reverend Clark.

"How about his friends? Anything stand out about them."

"One's southern from his accent," said the bartender. "We get all kinds in here but your man and his pals ain't the kind I like to serve. The only thing I can say about them is they is the wrong kind of customer. Ain't nothin' happened yet but a little bullying but when they get in their cups, my other customers stop drinkin' and make themselves gone. Let's just say they ain't the type is good for business."

Josh finished the shot while he thought of other questions. Before he could come up another the bartender spoke up.

"Son, I'll tell you this for free. I can see you ain't the kind to run with these fellers. They's the kind that finds trouble and you got a look about you says I hope you don't find your "friend" and his pals in my tavern. Fact is, I hope you don't find them at all. Here. Have one on me."

He produced a bottle from somewhere and poured out a rich brown liquor; poured it right to the brim.

"That's real Kentucky bourbon," he said with some pride. "Enjoy it and promise me you won't find those boys in my place."

"I don't mean to bring any trouble to you, mister. I was just curious if the man I know is in these parts. Not even certain if the two are the same. Thanks for the drink."

Outside, Josh climbed up on the wagon bench with Jubal.

"For sure the man you heard was Clark. He's goin' by Dan Higgins these days."

"He got friends in there?" asked Jubal.

"He's got a crowd he runs with but whether they be friends ain't certain."

"We goin' to look for him?"

"I don't know what I might say or do if I did," said Josh. "Let's take a tour of the camp and see if we see him or maybe Metzger's horse if he's still riding it."

They took a slow tour of the camp. No Clark and no familiar horse. Josh was hardly paying attention. The revelation the man who presided at the Bonner wedding was no preacher was a heavy weight. After an hour with no results they turned for home.

~ ~ ~

"Dan. Wake up, Dan. There was a man askin' questions about you down at Joe Allen's saloon. Wake up, dammit!" He gave the sleeping man a great shake and stepped back. Dan Higgins always woke up in a foul temper.

"Jesus, Pete. What the hell you doin'?" said the man known as Dan Higgins. He swung a vicious elbow and connected with nothing. "Who's looking for me? What did he look like?"

From a safe distance Pete replied, "Young guy, dark hair. Clean-shaven, but stubbly. Hell, looks like pretty much everyone else here but he's maybe twenty. Got into a wagon with some nigger."

"What did the nigra look like?"

"Hell, I don't know. There's precious few to pick from in these parts. You know these two?"

The big man wasn't absolutely sure but he'd be surprised if it wasn't that Bonner sprout and his darkie.

"I know a lot of people and you ain't told me much. They still around?" Higgins pulled on his boots, knocking over a mostly empty bottle in the process. He caught up the bottle and swigged a quick drink. He tucked his pants into the tops of the boots.

"I asked you a question."

"Yuh, still here. They was drivin' around the streets like they was lookin' fer someone or something."

"You should of come for me right away. What did Joe Allen say about me?"

"Just said a big man with a big voice and a beard comes in fairly regular, that's all," Pete replied. Pete liked drinking at Joe Allen's place and if he told everything to Dan, Joe would pay the price and that would end drinking in one more local saloon.

"Where was they last you saw them?"

"By the main gate. The man went in and the nigger waited on the wagon. You goin' to find them?"

"Somebody asking questions about me. Damn right I'm going to find them."

"Want me to come along?"

"If it was any of your business, you could come along. It ain't so you sit here and think on what else Joe Allen might of said about me."

Higgins stepped out of the tent into the dark. Pete started to think on where they would drink after Joe Allen's place closed up.

~ ~ ~

The man called Higgins didn't need anyone from the wagon train he deserted poking around for his former self, the Reverend Dayton Clark. He didn't need anyone spying out the horse he stole from the wagon train captain, either. If anyone from his past was looking for him, he needed to know who and why and then nip it off before people started asking questions.

There didn't seem to be, if he kept to the shadows, much chance of two men in a wagon finding him. He wasn't about to parade down the middle of the thoroughfare shouting out if anyone was looking for him. He'd steal along the streets behind the tents and stores watching the gaps. There were more people on the street at night and they all looked about the same. Two men on a wagon seat and one of them a darkie would be easy to spot.

After finding no wagon at the gate to the fort he decided to find a vantage point where he could watch unseen. Going into the fort was too exposed. He'd find a place to hole up. He stepped into the shadowy gap between a sutler's store and a butcher's shop. He couldn't decide whether the smell of dead meat from the butcher's was worse than the piss in the dark space between the two. From here he could see down one street and watch the main intersection. Eventually most everyone passed by this corner. Reflecting, he wished he'd bought the bottle to keep him company in his vigil.

He'd chosen his spot well. Before too many minutes went by along came a wagon loaded with goods. As the wagon passed a tent barroom with a lantern outside the entrance he could see the darkie driving. He was certain enough it was the scout. The other man was wearing a broad hat pulled down but in the scant light from the lamp he could see it was a young man, a common enough site in the gold camps. Put the two together and he decided it was Bonner and his man. He watched them pause by the saloon and peer inside. The younger man jumped down and stood under the lantern, looking in without being obvious. As he turned away the light fell full on his face. Sure enough, it was Bonner. The two talked for a moment and then turned down the muddy road to the south of the camp.

The big man slipped from concealment and followed the wagon down the road. Twice more they stopped by a bar and the sneaking about was repeated. At the south end of camp they continued on. He guessed they had gone into the freight business and were either headed to the Hangtown camp or the winter camp on Amador Creek.

Determined to pursue them, Higgins knew he would need a grubstake if he were to start over in another camp. He'd drunk up and gambled away nearly all but the clothes he stood up in. There wasn't time to work a swindle and even that would require more seed money than he had. In hard times he'd resorted to violence and this was hard times. All he need do is find some prosperous looking fellow and relieve him of his valuables. Finding such a man in a mining camp was a double-edged sword. The rich and the poor all dressed the same so it would just be a guess who to rob. The other edge was the robber was dressed just like the victim, making identification as difficult as culling the rich from the destitute.

After a bit of thought he decided a merchant would be his best bet. He crept amongst the rear of the tents looking for a darkened tent. Finding a row of three provisioner's tents he selected the middle one. Slow as the hands of a clock, he pulled the cords securing the tent flaps and slipped inside. He stood in the shadow, listening for the sound of sleep and cursing the noise from the street. Just as his nerve was about to desert him, he caught the stuttering sound of someone snoring and tossing in a bed. As his eyes grew accustomed to the gloom he spied movement on a cot set near the canvas partition dividing the store. Providence was truly smiling on him, guiding his feet stealthily forward until he stood over his victim. With his left hand he peeled back the covers over the dreaming man. With his right he raised a leather sap. A bald spot on the crown of the head was revealed. He put his hand over the man's mouth and was rewarded with eyes snapping open. At the moment the eyes found him he struck once, twice to be sure.

Once, while serving time on a chain gang, Higgins had met a pickpocket. The man practiced relentlessly, honing his craft for when he was released. Higgins almost laughed out loud at the memory. Picking a man's pocket was so much easier when he was unconscious. As he began to rummage through the mark's clothing his hand found some leather thongs tied to the frame of the cot. Tracing the rawhide he found they led to a pair of leather sacks. He weighed each with his hand and thanked the Good Lord for guiding his hand this fine evening. Before he left the scene he listened to see if the victim was breathing. Feeling the man's breath on the back of his hand he considered strangling him. He changed his mind, as there was no satisfaction in throttling the oblivious. God had smiled on his industry this evening but there was no sense in testing the grace of the Almighty.

Higgins was all smiles as he walked towards his tent. He kept a hand in each pocket, weighing and guessing the value of the two pokes of gold. He decided to stop off for a drink though he would not need John Barleycorn to help him find a peaceful sleep tonight. He'd get an early start and catch up to his quarry after a good breakfast.

No rush, he could catch up in the morning. It was time he moved on anyway. He garnered harsh words around camp and his reputation was spreading. The notions of justice in the camp were harsh and swift. The last thing he wanted was someone calling him out as a horse thief or to be dragged in front of a drunken kangaroo court. Hangtown had even a sterner reputation but there was plenty of wild country along the way where he could settle Bonner's hash and no one be the wiser. Already he'd skated by on flimsy but true accusations from miners. The accumulation of finger pointing was bound to catch him out.

He'd been on the run since leaving his given name of Eli Dixon and his Alabama birthplace behind. Over the years he'd developed a knack of sensing when it was time to skedaddle. No sense bathing in a kettle waiting for the water to boil. He arrived at his tent. Pete, Crowell, and Chapin were playing poker by candlelight when he came in.

"Boys, I'm done with Sutter's Fort. I met up with the two looking for me. They are friends of mine from Georgia and they offered me better prospects in other parts. I'm leavin' come sunup tomorrow."

"You gonna leave us behind just like that?" asked Ned Chapin. The card game, forgotten.

"You can stay or go as you please. I'm just saying I'm packed and gone after breakfast."

The trio started pestering him with questions. Over the time he'd spent with him, they'd come to depend on him for directions to scurrilous sources of income. Once more he told them he was leaving and they began protesting he stay with them.

"You boys take it outside. I need my sleep. If you be ready when I leave you can tag along. If not, it's been good to know you."

Dixon had always been a solitary man. He'd always relied on his guile to get by. In the camps the opportunity for swindles were rare. Soon she would be relying on his fists to earn and that was dangerous. Worse, his companions were starting to think they were too smart to be caught. Chapin and Crowell had enough undeserved confidence to think they could get by on their own. Likely they wouldn't come along. No doubt they would be stretching a rope or getting flogged out of some camp before the New Year was done. Pete had more sense or at least enough brains to know his own limitations. It would be good to have Stringer along but who could tell what that man was thinking. In the morning he'd see who was with him.

~ ~ ~

After breakfast Jubal was putting the mules in harness as Josh broke camp and buried the coals of the fire. The sun hadn't risen from behind the mountains enough to dispel the gloom of the forest. A wind had kicked up with the new morning and the branches above them clattered together as they set out. They hadn't gone many miles before their breath before them disappeared. There were high clouds blowing in but it was promising to be a fair day.

"Some of these trees is starting to bud," said Jubal, pointing into the branches.

"If that's the first sign of spring, I welcome it," said Josh. He wasn't up for a conversation, concentrating on whether the man they sought was the wayward preacher. Lots of things to be considered. They rode on in silence, just enjoying the morning.

From behind they heard the approach of a rider in a hurry. Soon a horse and rider appeared, riding quickly but at a comfortable pace for both. The rider slowed as he approached. Having experience with road agents, Josh drew his Walker Colt and lay it under the blanket in his lap. It was unlikely a single robber would take on two men but careful is as careful does. As he drew abreast of Josh, either the man was careful himself or a bold highwayman. In addition to the flintlock holstered at his belt he carried a brace of pistols in scabbards on either side of his saddle. He was surely dressed differently than the run of the average miner. Instead of the slouch hat the man sported a voluminous knit hat and instead of the wool shirt so common in the camps, he wore a bulky knit sweater. It had once been white or at least a natural weave. The sleeves and color were stained a dark gray. The rest of the sweater was trying to catch up.

"Mornin' gents," said the rider. "Where you headed?"

The rider grinned, showing a straight set of teeth stained to a shade matching his sweater. Josh didn't like the man's looks and felt no compunction against lying to him.

"Down the road to the camps to sell our wares."

"Hangtown maybe?"

"Hangtown certainly unless we sell out before."

"Absalom Peterson's the name. I know it's a mouthful so I just go by Pete. What's yours?

"I'm Josh and this is Jubal," said Josh. He regretted saying before the words were gone but it was just a courtesy common on the road. The man started to lean over to shake hands. Josh managed to press on the brake handle without being obvious. The man moved forward, no doubt aware of the slight.

"Hangtown then," said Pete. "Maybe I'll see you there."

"You're in a plumb hurry," said Josh. "You hear news of a fresh strike."

The man grinned. Josh was glad he wasn't close enough to smell his breath.

"No such luck. I heard there is mail being held for me. Haven't heard from my kin in months."

Pete flicked his reins and was gone.

"What do you make of that?" asked Jubal.

"That he was armed to the teeth or that he stopped to jaw with us?" said Josh, pulling the Walker Colt from under the blanket and sliding it back in the holster.

"Either of the two. You didn't seem to take to him any, lettin' the wagon lurch forward."

"These tracks between settlements ain't safe. You and Duncan know first hand and I put three more in the ground as they was robbin' those two brothers. Don't pay not to be careful."

"Suppose you be right. Cain't be to careful," Jubal agreed. He took the pepperbox from by his thigh and put it back in his coat pocket.

"Way Absolute Peterson or whatever his name was ought to come tearing back by here in the other direction later this afternoon." Said Josh. They both had a laugh over the idea.

But it was only a few miles along the road when they once again made Peterson's acquaintance, or at least spied him out. A ways off the track, too far to hail, a man was building a campfire. Even at a hundred feet it was difficult to tell one miner from another but next to the fledgling fire was the same bay mare with the white blaze and white socks, same as Peterson was galloping along on. The horse was washy from being ridden hard and there was no mistaking the saddle holsters or the knit hat the man wore. As they passed the man waved and the greeting was returned. No words were exchanged.

"Now why would a man all in a hurry to get his mail just stop to make coffee?" wondered Josh.

"Maybe didn't want to use up his horse," ventured Jubal.

"That horse wasn't even breathin' hard when we saw him. Now he stops in a meadow a hundred yards off the road and breaks out his tea service."

"Just looks like a plain old coffee pot to me."

"I just meant its peculiar. His behavior I mean."

"Reckon so," said Jubal. He turned his head to get another eyeful of the man and horse.

"What else I reckon is he ain't headin' to Hangtown or to anywheres else. I think he was just riding along until he found us. Now he's waitin' for friends."

"You think he might be Clark's man or whatever he's goin' by now?"

"Whether he is or he ain't we'd best figure it that way. This just don't seem right."

"You want to lay up somewhere's ahead and see?"

"No. That ain't on my mind at all. We both had run ins on the road and I ain't lookin' for another. What I want to do is get home before they catch us. From now till home we are teamsters and we're burnin' daylight and money by dawdlin'."

Jubal snapped the reins over the mules. He yelled "Gee" at them. It startled the animals from their reverie and they picked up the pace. Jubal had them trained well. The road was no more than a trace of convenience. He had to hold on to the wagon with both hands. When there were relatively smooth stretches, he ventured a look behind, half expecting the big preacher at the head of a dozen cutthroats on horseback.

CHAPTER FIFTEEN

If miners wishing to register a claim knocked on the door of the registrar's office, they were disappointed. The office was closed and a hand-lettered sign in the window affirmed it. No date of re-opening was provided. The registrar and his assistant were absent, intent on prospecting for a new claim of their own.

Just before dawn Duncan and Elizabeth crossed the footbridge over Hangtown Creek and headed upstream. Over the mountains the eastern sky was a shade of lavender fading to pink as the sun crested the peaks and erased the stars from the sky. The two prospectors came upon a few scattered tents and lean-tos with banked campfires trailing wisps of smoke. Before approaching a camp they turned off the footpath and stole into the forest. No doubt they awoke some campers as they pushed through brush and snapped branches underfoot. No voice challenged them. People stumbled around in the woods day and night. In any event they soon left the camps by the creek behind. They decided to rest until full daylight where a geological survey might be more fruitful. The early departure was just to avoid attention. They sat quietly, enjoying shadows appear and songbirds stirring as the day unfolded before them.

"The deep gravel diggings we are working sits well above this creek and they lie parallel to it but the dry diggings are in a streambed flowing in the opposite direction from the current one. No doubt some upheaval or shift in the bedrock caused this. We are seeking the point of demarcation. Most likely this will appear as a bluff or a short cliff, perhaps buried by millennia of erosion."

Elizabeth had heard Duncan tell her the same thing last night and before that at the office. Now they were in the field the concept was no longer in the abstract. The land may reveal its secrets to Duncan but it was just a long shallow descent on the right with a slope and some upthrust granite as the land fell away on the left. If she put her mind to it she could see where the land might have turned back on itself like a stairway that curved round at the landing. She didn't have Duncan's eye for the lay of the land. The trees, living and fallen, broke up the landscape as did the clumps of granite and tumbles of half buried boulders. She just couldn't unwind countless centuries of erosion and movement like he could. He would scurry from one clump of rocks to another like a squirrel seeking nuts, pause, look about and scramble off to the next spot that drew his interest. She followed along and tried to pay attention to his ongoing chatter. He was pre-occupied and in his own world so he didn't see the crude encampment about two hundred feet ahead of them.

"Duncan," she said in a stage whisper. He paid no attention. She raised her voice and repeated his name two more times before he turned to look at her.

"Ahead, on the right. See the campfire," she said. He swiveled around, reminding her once again of a squirrel, this time a squirrel wary of a predator.

The camp was little more than a lean-to of limbs laid against a cut bluff and covered with a canvas and a few pine boughs. A small fire was burning under a coffee pot hung on an iron frame over the tiny nest of flames. A man in a robe stood on the other side of the fire. Behind him was another man standing in the opening of the lean-to. It was a curious looking camp as there was no sign of any mining equipment. No pans, picks, shovels, or rockers. The men were not armed unless the one had something under his robe. Nevertheless Elizabeth put her hand in her satchel and gripped the pepperbox. The two parties just looked at each other as Duncan and Elizabeth approached. As they got closer Elizabeth saw the robe was actually a dirty cassock with a muddy and hastily mended hem. Could the man be a priest? If so what was he doing out in the middle of nowhere. The man stuck his arm out straight with the palm facing them.

"Please, come no closer," he said.

They were still too far for conversation so they took another ten steps before halting.

"Please, for your own good, come no closer. We have sickness," he said. His voice was imploring, almost desperate.

His words were effective. Duncan and Elizabeth retreated five steps.

"Do you need help?" asked Duncan.

"What kind of sickness?" asked Elizabeth. Unbidden her voice rose. Having lost her family to cholera she was very cautious to avoid the stricken.

"My name is Martin Clement. I am a Jesuit priest and I am seeking help for my friends at the Mission Santa Cruz."

"So you say, mister. How many are you and what kind of plague do you have? How many sick?" said Elizabeth as she tightened the grip on her pistol and stepped sideways near a large tree she could duck behind. As she did the man in the door of the lean-to, perceiving a threat to his friend, stepped into the light.

"Leprosy," said Duncan. "The man has leprosy." The single word sucked all the warmth out of the day and a cloud seemed to pall the sky.

Father Clement stepped around the fire, both hands out in supplication. Two more bodies appeared in the shelter but remained in the shadows.

"Please no closer. We mean no harm. We are lost and only need directions and...perhaps if you could spare some food?"

"Intending no harm doesn't mean you don't bring it," said Elizabeth. She had never seen a leper before but even giving voice to the word struck terror in her. The priest didn't look ill. The man who had stepped forward had some small lumps and some scale on his face but otherwise he only looked foreign. Shipwash put his arm on hers, hoping to quiet her outburst.

"I've seen this before. Let me deal with them, please," he said to her.

"Perhaps you better explain yourself, Father," he said to Clement.

"Yes, yes. Of course," said the priest. He began his tale.

"My friends are from the Sandwich Islands. Each has shown signs of the early stages of the scourge. We had heard there was treatment available in Alta California at the Mission Santa Cruz. The Abbot, acting on the rumor of treatment and because these men showed no symptoms yet, decided to send them to California and the mission. As they don't speak English, I was sent along."

"Kanakas," said Shipwash.

"As you say," said Clement, continuing his tale.

"On board the ship two of my charges began to exhibit the disease on their face and hands. The crew was nearly crazy, imprisoned they felt with lepers. With a rope they managed to snare one of my patients and hoisted him aloft and over the side. When they came for the rest, and probably me too, I beseeched the captain for mercy. I told him if sulfur were burned it would defeat the spread of the disease. He agreed to put us in the cable tier and they burned little pans of sulfur all around us. It is a wonder we didn't choke to death. Maybe that was their plan all along."

"I never heard of sulfur being used on leprosy."

"Neither had the captain, or for that matter did I but I convinced him and that is how we survived. However, we never landed at Monterey, our destination. To a man, officers and crew, it was decided to go to San Francisco, abandon the ship and go to search for gold. The winds were better for San Francisco and no one wanted to remain on board what they felt was a plagued ship. As we came into the bay, the crew put us in a small cutter and cast us off. We watched them sail away and said a prayer for their final Christian charity. At least we felt it was charity until we realized they wouldn't be allowed to land if leprosy was aboard. Then the tide turned and we had to row all night to keep from being swept out to sea. At night the wind turned onshore so we raised a small sail and went past the town, determined to reach Monterey. The wind died and the flood tide carried up the bay and away from the south arm towards where we wanted to go. We beached the boat and headed overland but now we are lost."

"You're about as lost as a body can get," said Duncan. "You need to cross the creek that's just downhill of us a ways and then head into the woods. Turn left and you will come to a river. That's the American. Find a place to cross and stay in the foothills. Maybe you can find a Mexican who will direct you to a Papist priest and he can help you. There's men camped along the creek and the river so wait till night and avoid any miners. I doubt you will find them any more charitable than your shipmates."

"And you? Are you charitable?"

"I don't get your meaning."

"He means food. He wants us to give him food."

"Oh, yes. Certainly. We'll leave you what we have but you need to leave these parts. Do it tonight as I will be back with men in the morning and we will burn you out and devil take the hindmost."

"God Bless the both of you," said Clement. "We will be long gone by next daybreak. Thank you. We all thank you."

"Its just the right thing to do," said Duncan. "Meeting you has not been a pleasure, believe me. You've taken the joy from the day and soured me for prospecting for a while."

Elizabeth emptied out the scant provisions she'd brought. She didn't even keep the containers or anything else except her canteen. Duncan did the same and they retreated. Once more Duncan warned them to be gone by the time they returned with others.

"Did you mean what you said about coming back with others?" said Elizabeth. "If others know there are lepers here they will shoot them down and burn the bodies. The priest too."

"No. That was just to get them gone. Tomorrow you and I will come back and burn that camp clean. Then we'll burn it again before we file a claim on it."

"A claim? I don't want to even think about that place, much less file a claim on it."

"Did you see the face of that bluff where the lean-to was?"

"I should say no. I was looking at the leper as I'd never seen one before."

"If you'd let your eyes ramble a bit you'd have seen that whole face was veined with white quartz. Those pitiful souls camped at just the spot we were looking for."

~ ~ ~

Instead of going back to the creek, Elizabeth and Duncan walked along the old watercourse towards their dry diggings. As they walked they passed the wood lot on the bluff above them. Duncan was again in his own world, absently describing the possibilities of exploiting a quartz claim. It was Elizabeth who noticed it first.

"Do you hear that?"

"Begging your pardon, Hear what?"

"Just listen."

"Branches rattling in the wind. Some birds. What did you hear?"

"Nothing else and that's the point. The timber lot is right above us and there is no sound of men working. They should have been at it by now."

They didn't speculate but continued on until, a couple hundred paces ahead they saw the entire company gathered by the exposed bedrock excavation. Finally they were spotted. Luder stepped from the crowd and called to them.

"Come quickly. You'll want to see this. Glory be!"

And glory be it was. The rubble from the overfalls had been removed and what was left was a natural dam comprised of large boulders that trapped material behind it. The men had rolled away the boulders and were filling buckets with black sand. The sand was being loaded on wagons lined up to take the finds to the wash area.

"Looks like we've struck it," exclaimed Fellowes. "This is even better than the bench upstream."

He produced a pan of what was being loaded up and offered it to the two new arrivals.

"Lord, you can just see the gold mixed in." He stirred his finger around in the dirt and gold glinted in the sun. He handed the pan over and Duncan repeated the exercise before handing the pan to Elizabeth. At first she thought they were all agog over some pyrite but tilting the pan, the glitter remained. Pyrite's gleam would fade as the reflected light changed on its surface.

"This is real isn't it? Just as it come off the shovel?"

"You bet it is, Mrs. Bonner. We brought a tub of water down. Why don't you wash that pan yourself."

Elizabeth sat down on a stump set by the washtub and began the slow, regular dip and tip action Texas Billy had taught her last fall when they first arrived. There were few pebbles to pick. The contents were a bit different than the black sand that was the harbinger of gold. This was similar but had a bluish cast. There was no silt. The water stayed clear in the pan and as she rocked, tipped, and spilled, she could see fine gold begin to accumulate behind the shallow ridge hammered into the pan's bottom. If the company hadn't been standing over her shoulder and watching the gold appear like magic she might even have heard some of the larger pieces of gold rattle along the bottom of the pan. Even without hearing them she could feel them. Growlers, she thought. She knew that larger pieces of gold, being individually heavier, sank first and indicated they were close to the source. As she washed, she imagined the timeless stream scouring away course down to bedrock and the gold tumbling along under a cloud of silt until it tumbled over the falls and was trapped by the boulders stuck in the narrow gap.

Finally, the pan was empty save for its treasure. There, like a smile in the bottom, was an arc of almost pure gold. There were half a dozen of the growlers, pieces no bigger than the nail on her pinky finger and a dozen more tiny individual pieces the miners called "pickers." She had seen only a few pans with more wealth in them and that was last fall, when she along with Josh and Duncan had cleaned out a similar cache in an afternoon and taken out over two thousand dollars.

"How much is here, do you think?" She asked, turning to Duncan. The men crowded around looking at the pan like children around a pan of fudge.

"I would say there is close to four ounces there. An eighty dollar pan if I'm right," he said. "You say there is more like this?" The crowd erupted in laughter.

"Barrels of it," came a voice from one of the men and another cheer rose up. No wonder there wasn't a soul sawing planks or felling trees.

Elias Fellowes, usually the most constrained of men, wore a grin as broad as the band of gold in Elizabeth's wash. He thrust a pan into Duncan's hands.

"See for yourself. There's plenty more and we ain't touched the bottom yet."

"Seriously?" exclaimed Duncan. "There should be cracks full of color once you do. I'd love to see it before you pry it out."

Duncan quickly and expertly washed his pan and with much the same result as Elizabeth's sample. The men cheered like drunken madmen. It was early and perhaps a few had already celebrated. Who could blame them?

Shipwash was as excited as any man present, but it did not mean he abandoned his discipline. He remained on the stump by the tub and cast his eyes toward the excavation above and upstream. If they were finding more than dust than the source was nearby. It would take a careful examination of the terrain. He would do that but for now he simply grinned back at Fellowes, at the miners, at Elizabeth, and at the golden smile in the bottom of the pan.

~~~

Despite Josh's imagination and the visions of pursuit he conjured up, the travelers arrived home without incident. They turned off the path before the bridge and worked their way down to the camp tents. They too noticed the lack of activity or people along the crude street but not for long. Before they even got to the first tent they heard the excited hullabaloo carrying to them from the wash site.

"That cheerin' ain't because they are washin' gravel," said Josh.

"I s'pose you want to go down there and make sure," said Jubal.

"Well, hell yes," said Josh but the wagon had already lurched forward. Passing the deserted tents of the Albany company, they slowed only to take the descending curve from the bluff and left towards the river. The uproar from the gold machines kept up a steady buzz and once more reached a crescendo as another pan of color was culled from the spoil it slept beside for ages gone by.

The whole company was crowded about one of the long toms. Some were shoveling ore from barrels into the upper end. A few men lined up along one side and, on occasion, plunged fingers into the passing current attempting to seize a spot of color that flashed before them. Each time they were successful, they hoisted aloft their find, their companions cheered. At the lower end of the upper section two men stirred the accumulation on the perforated plate with their fingers. Once in a while they found a piece of gold the men above had missed.

The real concentration of activity was at the lower end of the machine. Gold was being caught in the riffle boards and backing up. Two men with camp spoons were busy removing the line of gold before it piled up and could escape over the slats. A third man held a pan where they emptied the spoons. When filled he would hand the pan to whoever's turn it was to do the final wash. Taking turns, each man became the bringer of wealth. Everyone, Elizabeth included, hovered over the lucky crewman, watching riches appear as if by magic.

It must have been a great find. Elias Fellowes, the most stoic of the bunch and boss of the woodlot, was dancing a jig by himself. Each glance over the shoulders of his friends to gaze at the wondrous pans set him off dancing afresh. He still managed to be the first to notice Josh and Jubal's arrival in the wagon.

"Come. Come see! Its more gold than any of us has ever seen!'" yelled Fellowes before succumbing to the dance.

Josh had stepped down and was walking to the party when he noticed he was walking alone. Jubal remained on the wagon board, reins in hand.

"You comin'? However much they found, you own a part."

"You go on. They don't know I'm a partner and it's best they think I'm just hired on."

"Well, Dammit! Its time they found out."

"Ain't no time gonna be a good time for that. You go. The mules need tendin' to anyways." Not waiting for a reply of wanting to discuss it, Jubal pulled the team about and headed back to where the animals were picketed.

Josh thought him a stubborn cuss but was anxious to see how great the find might be.

The first thing Josh noticed was one of the men emptying a pan of washed gold into a Dutch oven. Typically, as the gold was washed the pans were emptied into a fry pan. The fray pan was then taken back to camp, put over a fire to dry it, and then put into metal cans to be weighed. The weight was noted and recorded into the ledger, witnessed each day by a different member. Today they were dumping fry pans half filled with gold, flake, fine, and picker into the Dutch oven. Crowding in and looking over shoulders Josh saw a mound of gold growing in the pot's bottom. The weight was beyond his guess but he could see this washing would be weighed in pounds, not ounces.

The men in the Albany company had reason to rejoice. The dry gravel diggings had been producing in fits and starts. The seventy percent shared out amongst the current twenty-one members had been paying them board and a daily wage. Men in the camp would work for wages only because the winter had shut down their prospecting. Once the canyons and streams could be worked, men in the camp would be departing to explore. With a find like this it was doubtful the men would leave. Josh had returned to camp, despondent he had spent almost all the accumulated wealth on supplies priced so dear as to break the company. For the time being the concern was gone.

Elizabeth was so enraptured with watching the gold appear in the pans she hadn't noticed Josh's return. When she did she ran to him and threw her arms about him.

"Isn't it wonderful? This is more gold than even we found on the Middle Fork last fall."

"I should leave camp more often. Appears I'm a jinx on the whole operation."

"I was saying the same thing to Duncan just this morning," she said. "We found another quartz vein like in that arroyo, too. Once we uncovered that, we decided you should be run out of camp for the Jonah you are. I'm sure the miners' court will agree but we will insist you not be tarred and feathered."

It had been some time since Josh had seen her so exuberant. He'd forgotten how much more fetching she was when excited. She kissed him full on the mouth and squeezed him tightly over and over. The men watching the washing were distracted by her antics and his discomfiture. Their laughter and comments were all in good humor but Josh disliked the public display. Elizabeth, usually not averse to being the center of attention, stopped her antics and for once, blushed as red as her hair. The laughter and hazing redoubled as Josh led her away.

"What about this quartz find?"

"I'll let Duncan tell you about it. I only have a vague idea of how he found it and less about what to do with it. Besides, there was an interesting turn to the tale that should only be revealed privately."

"Well, now you have to tell me."

Elizabeth would not be dissuaded so she changed the subject.

"Tell me of the goings on in the outside world," she said. "How are the Van Volks? Did you managed to get new clothes? How about shoes? What are the prices like?"

Josh knew her well enough to know the interesting turn would have to wait.

"The Van Volks have nearly doubled their business. They have a frame house behind the bakery and have hired help. They even have a cow. I couldn't help but think we chose badly when we decided to prospect instead of mining the miners. I couldn't find shoes or a cobbler so you will have to wear boots under your new Paris fashions. As it turns out, I have some news. It will have to wait for later, too."

"No!" protested his wife. "The day has been so good to us. You must tell all."

Knowing there would be no end to it until he revealed his news, Josh told her about Clark, now going as Higgins, living at Sutter's.

"I never laid eyes on him though we looked. Worse, I have a suspicion he's taken up with some hard men and they might be coming here."

Elizabeth's reaction was far different from what Josh expected.

"Bother on Clark or whatever he calls himself now. Damn his eyes and damn to hell with his band of thieves," exclaimed Elizabeth. "There is nothing he can do to us here."

"We already figured he wasn't no preacher and that means we ain't really married. Suppose he starts tellin' tales?"

"And what if he does? Joshua Bonner. Do you not know me well enough to know I don't give a bird's nest for what people think or say?"

"We should get married...again. In a church and official like."

"And we shall but the only churches are the Catholic missions and I'm not about to become a Papist so some black-robed friar can swing incense over our vows."

"People will talk."

"So they will. We are the richest people in all of camp and all the rivers around. Let them talk about that. We'll eat oysters and drink champagne while they wag their tongues like old biddies."

~~~

The company was still washing their pay dirt when Josh and Elizabeth managed to yank Shipwash from the crowd. Josh gave him a quick summary of the purchases and pressed the blue vial of quicksilver into his hand.

"That little bit was forty dollars and some of what's in there is our own gold besides. Don't think I ever made a stranger purchase."

"Forty dollars that will pay itself out many times over. I'll show you how it works down at the claims office. Actually I was thinking I will spend the night there. I may have to remain there for several days as the business has been neglected these past few days."

Living in the small camp with Jubal and the Bonners afforded little privacy for the married couple. Since the claims office had opened,

173

Duncan and Jubal had begun sleeping there when they got the sense the two lovers needed time apart.

"Elizabeth says you found a quartz vein and she wants you to tell me about it. Can we step up to the main camp so we can talk. I could use some food, too."

Duncan caught Elizabeth's eye and not in any discrete fashion either. Josh saw their exchange and how Shipwash was assured she hadn't spilled the news of the lepers.

"Yes. Yes, of course. Let us go now. Everyone is watching their fortunes being revealed," said Duncan. "Where is Jubal?"

"He's up there now unloading the wagon. You can tell us all and save another telling."

Elizabeth interrupted, "Let Duncan tell you first, and then you decide how much to share with Jubal."

Josh puzzled as to why he should learn first but figured the why would come with Duncan's telling

"I've recorded several claims, promising ones, for miners upstream of the creek by our camp. It puzzled me because we are working a dry riverbed that flows in the opposite direction. I concluded land upheaval must have created a point where the two met in some precipitous uplift or decline in the geology. If there were such a boundary it is likely a face of earth would be created much like in the arroyo we explored in the fall. Gold would wash down from the face of the bluff and on into the creek. Elizabeth and I got up early and went searching for such a place."

"And you found it?" said Josh, excited by the prospect.

"I was following clues in the contours of the land when we stumbled upon a lean-to set against a bluff. Camped there was a priest traveling with some afflicted with leprosy. I couldn't tell how many."

"Good Lord. One is enough to make my blood run cold."

Speaking the name had the expected effect on Josh, as it would almost any American. Leprosy was very rare in North America, but most Americans were acquainted with the wasting disease from the Bible. From Leviticus to Matthew, the Good Book told tales of those cursed to slowly rot away.

"They were seeking a mission to care for them. We gave them directions and some food. They are gone."

"You aren't tellin' me you sat down to lunch with them?" asked Josh in disbelief.

"Josh. This is no joke," said Elizabeth. "We never came within thirty feet of them. What food we had we left for them and came back. Now listen up."

Duncan continued, "What I noticed while talking to the priest was the shelter they built was adjacent to a large vein of quartz that ran up the side of the bluff. I could see no more but it's likely the vein may well be crevassed with ancient gold."

"It can stay where it lies," said Josh, involuntarily giving up a shiver as he pictured the site. "A pocketful of gold is no good to a dead man."

"Our plan is to return with lamp oil," Duncan explained. "Toss brush onto the site and burn it clean. Fire will purify the camp and we can take samples from the quartz. It may take black powder and that will serve to further remove any trace of the pestilence."

"And you haven't told the others yet?" said Josh.

Elizabeth replied, "No, and once it's burnt clean we don't see any need for them to know, either."

"You don't think a fire and an explosion might raise some questions?"

"By then any trace of the disease will be gone. We can just tell them we had to burn the brush away from the quartz and the explosion will be part of the exploration and that part is the truth."

"The lepers have had the pestilence since the day they set foot in Alta California. If it's going to take hold, nothing we do is going to stop it. At least we are purifying the place where they slept," Elizabeth said.

"Every trace must be burnt up," agreed Josh. "It is the only way."

"You can't tell anyone. If word gets out we even saw some lepers we will be permanent outcasts."

"Well then, when you go to do the burnin' I'm going with you. You two are liable to set the whole woods afire."

"You aren't afraid?" asked Elizabeth.

"Course I'm afraid but if you got it, I'll eventually get it unless I kick you out of my bed."

Elizabeth laughed. "You always did strike me as a selfish man."

With the matter settled, Josh grabbed some bread and some ham, took fixins' to Jubal, and they went back to watch the magic of the gold appearing. While gathered around the washtub Josh reflected on leprosy. If his woman and his partner were sick, then so was all the rest of the company. There was nothing to be done. If they were going to get it, they would all at least die rich. He wished Doc Bingham were here so he could ask him.

CHAPTER SIXTEEN

By the next morning, news of the rich findings in the dry creek had somehow spread to the main camp across the river. When the Albany men arrived back at their washings the embankment above them was lined with miners. It didn't appear anyone had visited in the night and taken even so much as a bucket of the rich ore. The claims rules, at least for the time being, were holding. It couldn't be helped that miners would come to watch. As a precaution no member ventured back to the source of their riches. Nor would any member admit to slipping out of camp to celebrate their new wealth a few drinks in a saloon. Still, the word was out and the curious gathered to watch the goings on.

With the distraction no one noticed three people slip away into the woods laden with prospecting tools, blankets, and a metal can of lamp oil. The trio trudged down the length of their claim and past the cairn of rocks that marked its end. Not ten steps beyond groups of miners were poking about in the dirt and scouring the hillsides for likely places to prospect. Duncan, Elizabeth, and Josh left the old streambed and dropped down to where Duncan had explored the day before. As they approached the creek, men were scrambling up and down the banks of the creek. No one seemed to be using any method to their prospecting. It was if news of a strike set off a frenzy as wild and uncoordinated as kicking a nest of hornets.

Men were digging at the foot of nearly every bluff and washing a test pan in buckets and tubs of water they had carried from the nearby creek. If they found anything promising they would move along the base of the slope until they found nothing. They would then, using the limits of successful prospect pans, move up the hillside, pan by pan in a narrowing triangle towards the top. Gold, when released by the earth would wash down a hillside. As it moved it was not in a straight line but in an ever expanding swath. The wide end of a rough triangle would lie at the bottom of a slope and taper up to wherever the source was. At best this was hit and miss and a single pan of color was enough to start men digging like badgers, almost always to no avail. Those with some experience would follow the rifts and folds of the landscape, searching for a spot where it appeared an ancient rill of water had carried down a slope to a resting place in a depression or small bowl on the slope. Often thick brush or trees that grew from the pocket of groundwater or subterranean flow concealed this. As much as the prospectors studied the lay of the land, it still remained a matter of pure luck.

Duncan was well known in camp. His background was known and as the first to exploit the dry gravel diggings above the American were well known. After the pocket currently being washed men looked up from their random diggings and began to follow him like a Biblical prophet. Shipwash was at a loss. He couldn't order them to leave yet he didn't want to lead the whole camp to a likely spot he hadn't examined. There was nothing to do but to press on. Eventually they arrived, with a dozen miners in tow, to the leper's shelter by the quartz vein.

"Keep walking," he said to his companions.

About a hundred feet away they stopped. Duncan did some pecking away at the rock with his hammer and then turned the findings over slowly in his palm. Studying the land he moved back towards the quartz vein, repeating the ritual until he had the full attention of the miners observing his research. Finally, he picked a spot and started piling brush against the bluff. He added some small dead branches and primed the pile with a little lamp oil before lighting it and stepping back to watch the results. To sustain the blaze, he occasionally tossed on more dead branches. Finally, the fire subsided and left a blackened surface. Duncan stepped closely and examined the scorched earth. He puzzled over it, even going so far as to put chin in hand and lean close to the slope. Next, he took his rock hammer and scratched a deep vertical groove in the dirt. He leaned in, peered closely and put his finger in several places as he ruminating over the evidence.

Finally, he called to the spellbound crowd, "Come over, boys. Let me show you."

The miners, including Josh and Elizabeth, quickly gathered around to better hear the wisdom being imparted.

"Building a fire helps make the geological striations more visible, as you can plainly see here."

He pointed to several different points in the dirt. The men shuffled in. After a few moments men began to wisely nod but no one said anything.

"While this does not directly give an indicator of the color, it does draw a picture of the land's history and movement. Let us move on and repeat the experiment. The miners scattered to gather brush and branches and the illustration was repeated twice more with no more conclusive results than the first demonstration.

"Hah, this is interesting," said Shipwash as he approached the leper's campsite and the diagonal run of white quartz. "This might be tricky. Perhaps you might let me set and tend the fire myself, please."

The miners scurried to gather materials as Duncan perused the rock face and made a show of placing the combustibles to the best scientific advantage. He lit the fire and stepped back to observe. Quickly it became apparent the engineer was reckless in his construction. Fire spread across the ground and lit the stockpile of fuel in the immediate vicinity.

"Oh, I must have spilled lamp oil all about." Men, don't try to put the fire out just keep it from spreading. Some of you up the bluff so embers don't carry away and burn down the whole forest."

The miners began clearing fuel away but it still burned for a good twenty minutes before the fuel was exhausted to slowly flaring sticks and hot ash. Duncan stepped carefully to the quartz and began scratching with his rock pick.

"As we all know, the presence of quartz is often an indicator of gold. I was hoping to see some exposed by the fire but am disappointed as there are only small traces near the toe. He chipped away and produced a rock with a bit of gold clinging to the freshly cut face. He tossed the specimen to one of the miners, as if to dismiss its value.

"Perhaps enough to warrant picking away but this is hardly the source of color we seek. Pick away at what you can and we'll try one more burning."

The miners moved in and found some samples Duncan dismissed as incidental and hardly worth the labor. Many of the miners hadn't seen lode gold before and were excited to whack away at the quartz with some little success. Duncan stood with Josh and Elizabeth watching the miners politely trying to nudge others away from the meager findings.

"I couldn't follow your explanations. I'm guessing it was just to distract them from our purpose," said Josh.

"I'd be very surprised if any of it made sense," said Shipwash. "It was all pure blatherskite. Just made up taradiddle. Do you think they bought it?"

"Putting a few flakes of gold in their pocket at the end of the day does lend authority to your performance," said Elizabeth.

"It may not be all humbug. There is gold in the creek below and I'm certain there are quartz reefs feeding it but from where I haven't yet a clue. This land has been tossed and shifted for endless centuries. I was hoping to find a slope with a pile of scree at the toe. This one does not look promising from what is exposed though there are empty fissures that have been hollowed by erosion. This appears to be a broken remnant but whether the rest is horizontal, vertical, upstream, or down from here I have no clue. There could be a reef of quartz full of gold six inches under our feet or twenty feet above or below us. The only way is to tunnel in and follow the white rock wherever it leads. We have the manpower but alas, we are not equipped to either tunnel or to separate the gold from its quartz home. We don't have even a rock drill so we could set a charge and blast away at the quartz.

"Well, what shall we do now?" asked Josh.

"We shall repeat our experiment one or two more times until the crowd loses interest," said Duncan. "Mark my words, most of whatever gold is in this country will be extracted by tunneling. For now, we shall return to our dry diggings and try to accumulate enough capital to take advantage in the future."

~ ~ ~

Jubal did not accompany his friends and they did not explain where they were going except to say they were sampling prospects. The rest of the men were washing gold from what they were calling the honey hole and he knew he wouldn't be welcome there. It didn't mean he was going to waste the day away.

Jubal was as certain as anything in life the voice he had heard at Sutter's was Reverend Clark's or Higgins or whatever he was going by now. He didn't need to set eyes on the big man to know he was near. Ever since their encounter with Absalom "Pete" Peterson on the road, he was just as certain the man and his friends were on their trail. What he wasn't positive about was whether they had already arrived in camp or were still on the road.

If Clark and his crew had already crossed the bridge into the camp over the river there was no use in going to town to look for him. Clark and his people would be on the lookout for a black man. Jubal had only seen one other black man in the camp and that was only at a distance. If Clark had eyes looking for a black man it was more likely Jubal would be found instead of doing the finding. Going to camp was out of the question.

Instead, he set up a vantage point in the trees by the approach to the bridge and made himself comfortable. He was provisioned, dry, and concealed from view. He was prepared to wait as long as it took if it would give him and his friends the upper hand.

Several travelers passed his post but mostly pairs of men, some he casually recognized. Half a dozen wagons came and went but all were freighters. No big man or man in a knit hat and sweater. Jubal was not about to quit and soon his steadfast patience was rewarded.

Five mounted men, leading three pack horses approached with "Pete" riding ahead like a scout but hardly more than fifty feet in front of the van. If Jubal had any doubts about the scout they were wiped away when a familiar voice shouted, "You might be ahead of us but you ain't going to beat us to the whiskey. I'll ride right over you should you try."

His companions laughed, not so much at anything funny but because the leader had made the joke. Peterson reined up until the rest of the men approached close enough for Jubal to identify them. Clark had lost the untamed beard that had given him the look of a Bible prophet. The beard was trimmed close or at least closer than most men in camp. He still wore his black coat and collared vest. They were as clean as could be expected but there was a patch on the right elbow. He'd changed to the crushed and shapeless slouch hat that was almost universal in the camps. Most telling was he was still riding Trinket, the gray he'd stolen from Leland Metzger back at the Big Sandy. With his size Clark would be easy to pick out in a crowd. Two of the others looked and dressed like everyone else who was seeking gold. One of them had a newer hat, flat brimmed like a plowman. The other was lean with a long face, sported a blue kerchief, but was otherwise forgettable. Both wore identical gray cloth coats. Plowman rode a dun mare. Long face rode a black stallion with some good blood. That would have to do.

The last would be easy to single out. He was draped in a long tan capote with a sewn on cape around the shoulders. His hat had a rounded crown. If his dress was not distinctive enough, the man in the capote was even more unique. He was gaunt and clean-shaven except for a big broom mustache hanging over his upper lip and maybe hiding bad teeth. His blue eyes never ceased looking around. His mount was the same color as his coat, as if he'd bought either one or the other to match. His tack and saddle were well-cared-for as was the double-barreled coach gun in a saddle sheath. The man radiated menace and no doubt men stepped aside as he passed. He'd stand out in camp like he was on fire.

Clark said something more to Peterson and the men laughed again. It was obvious Clark was the leader. Equally obvious was the man in the capote no more smiled at what was said than an axe blade could smile. Here was the man who kept order, no doubt of it. Jubal was reminded of Joe Sweeney and his crew at Fort Laramie. There was some small talk about what they would do in camp. The chatter was interrupted by capote man.

"Quit your jabberin' and let's get a move on? I want to settle in and get some sleep."

"The boys were just looking forward to a new place, same as you, Stringer," said Clark.

"Then let's get over that bridge and we can talk about it when we find a hot meal."

That settled it and the men clopped over the bridge and towards the main street of the Hangtown camp. Jubal at least knew the men had arrived and some description of them. Importantly, he knew they were going to get fed and there were only a few places in camp that served as restaurants. That knowledge could serve to his advantage. None of the eating-places would let him come in the front and be served but there was at least an even chance he could approach from the rear and be served. If he was careful he might be able to see those inside without being detected, or even better, he could find their horses while they were eating and making plans. Still, there was some risk for a black man alone and on foot in the camp. It didn't take him but a moment to decide. The intelligence gained would be worth the risk. Keeping his eye on the tan capote and horse he let his quarry lead him across the bridge.

~ ~ ~

"So we're all agreed the leper's camp is burned clean and there's no need to discuss it again?" asked Duncan.

"I don't know what else could be done but is there any need to go back," said Elizabeth. "You said there was nothing there."

182

"I don't have much hope for that particular reef but a closer evaluation might well point us to more promising ground."

"I can dig and swing a pick as well as the next man but I'd have no idea what I'd be looking at," said Josh.

"I gather you are reluctant to go back with me and explore."

"You gather right. We both lost our families to cholera and I'd reckon take a long walk around anywhere there's been pestilence." Elizabeth nodded in agreement.

"I'm no doctor but burning seems to be the answer for most pestilence," said Shipwash. "You needn't bother anyway. I simply want to take some samples from further into the drift. If there is color it may lie concealed in the strata." Duncan saw the term was unfamiliar to his friends.

"You saw the layers of earth and rock in that slope. The quartz vein ran in one layer or strata. I intend to find the matching face. Think of the layers as a cake. The movement of the earth has removed a slice and I want to find it. The quartz can be thought of as the frosting between layers."

They had been walking as Duncan educated them and they arrived back at camp, still abandoned.

"If no one is here, they must still be washing out good pans," said Elizabeth. "Let's go see how much we've made while we were setting the woods afire."

"You two go on and count your treasure. The day's walk has irritated my leg. I've enough energy to make it to my bed."

"We can go with you if you need a hand," said Josh. "I need to speak with Jubal anyway."

Duncan replied, "No need. The leg is stiff but not debilitating. If Jubal is at camp, I'll send him along."

They parted ways. Josh and Elizabeth watched Shipwash until he got to the footbridge. He was walking tenderly but hardly hobbling. He turned before stepping across the creek and waved. They waved back and went to watch the wealth accumulate. They'd seen enough bare dirt today and the sight of gold smiling back from the bottom of a pan was never an unpleasant way to end a day's work.

~~~

There was a commotion in camp. A miners' court was to be convened and the men in camp were distracted. Normally, Jubal was wary of walking the camp streets, mindful of having to step aside and acting all docile among the white miners. The preoccupation with the pending court proceedings let him pass amongst the crowds with little more than the occasional hard stare. The silent challenges meant nothing to him. He was used to them and simply averted his eyes, awarding a meaningless victory to the white man. While it galled Jubal to have to be acquiescent in these encounters, inside he smiled. Unknown to the populace or even the Albany partnership, he was undoubtedly one of the richest men in the camp. While the whites who looked down on him were measuring their wealth in pinches and spoonfuls, he could measure his in pounds. After today he would be even richer as the day's wealth would be dried, measured, and divided after supper. His allotment of the dust would again later be divided in their separate camp and he would add it to the one of the leather pokes buried under his bed. He was as rich as any white man he had ever known yet he couldn't spend a dollar's worth to buy a meal or a drink in a public house. Little matter, he had no desire for the society of other miners and there was little enough to buy in camp no matter how much gold he slept above. Luxury was just not available no matter the ability to pay.

Over the heads of milling men Jubal saw the man on the dun horse dismount. Jubal slipped away between tents competing for hardware business. He followed his nose to the kitchen of a business serving out an ongoing stew of what vegetables became available and what they claimed was a variety of fresh game and hot biscuits. He stuck his head through the back flap of the tent and asked if could buy some biscuits and a mug of gravy. He offered a pinch worth two dollars, holding his "walking around" poke in one hand and a mug in the other. He expected to be cheated and was not disappointed. One of the kitchen help squeezed a pinch worth at least double the offer, thereby cheating his employer as well as the customer. Jubal was able to see into the front of the tent where Clark and his men stood in line with other miners. The kitchen help came back with a mug of gravy from the stew and two hard biscuits. Jubal thanked him like he'd done him a favor and retreated.

The first thing he did was to throw the gravy on the ground and wipe his mug clean with a nearby tent flap. Any restaurant that advertised fresh game usually featured what was identified as squirrel. The biscuits were yesterdays and rock hard, destined to be added as thickener to the stew. Jubal ground them into the mud. He took up station down the street, waiting for the newcomers to come out again. He would follow them at least partway to wherever they were going to set up camp. As long as he moved about some he shouldn't be noticed.

He hadn't been at his post for five minutes before his plan went awry. The miners' court was convening not a hundred feet from where he stood. It looked like the whole camp was walking right past him. The kind of justice meted out in the court was not something he wanted any part of. He retreated to behind a row of tents and made his way to the bridge. The success of his reconnaissance would be limited to knowing Clark was in camp and who was with him.

~~~

The division of the day's gold had become a ritual conducted before the evening meal. The gold was ceremoniously placed in a fry pan and dried over the cook fire. The residual water would steam away and, still hot from the fire, the gold was weighed. Then the total was written down in a ledger before all present. Once cooled, the dust was poured into a powder horn, any pickers or the rare nugget went into a leather poke and placed in the custody of the captains. Once the ritual was concluded, the evening meal commenced. The mood of the diners was directly tied to the amount of the day's measure. Today's meal, a main course of goat roasted on a spit and the ubiquitous flapjacks with molasses and black coffee would be a joyous one. Goat was a rare enough treat but each man present was going to eat his meal a bit over a hundred dollars richer even after rough calculations for deducted expenses. Those were kept in another ledger for the every other Sunday settling up. The talk at table was mostly a discussion of expenses and what each man would do with his wealth. The day's work had not been exhausting and tomorrow looked like more of the same, just counting money. A celebratory drink was called for. A small cask of brandy was produced, tapped, and toasts drunk to the future. After the brandy was downed, a banjo and fiddle appeared. The banjo was played without much talent but with a compensating enthusiasm. All in all, this day was considered the best since the partnership was formed in the cabin of the *Julianna Dolce*. To a man, each promised to tell his children and grandchildren of the day he first became rich.

"I want to go back to our camp," Elizabeth whispered into Josh's ear. "Let's go."

"Why? Everyone is having a good time."

"That's why. One more drink and someone's bound to ask me to dance. If I refuse, it will appear rude. If I say yes, I'll soon have every drunken miner tromping on my feet while those two saw away at whatever they think they are playing."

"Well, no one is going to tromp on my wife's feet but me. I'll say our good-byes while you slip away."

Elizabeth stepped away from the light of the mess tent and waited while Josh shook the required number of hands and joined her. The night was clear and the stars served to guide them to the creek bridge and to their own camp. There they found Jubal waiting for them.

"Clark is here in camp. He's still ridin' the horse he stole from Captain Metzger. That Peterson character was with him, three others, too."

"Damn," said Josh. "We was right. He followed us here."

"If you never saw him at Sutter's, how would he even know we are here?"

"We were askin' about him in a bar. One of his friends might have overheard us."

"Even so, why would he take up after you?"

"After us, you mean. As to why, I couldn't begin to guess."

"He's fallen in with some bad folks," said Jubal, "and he appears to be in charge. You seen the one goes by Pete. There's another he called Stringer. Lookin' at him, he chills me to the bone. There's two more but they just look like miners fallin' in with the wrong bunch."

"Maybe he wants to stop anyone from telling about the stolen horse," Josh suggested.

"If that's the reason, it would make sense to put as much distance from us as possible," said Elizabeth.

"Could be you, wife. You two was always at odds. You know how he looked at you, too."

Elizabeth made a little show of saying how she'd put a rougher man than Dayton Clark in the ground. What she said was true but the bravado seemed more than a little forced.

Jubal put an end to the speculation.

"Whatever reason he be here, it ain't to do The Lord's Work."

CHAPTER SEVENTEEN

If the subject of the partners' speculation had been asked why he'd pursued Bonner and Jubal, he probably couldn't truthfully answer. Events were unfolding in Hangtown that could make a dedicated rogue like Clark think about his future.

The five travelers hadn't been in the tent saloon for a quarter hour before the commotion in the street left them the only patrons at the bar. Stringer asked what was going on. The bartender, hardly at ease with his customers, told them about the convening miner's court. He was anxious to close up and be rid of them.

"There's goin' to be a miners' trial at the vacant lot just down the road," he explained. "A sutler was found out to be usin' shaved weights on his scales. Cheatin' the customer."

"I suppose that's a practice exclusive to storekeepers in these parts. A bartender would never cheat his patrons now, would he?" Clark asked.

"Some bartenders will put some tallow under their nails but this is an honest establishment," said the bartender. He didn't like the implication and he didn't like being alone with this crew. He displayed his clean hand as evidence of his honesty. Then he had a better idea.

"If you gents ain't never seen the miners' court, you'd be missin' something. I'm fixin' to close up myself. How about I pour you each a drink on the house for the inconvenience?" He produced a bottle from the shelf behind him. "The good stuff, genuine Kentuck' bourbon."

"I can be inconvenienced a mite for a free toss of good bourbon," said Pete. "What's goin' t'happen to this cheatin' storekeep?"

"Well, he's guilty for sure," said the bartender as he poured out the shots with an unsteady hand. "Otherwise there'd be no reason to have a trial, would there." They all laughed, save for Stringer.

"That sounds like the law to me," he said, putting down a Mexican eight-*reale* coin on the bartop.

"Oh no, friend. I said this round was on me."

"And we appreciate it, friend," said Stringer. "This is for the first round. On me, boys."

A silver *reale* was below the going rate for five shots of trade whiskey. The bartender picked it up and considered saying something until he looked at Stringer's eyes. He looked at them because there was no looking into them. They were as flat and lifeless as a fish. Clark could see Stringer was testing the man. They didn't need trouble in a new camp.

"You didn't say what was going to happen to the cheat."

The bartender looked at the big man.

"They don't call this place Hangtown for nothin'."

"Well. I think we'll just stroll down and watch the goings on," said Clark. "Why don't you close up and come with us?"

"That's a nice offer but a trial and a hangins' good for business. I'll just stay here and get ready for the crowd," said the bartender. He just wished they would leave.

"Suit yourself. Maybe we'll see you later," said Stringer. "Come on boys. Let's see how the law works in these parts."

The bartender watched with relief as they walked out of his tent. Business was good enough he didn't need to invite them back. He picked up the Mexican *reale*. It wasn't gold but a minted coin was rare enough he didn't feel shorted.

~~~

If the newcomers attended court with the hopes of seeing a man hang, they were disappointed. There was no doubt about the man's guilt but it was decided the theft was not by force but by guile. The sentence was to be a flogging of forty lashes, a fine of five hundred dollars, two ounces of gold to the man wielding the whip, and banishment from the boundaries of the Mining District. There were no actual boundaries established but the flogging would teach the guilty man distance from the South Fork of the American River was a wise course of action.

The convicted man was stripped to the waist and lashed to a nearby tree where the sentence passed not ten minutes before was read aloud would be carried out. There must have been friends of the prisoner in the court as it was determined to use a stock whip instead of a teamster's bullwhip. Fifty lashes with a bullwhip would probably have killed the man and been a much crueler sentence than hanging,

189

dragging out the punishment interminably. The miners were not cruel by nature but they lived in a harsh environment and crimes offending life and property must necessarily be severe and certain. A Mexican stockman was selected to administer the discipline. Some objected to a Mexican being chosen to whip a white man, but the man's expertise with the specialized instrument was well known and the objections were overridden.

The witnesses crowded about the scene, pushing for a closer advantage. So close did they crowd the executioner complained they impeded his swing and they slowly gave him room. The first blow fell to a ragged cheer from the crowd. Whether this was from a thirst for cruelty and blood or from a thirst for whiskey is anyone's guess. By the third blow, the condemned man's resolve not to cry out abandoned him. He howled piteously but did not cry out for mercy. By the time the fifth or sixth blow was struck, the crowd was silenced. The Mexican laid the stripes with the ease of an expert. Each lash landed between the shoulders. Not a one fell on the prisoner's shoulders, neck, or arms. The skin on a man's back is thicker than on those extremities but as each stripe was laid, welts erupted one after the other. As one lash overlaid another the flesh failed and each fall of the whip brought blood. Twenty lashes in and his pants were crimson to the seat.

Crowell and Chapin stood between Clark and Pete. Stringer was in front of them. Neither had ever witnessed a flogging and they began to gasp and cringe with each fall of the whip and every howl of the prisoner.

Stringer turned to them, a sneer of contempt on his face.

"I'm guessing this is the first time you've seen a man striped?"

"The first and the last time for me," said Chapin. Crowell nodded his assent.

"First time I ever saw a white man whipped," said Clark. "Back home it was common for a nigra who sassed to get a half dozen or so."

"Where was it you said was back home? I forget," said Stringer.

"In the South."

Sometime with maybe a dozen strokes left the prisoner lost consciousness, a mercy to him and to Chapin, Crowell, and most of the spectators. Before the prisoner was cut down, he was doused with several buckets of water. His pants were stained pink and his back still

190

oozed blood. He was laid face down in a wagon and driven away. His back would be sponged with a dilution of vinegar and bandaged with what was available. As soon as he could move by himself, he would leave the Hangtown camp.

"Why the hell did we ever come to such a place as this?" said Crowell.

Both he and Ned Chapin had been prospectors whose claims did not pan out and had fallen in with the other three ruffians. They both fancied themselves as sharps with cards and petty larcenies. Their small successes had not prepared them for the consequences of failure. The administration of justice in the camp was not just a lesson for the cheating storekeeper.

The lesson was not lost on Clark either. He was having a difficult time recalling why he had pursued the two men here. Once again his temperament had betrayed his common sense. Enraged by the knowledge someone from his past was prying into his affairs, he'd set out to teach them not to meddle. He'd just witnessed a man beaten into oblivion for cheating on his measures and now he'd ridden a stolen horse into a camp where the only witnesses to his crime resided. Trinket was a good mount and he would regret having to sell him to someone passing through. Once done he could pursue his stock and trade, the swindle.

With the flogging concluded, the crowd dispersed to the nearest saloons. The five new arrivals adjourned back to the tent where they were drinking. They found the bartender is a much happier frame of mind.

~ ~ ~

Duncan, after the day's gold cleanup was done, came back to the camp with the happy news the partnership was richer by nine ounces of gold, a value of one hundred and eighty dollars. The men digging in the hole below the old overfalls had moved laterally and found the watercourse continued on into the sideslope. It looked promising though not as rich as what had become known as The Honeyhole. Duncan interrupted their digging to direct commencement of the bluff shoring above where they were digging. Further, the water level in both the American and the creek were dropping. Soon the diversion channel would have to be lowered so they could continue to wash. Gold mining always presented more arduous labor that didn't directly result in wealth. Even the well-washed findings required more work.

"While the final washing and drying of the gold is being accepted as an ounce for the purposes of commerce, it is still far from what could be considered pure. No matter how much we wash and sift, a contingent of iron and other heavy materials will remain behind. To obtain gold in its pure form, it must be further refined. No doubt you were wondering why I asked you to obtain some quicksilver for me."

"I've heard of it being used as a physic when a person is bound up," said Josh. "I bought it from a doctor so…" He let the rest go in deference to Elizabeth's presence. Once again, his wife would surprise him.

"I know doctors use quicksilver to treat the French Pox," she chimed in. She was not about to inquire whether Duncan's purchase was for any such reason.

"I'll save you asking," said Duncan. "I am, other than this stiff leg, as hale and as fit as a man can be living as we do. No, our application will be in the laboratory of metallurgy. Let us step outside and I will astound you."

The trio followed Shipwash to their cook fire where a small table stood nearby. On the table was a stone mortar, a ceramic saucer, a leather poke, the small, blue bottle of quicksilver, and a curiosity made from a funnel with a length of coiled copper tubing soldered to the spout end of the funnel. Four short stumps of wood to serve as stools were set about the table for the demonstration.

"Jubal, hang up the lantern there so we all can observe," said Shipwash, the delight of anticipation peppered his words.

When all were situated he poured about two tablespoons of shining fine gold dust into a saucer. He then unstoppered the blue vial and poured out an equal amount of mercury. The liquid metal glimmered brightly in the firelight.

"I've never seen the like," said an astonished Jubal. "When you were talkin' "quicksilver" it was just words I'd never heard before. Whoever named that stuff knew what they was doin'."

"It's also known as cinnabar," said Duncan, laughing. "I like the sound of the word." He spoke the name as if naming an exotic potion from the mysterious Orient.

"You probably have seen it before in a thermometer," said Josh.

"I seen a thermometer before but it was a dial on a steam boiler. Never seen anything like this, though."

"Then prepare to be amazed," said Duncan.

With the pestle he began to work the two shiny elements, one liquid and one a solid, together. Within moments the gold vanished, literally dissolved into the liquid. Methodically and in ever decreasing amounts, Shipwash added more gold, mixing it until the gold was dissolved and the liquid metal had transformed into a lump, firm and almost dough like. Duncan picked up the lump and placed it in the mortar and bedded the mortar into the coals of the fire.

"Simms, one of the wood cutting crew, I found is also a tinsmith and he fashioned this retort for me." He placed the mouth of the funnel over the mortar and guided the open end of the copper tube into an empty rum bottle propped near the fire pit.

"Why, you are making a still. My father used to make whiskey in a copper still back home," said Elizabeth.

"This is the exact same process but is designed to recapture the cinnabar as it boils away and condenses in the bottle. We probably should step away during the transformation. The fumes are extremely toxic."

For the first minutes there was little to see except the shimmering heat rising from the red coals. Soon though, a drop of quicksilver formed at the lip of the tube, grew, and dropped shining and pure into the bottom of the bottle. Fumes began to flow from the tube and instantly dropped to the bottom where they became liquid and joined the slow, steady drip from the tube. The spectators were transfixed.

"Lord be with us," said Jubal. "This be magic like I never seen. Black magic, I'm guessin'."

"Gold magic," whispered Shipwash, as much to himself as to his audience.

"By God, it is gold magic," exclaimed Josh, catching the spirit of the event. They all laughed briefly, albeit a bit nervously.

Before too long, the drip and the fumes ceased. About two tablespoons of quicksilver lay in the bottom of the bottle.

"Normally, an iron receptacle would be used. I couldn't resist using the bottle for the demonstration." His audience nodded obediently and with respect for what they had witnessed.

Duncan picked up the white saucer and pointed out the leavings, a black dust of perhaps a quarter teaspoon. He passed it around.

"From what remains, I would say the gold dust we started with was about eighty-percent or so pure. This residue is worthless," he said as he cast it aside with a disdainful flourish. He then removed the funnel and tube and picked up the mortar with tongs. The bottom of the vessel was nearly pure gold, still unmelted. He shook out the refined gold, gently tapping the mortar on the edge of the saucer.

"Quicksilver will also converge with lead, copper, and silver so we cannot be certain this is completely refined. The fire was nowhere nearly hot enough to melt anything but lead and I see no trace in our sample. I would guess this is at least ninety-five to ninety-seven percent pure."

He passed the saucer around to three sets of admiring eyes.

"If that ain't magic, it's sure a kissin' cousin."

"Hardly magic, Josh. What you see is science at its best."

"People told me about science but I never believed. Now that I seen it, it still seems like magic to me," said Jubal. He was slowly shaking his head, not in doubt of what he'd seen but as if he had witnessed something contrary to his known world and thereby unnatural.

"You can see now how this process can be applied to establishing the value of a claim," said Duncan. "I can take the dust paid for the claims recording and, marking the claims on a map, see where the drift of paying ore lies. Hah, I should be paying the miners instead of them paying me."

"Some miners don't wash as clean as others," offered Elizabeth.

"Poorly worked pans are readily apparent. If you wash each sample when submitted for payment, the wash will be consistent. Soon a pattern can be developed on a map."

"I notice you didn't say *we will wash the samples*."

"I have something to announce."

Elizabeth interrupted. "I knew it. I knew it. It was plain to see when we were out looking for that reef or drift or whatever you call it. You want to go back out prospecting."

"I didn't think it was so obvious but you are entirely right. Sitting in the claims office day after day waiting for someone to come in with their findings and record their little piece of the pie makes me feel like a dog in a kennel tearing at the confinement. The dog needs to be on the hunt and so do I. I'll shrivel up like an old potato. Get soft and rot if I have to sit behind a desk sorting papers and sticking tacks in a map. My purpose is to find the color and I must follow my purpose."

"The miners won't accept my signature as valid on their claims. They might not accept Josh's either, being so young," Elizabeth said.

"A trifling matter and one I can easily resolve with the Mining Commission," said Duncan. "The only operations filling their pans with gold is ours in the dry diggings I discovered. It should be no problem to convince the camp it is better for all if I am out turning over rocks instead of turning over pages in a ledger. I certainly can convince them Elizabeth Bonner is a much more attractive choice as registrar than Duncan Shipwash. You and Josh will take the majority positions and we'll have the sign repainted."

"I can see you've given the details a good goin' over," said Josh.

"Indeed I have. You simply let me examine the samples from the claims from time to time and I will lead us to new veins of color. We shall all be rich."

Jubal had been silent during the exchange but now spoke up.

"Guess now is as good a time as any to speak up. I got something to say."

The trio turned to him, waiting.

"Once the passes are open, I aim to leave."

Josh and Elizabeth certainly hadn't seen this coming. Since leaving Illinois and all during their trek west and their time in Alta California, Jubal was there at their side. Seldom was the day they hadn't shared their meals, their camp, and the day-to-day labor of surviving. If Duncan's plans were unexpected, Jubal's announcement was life-changing for them all.

"Where are you going? Back to Cairo?" asked Josh. As far as he knew there was little for him there.

I'm going to try and find my wife and child. I can't go myself but now I can pay someone. Thinking I might join up with the Railroad. Mebbe go to Canada."

"The Railroad?" said Josh. Jubal had never ridden a train. He'd been a river man as long as he'd known him.

"The Underground Railroad," said Elizabeth. "There were people even in Cairo that were "conductors" spiriting slaves out of the slave states and up to Canada. You didn't know that?"

"I heard of it but didn't know people in Cairo were in on it."

"It was more a country thing than a town thing. I didn't know who was in but I heard stories of slaves moving through at night or hidden in barns."

"Why didn't you go through to Canada when you first come over the river 'stead of workin' for my dad?"

"At first I thought I could go back and save my kin. I was all for it then but soon I saw it wasn't anything I could do so I took work with your dad so I could be on the water. Maybe help out with transport."

"Did you? I mean go across and help runaways. Who in Cairo was part of it?" asked Josh. This was turning into a day of revelations.

"Ain't sayin'," said Jubal. "Ain't sayin' whether I helped or not. Ain't sayin' I even knew anyone. That's what they mean callin' it underground."

Jubal had been part of the Bonner household for going on eight years now. When his father first hired him, Jubal was vague about his past but the family deduced he had left behind an expectant wife. Now, he as much as says he was working for the Underground Railroad. Josh didn't care one way or another but he was disappointed Jubal didn't trust the Bonners enough to tell them. Coupled with the announcement he was leaving for another country was quite a bit to choke down all at once.

"Can't you just stay here and hire someone to go find them?"

"Don't like it here. I got to do this myself."

"I'll be the first to say this is rough living," said Elizabeth, "but all your friends are here."

"Best friends a body could have, too. Thing is, this ain't no place for a colored. I got more money than near everyone in this camp but there's not much to buy and I couldn't spend it if I wanted. Can't go into a saloon or a place to eat except to go to the back. Can't own land or work a claim on my own. What do you think those Albany boys would do if they found out I got as much from their labor as they did? You know exactly why you can't tell them I'm in the partners. Ain't it so?"

"Jubal, if anyone has brought you grief, tell me their names," said Josh.

"Ain't none of them callin' me boy or nothin' but none will sit down across from me at suppertime. None offer me a drink or to help with the kitchen work. It ain't a bother to me. Been walkin' careful round white folks all my life. Ain't complaining and I know it's the way it's got to be. Just sayin' I ain't got no place here so I gots to go." He paused to gather his thoughts before continuing.

"You've seen what they done to those Frenchies built the bridge. They was white but they got run off cause they weren't Americans. Only thing makes a black man better than a Chinese or a Mexican is I speak American and that don't count a lick. When I was a slave I was just a field hand and I knowed my place. There was rules and if you followed them, you was fine. In Cairo there was places for whites and places for blacks. Everyone knew which was which you stayed with your own folks. Any troubles was worked out by your own people. Folks got along that way. Ain't no place for me. Don't want to be with the Chinese or the Mexicans. Ain't no place and ain't no rules you can hang your cap on, neither. Ain't no law here but hangin' and whippin'. I been whipped. You know that. I felt the lash back in Missouri for stealin' food for my woman when she was carryin my child. What law there be is whites. A white man could shoot me down in the street and tell that I put up some sass and that would be the end of it."

"Jubal, I can't believe people are so callous such a thing could go unpunished," said Elizabeth.

"Wouldn't matter much to me though, would it. You both young but you already seen more ugly in folks than most people see in a lifetime. No, there's no place for me, and no rules I can count on. I have to leave."

They couldn't find fault with Jubal's thinking. Ever since the Americans won the Mexican War they just moved in and took over. People were arriving from all over the world but the Americans were clearly in charge. The most ragged prospector, scrounging for a potato or a flapjack was considered lord and master over every South American, Chinese, or South Pacific Islander. Miners and merchants were overrunning the *Californio patrons*, holders of vast tracts of land and livestock, their land grants laughed at. Sutter, who had opened his lands to the new settlers, was being bankrupted. Many thought this was shameful but there was little they could do.

The native Indians were barely considered humans. The missions had enslaved them, the ranchos had exploited them, and now the Americans had run them out of the hills and into the north of the country. Except for the few remaining at the *haciendas*, it was rare to even see a native Indian. The Indians had a long history here under the rule of the conqueror. Now the conqueror had been conquered. The wise choice for the Indians was to move on. Jubal was simply taking the obvious and wisest course. There was no changing his mind.

"All right. Jubal is leaving at the end of the month so we will settle up the partnership against expense," said Elizabeth.

"You will still be a partner. Get us word where you are and we'll get your share to you," said Josh.

"Ain't gonna do no such thing." Jubal shook his head in vehement protest. "Your daddy took me in as a runaway and paid me for the work I did. You kept me on and I learned to scout. Paid my way with my work. I done my work here, and you made me the richest nigger in California. I ain't about to take no money when I'm long gone and ain't doin' a lick to earn it."

"You're part of our partnership. It's the way a business works," Josh protested.

"A farm with slaves is a business getting' by on the work of others. If I took gold for doin' nothing while other men worked with pick and shovel, why that's just rubbin' up too close to slave and master for my comfort."

The long discourse had emptied Jubal's sails. Normally an almost silent companion, he'd been tossing this back and forth in his mind. Once he let fly with his announcement, everything that followed was more than he'd planned on. As a sailor might say, he was left "in irons". He left without another word.

"That was quite the soliloquy," said Elizabeth.

"Quite the what?" said Josh, still stunned by his friend's revelations.

"I gather you had no idea of his feelings," said Duncan.

"I'd seen the looks he received while we would be out buying provisions," said Elizabeth. "Seeing a black man keeping company with a woman galled a lot of men who hadn't spoken to a woman in months. I saw the looks and heard the insults spoken behind us as we passed. I can only guess what it was like on his own. It's a sorry thing and I hate to see him go under any circumstances."

"None more than me. Jubal was a part of my life like breakfast or dinner. His mind is set but I wish I could change it."

The topic of Jubal's leaving was thus concluded. Josh and Elizabeth retired to their shelter. Duncan sat alone by the fire. He stared into the dying coals for some time before banking the fire and turning in. In his mind he planned the changes to the sluice gate and the shoring of the bluff over the honey hole. The association of four was now broken. It was not the only company with unexpected reductions.

~~~

Clark and his men had spent most of the evening drinking. They moved to a spot under some trees just north of the camp. They didn't even bother with a fire. They staked a canvas above where they set out their bedrolls and passed out beneath it. They awakened as the sun came up but pulled blankets over their splitting headaches and went back to a fitful sleep.

When Clark finally arose his hangover was awaiting him. He got up, splashed some water on his face, rinsed the sour taste of old whiskey from his mouth and stepped behind a tree to relieve himself. He didn't notice anything amiss until he returned. There was only flattened dirt where Chapin and Crowell put their beds. They were gone in the night. Pete was still snoring away. Stringer was awake but not yet standing.

"Guess those boys weren't cut out to be gentlemen of leisure," he said.

"Sleeping on the ground with a piece of canvas for a roof ain't my idea of leisure."

"Well, we just now getting started making our fortunes, ain't we. Give Pete a kick so he can start a fire and make coffee," said Stringer, rolling over and pulling his capote over his head.

"I ain't your damn butler and I'm just as ruined as you. We ain't broke so let's go find us some breakfast and a place with a roof to sleep."

"I'm with Pete on this one," said Clark, kicking Stringer instead. "Get up and we'll go see where men of leisure might find an opportunity in this camp."

Stringer managed to get to his feet, unsteady and still reeling. "I could go for a card game."

"Its Tuesday. Ain't nobody playin' cards on a Tuesday but sharpers. Hell, I can barely see you much less hold a hand of cards. My eyes is so red they may start bleedin'."

Pete was cinching up his horse and securing his gear. "There was a livery, leastwise some corrals just after we crossed the bridge. We can board them there. Then we eat. I could use an eye-opener to cut through this fog in my head, too."

CHAPTER EIGHTEEN

Josh and Elizabeth awoke to find Shipwash gone from camp. This caused no alarm. Often he would disappear into the wild for a few days prospecting. They were surprised somewhat when he returned just before dusk on the same day.

"I went down above the creek looking for the rest of that reef of quartz. I had no luck and what was worse I found four men camped at the quartz vein by the leper's camp. They were busy scratching away at the bluff and had managed to get behind it and break out some samples. Seeing my approach they were anxious for my opinion. Their labor produced some color in some small fissures. They were breaking up the rock and picking away at the gold in the fissures. I took a look back where they were trying to follow the drift downward and discovered its end. They said they were going to follow it back into the hill. The project didn't look promising and nothing I said could discourage them as they were picking out enough to show a profit for the day."

"What was most discouraging was how ill-equipped anyone is to commence mining a vein underground. I don't know how long the placer claim will pay out but those who are willing and able to prise the gold from the lodes to be found below ground will claim the real riches. Even if a find could be extracted with powder, pick, and shovel, the riches remain in the rock. The rock needs to be crushed down to dust and then washed."

"We were able to take out quite a bit from the arroyo on the Middle Fork," said Josh. "We didn't do much more than pick out what was there and crack a few fissures loose with a hammer."

"Believe me, Josh. We just scratched away at the surface. The exposed gold bearing quartz is what is eroded into the placer holdings all through the Sierras. The real wealth is in the rock and underground. Capital and labor is what is needed to follow the seams through the earth, extract the rock and then crush it. Men to dig, timber to shore the tunnels, and most all, equipment to crush the rock. The most primitive means of crushing is to set up stones like a gristmill. One round stone on edge is run around in a circle as it rides over the horizontal stone. To really crush ore, a stamping machine is needed and a steam engine to run it. I doubt there is a stamping operation within a

201

thousand miles of here. Even if we could import one, it would have to run day and night to be profitable. We have the arroyo on the Middle Fork but we don't have the capital to exploit it. The claim will have to wait for another day."

~~~

Jubal and Shipwash were driving the cart to Hangtown camp. With both planning to leave they needed supplies. It was agreed Jubal was to take the cart with him but he would have to provide mules himself. Duncan's plan called for the purchase of several casks of black powder and slow match. Mules and powder were the main objectives but they would need supplies for living on the trail as well.

The weather was warming, the rivers were subsiding and Hangtown was a melee of miners preparing to head into the hills. Supplies would be scarce and expensive. Duncan would dicker for the supplies. Jubal would pose as his hired man. After crossing the bridge they drove towards the livery where it was hoped a pair of mules could be haggled for. Right after they turned in the gate, Jubal drew the cart abruptly to a stop.

"There's some men followed Josh and me from Sutter's. They be bad men and they're standing right in front of us."

"Those three?" asked Shipwash, recalling his cutlass was back in the tent.

"There be two more but I don't see'em anywheres. Shit. They seen us."

Duncan saw one of the three, a bruiser of a man in a black coat, break into a grin and begin waving as he paced down to where they were stopped. Noticing his departure, his companions turned but did not follow. Clark kept walking, his teeth white against the stubble on his face.

"Jubal," he said in greeting. "Are you no longer with that Bonner cub? Whose your friend?" Clark stuck out his hand toward Shipwash. Duncan took it just to be polite.

"Dan Higgins. Pleased to make your acquaintance." He didn't even look at Shipwash, instead staring down Jubal as if defying him to challenge. Jubal was not cowed in the least.

"What happened to the right Reverend Dayton Clark?"

"A sad thing. He died crossing the Sierras. We traveled together and I said the right words over him when I laid him to his final rest." Clark smirked as he lied. He was pushing just to see how far he could push.

Jubal played along knowing he was indulging a dangerous game.

"I see his horse survived."

"Didn't see any sense in shooting the horse just because the rider passed away."

Going further would create the circumstances he most wanted to avoid. Any reply would necessarily result in calling Clark a liar and a horse thief, neither claim could he prove.

Duncan did not know the history between these two but it was obvious the man was baiting Jubal into some sort of confrontation.

"Mr. Higgins. I have business with the livery owner and much to attend to today. Pleasant as it may be to reminisce with my hired man, I am afraid he has work to do. Perhaps a later time would be more convenient?"

"My oh my. Listen to the snuffer. Supposin' now is when I find convenient?"

"I take it then you have concluded your business with the livery owner."

"I reckon not."

"It has been my experience when a man attempts to do two things at once, both endeavors end rather shabbily. No doubt you are familiar with shabby outcomes, sir."

"I don't think I like your attitude," said Clark. His face was starting to flush, replacing the gray pallor of his hangover.

"I've suffered that complaint all my life. Alas, there is little I can do to curtail it."

The last was all it took. Clark surged forward, seizing Shipwash by his coat and dragging him from the wagon.

"You Brit bastard. You're going home in the back of the damn wagon." He swung a vicious club of a fist at the smaller man. Duncan stepped inside the punch and skillfully slipped sidewise.

"Get ready for a beating, you slippery shit," bellowed Clark, charging his adversary.

Even with his bad leg, Duncan was able to avoid the charge. He retreated several paces away.

"I'll not brawl with you here in the mud, sir. I will accept your challenge, however. Where may my second call upon yours?"

"Challenge. What are you talking about?"

Duncan stepped to the middle of the stable yard to shout his announcement.

"This gentleman has challenged me to a duel and I have accepted. I will allow him until tomorrow to rescind his challenge and apologize. Barring an apology, we shall meet again at a time and place to be determined."

Clark was completely flummoxed. When he'd spotted Jubal he thought he would just have a little fun teasing him. Before he'd even got going the Englishman had interceded and within the blink of an eye he was somehow involved in a duel. Clark was not unfamiliar with being in a fight. He was not afraid of a fight but he went to particular cautions to only enter a match he was confident he could win.

Growing up in Alabama the occurrence of duels was commonplace. They were the provinces of the upper classes where duels were fought over land or debt. As it was lowborn to fight over material things, reasons of honor or insult were manufactured to make the encounter an honorable combat. Being the son of a Baptist minister precluded his own participation. He was nowhere near highborn or landed enough. The young gentry fairly gloried in the idea of a duel. Many were fought but only a few participants died. Honor was satisfied by participation or by drawing blood. Standing before an opponent and being fired upon was considered the height of valor. The seconds and witnesses would determine a winner if no shot struck home. As a young man he fought other youths. The ritual dictated by the *codes duello* were followed but the actual combat was always fists, usually in a neutral party's barn. Without meaning to, Clark had become the challenger in a duel with a stranger. The realization of his situation left him without words as Jubal and the Englishman turned the cart from the livery yard.

"That worked out rather well, don't you think?" said Shipwash.

"You got yourself mixed up in a fight to the death for next to no reason," said Jubal. "How do you figure things turned out well."

"Oh, don't be so concerned. Duels seldom result in death. When they do, it's almost the result of a lucky shot. Or an unlucky shot depending on whether delivering or receiving."

"You gonna stand up and let a man shoot at you because of me. Why would you do that?"

"Because you are my friend and you needed help. I'm not unaware of the prejudice you are subject to. I experience some myself just for being English instead of American. Besides, I'm not going to let anyone shoot at me."

"Isn't a duel with guns?"

"Most usually. You have witnessed I have some expertise with the blade. As the aggrieved, I will insist on cutlasses and daggers as the instruments of satisfaction. Other than the military no one carries a sword anymore." Duncan laughed as though he had not a care in the world. Jubal just puzzled at his companion. The Englishman was always surprising him.

~ ~ ~

"What was all that to do about?" asked Stringer. He and Pete walked down to where their friend was standing after he didn't come back to the livery.

"That was the darkie we followed here from Sutter's Fort. I don't know the other from Adam."

"He ain't who was with the nigra when I saw him on the trail," said Pete. "He was with some young fella with a snippy attitude."

"Appears he's working for an Englishman now. The limey butted into my business and I saw fit to set him to rights."

"What's this about a duel?" Pete asked.

"He thinks I challenged him and he wants to stand off twenty paces and shoot it out. There's rules to be followed and I'm happy to oblige him."

"So you come down to mince words with the colored boy and end up in a gun fight?" said Stringer. "Now that's what I call havin' a situation in hand." Clark fumed at the implication but he swallowed his bile and kept quiet.

"Golly. I heard of duelin' before but never thought I'd see one," said Pete.

"The rules say he sends a friend, called a second, to see my second and they make the arrangements."

"I'd be pleased to be your second," offered Pete.

"No offense, Pete, but sometimes these duels can get..." Clark hesitated, "tense is what I'd call it. The seconds can get involved in the feud and I'm picking Stringer to stand for me. Not that you ain't got the sand. Boney here just got more kill in him."

"Hell, I killed before."

"I'm sure you have, Pete, but some folks gun play just come to them more natural."

Stringer found that funny.

"You got a way with words there, Higgins. I'll stand for you, certain."

"Let's find a place to sleep and sit down to a meal," said Clark. "That bastard's second can look for me. I aim to be easy to find."

~~~

Duncan gathered up Josh, Elizabeth, and the Albany officers to relate the tale of the encounter with Clark and the subsequent duel. Josh jumped at the chance to be Duncan's second. Both Duncan and Elizabeth objected.

"Hell, I ain't afraid of him."

"No one is saying you are. By asking one of the Albany officers to deliver terms, then they will know we have others on our side. Perhaps others could accompany Jack."

"Why pick Jack Luder?" asked Josh.

"Jack's been in the military as have some of his men. Sending him as both my second and an officer in a mining enterprise will show the four of us are not alone," said Duncan. "Besides, he has a sword. I doubt my adversary has access to one and I believe Jack would lend his to a good purpose. Jack, I've hastily assumed you will serve as my second. I hope I haven't imposed myself."

"Not at all," replied Luders. "When it comes to the preservation of a man's honor, I would be proud to serve. My sword is at your disposal."

"All right," conceded Josh. "You make a good argument but damn, I sure would like to see Clark's face when he finds out he's goin' to be in a sword fight."

"Still, I'm going to the duel," declared Josh. He looked at Elizabeth as he spoke. He wasn't looking for her approval but just to let her know his intentions. She said nothing. Her face was a blank slate. Usually that was not a good harbinger.

Luders did have a question. "Once you've accepted the challenge and I deliver the terms and place, I will inform him of your choice of weapons. It's customary to offer the challenger a choice between two weapons. Suppose he picks your cutlass? It's obviously of better manufacture than my own."

"That won't happen as I'm not going to offer him a choice. Tell him the matter will be settled with swords and daggers. He'll say he doesn't have a sword and you offer him yours, and I thank you again for volunteering it in service. Suggest he can either apologize publicly to me for his offense or he can accept what is offered and use the time left to practice."

"Swords *and* daggers is most unusual. Why insist on both?" asked Luders.

"It's certain this lummox has no skill with the blade. He will undoubtedly rely on his size and strength to win. This will mean a headlong charge and a slashing attack. By insisting on knives as well he will feel obligated to carry both. Insisting on two weapons will hinder the charge and prevent using the sword two-handed. Tell him he can provide his own knife."

Luder had to laugh out loud. "Damn! This isn't your first dance on the field of honor. Glory be. I never would have guessed."

"As you know me better, you will find out that I am handy with more tools than my little rock pick."

"I ain't surprised," offered Jubal. "I seen him do away with two rascals on the trail like a man swattin' flies."

"Yes, yes. Thank you my friend for the vote of confidence. Now let us determine where the field of honor shall be."

"Maybe on the hill south of camp. It's nearer the graveyard," said Weber.

"Oh! Don't even joke about this business," exclaimed Elizabeth. "This may not turn out for the best."

Shipwash chuckled. "Thank you for the vote of confidence, my dear. Tell Clark I will meet him Monday morning at the French Bridge over the river. We shall meet at each end. This will, I believe, inspire his charge yet still give me room to manuever. Yes, the bridge is where we shall meet."

"What about your leg?" asked Fellowes.

"Do you mean this trifling limp? I think you will find I am full of surprises."

"Sounds like you got a plan," said Josh. "Just hope it's a damn good one."

Luders stood up to leave. "Guess there's nothing to do but go deliver the terms."

"I'm going with you," said Josh. He stared at his wife in case she objected.

"Well, go ahead," she replied. "Jack doesn't know what Clark looks like and you best get a look at this man in the mysterious capote."

"Hell, you have a few surprises of your own, I guess."

"Just promise me all you will do is deliver the terms."

"I promise. I won't say a word and I'll tip my hat when we leave. You have my word."

~ ~ ~

True to his word, Clark was easy to find. He and his two companions had set up camp just outside the Hangtown camp. The place they picked was just down the street from the claims recording office. Whether this was accidental or selected with purpose was anyone's guess. The new arrivals had made an impression on the camp and Jack's inquiries on the street were answered with not only directions but with a caution. The trio just didn't look right. One man they asked said he moved his own camp because they had set up near his. He attributed his intuition as a gift from his grandmother who could spot the Mark of Cain on a person and had passed it down to her progeny.

Luders hailed the hastily constructed lean-to from a cautious distance. The one called Pete, ever the tireless lackey, appeared and invited them to enter. Luders spoke, declining the invitation.

"We'll do this here in the street. There is nothing about an affair of honor that needs to be hidden from the public eye."

Clark burst from the tent, followed by Stringer.

"Fuck your affair of honor. Just tell me when and where I'm to kill that hamstrung Limey bastard. I aim to shoot him in the guts."

Luders did not approach. "I choose to believe we are all gentlemen here. I…we are here to either accept your apology or to deliver the terms according to the recognized rules of the duel."

"Apology, hell. Let's get on with it."

Clark's outburst had elevated the tension to near breaking. As unobtrusively as possible, Josh let his right hand drift down near his holstered revolver. He wasn't inconspicuous enough. Stringer edged around Clark's side, letting his hand drop and flexing his fingers. His gaze landed on Josh's and the younger man knew he was in the presence of a life-taker. Stringer opened his eyes wide, making himself look like he lived on the edge of crazy. The look was calculated to intimidate and wilt a man where he stood. Josh was not so foolish as to feel no fear but damned if he was going to let a man break him with a gimmick look. He didn't react except to slow his breathing and widen his stance. He'd promised his wife there would be no gunplay. The promise was becoming a dicey proposition.

It was the interest of the nearby miners that defused the confrontation. Miners, hearing the exchange, began to gather at their tents and in small groups. Josh noticed no one was standing behind Stringer or his companions. He dared not take a look behind his. Were these men so curious or so bored they would be drawn to a place where bullets might fly. A voice from his right finally broke the tension.

"This must be those duelists we heard about. I know the youngster. I seen him snap shoot two highwaymen to death at near a hundred yards. One second his hand was empty and the next second two men was dead as fence posts. Saved our lives, sure."

"It was just as he says. I was there and my brother is speakin' the plain truth. Damnedest thing I ever seen."

Josh recognized the voices. It was Silas and Erby Pratt. Their declaration set off a murmur amongst the gathered miners. More importantly, Josh saw Stringer abandon the crazy look. He didn't blink but it was enough to defuse a bad situation. Clark glared at Josh, not quite believing what he'd heard but unwilling to risk more than a hard stare.

"All right. Say what you come to say. I'm ready."

Luders announced the time for ten o-clock on Monday morning. Clark agreed.

When Luders said the duel would be start at either end of the French Bridge, Clark looked puzzled but agreed.

"I shall serve as Mr. Shipwash's second. Will you name your own?"

Stringer stepped forward. "Name's Dobson Stringer. I'll do it."

If the seconds were supposed to shake hands, it didn't happen. The two exchanged barely perceptible nods.

"Mr. Shipwash has selected bladed weapons for the engagement. The opponents will face each other with both sword and dagger."

"Swords, what the hell kind of nonsense is this? I ain't got no damn sword. We fight with guns where I'm from. Ain't going to…"

For one of the few times in his life, words had abandoned Clark. He was flummoxed completely, turning to his two companions for some sort of support. What that might be was elusive.

"Mr. Shipwash anticipated you might not have a sword so I have agreed to present you with my own. I carried it as a member of the New York State Southern Militia. It is virgin, having never drawn blood but nevertheless a capable weapon. As to the dagger, you are free to bring any knife you choose, daggers being in such short supply in these parts."

Luders had kept the sword concealed in a rolled blanket and he withdrew it and presented it to Clark, stepping off half the distance between them. He held the sword over his arm hilt first. Clark hesitated but a moment before regaining his bravado. He accepted the sword, unsheathed it, and waved it about with a flourish enjoying the sound as it cut the air.

"This sticker'll do." He ran this thumb across the edge, looked critically at Luders. "Might have to give this a turn with an oilstone till it meets my standards."

Luders gave a short, formal bow. When he stood, he found the point of his own sword pointed at his chest.

"Tell your Englishman I'm going to open up his belly with your sword and then stick a knife in his ear come tomorrow. He'd best spend his time making peace with his Maker."

Those words ended the honorable exchange of dueling particulars and both parties retreated. Josh caught the eye of the Pratt brothers and gave them a grin.

"You could say things was getting jittery back there till you spoke up."

"That was Erby," said Silas. "He's the quick thinker in the family."

"Sorry if I turned the story into a bit of a stretcher."

"Served its purpose. I'd say we're even up now."

"Like hell," said Erby. "How's about we buy you and your friend a drink or two. I know a barroom keeps a good bottle or rye below the bar."

"Done!" piped up Luders. "I could use one after that. The Clark fellow has a temper you could broil a steak on."

~ ~ ~

Not wanting to cause worry, Josh and Luders soon wished the Pratt brothers good luck and returned to their camp. Luders told the tale to his friends and Josh slipped away across the bridge at the creek and found his wife pacing the floor of their shelter, arms crossed and her eyes, bright, on the verge of tears. As he entered she turned to him, tried to look cross and failed. She threw her arms around his neck and her tears flowed freely on his shirt.

"I was so angry at you for going with Luders but now I'm just so relieved you returned safely."

"If I recall, you said I should go 'cause I know what Clark looked like."

"You should have been able to tell I didn't mean it. You shouldn't have gone."

"I promised I was going to let Jack do all the talking."

Josh wondered how long it take before the story got out how dicey it had been. Probably not long but damned if he was going to tell her. She was near blubbering. One thing at a time.

"These past couple weeks I don't know what's come over you. I feel like I'm walkin' on eggs. How'm I supposed to guess you say one thing and mean the opposite? What's come over you?"

Elizabeth blurted back something but her face was buried in his shoulder.

"Come again."

She stood upright and looked at him through eyes misted with tears. Her face was blotchy and almost trembling. She could have still been angry but he didn't think so. She took his face gently in her hands. Her fingers played lightly on his cheeks. It took her a few moments to find her voice amidst the occasional sob.

"I'm going to have a baby. You are going to be a father."

Since the time Josh had been with Elizabeth part of him accepted he would someday hear she was pregnant. The idea had always been an abstract and occasionally he would play out this announcement and his reaction in his mind. The reality was so profoundly different than he imagined, he could only gape. Joy, worry, fear, apprehension, responsibility, and questions of the future ran all together through his thoughts at once. He couldn't focus on any one of them long enough to think coherently. He could only stare back at her. Finally, behind the tears, behind the blotchy face and runny nose, he could see the joy of expectant motherhood appear.

"Truly? Are you sure? How can you know?"

She wiped her face on her sleeves and let loose a little secret laugh.

"Yes, yes. And I know. Didn't your mama ever tell you anything?"

"Nope. She never told me nothing about women things and my father never let on if he knew. Really, you…we are going to have a baby? What kind? I mean…"

She was calm now, tried to put on a serious face.

"Men are so silly and helpless sometimes. Yes, a baby is on the way and I figure you will be a father before next Christmas. I won't know till I see a doctor."

Josh had begun just nodding along. "Right. A doctor. There's no doctor here. We will have to find a doctor."

"I don't need one tonight but I should see one soon. Oh, I wish Doctor Bingham had come to California with us."

"He's in Oregon. We can send for him. We've got money enough he'll come."

"And I'll bet he'll come if we asked. I think he wanted to when we split but Hattie made him go on. We can talk about that later but we have to consider some changes."

"Changes, of course. Whatever you want."

"I'm saying we can't stay here. Can't have our baby born in a half-cabin, half-tent. Even one with so nice a little stove as we have. We're going to have to go someplace settled, someplace not a wild camp. Do you want to tell your daughter she was born in Hangtown?"

"A daughter. You're going to have a baby girl."

"Or a boy. Maybe both." She laughed aloud as the possibility tried to sink in for Josh.

"We'll go wherever you want. We've got money enough but if we leave, what happens to our claims? A claim that isn't worked by the owner reverts to the first who records paper on it."

They were puzzling this out when a voice asked if they could come in.

Timely as ever, Duncan had arrived with a solution.

~ ~ ~

"I've just left meeting with the officers of the Albany partners. Luders told me of your encounter with my dueling companion."

Josh shot him such a stare Duncan couldn't help but know the confrontation should remain hidden from Elizabeth. Without acknowledging Josh's hint or missing a beat, he got straight to his purpose.

"As we've discussed, I'm going to be leaving camp soon. It may be as soon as Monday morning." He allowed himself a small, wry smile as he attempted to joke about his possible demise.

Elizabeth didn't see anything funny about it and her eyes began leaking again.

"Don't even try to joke about such things."

"I'm sorry, my dear. My attempts at levity often come across awkwardly." He looked at Josh, puzzled.

"I'll tell you later."

Duncan let it pass.

"Earlier I ventured down to the end of our claim and as far as the quartz vein we explored some days ago. Once again, I was looking for auriferous signs with the intent to establish a further claim. To my dismay, the entire area is now populated with prospectors who apparently believe I am possessed of the Midas touch. Men have begun excavating the vein and have taken up residence in the tunnel. Such tunnels and prospects are all along the ridge down to the creek. The men who live in them have taken to calling them *coyote holes*."

"What was most distressing was I ran into two of our Albany partners, Dryden and another man whose name escapes me. I did not stop but to exchange greetings. I grow concerned where two men who are pulling a steady and laudable income from the deep gravel claim would abandon their interest to strike out on their own. This gives me great pause regarding the future of our entire operation here."

Duncan paused, inviting comment. Elizabeth was still collecting her wits. Josh shrugged his shoulders and motioned for him to continue.

"I have to ask, with the weather improving and miners soon leaving for the upper rivers and streams, how many men will be content with what they have and how many will follow the next rumor of a strike, willing to abandon their share to chase a dream."

"That doesn't make sense to me," Josh said. "We've pulled out plenty of hundred dollar pans. The men are making many times what they would at home and the deep gravel is a proven claim. Who would give that up to go freeze in a river for maybe nothing?"

"Once a man gets touched by the fever for gold, there is no cure. I would offer up myself as one of the afflicted. I would rather roam the hills with pick and pan than sit in the claims office and watch men bring me their gold and tales of their adventures."

"We already talked about taking the majority in the registry so you can explore," interrupted Elizabeth, now returned to her more familiar, rational state.

"Let me continue. Consider one of those hundred dollar pans. Our separate partnership is ceded thirty dollars right from the start. The remaining seventy dollars, assuming even twenty partners means each of the Albany partnership receives but three and a half dollars and from that the costs of food, shelter, and equipment must be deducted. Even if our claim continues to produce at the present rate, the man who is digging and hauling can't have expectations of more than twenty or twenty-five dollars a day. Measure that against washing out a hundred dollar pan all for yourself. By high summer, twenty dollars a day will be laborer's wages and jobs will go begging even at that."

"You didn't come here just to tell us things might fall apart." Elizabeth was her practical self again, at least for the moment. "What are you suggesting?"

"Not suggesting. I'm doing. I'm willing to sell my share of our partnership and I will offer it to you first before approaching the others. This is simply a courtesy. If I were you, Jubal too, I would suggest we divest our entire interest or at least a substantial part of it to our partners, or, if they decline, to the highest offer. Thirty thousand for our thirty percent seems appropriate. How say you?"

"The whole company together doesn't have that kind of wealth."

"I'm willing to take a note for what they cannot raise. Consider the alternative."

"The Albany company will dissolve and our claims revert to the first who sticks a shovel in the ground," offered Elizabeth.

"Precisely. At the least their steadfast partnership will be greatly reduced. No doubt there are members right now contemplating selling their interests to others. If we move quickly each member will not only increase their percentage but will be obligated to retire the note."

"They might cheat us of any part we keep," scoffed Josh.

"I would hope they are honorable men but consider the alternative. The work is abandoned for lack of labor and we lose everything."

The young couple exchanged looks. Elizabeth spoke for both of them.

"Yes. Negotiate all our percentages as a single purchase. We should like to retain some interest. I consider myself as a savvy person at the bargaining table but they respect you. Whatever deal you come up with is fine with us. I'm certain I speak for Jubal, too."

"There's another reason we are willing to sell. Go ahead, wife. You tell him."

Elizabeth beamed. "I am going to have a baby, and Hangtown is no place to birth a child. We are leaving the hills for…well, I'm not exactly sure where."

"My dear, this is such wonderful news." Shipwash gathered them in his embrace and they celebrated with a drink. Elizabeth demurred but still accepted a sip as toast. They then got down to discussing their options for selling off the claim. Once concluded, it was decided Duncan would sell his half of the claims registry to Leland Weber. The former legislative assistant was better suited to working with a nib and inkpot. The Bonners agreed to give up part of their share to sweeten the deal.

CHAPTER NINETEEN

Monday, this most auspicious Monday, dawned like any of the recent days. The sky was as blue as the day before and the same scattered, puffy clouds cast intermittent passing shadows on the land as a light breeze scattered the winter's dead leaves and rattled the branches of the trees and their newly formed buds. Birds trilled and sang. Men awoke, prepared the morning meal and concluded Spring had finally taken hold in Hangtown. More than talk of the weather, the conversation ran to the impending duel at French Bridge.

The practice of the duel had largely fallen out of favor except in the American South. Even there it was conducted in secrecy because of newly enacted prohibitions. Most were familiar with the history and even the concept. Duels with pistols were the rule. A formal combat with edged weapons was an event many of those present would later tell to their grandchildren. The migration to the bridge began early. The anticipation was as high as Independence Day. Many commented on the holiday atmosphere and how it differed from the rather grim proceedings of the Court's floggings and hangings. This was blood sport, better than the rat pit and more deadly than a prizefight.

Ten o'clock arrived and went without either combatant making an appearance. Soon, as is common within a mob, speculation arose the whole affair was just a rumor started in a saloon. By quarter after the rumors were put to rest as Duncan and his second arrived, followed by the miners from his camp. As if on cue, Clark, Stringer, and Peterson appeared, followed by curiosity seekers. Where their allegiance aligned was anyone's guess. Touts circulated and shouldered their way through the gathering, offering an opportunity for those inclined to support their favorite. The odds were three to two on the big man. As in a fistfight, size counted and Clark outweighed his opponent by a good fifty pounds. The odds increased, as Duncan appeared, hobbling along noticeably on his bum leg.

The crowd parted for Clark as he approached. Not a few called out encouragement but most retreated as the big man was already waving his blade over his head and throwing phantom jabs with a wicked looking skinning knife. Clark was a showman and he worked the crowd for all he was worth. Barkeepers abandoned their shops and plied shots to willing customers. The crowd closed in behind Clark and his entourage. They didn't come too close. Clark's second was perhaps even more imposing, the kind of man its best to keep your distance from. Several men ran across to the less crowded north end. The mob, other than a few raucous drunks, hushed as the seconds left their champion's side and met in the middle. Whatever was said could not be heard but those who had knowledge of the *Code Duello* explained the last minute opportunity for an apology was being offered and the conditions determining a winner would be set. The first to draw blood was the generally accepted determinant. Two barbers, the camp's answer for medical assistance, came forward and were introduced. A choice was offered and each barber joined their respective sides. The seconds withdrew and the combatants took their places. Sixty feet of rough planking separated the two.

Clark kept up his bluster, shouting the same few insults across and telling his opponent to make peace with his God before being opened up for the world to see his vitals. Some bettors, wiser than others, perceived the bravado for what it was and quietly placed wagers on Shipwash. Odds were at four to one against the smaller man.

Duncan removed a cloak and handed it to Jack Luders, revealing a British cavalry officer's dress tunic. He drew on leather gloves and withdrew his sabre from the scabbard offered by his second. He let the blade drop to his side. By contrast, Clark wore trousers over gray long underwear. His paunch, while not substantial, was a contrast to the slim physique of the man facing him. The odds dropped and a quick flurry of betting ensued before the crowd grew silent. It was time.

The combatants faced each other and Clark quit his harangue, instead glaring across the field of honor. The birds no longer chirped. The noise of the gathering crowd had dispersed them. The breeze still sighed through the tree branches, and the river burbled and splashed below. Duncan raised his sword in salute. Clark pawed the ground like a bull and let out a heathenish howl. Then he charged.

Duncan allowed him four or five steps before he began a measured pace forward. The attention of the crowd was on the big man and cheers anticipating the clash drowned out those despairing the violence they were about to witness. The crowd on the camp end pressed together, welling forward. All attention was on the mad rush of the bearded giant, a barbarian released.

Those on the other side were silent. Those who watched the man in the red tunic advance later said they were struck by his poise. A few noticed the slight hitch in his walk diminished with each step. He'd raised his weapon until the sword pointed into the bright sky but offered no counter to the certain death now only a few paces away. Had he resolved himself to death and was simply being gallant in his last moments. It appeared so. Elizabeth, the only woman present on this side, let a dismal wail escape from her and leaned back against Josh for support. She did not look away. No one looked away.

Clark saw victory before him. His sword was held high, behind his head and ready to deliver death like a hawk pounces on a mouse in the field. The skinning knife was held out to his side, balancing him as he prepared to hack down the smaller man.

Six feet separated the two when Duncan drove forward. There was no sign of a limp. He brought his blade up straight before him and clutched it with both hands. Clark took a short leap and his weapon descended in a wicked blow from arm's length. A growl of triumph would be the last thing the Englishman would hear.

As the blade slashed downward, Duncan sprang forward, stepped neatly inside the blow and, throwing his bad leg straight forward, falling to his other knee. He held his sword out flat to deflect the vicious blow. It never came. Clark saw the deception at the last moment and tried to bring his blow down straight. He succeeded in delivering only a glancing blow to Shipwash's shoulder with the hilt. He tried to arrest his charge but his momentum flung him forward.

With his leg still forward, Duncan rolled on to his left hand for support. As Clark stumbled by, he brought the sabre up and forward in a blur, striking his opponent on the side of his shin and opening a long, diagonal gash along the calf. Clark lurched forward a step until he brought weight on his wounded leg. He toppled forward, the knife skittering away on the planks. The savage growl became a grunt as Clark looked at the ruin on his calf. Before he'd been able to roll over, Duncan was on his feet and coming towards him. Before Clark was aware of it, Duncan's boot was on his wrist, pinning his weapon to the ground.

"Now we both have bad legs. Do you wish to continue even without your prior advantage?"

Clark didn't answer. He released the borrowed blade and sat up, clutching at the wound as if he could bind it back together with his hands.

"Look what you done to my leg, you sneaking shit. I'm bleeding to death."

"It's not spouting so the artery is intact. It's a severe wound but the barber you chose looks competent."

The pain set in and Clark let loose an agonized bleat that served to summon the barber to his side. He swatted Clark's arms aside and affixed a loop of cloth above his knee and wound it tight with a stick. Clark pounded the deck with his bloodied fists.

The crowd was stunned. The combat hadn't lasted ten seconds from the time Clark pawed like a bull to him thrashing on the ground like a fallen horse, his defiant howl reduced to whimpering curses. As a blood sport spectacle, the duel had disappointed. Expectations were for a drawn out fight, the combatants bloodied and beaten until one lay dead or crying for quarter. They came expecting an affair like a prizefight and instead witnessed a knockout before either fighter even broke a sweat. Indeed, Shipwash had not even drawn the knife from the sheath at his belt. It took far longer than the fight itself for the throng to realize what transpired and then they broke into cheering. Those who had backed Clark made noise about cheating, but they were silenced by those around them.

Duncan turned to the mob on the Hangtown side, held the hilt of his sabre to his chest and rewarded them with a short bow. He retrieved Luder's sword and swiveled back to his own supporters. He kicked the skinning knife into the river as he passed.

"Lordy, that was slick," exclaimed Josh. "You just made yourself King of Hangtown."

Duncan's laugh was one of relief. "I must admit everything went as I planned. If it hadn't, the outcome could have been perilous. Jack, thank you for the loan of your sword. I believe it is undamaged."

"Can't say the same for you, you're bleeding." Elizabeth pointed to the back of Duncan's trousers."

"I'm afraid you are right. I took quite a painful splinter in my rump when I hit the deck."

Josh joked, "Appears Clark drew first blood then. He should be declared the winner."

"Let's keep this amongst ourselves. It might start a controversy among those who wagered."

Jack Luders leaned in and interrupted. "Look who's coming."

Stringer was approaching. Looking him over, Josh didn't think he was armed. Still, he had to resist letting his hand fall towards his holster.

"Ah, Mr. Stringer. I hope your champion is not too badly injured."

Stringer ignored Duncan's inquiry.

"That was low down. From the way you forced him into a duel, to the way you played on his weaknesses, to the sneak's trick you used to gash him."

He leaned in and glared at Shipwash.

"The nature of combat is to exploit your opponents weaknesses. Someone famous once said that but for the life of me I can't recall who it was just this moment."

"I'm calling you a pile of stinking English weasel shit. How about you and I have a go at it?

"The duel with your friend served a purpose. I could as easily killed him in as much time as it took to wound him."

"Clark is a brute and a bully. He's bigger and in better health," Elizabeth interjected.

"You stay out of this, missy. I don't need to listen to some doxy pretending she's a married woman. You think he didn't tell me?"

Elizabeth's hand was already in her bag. The metallic double-click of her pepperbox being cocked was heard before Josh could drop his hand to the Colt. Stringer smirked at them as he opened his capote, showing he was unarmed. He stared hard at each in turn. His breathing was audible, slow, and measured as if struggling to keep himself under control. The exchange was escalating into a confrontation and drawing the attention of the Albany boys. They began to sidle over and form a ring of protection around their champion. Stringer saw what was happening but was determined to get in the last shot.

"You made an enemy today, an enemy for life. I ain't talkin' about that Lummox Higgins, neither." Stringer gave each his crazy-eyes routine, turned on his heel and never looked back.

"He did that eyeball routine when I first met him," said Josh. "Bet he thinks it gets him somewheres."

"It's just an act," replied his wife. "His regular look is what scares me. Like there's something malevolent inside him looking for a way out."

"You're right, of course," said Duncan. "He's a dangerous and unpredictable man and an enemy this English pile of weasel dung can do without. It may appear cowardly but I think it best we depart camp with as little attention as possible."

"You should've finished Clark, and I say its best to have it out with Stringer now."

"And I say you are going to be a father and Duncan's right."

"You mean we just sneak away?"

"That's exactly what I mean. If he stays in Hangtown, odds are he'll end up dancing on the end of a rope within the month. That man isn't right."

"Say, if its not much bother, I can feel blood in my boot. Perhaps we might retire. Would one of you summon the barber, please?"

CHAPTER TWENTY

The final days before the friends put Hangtown behind them passed without any further encounter with Stringer. The four of them made several visits to the claims registry located on the same dirt street as Clark's, Stringer's, and Peterson's. From a distance they had seen him watching them, staring them down, no doubt with his crazy eye routine. It went no further than that.

Since the duel the trio were becoming near outcasts in camp. Those camping near them had pulled up stakes and moved to quieter surrounds. The Pratt brothers were among them. The two stopped by the office telling a tale of drunken shouting matches and hangover induced bickering emanating from their tent. Their only visitor had been the barber tending to Clark's wound. Even his visits became shorter and shorter before he too cut off contact. When Clark was in his cups he bellowed hollow threats of retribution. Sober, he berated his companions for neglecting him. Peterson was observed buying laudanum but whether it was too placate his injured friend or to escape his wrath was unknown.

Spring had set the camp in motion. Miners were equipping themselves for the approaching mining season. The roads were becoming a steady stream of new arrivals. The greenhorns dressed in the requisite heavy trousers, wool shirt and felt hat. The difference was their gear was new and served as a flag to the tradesmen to raise their prices. In the saloons the veterans explained this to the novices and not a few were persuaded to trade their fine new duds for the faded and *experienced* clothing of the experienced prospector. For those who had spent the winter in camp taverns the fresh arrival was their natural prey. Sage advice could be had for the price of a drink. Bad advice was the same price.

The Bonners had little need to purchase more than provisions to get to the next settlement. San Francisco, as it was now known, was their destination and what they would need was cheaper at the coast, saving the cost of freighting goods inland. They kept the planks and spars from the *Julianna*, loaded their precious stove and their household goods on the wagon and covered it with the sails and canvas they'd spent the winter under. Everything else they offered to Jubal and Duncan whose needs were much like those of the prospectors preparing for the coming season. The rest went to the Albany men.

One item of note they loaded was a barrel of flour. They weren't planning on a lot of baking on their journey to the port city. On their odyssey over the plains a barrel of flour had served as their bank and repository for their valuables. The money belt of Elizabeth's father went into the barrel but this time was joined by a fortune in gold. The young couple were, by the standards of the day and even those of the gold fields, quite well off. In addition to their own treasure they carried a sizable piece of Duncan's gold. Jubal left some with them but retained the bulk of his wealth for his own use. He was destined for a much longer journey back to the United States or perhaps Canada. He was a man with plans for his money and would send for the balance when he was settled. Duncan, always a light traveler, entrusted an amount nearly equal to the Bonners into their hands. Surely someone of enterprise would start a bank. If not, who would suspect these two young people of safeguarding tens of thousands in gold?

Duncan did have one oddity in his gear. He'd purchased two casks of gunpowder, a rock drill and a long coil of waterproof fuse. Questioned, its use was revealed.

"That short, dry arroyo where we picked out the exposed veins of gold is probably as rich or richer than even the deep gravel claim we worked over the winter. If we are fortunate, it remains undiscovered. No doubt the banks along the Middle Fork of the American are even now being swarmed over by miners like our old friend, Texas Billy. They will certainly be working the placer holdings and have no idea of the riches lying within rifle shot of their camps. It will take labor and machinery to exploit those reefs. Neither are readily available so my intention is to secure the arroyo for our partnership until we can register a claim and work it. In the meantime, these barrels should be sufficient to bring down the slopes above the mouth of the gulch and preserve it for ourselves. Jubal, can I entice you to accompany up the river beyond where you once rescued me from the flood?"

"What man doesn't like blowing things up? I ought to pay you for the chance to go along."

"It's settled then. Our friends from Albany have planned a bit of a celebration in our honor. I insist you attend with us."

"No, I ain't gonna fit in at no party like that."

Elizabeth, always eager for some controversy, piped up. "You're going with all of us. You worked cheek by jowl in the mud over the winter, and if they won't seat you they can all line up and kiss my behind."

"I think you might find some willing takers to your challenge, dear wife. You have a mighty fine behind."

"You've been drinking, haven't you, dear husband? You don't need to be discussing my behind even with our best friends." She was right of course but she laughed through the blush on her cheeks.

"Jubal, let us go across the river and secure several bottles of reputable popskull. I'm certain a few drinks under the belt and the Albany boys will be like long lost brothers."

~ ~ ~

For the party three goats had been secured and were being attended to over a slow fire. In his honor a spicy rice dish was being prepared according to Duncan's specifications. A kettle of dried peaches was being resuscitated in a pot. They would become a streusel dessert. Lacking butter, bacon fat would be used in the topping but by the time it was served, most everyone would have drunk enough it would hardly be noticed. The arrangements were nearly complete when the four friends arrived bearing a cask of brandy and a dozen bottles of local mission wine, some trade whiskey, and three bottles of the locally produced Mescal, shipped up from the southern mining district.

"Jubal, you sit on my left and damn anyone who objects." Elizabeth's pregnancy had not affected her obstinacy. Jubal, well familiar with her nature, readily but uneasily complied. There were some looks and three or four men moved to tables as far from the table of honor as they could. As Shipwash had predicted, any objections to Jubal being at table were forgotten within thirty minutes of the first cork being popped.

"I count seventeen of your company remain, Duncan remarked to Luders. "Will you be able to keep your partnership intact?"

"I don't think we will have any more quitters. Dryden and Hanes took off to work a quartz vein they discovered but realized two men living in a hole and digging a tunnel that might collapse on them wasn't a paying proposition. They skedaddled back. They've been the most active in discouraging others to take out on their own."

"Two of them rascals that took off in January and then crawled back have lit out on their own," interjected Josh. "They came to me trying to buy my shotgun."

"We tried to talk them out of it, but they wouldn't listen. We even told them they couldn't come back a second time but they were determined. We got two men down with fever, not serious, but they weren't well enough to attend."

"Some time tomorrow, after most are approaching sobriety, I'd like to walk our entire claim with all in attendance. I'll explain where the best prospects are and how they should be worked."

"Much appreciated. They are, for the most part, quick studies. You've set them on the right path and this shindy is a reflection of their gratitude. You too, ma'am. Josh and Jubal, too."

Jubal and Elizabeth recognized they were being spoken to but were seated far enough away they couldn't hear over the ruckus. Both held up their glasses and laughed as Luders tugged at his hat in acknowledgement.

"Glad to see you're loosening up a bit."

She touched glasses with Jubal, toasting nothing. The gesture seemed a bit too familiar to Jubal but he couldn't refuse. He looked about, expecting some hard stares. Instead a few men nearby lifted their glasses and smiled. Nervously, Jubal returned the gesture but didn't risk offering to touch glasses. All in all the party was proceeding better than he ever imagined. Elizabeth was exchanging some nonsense with the miner seated across from her. Jubal was concentrating on his plate when the man on his left nudged him.

"I hear you are going to head east once the passes are open. Some of us are wondering if you would carry letters home for us. Of course, we'll pay you for your trouble."

"I ain't figured just where I'm headed. Might even go to Canada." He wasn't sure he should even share that much but the words were already gone.

"Eventually though, you will come across a post office. If you would simply put stamps on them it would be a great service to us. We've had no contact with the States in months. Our families must be wringing their hands in despair."

"I reckon I can. Can't guarantee nothin' though."

"Of course not. Dwayne Cole," he said, offering his hand to seal the deal. "We worked together hauling ore to the wash."

This was turning into one of the strangest days in Jubal's memory. He tentatively stuck out his hand and the man shook it enthusiastically.

~~~

There were no early risers the next morning. Trees would remain uncut. Shovels and picks would remain where they lay. No one would feed the toms or wash even a pan. The party carried on past midnight. The food and drink kept coming. A fiddle and a jew's harp were produced and lamentable renditions of some popular tunes were rewarded with raucous applause. Elizabeth was enticed to dance with Duncan and soon she was beset with offers to be twirled about the dirt floor of the mess tent.

Given her condition she had refrained from the offers to refill her glass. She'd limited herself to two glasses of wine, judiciously sipped. She obliged many of the requests to dance. She didn't want to refuse anyone, but the demands of polite society were soon exceeded. Josh, at last, came to her rescue. He took a dance and skillfully worked their way to the fringes of the party. As the violin squawked its last long note, he thanked each and all for a wonderful party and bid them good night. There was some good-natured booing following them into the evening.

Once again they were sleeping under the wagon. Josh had his arm slung over her as she awoke. Gently she moved him aside and lay contemplating their departure and the last details. Eventually she arose, found some privacy behind a stand of scrub oak and conceded the day had begun. When she returned Josh hadn't moved but two men stood off a polite distance from the wagon. She motioned them over and they exchanged banalities about the last night's party, the morning and the weather before getting down to business.

"We were wondering, ma'am, if we wrote some letters if you would take them to San Francisco and maybe put them on a ship bound for home?"

"I'd be pleased to but isn't Jubal going to carry your letters?'

"He is, but that's a dangerous road." He produced a thick packet of envelopes and a pouch of gold dust, offering to her. "We've all written duplicates, figuring there's better odds that way."

"Is this all? We're getting ready to leave."

"This is most of them but some is still scribbling."

Josh was awake and watching the exchange.

"Where you figure on posting those?"

"I haven't any idea but how could I refuse?" She tucked the bundle into a satchel underneath the wagon seat.

"Well, guess there's nothing to do now but get the team hitched and get on the road."

"Duncan is out with the company, giving them last minute instructions. We'll leave after, if he doesn't take too long."

~ ~ ~

Even the friends' best efforts could not get them ready to leave before almost noon. Interruptions and small details dogged them right up until they were mounted and the last packet of letters was delivered. Well-wishers lined the way out of camp as the procession set out. Josh and Elizabeth led the way in the big wagon with Natchez and two mules in tow. Jubal followed with the cart and Chicory. Duncan, aboard Cyrus rode behind with another mule. The two kegs of gunpowder discretely hidden under an oilskin cover. As they progressed the men tagged along on foot as far as the junction with the road to Sutter's. Before they made the first turning the friends all turned for a last look and were greeted with a cheer and waves. Hangtown was now a point of departure, no longer their home.

The road to the fort, as always, was well-traveled. The surface was firm but rutted and muddy. Last season's leaves were strewn across the way, overlaid together like some crazy mosaic. In just a few months, the surface would become a shootop deep passage of sand and dust. Every foot, hoof, and wheel that passed would leave a cloud hanging in the air for minutes after their passage. The mosaic of leaves today carpeting the road would be crumbled away and become part of the grit in the mouth and on the teeth of the thousands of men and wagon teams marching inexorably along. Today the road was full of fresh faces, new boots, and virgin picks, shovels and pans. The newcomers came alone, in pairs, and in small groups. All the new arrivals were eager and confident. They greeted the friends' procession with the valiant enthusiasm of new soldiers marching to glory in their first battle. The friends were reminded of their first encounter with the Greater Albany Argonauts. They exchanged greetings with the novitiates, answered their questions with brief replied and wished them good luck. Soon it became tiresome and they speculated amongst themselves how many of the fresh new faces would survive the next year.

On occasion they met a freighter hauling supplies to the far-flung outposts in the hills and canyons. The exchanges were brief. A nod of the head, a tip of the hat, and a brief query about the road ahead served them well. Several times they encountered a grizzled miner in ragged attire and leading a mule laden with the necessities of prospecting. Beside and behind the veteran clean-shaven faces dogged the drawn and bearded miner like geese gathered around a farm wife with her sack of grain. As these swarms passed our friends they looked at them with pleading eyes but there was nothing to be done. It was agreed amongst them they had the better of it with the new ones and thanked heaven they were traveling away instead of to the gold.

Josh had settled into a morose mood, not entirely because of the endless barrage of questions coming their way. He huddled down in his coat and pulled his hat down as far as it would go. Elizabeth, used to these dark moments of his, remained silent. She knew he would finally reveal what ailed his mind and eventually he spoke.

"I don't like leaving Clark and especially that Stringer character behind us. Can't much get the idea we are being pursued out of my mind. We ain't seen the last of that crew."

"The best thing we can do," suggested Elizabeth, "is to pull off into the woods and ambush them as they pass by. Then we just drag the bodies off the road and move on. Who's to stop us?"

The remark brought Josh out of his reverie. He turned towards her and was greeted by an evil glint and a devilish smile on her face.

"You ain't serious, are you? You're just having a bit of fun cause I'm bein' moody."

"Let's do it. It will be fun." She was rewarded with a knotted and uncertain look on the face of her man. She poked him in the ribs and laughed. Jubal and Duncan looked up, wondering what had precipitated the mirth.

"Clark's laid up for at least a couple more weeks and I don't think the other two have the gumption to leave him."

"You heard Stringer. That man is dangerous."

"I've heard Clark roar and stomp. They're two of a kind and Peterson wouldn't make a move on his own."

"I'm just sayin' I feel better tracking a deer than being the deer. The hunter can sleep easier."

Elizabeth decided to let the other two in on the joke.

"Josh thinks Clark and his wolves are on our trail. He wants to hide out next to the trail and cut them down as they pass. What do you think?"

"I never..." exclaimed Josh

Duncan and Jubal put on the same concerned looks Josh had. Elizabeth roared with laughter. The gloomy cloud over them dissipated and they met the next approaching clean-shaven faces with good cheer and helpful advice. The mood held until they approached the fort. Sutter's had always been a busy place but it swarmed with humanity now. It was like a hive of gold-hungry bees buzzing about a hive. They pulled off the road before they got any closer and camped. They would press through tomorrow.

And press through is literally what they did. The enclave near the fort was a mad sea of human commerce. Merchants brayed their wares and prices. Newcomers dismayed as they parted with their savings at astonishing prices, confident they would win back their investments in a few days. Gold dredged from the rivers last season and hoarded throughout the winter went for new supplies. It took three maddening hours to inch their way through the melee. Finally they were on the trail again, this time headed in the same direction as the gold seekers.

Ahead of them a company of men sang a bawdy song. Others stopped to repack sloppily tied packs that leaked equipment onto the road. Several inquired of the friends where they were from. The reply of "Hangtown" furrowed many brows and brought more questions. Even the grim name could not dampen the confidence of those who knew that golden dreams would soon be fulfilled.

Eventually, the friends parted company where the Middle Fork of the American River intersected the road. They had talked amongst themselves and made plans so the parting was brief but heartfelt. Jubal and Duncan turned towards the narrow gulch and their mission. The Bonners turned westward towards San Francisco and the Pacific. Duncan had described the ocean to them. Nothing could be so great as the vast continent they had crossed nearly a year earlier. They were anxious to take in the enormity of it for themselves.

THE END

ADDITIONAL CONTENT

Since the publication of **HANGTOWN** I have added two short stories continuing the Bonner saga.

The titles are:

INCIDENT AT BLUE LEAD CREEK: Josh protects his interests in other mining operations he owns an interest.

VIGILANTE STREETS: Lawlessness is rampant in San Francisco. Josh is called upon to help form and lead a Committee of Vigilance.

If **HANGTOWN** is the first novel of mine you've read, you won't want to miss the first two installments of **THE PLATTE RIVER WALTZ**

I've also added a bit of a teaser following this sample from **ORPHANS IN THE STORM**:

CHAPTER ONE

May 30, 1848

Dear Uncle Virgil and Aunt Martha,

I write to you from four days' trek west of Fort Kearney. I am in the Indian Territories now, near the Platte River. It is better this sad news come from me than by a traveler from these parts. Mother and Father did not make the journey. The cholera took both their lives, which was present in St. Jo when we left and has been with many emigrant parties on the trail. Father showed first signs about the time we made afternoon camp on Saturday the twenty-fifth and was quickly consumed by fever and the purging of the sickness. He was gone before the sun arose on the Sabbath. Mother tended to him well during the night and was with him at the end. On Sunday afternoon, Mother became ill and I feared the worst. Mrs. Gresham, who you may know, tended her along with a Dr. Bingham from a Missouri train encamped nearby with sick people of their own. He gave her barberry and an opium pill, and it seemed she rested comfortable and that the malady would spare her. Our party remained at camp as two other wagons took sick with the cholera. Mother stayed quiet till Monday afternoon when she awoke in a delirium for about an hour and then quickly slipped back and soon died. I was with them the whole time but thankfully am not sick. Mr. and Mrs. Hampton along with their boy James died from the disease, too. I didn't know this until they were gone. I was with my own kin, as would be fitting.

They was buried near a cold water spring next to the river along with the Hamptons. All except the father from a family of the Missouri party, name of Cooper, perished. There was a mother, a daughter, and a baby boy. All were given Christian rites by a Missouri Methodist preacher name of Clark. It was as pretty a resting place as any at home. There were some willow trees within a glade where we laid them down and green grass all around.

Elizabeth Hampton survived without affliction. She will travel on with the Clark preacher and his wife at least as far as Fort Laramie 'cause there is no one on the trail going east who she could safely travel with.

The Hamptons were from south of town near you, and you may know their people and can tell them of their loved ones' passing. Please let the Greshams of Cairo know that theirs are all right and how Mrs. Gresham was an angel to all the stricken. Mr. Gresham was not so Christian as he feared for the cholera coming to him and his. Their people maybe shouldn't know this as he was always liked about town but is much changed after only a month on the trail to Oregon.

I am left now with our hand, Jubal, and our stock and wagon. I have thought this well and have chosen to stay on the path to Oregon. I do not want to return to Cairo and be the orphan Bonner boy. My Father said this trip will make a man of me and that is a part of my reason for going on. I want to make my fortune like my brother, Ned. Perhaps I will meet him in Oregon as he has shipped on a steam packet out of New Orleans and is destined to stop for trade in California and Oregon.

I send this back with a family who has also suffered and has given up. I hope this letter reaches you, and I will try to write again from Fort Laramie.

Your nephew in sorrow,

Josh Bonner

Josh Bonner wasn't tired of walking. He was just tired of looking. For over an hour, he had been staring only at his feet as they trudged through the new grass of the plain beneath him.

For the last ten minutes or so, he had been concentrating on a white pebble picked up between the sole and toe of his boot. It wasn't that his boots fascinated him; it was just he dreaded looking up again at the endless vista of shifting green buffalo grass against the constant horizon. Nothing ever seemed to get any closer.

It had been seven days since he had buried his parents near the spring on the Platte. He was glad for the copse of trees near the gravesite. It was a peaceful place and made a landmark in this changeless sea of waving green and the occasional stunted tree. It was almost time for the afternoon camp, and he would be grateful for the reprieve despite how despondent his evenings had become.

The dreg ends of the days were the worst. With them, he had the dragging hours of the evenings to think about his parents and to entertain doubts of his decision to push on. Sometimes, it seemed every step was a chance to turn about.

The mornings, strangely, made everything seem right. Each day, he was thrilled by the bustle of having breakfast in the open and by the breaking of the night's camp. Packing, getting the mules from the picket line, and helping Jubal hitch the team to the wagon renewed him. Best of all, the affairs of the new day took him away from his misery and doubts.

Jubal watched Josh from his perch on the wagon. He held the reins loosely and let the mule team plod along. The river was just out of earshot to the right, and Josh walked aimlessly abreast the wagon about five rods distant. There wasn't much for Jubal to do in driving the wagon. The mules had steadied to their task in the past few days. Still, at night he picketed all the animals lest they get a notion to return to their old homes along the Missouri River. Other than an occasional flick of the reins he had little to do but watch the miles roll under the wheels and wonder about the young man pacing alongside.

Josh Bonner had changed more in the past month than in the seven years since Jubal fled slavery and had become a part of the

Bonner household. When they first set out for Oregon from their home in Cairo, Illinois, Josh had been just a boy, all full of himself and brimming with jump for the venture ahead. Since the deaths of Mr. and Mrs. Bonner he had seemed still a boy but one changed beyond the pain he must feel. Jubal was surprised that Josh decided to continue on.

After burying his folks, Josh sat for nearly a whole day by the bank of the river and wouldn't brook any company. Everyone knew he was crying but striving to behave as what he thought a man should. He wouldn't let anyone see his grief and turned away if any of the party tried to approach.

At that day's end he returned to the wagon camp to eat a sparing meal in silence. After an hour or so of poking the fire with a stick, he quietly announced they would go on. Surprisingly, neither the captain nor any of the other emigrants questioned Josh nor tried to dissuade him. They just passed glances around, shuffled about, and that was it. Nobody looked to Jubal, as they wouldn't pay any attention to a black man anyway. Even if anyone had bothered to ask for his opinion, he probably wouldn't have been able to tell them how he felt about the casual way the whites allowed even a boy to decide what to do with his own life. Perhaps it was the offhand way Josh spoke up or the determined set of his features that discouraged comment. As for Jubal turning back on his own, that wasn't even a consideration. Jubal had nothing to return or go back to. Worse, some of the emigrants were from slave states and might not take well to him walking away like a free nigger.

A flicker of movement ahead brought Jubal back to the moment. Shading out the sun with his hat, he saw amidst the glare the shimmering form of a rider approaching at a fast trot. As the dust rose around the rider, it was a few moments before he could pick out the scout returning on his roan gelding. He sure was coming back at a faster gait than he had left with that morning. Something had happened on the trail ahead.

"Mr. Bonner!"

No response.

"Mr. Bonner! Lookit! It's Monsoor Delcroix a-comin' back!"

Josh had heard Jubal the first time but didn't register it was him he meant and not his father. At the second hail, he realized he was the only "Mr. Bonner" left. He looked to where Jubal was standing and pointing, then stared off in the direction he was gesturing. He could only see a wispy cloud of dust he guessed to be about two miles distant. He ran to the wagon and vaulted up for a better vantage. Jubal halted the team and moved over as Josh stepped onto the wheel and into the bench box so he could see.

Closer than he'd thought but still some distance away, Josh saw the rider and could tell by the horse and outfit it was the scout, Delacroix, returning with some bit of news. By the way he was riding, he had seen something worth tiring his horse for but not so fast as to alarm the train. Josh's wagon was in the fore this day, and he decided to halt and let the others draw up. He raised his hand in a signal and stopped.

Their original party of three wagons from Illinois, the Bonners, the Greshams, and the Hamptons, had joined up with the Missouri party led by a Captain Metzger. In this party were Dr. Lemeul Bingham and his wife, Hattie, the Parson Clark and his wife, and six other wagons of people he hadn't met yet. It seemed to Josh that one of the names was Oroville.

Altogether there were about fifty people including the Missourians' half dozen or so slaves and about eighty head of mules, horses, cattle, and oxen. Elizabeth Hampton's wagon was being driven by one of the parson's slaves, Ely.

Another of their slaves, a woman named Dinah, helped with the camp chores.The men had all gathered and stood shuffling about, speculating on the news the scout was bringing. Most huddled around Captain Metzger and many brought their guns. They were checking their priming as they talked. In these parts, any news or change carried the prospect of danger. Josh carried no weapon, as the carriage of the scout didn't seem to indicate any threat was close at hand.

Josh sidled up to Mr. Gresham, who stood slightly away from the group, enough that he didn't seem a part of it.

"Mr. Gresham, what do you think the scout has seen?"

"Either Indians or buffalo, I reckon, Joshua. The weather's clear, and I expect we would have smelled a fire on the wind."

"Well, we ain't seen sign of either so far, but I expect we'll have our fill of both afore we get to Oregon," said Josh.

"Reckon that right enough. I wonder what Metzger's plans are."

Gresham's remarks about Metzger's as yet undisclosed plan seemed tinged with some hostility. Mr. Gresham apparently felt he should have been the captain, but the others had already elected Metzger their leader before the Cairo party joined them.

Delacroix rode up to the milling group of emigrants and they crowded about, all probing him with their questions. The scout could see they were on edge, and it would do no better talking to them than to a jabbering flock of crows.

"Nothing to worry about, men, but I'll need to talk to the captain," he said.

This didn't do much to quiet them but did give him the opportunity to take Metzger by the arm and lead him aside. Metzger saw what the scout was about and raised his hand to quiet the others.

"Hold off, boys. I'll talk to Delacroix and then we'll see what's to be done, if anything."

He strode away a few paces with Delacroix and turned his back to the group.

"Well, Delacroix, what did you find up ahead that's worth lathering that fine horse of yours?"

The scout replied, "'Cap'n, I espied some Indians up ahead." He slapped the brass spyglass he carried on his chest. "I didn't bother to make their acquaintance, only seein' but two. However, they was travelin' in a peculiar manner."

"Thunderation, Claude, I've never been in the Indian Territories, so maybe you better explain 'peculiar' to me," Metzger retorted.

"I means peculiar in that they was bein' watchful but movin' too fast to be scoutin' game. I think they was runnin' from something."

Metzger asked, "Are they headed this way?"

"*Oui*, there is a place about a mile ahead where one could ford horses, and this, I think, is the place to which they ride."

"And do you think there are more than the two you saw?"

"I believe so, *Capitaine*. If there were just the two, they would travel close together. They were some distance apart and one seemed to be watchin' the land about while the other scouted the river. I don't think they saw me."

The captain thought a moment. "We'll stop here, then. I don't want a party of Indians able to come up behind us where they can run off our stock." He spoke loud enough for his voice to carry to the milling settlers.

All the men had been straining forward, trying to overhear the scout's report. The mention of Indians didn't do much to placate them.

"He still didn't tell us what's come up. He ought at least to do that much," Gresham muttered, mostly to himself.

Josh made no comment. He knew Gresham resented Metzger's being captain. When they steamed up the Missouri, the three Cairo families had chosen Gresham as their leader. He had been a selectman up until the last election, and it had come natural to pick him. As near as Josh knew, none of the people emigrating had been any farther than Cincinnati except his father, who had been to New Orleans as part of his steamboat enterprise. Josh figured floating to New Orleans on a boat didn't qualify. Josh hadn't voted. Gresham seemed as good as any other to him.

When the two parties allied at the camp where his parents died, Metzger had already been the elected captain of the Missouri families. When they joined up, no one had asked for a new election. They had just been soaked up, Gresham's captaincy and all. It was a risky thing, asking a group with disease to come on with them. Metzger could have been voted down then, but he hadn't. Josh was grateful but a part of him wondered at the wisdom of such a decision.

"We'll stay below the ford where we can keep an eye on them till they pass. Thank you, Claude," Metzger announced.

Dismissing the scout, the trail boss wheeled back to the anxious faces awaiting him. As the throng parted, he strode amongst them and began to outline the situation.

The guide watched Metzger being surrounded by the nervous greenhorns, like chickens to a housewife with corn. While they were distracted, he ambled up to retrieve his horse. He softly stroked the horse's nose and led it away to the riverbank.

Kneeling by the horse as it drank, he commenced to refill his canteen, keeping his eyes westward toward the distant ford. The roving band wouldn't be any bother, but it was always wise to keep your eyes and ears open in these parts. The two he had seen looked from their topknots to be Pawnee, and while it was not unexpected to see Pawnee so near the Platte fords, the Sioux considered this their land. From the way these two were behaving he reckoned them to be scouts for a raiding party looking to put some distance between themselves and a pursuing party of Sioux, probably Oglala. He sure couldn't begrudge them their haste. The Pawnee and Sioux were hereditary enemies and they wouldn't be touching with coup sticks if they met up. Revenge for old murders, stolen horses, and stolen women would turn any meeting between those two into a hair-lifting party, certain as sunset.

He surmised it was just plain orneriness that sent the Pawnee this far north. There were plenty of *buffle* for them all, and there was water and land enough on these prairies for all the tribes. Old habits didn't die easy, he figured.

It was good for the emigrant trains that the Lakota had pretty much driven the Pawnee south near the Kansa River. As long as they were busy cutting each other up, they generally left the trains alone. The Sioux, while more numerous and therefore potentially much more dangerous, seemed to abide the whites who just passed through their lands. As long as they could trade for blankets and knives and be allowed to steal a horse now and again, they remained tractable enough. Sure, they would probably kill a lone hunter or scout, but as long as the whites traveled in groups and didn't wipe out more game than they needed, travelers were tolerably safe.

Delacroix walked the gelding up the short embankment and back to the train. He saw the men had gone back to their wagons and were commencing to form into an open corral where the animals would be protected. Metzger had gotten them doing the right thing without much of a fuss, and the scout was grateful the crisis had been averted with no further bother. So far, Metzger had been an easy man to lead. These people were fortunate to have picked Metzger as their headman. He had a natural ability to command but was smart enough to know he didn't know his way past St. Louis. He usually listened to Delacroix's advice, even beyond which direction to go.

The year before, he'd taken a party of fifty-five from Ohio to Oregon who had picked a rich farmer as their wagon master. Even when they had gotten as far as the Salt Lake, he still thought he could buy his way across the country. Worse, the skunk—Perkins his name was—turned out to be a Mormon hater. Not that Delacroix knew or even cared much about the Saints' religion, but he did know they would need their help by the time they got far. Blowhards like Perkins were dangerous on a journey like this, and it was asking for disaster to have one in charge. In spite of the rich Ohioan, the scout led them through. At least he led forty-nine of them through. Of the six that had died, three probably would have anyway. Two others had died needlessly, and one more had died viciously because of their damnfool captain.

The only real complaint Delacroix had about Metzger was he let the Illinois group join up with them. Delacroix didn't know anything about treating cholera, but he did know it best to keep your distance from any fever or disease. However, the malady seemed to have passed over them. He surely hoped so. One of his bonuses as trailblazer was to be fed at each wagon in turn. Today he was to eat from the camp of one of the *morte* wagons, the one in which the steamboat mechanic and his woman had died.

He had been watching the boy and the black for signs of cholera. There didn't seem to be any, and he did admire the boy's pluck for going on. The black seemed like he could handle himself in a fix. All told, though, he would rather camp with the red-haired Hampton girl. She seemed a likely wench to take care of a man on a lonely night. And her breasts! *La Tetons Grand*, he joked to himself and smiled.

Leland Metzger was pleased with the train's progress so far. Except for forming up into a U-shape with the livestock picketed within its confines, this day's camp was much like any of the previous ones. He was glad a potentially dangerous panic had been so easily thwarted. His people settled down after the first talk of the Indian sighting. The news sent the menfolk scudding to drive the women and children to the wagons. Now that the task of corralling up was complete, the usual routines of the afternoon camp were commencing, albeit with an air of nervous anticipation.

While it would have been pleasant to congratulate himself on his own handling of the crisis, he knew he was as green as any of the rest. Visions of a butchering party of savages had raced across his vision when he'd first learned of the nearby Indians. However, the quiet confidence of the pilot quickly settled his nerves and let him think clearly about what was to be done.

When he accepted the captaincy of the expedition prior to leaving St. Joseph, it was the reputation and the qualities of the Western guide that had inspired him to service. He now felt this dangerous journey could be completed. After all, Delacroix had led three other groups through to Oregon City, and they should consider themselves lucky they were able to hire him for the trip. Although he had heard good things spoken of him in St. Joseph, he didn't really know much about him. He had been told he was the son of a French *voyageur* trapper. Delacroix told him he had been to Oregon and California before with Fremont in '43. He sure looked and smelled like a trapper.

It was good luck they had a surgeon amongst their group of farmers, merchants, and clerks. He guessed he had old Doc Fletcher to thank for that bit of luck. If he hadn't had all the birthin' and buryin' business in Monroe County sewn up, Doc Bingham would probably still be at home settin' busted legs.

Home! That was somewhere ahead of him now in Oregon; unless he wanted to consider the wagon he, the missus, and their young'uns slept under as his home. Rough as that might be, it seemed to him better than the shabby rented house they had back in Monroe. Being the constable in Monroe hadn't been half-bad, but the townsfolk sure begrudged him his keep. Most of his job was keeping drunks off the street and transient scalawags moving on down the road. It had surely been a thankless job, but lately it seemed there were plenty of other men who wanted it. Chief amongst these was the cousin of the county sheriff, Bill Archer. Archer was about to put him out of the job anyway and the hundred dollars in gold he had offered him for an early retirement was all the convincing he needed to move on. A hundred dollars! That, and the guff his wife had to take from the wives of the other town officials who didn't think Claire Metzger was quite good enough for their parlors. Hell, they had been about ready to pack up and git even without the ten gold eagles Bill Archer had slapped down on the constable's scuffed desk that Saturday morning in March.

Delacroix wasn't around when Metzger stopped at the Bonner wagon.

"Where's Delacroix? Ain't you supposed to feed him today?"

"He be on the rise on t'other side of this wagon here. 'Spect he'll come for his supper when he's done Injun watchin', Cap'n, suh," Jubal replied, indicating where with a swing of his head.

Metzger noted Jubal was fixing two sleeping places under the wagon. True, it was on the ground, but a nigger shouldn't ought to bunk up with a white man, even out here. People sure got some strange ideas from living across the Mississippi in Illinois.

Josh stepped around from the other side of the wagon. One forearm was dusted with flour and held a canning jar dusted white.

"I suspect he'd rather watch for Indians than spend much time down here with us. I'm hopin' some of Ma's put-up peaches with his bacon and potato might friendly him up some." Josh held up the floured jar.

"Mebbe' you ought to pass some out to the other wagons, too. I don't see anybody crowding your camp here," said Metzger.

He paused to see how that set with the boy. Asking to hook up with them hadn't been received well by the rest of the Missourians. He had, however, elected to let them come on after Doc Bingham assured him once the cholera had killed whom it might. There was no further danger from it cropping up again. It was like the pox. After you were once exposed to it, you were safe in the future. Even now, he was considering sending the Hampton girl back to Fort Kearney with the boy and his nigger as escort. He couldn't care what the others might say about the arrangement.

As though Josh was reading Metzger's mind, the boy spoke up.

"Captain, if there were still cholera about, Jubal and I would both be dead. The rest'll see so in a few days, but I don't expect any of the womenfolk to be bringing over any pies. I mean to press on, be it with you or alone."

"You all are getting by, then?"

"We're gettin by. Jubal helps fine," Josh answered.

"Now, you be tying off your stock to the wheels tonight. A picket stake might pull out if there's any excitement. I'd just hobble that sorrel of yours. You might need to saddle up right quick-like if there's trouble later," Metzger cautioned.

"You 'spectin' trouble later?" Josh asked.

"Just putting careful ahead of wishing, you see."

"I'll be ready if you need me," Josh said assuredly.

"Good thinking, boy. Now, I've got to see the Frenchy."

As Metzger turned, Delacroix appeared from in front of the wagon.

"Our company's come," he stated evenly. "Don't raise any call. They are at the ford and just mean to pass, I'm sure. Come have a look."

Without waiting for comment, he slipped away back the way he had come. Metzger stepped off after him, and Josh, unbidden, followed several paces behind.

As Josh got to the base of the knoll, he saw in the failing sunlight that Metzger had taken the spyglass the scout produced and was looking toward the ford about three-fourths of a mile distant. Using his hat as a shade, Josh could make out four horses in file crossing the whirling river. The horses were sunk to their chests and seemed to be losing some ground to the frothing current. Each horse appeared to have a rider lying low on its back. As the horses emerged from the water onto the sandy bank, he saw two of the animals had swimmers hanging to their tails. When all were ashore, the two extra swimmers leaped up behind the riders who had swum them across and all six immediately rode off through the knee-high grass.

Metzger peered through the glass until the Indians disappeared behind a low rise. He handed the glass back to the scout, who turned and proffered the telescope to Josh.

"Ever seen an Indian before, boy? Take a spy through this," the scout offered.

Josh accepted the battered instrument, put it to his eye and scanned about until the party reappeared in the distance. He had seen Indians before, mostly as they traveled up and down the river on steamboats, probably to trade. Other than their long hair and dark complexions, the ones he had seen before could as well have been white men. Close up, one could see the medicine bags and beaded ornaments they wore around their necks, often in addition to the cravat a white would wear. His father had pointed them out as tame Algonquians or Kansa, who years before had treatied with the government and had taken on the white ways.

When Josh focused the spyglass he had his first gaze upon wild Indians out in the territories. The sight more thrilled than terrified him.

Mounted on calico ponies smaller than the draught horses he was accustomed to, they seemed fleet of foot even under the extra burden half of them bore. Patched with white and tan, they gracefully carried their riders. As they emerged suddenly back into view, the Indians' ponies struck off directly across Josh's vista. The riders were intent upon their course, never even glancing toward the train or the watching men. Josh was certain they were aware of the emigrant party. How could anyone miss the wagons and eighty head of livestock? It was puzzling to Josh why they wouldn't even look over. Did they hold the whites in such disdain, or were they hoping to remain invisible to the surveying eyes?

Josh recalled hiding from his father in the boatshed for some misdeed and squeezing shut his eyes as his father peered over his hiding place. A child's reasoning told him he couldn't be seen if he closed his eyes.

"Guess those gents didn't do their chores," Josh remarked absently.

"What are you saying, boy?" Metzger said, turning his gaze on Josh.

"Nothin', sir! Just thinkin' out loud."

"Hrumph," snorted Metzger.

"Them rascals be Pawnee, sure," broke in Delacroix. "You can tell by their leggings and hairpieces. They stick part of it in the air with paint and bear grease and shave off the rest. Maybe they feel it makes their scalps less appealin'."

Delacroix could see the greenhorns were impressed with this bit of plains knowledge. Of course, he could tell them that buffalo came from mating horses and bears and they'd probably sell the story to a newspaper. What the hell, let them think he was Kit Carson himself.

"They're sure movin' like the devil's come for supper," said Josh.

"If the devil had Sioux on his trail, he'd be making quick time, too," Delacroix retorted.

"What're we seein' here, Delacroix?" interrupted Metzger.

"It appears, *Capitaine*, those Pawnee came up north for some fun and got a taste of Sioux hospitality. T'would expect they left some of their companions behind to pay the bill," the scout replied. "We may see some Oglala if they don't pass us in the night."

"Does that mean trouble for us?" inquired Metzger.

"Not likely, but they will steal something if they can just to say they did it. They see it as a point of honor to be able to come and go without us knowing. Stealing something would just go to prove it."

Metzger motioned them back and nodded toward some approaching men. "Let's head back to camp. I'd best be tellin' everybody their scalps are still safe." Metzger left the scout and Josh to themselves.

"Mr. Delacroix, we've some fine peaches to liven up your supper. Hope you'll like 'em," Josh invited.

"Mighty fine, boy—and I'll bring something to the fire to liven yours."

The scout untied a sack from his saddle pack, reached in, and with a glint in his eye, produced a rattlesnake as thick as his wrist and about five feet long. He held it by the head, pressing down so the fangs dripped yellow venom. It was hideous.

"Always happy to share with those that haven't any. Let's go eat."

"Oh, sir! I couldn't eat snake any more than I could eat crow," Josh squeaked.

"Can't blame you to that point, boy." Delacroix was warming to his fun. "Crow meat cooks up a mite too strong for good eating, but a baked rattler is as sweet a plate as you'll find." He looked at the stricken young man and added, "Don't get smarmy there. After you eat nothing but bacon and hard biscuit for two months, you'll be looking for snakes and such and a-licking your lips."

When they arrived back at the wagon, Jubal was crouched at the fire tending some biscuits in the collapsible tin oven. He had a bacon slab sizzling on a skewer over the low flame. Josh pulled up a crate, sat down, and casually turned the bacon spit.

"We saw some Pawnee Indians, Jubal, on the run from a scalpin' party of Sioux."

"Everybody else see'd 'em, too, Mr. Bonner. That's as close as I ever want to be to Indians if they cause as much carryin' on as they did here. You'd a thought a circus was passin' for all the ruckus," Jubal replied, winking.

Suddenly, Jubal's mouth fell to his chest, his eyes bugged out, and he fell on his backside. Silently working his mouth, he peered over Josh's shoulder. With feigned disinterest, Josh nonchalantly turned to look behind him.

Delacroix cut the snake's head off and tossed it near the fire. He planted one foot on the tail and had the snake stretched out like a washtub banjo. Beginning at the tail, he slit the snake along its length and proceeded to gut the carcass with a callused thumb.

Josh finally found his tongue. "That's a right big snake, mister. Is there more on the road ahead?"

"Been seeing 'em regular now for two days," Delacroix replied. "This one about threw himself at me, so I couldn't refuse. But, *oui*, there are more. It's spring and they are out of their nests. We'll see many more than you'll like. I wouldn't worry much, though. They will git quicker than they are likely to strike—and they always shake their hips first."

With that, he picked up the rattle and shook it mischievously next to his face. The image of the slick gutted snake looping below the Frenchman's creased face was eerie in the gloaming light. The scout set the carcass at the edge of the coals. Josh squinted his eyes shut for a second, hoping the disturbing vision would vanish.

Josh could see, short of convulsions, he was in for a taste of snake. He looked toward Jubal hopefully to see if he had any ideas. It appeared, for a black man, Jubal was a little green about the gills. His return glance didn't seem to hold any promise of escape, and Josh reckoned there was little hope of avoiding the tracker's preparation. Picking up the dishes, he handed them around.

"May as well have some sowbelly whilst we're waitin'," he said. Josh picked up the cup that had been catching the drippings of the sizzling slab bacon and mixed in some flour to make gravy. Jubal handed around biscuits from the tin oven and began slicing the meat.

"Don't get full bound. There will be plenty of *serpent* for everyone," Delacroix admonished as he accepted his plate.

Delacroix peered over the rim of his coffee cup at his dinner companions. While rattlesnake was not his favorite meal, the amusement it afforded him with the greenhorns could soon make it one. Those who had never traveled the Oregon Road departed with the impression they would eat fresh antelope and *buffle* throughout the journey. There were buffalo to be had, surely, but farther west. The antelope, however, had become skittish with so much activity, as had the birds. Only a skillful and patient hunter could bring in fresh game and then only from far afield of the road. Coffee, bacon, and hard bread were the fare for all until the buffalo herds were discovered.

The tracker, upon finishing his dish, set it down. "Dinner's ready," he said, lifting the carcass gently from the coals.

Jubal sensed the guide was having his fun at their expense. He knew Josh and he were going to eat snake tonight, or the Frenchman would brook them no peace all the way to Oregon. Well, he could try it once, but he wasn't about to take up any foreign habits.

"Mr. Del'croy, let's serve up that thing and be done with it. I want to turn in and dream 'bout sweet tater pie."

Delacroix replied, "Any preference for which end we start on?"

"The end without the poison will suit me," Josh piped up.

The scout drew his knife and sliced portions of the snake onto plates.

"It looks and smells better than I expected," said Josh, "though I have no standard to rally to."

He watched as Delacroix fingered loose a chunk, blew on it, and dropped it into his mouth.

"Don't let it cool too much, boys. It loses some of its flavor."

Gingerly, Josh slipped loose a morsel, lifted it to his mouth, and cautiously took a bite. The texture was firm like channel catfish back home, and the flavor was mild. Josh snuck a peek at Jubal and hoped his own face didn't look at all like what he saw.

"Welcome to the trail, *mes amies*," chuckled Delacroix between bites. The scout rose and strode away from the fireside, licking at his fingers noisily. He would leave them so they could spit the meat out beyond his seeing.

"Damn him," Josh growled. "I ain't about to let that blasted Frenchy make me for a fool. I'm gonna eat at this snake until that trapper thinks we have it for Sunday supper twice a month."

"But, Mister Josh, the Frenchy ain't here to see us eat it," said Jubal meekly.

Josh grinned. "I'm glad you said 'us,' Jubal. Let's split up this worm and have at 'er."

"Mister Josh!"

"And don't be sickin' it up, neither," Josh admonished. They began eating.

As they were collecting the dinnerware and finishing up with the coffee and the peach preserves, the scout returned and helped himself to a cold biscuit and some peaches. The fact the snake was mostly gone didn't escape him. Josh was leaning back and wishing he had saved a bone to pick his teeth with. The trapper squatted at the fire and waved his cup at them offhandedly.

"You are lucky, *mes amies, Le Capitaine* Metzger is posting extra guards tonight but is sparing you two. Perhaps you are too young and you are too dark, eh?" He pointed at each in turn.

"Probably he doesn't want any snake eaters pokin' about his wagons," Josh snapped back.

Josh and Jubal rolled their gear out under the wagon. Each had a buffalo robe, bought in St. Joseph, for a ground cover. They pulled blankets up over themselves and balefully stared at their guide, who was laying out his own worn robes.

Delacroix smiled to himself. He was beginning to like these two. The boy had sand, and Jubal seemed an able and willing hand. They had taken the edge off his joke by finishing the snake, but he had enjoyed himself. One had to make do for pleasantries while on the plains. The trapper banked the fire and began to uncoil a stiff rope around his bedding. The inquiry was only moments in coming.

It was Josh who asked, "Now, why would a man make a rope circle around his bed, I wonder?"

"The snake, she hunts at night, but she won't cross the rope because it smells of man," Delacroix explained seriously.

"Snakes be damned! You must think me a fool fer 'em!" Josh snorted, turning his back to the fire and his tormentor.

"Durned French beaver skinner," he muttered to himself. He did, however, plan to get up and grab a rope out of the wagon as soon as the camp grew quiet.

A SAMPLE OF **DEADLY TALLEY**

CHAPTER ONE

I spent the afternoon in Modjeska Canyon by a vacant vacation cabin...vacant except for the decomposing body on the back porch. A passing jogger had caught a whiff of something foul. After discovering the body and puking on his Reeboks, he phoned it in. When I arrived, there was already a deputy stringing yellow tape around the house. Together we leaned on the hood of the county Crown Vic and waited for the forensic team to arrive.

A cursory examination didn't reveal much: no ID, defensive wounds, or ink. Considering the weather was mild, I figured the guy had died there within the week. Decomposition was progressing well. At this point, it wasn't obvious whether the deceased was a local wretch or an illegal alien wretch or whether there was even a homicide at all. There was nothing conclusive and it would take an autopsy to disclose any latent wounds or trauma. My gut feeling was the deceased had simply fallen ill and crawled up on the porch seeking shelter from the damp and chill of the evenings, but I didn't put gut feelings in my reports. It was possible forensics might reveal an identity, but from the looks of it, I wasn't going to expect much. I rolled the cold hand in mine and glanced at the fingers, doing a quick evaluation of the state of decomposition and whether the lab would be able to get good prints. The body bag guys and the forensics people arrived nearly together. The usual exchange of dead bum jokes was traded and I turned the case over to the lab techs before departing.

From the cabin in Modjeska, I descended to the flatlands through Santiago Canyon to Santa Ana downtown. At CID headquarters, I parked the County car, found my locker and put my field notes from the day on the top shelf. My report could wait until I got some preliminary information from the coroner or forensics. If they determined there was no crime involved and no ID established, the guy who crawled up on a stranger's porch to die would become a few paragraphs in a police log and either go up a crematorium chimney or end up in an anatomy class at UCI. I straightened up the files on my desk and shut down for the day. In the parking lot, I unlocked my vintage El Camino. Just starting the V8 and listening to the mellow rumble of the pipes always made me feel the workday was over. I pointed the hood toward the freeway and home.

I tapped the button for the El Camino's wipers. They clattered over the glass producing little more than a rasping noise. I hit the washer and was rewarded with a spray of water that smeared the accumulated gunk into streaks.

The windshield was glazed with tire smut and diesel fumes blown from inland Orange County to the beaches by the Santa Ana winds. I hate the winds that carry the stink of industry to my little beach town. Who am I kidding? Newport Beach is no longer the little town I grew up in. It's a ritzier parking lot in the summertime with oiled bodies staining the leather of Range Rovers that will never leave pavement behind.

Newport has always been snobbier than the rest of the county but it's getting intolerable. Still, I was glad to be heading home to my board and batten bungalow on the peninsula. I'd be able to wash the car and get the grime of my job off at the same time.

After twelve years on the streets as a sheriff's deputy, finally I'd worked my way into the Criminal Investigations Division. As a homicide investigator I spent only about half of each day with my butt planted in the seat of a car; there was a lot of freeway time. Though there wasn't much of Orange County left that wasn't city, the sheriff's department provided police service for many of the smaller towns. In addition, they caught the calls in the remaining unincorporated parts of the county, mostly the remote canyons and isolated urban pockets that none of the cities would willingly annex.

~ ~ ~

I flicked the wipers and again watched windshield muck get rearranged. The drive home is my reflection time, the time where I let the job of homicide investigator slide away. I pondered the dead man at the cabin. Was there someone who would miss him, wonder where he was? Maybe the guy was on the run from family or the law. He could simply have been a migrant. Likely, unless someone was missing him or unless someone had paper out on him, it would never be resolved. Lives went astray without warning. A person could be living a normal life, a cog slips, and all that seemed secure gets ground in life's gears. Years on the street had taught me at least that much. I wondered if the dead man, as he lay dying on the porch, wondered how things had gone this far wrong.

~ ~ ~

Twelve years I'd spent trying to get to the Criminal Investigation Division and the last three regretting it. As a street cop I'd quickly become bored dealing with the parade of misdemeanors, petty thefts, and endless tedium of the domestic violence cases. On the occasions when I was responding officer at a major felony case, I always envied the detectives who showed up to manage the investigation. From the first time I roped off a perimeter around a gangbanger gunned down in an alley, I'd aspired to take the badge off my shirt and hang it on my belt. Nowadays I just wanted to take the badge wallet, toss it on the dresser at home and sit on the back porch watching the pleasure boats circuit up and down the channel.

~ ~ ~

I followed a BMW convertible down Balboa Boulevard. Two girls in baseball caps, sunglasses and little else, cruised, on the prowl for whatever young women in Beemer ragtops might desire. Obviously, they weren't seeking young men. Suitors in baggy shorts and flip flops whistled and hooted to get their attention. They didn't get even a glance in return and the young men awaited the next carload of honeys to come along. It's a ritual as old as Balboa Boulevard.

I turned left off the Boulevard. Just getting off the main drag is a tonic. The pace of life rolled slower and became just a bit more mellow on these narrow side streets. I always pressed the garage door remote before I get home. I liked the door to be open when I arrive. It's as the house were welcoming me home. I idled the muscle car inside and relished how the motor sounds resonated off the walls. The space normally occupied by Laura's Miata was empty; I was the first one home. I sat for a moment in the garage before going into the house, leaving the door up for when Laura returned. Stepping inside, I emptied my pockets into a bowl on the sideboard placed there for the purpose. Trading shoes for *huaraches*, I cracked open a Sierra Nevada and dropped into an oversized deck chair. An Egg Harbor sedan chugged by just inside the channel buoy. A crew member in the cockpit held up a long neck in salute. I returned the greeting and settled in. All was right with the world. It looked like the brightwork on my Bayliner Flybridge cruiser could use some attention. I decided to finish this beer and then fiddle about with the boat.

~ ~ ~

The next thing I knew, I was startled awake, hating the momentary disorientation of not immediately knowing where I was. The garage door was closing and the noise disrupted my nap. It was nearly dusk, too late to wash the car or tend to the boat. Night had settled over the peninsula, the beachgoers had departed, and I was missing the best time of the day. Laura came in from the garage, one temple of her

250

sunglasses in her teeth and arms loaded down with groceries. I spied a loaf of Italian bread poking from one of the sacks. That meant spaghetti for dinner.

"See if there's a decent bottle of red wine in the pantry. I don't want to have spaghetti without some *vino* and I forgot to get wine at the store."

There wasn't, so I ended up going out again while Laura browned Italian sausage and started dinner. Afterwards, we opened a second bottle of indifferent merlot and sat out on the deck. By eight o'clock even the boat traffic had gone and we watched the reflections of the homes on Balboa Island wavering in the current of the channel. Occasionally a boat slipped by, returning from a coastal cruise or an early end to a pub crawl. Fog looked likely, marking the end of the Santa Anas. It was already starting to get chilly.

"Did you have a nice day?" Laura asked.

I smiled and gave her a knowing look. Laura knew I didn't like talking about the job and only wanted me to offer a casual reply because she wanted to talk about her day. I obliged.

"Just the usual mix of bad and boring." I hesitated, just for effect... "and how about yours?"

Laura is a technician with the Sheriff's CSI office. We met years before I became a detective. I was the responding officer at a homicide and she was the tech assigned to the case. It always made for a good story when people asked how we met. Now that I'm a detective, we are prohibited from working together on a case since we'd risk compromising the evidence.

"Today was my first day of testimony in the Swain case. There was a sketch artist in court and he drew me. I wonder if I can get it after the case is over. I can't contact the guy but maybe someone from your office could speak to him."

Ordinarily, giving testimony was not an event to get excited about, far from it. The Swain case involved the drowning death of Abby Swain, aka Abby Deer, network affiliate newscaster wife of a locally famous restaurateur. Abby had been discovered tangled in the mooring lines of the Swain's motor yacht, an accidental drowning was presumed. It was Laura who had dug a little deeper after finding bruising around the ankles. The bruising had been attributed to the victim's struggles in the water. Laura was suspicious because the bruises were too symmetrical. This led to more lab work that determined the water in Abby Swain's lungs was not ocean salt water but saline from ordinary bath salts. The Coroner's office reversed their finding of accidental death and concluded Abby had been drowned in a bathtub by someone lifting up her feet and forcing her head underwater. Eventually, Alan Swain was charged and the forensic testimony was key. While it was a good bit of forensic work, the small notoriety of the deceased had garnered media attention and Laura was going to enjoy her brief stint in the public spotlight.

"I wasn't called until late in the day, so I didn't get to do much more than establish my *bona fides*," Laura continued. "We'd only gotten into the recovery of the body when the judge called a recess."

"Don't look for this one to be just cut and dried forensics. Swain has good attorneys and they are going to challenge you on every point they can. They will go out of their way to make it personal trying to rattle you into contradicting your own testimony."

"Rebecca warned me about what the attorneys will try."

Rebecca Jamison was her supervisor and normally would have gone on the stand herself, but Laura was being given the opportunity as it was her intuition that turned an accidental unattended death into a homicide.

I didn't want to get involved in shoptalk, even if it wasn't strictly my shop. I was mildly lit from the wine and had already slept for a couple of hours. I got up and offered Laura my hand. She was still prattling on as I led her to the bedroom.

ACKNOWLEGEMENTS

For an author, the contributions of an editor cannot be extolled to the extent they deserve. I would be remiss if I didn't credit Samantha Ettinger for her endless patience in bringing Hangtown to its final form. Besides correcting the litany of grammatical errors I plagued her with, her enthusiasm for the project kept me striving to improve the story. While complimenting me on some passages, she never hesitated to rap me on the knuckles when I stumbled. Thank you, Samantha. This book would never have happened without your guiding hand.